Finally Found the Words

RIVERBEND HIGH
HAPPY ENDINGS
BOOK 2

M.C DANIELSEN

Finally Found the Words

This is a work of fiction. Names, characters, places, and incidents are either products of the author's imagination or used fictitiously. Any resemblance to actual events, locales, or persons, living or dead, is purely coincidental. The author is not affiliated with any brand name mentioned in the story. The author is not endorsing brands or places with mentions in the book.

Cover design by GetCovers

Interior images were created by the author. This book uses open-source typefaces from Google Fonts, licensed for commercial use. Printed in the United States of America

First edition, September 2025

ISBN - Paper back 979-8-9991058-3-7

ISBN – Ebook 979-8-9991058-2-0

CONTENTS

Evan & Aniko

I knew you'd be good parents, but the reality of it is stunningly beautiful.

END OF MAY TO MID AUGUST

1

Spa-Themed Flirting

Tyler

Summer plan energy buzzed on the last day of eighth grade. The reality of summer hit with the ringing of the final bell. Kids spilled out of classrooms like soda from a shaken can, foaming and fizzing out to summer freedom.

I tossed my backpack over my shoulder. Emptied of the school year the weight was light. For most kids that lightness? It hung around all summer. I mean, no homework—awesome? Check. No alarm. High-key wanting no morning alarms for life. Check. Knowing that's unlikely, IRL. Duh. Pickup games. Check. Camping trips with Gramps. Check. I mean, my grandpa is cool. He slaps. The unease of not having a routine. Check. Worry twined around lightness. Why? Well, my backpack never emptied of everything.

Here's the thing. I've always liked routine. Knowing what's around the corner, what's up next, with the alarm going off at nasty o'clock in the morning. Check, check. Summer's kind of sneaky, slinking in with the promise of freedom and no worries.

No one guarantees you'll be safe and free. Right? And without classes, teachers, and homework filling up my big brain? Worries forced in and occupied too much of my mind. My worries—Mom, the safety of whatever job she was working; the unknown we'd been ducking for as long as I could remember. Most kids enjoy the freedom and the unknown of summer. The unknown's not exciting in my world, the unknown brings bad stuff.

The hallways thinned out, a few people lingered. Enough students to pretend the last day hung around. I spotted Ivy heading for the back doors, cello case strapped like huge weapon.

"Have a great summer, Maestro!" I called. "Crush it at camp. Or play it at camp. Or... how do you win at music camp?"

She didn't slow down. "You don't. That's the point."

"Wait, I've got it! Break a string! No, break a bow!" She stopped and looked back.

"Don't want to break anything, but thanks, Tyler." She walked out laughing at least. *Thanks*, as if it was an obvious compensation for my idiot, oblivious best bro. Earlier in a hall Aiden and I threw lazy fist bumps as we passed.

"Later, man."

"Yeah, later."

Nothing more. He looked chill, like always. Did he ever find Ivy? Did he attempt to find Ivy? A not unknown fact-he ended eighth grade still an oblivious idiot.

Drew passed by with his earbuds in, ranch-sized backpack slung over a shoulder. I imagined a couple thousand calves waiting on him for vaccinations, cuddles or lullabies to fall asleep to. What do calves need? I live near, around, and surrounded by farms and ranches, but didn't know much. I did know that Drew, the ranch kid, his take on summer freedom was different like mine.

"Hey!" I called. "You free for a pickup game next week?"

He slowed long enough to say, "Yeah dude, well maybe. Depends on what's doing on the ranch."

"Fair. I'll keep your spot warm."

I found Nate parked near the trophy case, backpack dropped near his feet. He worked a Rubik's Cube like it offended him and twisting would get an apology from it.

"Cube giving you any patterning ideas for basketball plays—like graph theory but with more elbows? Don't forget I'm the buffest node." He didn't look up.

"Trying to beat my bus ride record."

"Still three moves behind," I tsked.

He glanced up, a smile tugged the corner of his mouth. "Maybe. Or maybe that's what I'm letting you think. Strategic misdirection. Nerdiest node makes the winning shot."

"Trash talk from Berglund? Man, summer's already getting weird. Wait—trash talk? Or math talk?" I paused. "Oh. It's Mash talk, dude!"

Nate snorted. "Please don't say that in public."

"Only if you keep your calculations to yourself. No mental mathing me into humiliation."

"Deal," he said, twisting the cube again. "But I'm always calculating in my head."

"Now it's Mash Talk and Math Threats. Or mather... thre... mea... mes... never mind."

I turned the corner—and my eyes found Emilia at her locker. The sunlight streamed down around her and angels sang. A butterfly flitted by and caressed her cheek with its wing. Oh, come on! That doesn't happen IRL. But my heart beat faster, and my gut did trampoline jumps. She didn't need sunlight and angel voices. She was real. Fun. Quick-witted. Could put me in my place. And stupid pretty, observed and noted by me, more and more the past year.

And now I needed to cling to the thirty seconds left before summer pushed us to different corners of the galaxy. Okay, fine, a twenty-five-minute ride from my house to the Preston farm. No full license yet, and no one could beam me to her. It might as well have been light years getting between us this summer. So, of course, I opened with sarcasm.

"Planning to cause any trouble this summer, or gonna laze around like usual?" I teased, leaning against the locker next to hers. "Because you live on the Preston Family Spa and Day Lounge right?"

She rolled her eyes, a grin spreading across her face. "Should I be worried you converse about spas and day lounges?"

"Guys can rock good skin too, you know," I said, rubbing a hand over my left forearm. "Keeping this baby-soft epidermis takes some work. I've been keeping tabs in case any local farm families decide to open a dream vacation spa and oasis combo. I'm the guy to influence the heck out of my vacation time there."

Emilia looked at me. "No official spa plans yet," she said, "but you're welcome to come roll around in the manure pile any day, Tyler."

"Hard pass on cow poop. The bath bombs lineup though, I'm in when you have some merch... No spa, so you're back to the age-old choice, world peace or world domination. I'm guessing world domination. Billions of people to boss around. That's your vibe."

Since third grade teasing her had been high on my list. When we first met she prickled at me like a porcupine. She learned I'd never pick on Ivy and our back and forth began. Now, her laughter had been harder and lingered longed. Made me want to be extra enough to prolong it. The feels about Emilia grew at a scary, steady rate since the beginning of middle school.

"No trouble-making at the Preston farm from me. I leave that to the sibs. As far as bossing goes, Mamá es major league. I'm still in the minors. I'll be bossing cover crops and fields. Telling the alfalfa, 'Grow, heal the soil! Regenerate!' And you? Spending all summer working on getting some actual jump in your jump shot?"

"Hey, my vertical is legend." I protested, smiling too wide for the jab to sting.

The idea of not seeing Emilia much over the summer stuck in my mind and nagged at me all day. I wanted to say something, maybe suggest hanging out more—but the words tangled up somewhere between my brain and my mouth. I hesitated, fiddling with the strap of my backpack, trying to gauge Emilia's interest level in spending time together over the break. She leaned back against her locker, arms crossed waiting on me like the last seconds of the school year meant nothing.

"Regenerating alfalfa? What is that anyway? Kind of sounds like a superpower."

Emilia tilted her head giving serious thought to my question. "It's not just alfalfa. We rotate in cover crops to rebuild the soil microbiome, retain moisture, and suppress weeds. Also good for carbon sequestration."

I blinked. "So... yeah a superpower."

She laughed. "Yeah, I guess if spreadsheet usage for planning cover crop rotation is a super power."

The laugh she gave, oof, hit me center mass. Another reason I crawled into summer rather than raced. During the school year? I heard her laugh at least once a day. And most days, the cause of it? Me.

"Besides cover crops, I need to spend a few days making Ivy feel guilty about being gone so long this summer."

"I'm going to text you stupid farm questions all summer. If you're a genuine farm super hero you need to practice being patient. And I don't want to lose my getting on Emmy's last nerve mojo."

She laughed again, soft this time, and shook her head at hopeless me. Hopeless me puffed up, oddly proud.

"I think that's hardwired into your personality. You'll be good unless you short-circuit. Jenna's decided she's our summer social coordinator—expect a group text by Friday. Movie night. S'mores. Possibly a themed snack spreadsheet and a request for color coordinated socks."

Thank you, Jenna. My heart tripped in relief at the idea of seeing Emilia this summer. Cause, man my heart needed a glance of her more and more to want to beat on. All the feelings welled up and smacked together; the resulting sonic boom disconnected whatever neurons wired the smarter part of my brain to my mouth.

I opened my mouth and said, "I hope the themed snacks aren't for Oppenheimer. I eat clean to keep this shape and radioactive isn't on my nutritionist's plan."

"Nothing nuclear for snacks," she agreed, stepping back. "You wreak enough havoc as is—we don't need you becoming more dangerous."

She paused while my brain waves stuttered out, Tyler, you are stuuupid.

"My mom's here. Gotta go. Later, Tyler."

And I think I said goodbye—though I'm not totally sure, because my next aware moment found me mid-pickup game at Simmons Park, trying to remember which net to score on.

> **Tyler's Brain:**
> When I called you stupid it wasn't a request for performance art.
> **Tyler's Heart:**
> Dude, you've got to stop letting sarcasm do the talking when your entire emotional system is in full-on Emilia's presence mode. Ask her if she wants to do something or hang out this summer. Like a normal human being with feelings.
> Tyler's Brain:
> I mean, can he do normal? Maybe he needs to take the manure pile option.

2

Kicking Zombie Butt

Tyler

A couple days into summer I rode my bike Aiden's. It clinked against his porch as I parked.

"Yo! Ready to kick zombie butt?" Aiden grinned big as he swung the door open. We dumped ourselves onto the couch, the game's loading screen on the TV. He'd bought the latest Zombie Skirmish game. Both of us ready and pumped up to see the action.

"Ready to get schooled?" he teased, tossing me a controller. As he watched I pulled my own controller out of my backpack.

"Dude my extra controllers are not sticky."

"We'll see if you can beat me when I've got my own," I smirked at him.

We dove into undead digital chaos. I used a momentary break in the intense action to ask Aiden a question. I knew it would make him defensive.

"Hey, did you catch Ivy before she left for camp?"

"No, I, uh, missed her," he said with fake casualness. "Timing didn't work out."

I paused trying to see his expression. He avoided eye contact.

"Aiden, she's been your best friend for ages. She's always been there for you. Keep it up and you're gonna lose that friendship. Dude, not saying goodbye? That's a disturbance along the fault lines. It doesn't seem bad now, but the earthquakes will destroy everything."

He paused too, his usual confident demeanor flickered off. "I know, I know! I didn't mean to be a jerk and miss a goodbye. I just... I forgot. Always got a lot on my mind."

"You can't keep anything in your mind except basketball you mean, right? Bro, it's a great game. I love it too, but so many things are more important."

I didn't understand his hyper focus on preparing for tryouts in the fall. Aiden played with natural talent and worked hard. He was a shoo-in, maybe would even have the MVP at season end. If not as a freshman, the year after. He played that good.

Annoyance pricked at me. He could be hyper-focused because everything else for him was safe and secure. Except Ivy's friendship. He's in danger of losing her. I guess when it's been easy without loss it's harder to put the best things first.

"Maybe I should text her or something," he mumbled, almost to himself. More than clear he been pushing it away, ignoring everything.

In an obvious shift he blurted out, "My folks are having twins in October." That diversion tactic worked.

"Twins? Man, that's intense!" I said surprised. "How are you feeling about all that?"

He set his controller down and leaned back. "It's a lot. I'm excited but kind of overwhelmed, too."

I nodded. Overwhelming? Yeah. "You'll be a great big brother."

He smiled." Thanks, Ty. I hope so."

We picked up our controllers slipping back into the game's rhythm. The room filled with virtual explosions and our cheers and groans. Aid was clueless about the importance of the simple stuff. Like now, the two of us gaming. Existing in a little world of us against the zombies. The kind of thing that vanished easily. The afternoon slipped past. I packed up my things. Slinging my backpack over my shoulder.

I turned to Aiden. "Look, I'm gonna say this now then let it go. You are on the edge of blowing up your friendship with Ivy. And I've always thought you guys would be more than just friends. You're going to be full of regrets if you don't fix this."

"Okay, yeah. I know." He sounded defeated, which I didn't understand. He'd given up already?

"Hey! Enjoy basketball camp. Though without me how could you?"

He grinned. "It's a couple weeks, dude. I'll survive without your bubbly presence. Enjoy your camping trip. See you when we're back."

"For sure," I replied, stepping out into the cool evening air. "About to request some tips from my game but never mind. It's all here and I'm ready to go." I spread my arms wide then thumped my chest. I heard Aiden scoff at me, but it was with a smile. I hopped on my bike and started off.

"See ya, Pedersen!"

"Later Alred!"

Peddling home, a strange mix of contentment and worry pinged prickled. Time hanging with my best friend? Awesome. Aiden's a solid guy—loyal, easygoing, clutch in a crisis. Watching him about to screw up with Ivy? It made me twitchy. Because when it comes to Ivy, who mattered, his blind spots were gym-sized. I wondered when Ivy would get tired of making excuses for him. If she did, Aiden would be blown away. I wasn't sure I'll if I'd feel bad for him. You lose important stuff when you don't look after it.

3

Fish Ghosts

Tyler

Mom wouldn't be home when I headed back from Aiden's. Out working I knew, like always. Bustling from one job to the next, making ends meet. Her jobs—a thick strand of the worry pulsing in my mind. It had been there since I started understanding our life.

Mom, man. She'd always done so much for me. Best of all, brought us to Gramps and Gramma, our safety net. They made sure Mom and I had all we needed. We had a basement apartment in their house. They filled gaps when Mom couldn't quite cover it all. If mi Mamá was less proud they'd do more. My grandparents respected that and didn't push. Gramps sat on the front porch reading a newspaper. His glasses slid to the end of his nose, forehead furrowed in concentration. The reading furrow that appeared whatever he read.

"Hey Gramps! Got enough light to read? Don't hurt your eyesight. You want to bait your own hook, right?"

Gramps looked up, face smoothing as he smiled. "Oh ho, the Smart Alec returns home. I'll be able to bait my own hook and out-fish you, mister."

"You can always out-fish me in the stories anyway, right?"

I stopped next to the porch and leaned my bike against the house. Gramps put his arm around my shoulder, giving me a hug.

"You're kind of a smart mouth, but I'm looking forward to our camping trip."

"Me too, Gramps."

The garage smelled like motor oil and grass clippings. At stupid-early-o'clock in the morning the ghosts hung in the dark, cobwebbed corners. I'm talking fish ghosts—the ghost of every fish that caught by an Alred in the last fifty years. Nothing scary about the scaled apparitions. The Alreds, with fishing poles in hand, conquered, according to Gramps' lore. No evidence backed up his claims. And Gramps' stories got fishier with each telling.

I stopped and pulled out my phone. Stupid-early-o'clock seemed a great time to remind Emilia that I existed. And it had been over seventy-two hours since I'd seen her.

> **Me:** Do farm superheroes get up earlier than beefy fishermen?

> Picture attached: Tyler wearing a life vest and Gramps' fishing hat.

Last night we'd loaded up everything into the truck. Now I waited on the cooler Gramps and Grams were in the midst of filling up. Next? We'd head off to our annual *Gramps and Ty Fishing Fun and Failure to Catch Weekend.* Gramps paused on the top step from the house, patting his pockets, as if a winning lottery ticket should've been there.

"Wait—nail clippers. I forgot the nail clippers."

I blinked. "We're camping, not attending a manicure convention."

"You say that now," he said, already turning back toward the house. "But let me tell you something about your dad."

Here we go. "Summer of '88. We out at Lake Upsilon, just me and Adam. He was ten, all elbows and energy, thought it'd be fun to scale the bluff behind our campsite barefoot."

I followed him back into the house, already smiling. These stories always got me.

"Slipped on a patch of moss, jammed his big toe so bad I had to trim half the nail so he could get his shoes back on. I used what

I had—my pocket knife. That boy yelped like a chicken getting its feathers plucked. Said a string of swear I wouldn't have thought he knew."

"Uh-oh."

"We made a pact that what's said at camping, stays at camping. And then?"

Gramps opened the drawer by the sink, still talking. "That Christmas, your dad gave me the world's ugliest pair of nail clippers. Bright orange plastic, shaped like a moose. Antlers and all. Came with a keychain that played Jingle Bells when you pressed it."

He found something and held it up. "This is my favorite pair," he said, handing them to me. "Camo green, bulky, and they've got a tiny flashlight on the end. Gave me these the year he graduated basic. Said, 'Now you can perform wilderness surgery in the dark, too.'"

I turned them over in my hand, the little flashlight flickering on with a squeeze. My throat tightened, but I nodded. "They're awful."

"Right?" Gramps laughed, taking them back. "Best of our traditions." He tucked them into his shirt pocket and gave me a wink. "Now we're ready."

Ready after checking for the third time for bug spray and citronella candles. Gramps turned into a big baby bitten and itchy. Grams said, "Well, I married you knowing a lot of things. I didn't know you a whiner about mosquito bites. After 40 years, that's one thing I'm tired of old man."

This year we headed up near the Canadian border to Lake Metigoshe. Gramps' favorite place-clear water, quiet trails, and so remote you could hear you DNA building cells. The noise of North Riverbend wasn't much so it wasn't the quiet that drew Gramps. Maybe the farther away we fished the more he could embellish his fishing stories. Seeking quiet? Not something I did. When it got quiet my brain got loud. That's when I opened my mouth and stupid came out like at Emilia's locker. She smiled at me and I responded with the world's weirdest spa-themed flirting.

Gramps hoisted the final cooler into the truck bed and dusted off his hands. We climbed into the faded blue truck. I leaned my head against the window as we rolled out of North Riverbend and onto the highway. The town blurred into buttes, hills, occasional shallow canyons, and stretches of prairie. We passed farms with hay bales stacked like giant marshmallows. The scenery gave way to the wilder space of the Turtle Mountains. Space that made your thoughts feel both smaller and bigger.

My phone vibrated in my pocket a couple of hours on the road. I didn't bother with stealth. Gramps didn't catch the biggest fish, but nothing else got by him.

"Not gonna have much signal where we're camping you know."

"Yeah, Gramps, I know. Just...," I heaved a dramatic sigh. "Please don't take my phone yet. I need a few more minutes to admire my bars."

Emilia answered my text. Somewhere else the response would've been shooting an imaginary basketball. Nailing the perfect net-swish sound. Followed up with, "He takes the shot... NOTHING BUT NET!"

My grin had to be reflecting enough sunlight to make Gramps reach for his shades. Well his weird slip-over-the-glasses things that only grandfathers rocked. I scrolled to her reply.

Emilia: Farmers spring out of bed with the sunrise singing cheery songs. You know that, right? #basicfarmlifefact Here's the real definition of beefy. Meet Claudio.

Picture attached: A massive bull standing by a fence, looking like he wanted to be in charge of ending someone's summer breaks for all eternity.

I thumbed out a reply.

Me: Fine, beefy's out. Sizzling. Hot. Wowzer. I mean—there are SO MANY adjectives. Respond fast, I'm about to lose all my bars. Better yet, if I lose reception it gives you a few days to come up will all the ways to adjective me up and admire me. Friendly hint: you'll need to switch to pen and paper.

I lost reception but looked forward to picking that convo up in a few days.

We set up camp—a practiced rhythm. Tent staked. Fire pit ringed with rocks. Gear stashed. Dinner cooked over flames that smoked just right. After we ate, Gramps passed me a root beer and leaned back with a kingly sigh into his throne of a camp chair. The sky went dark slow, popping out one star at a time. The lake shimmered gold and navy, then just darkest navy. Across the water a country playlist became background music for memories.

"You've been quiet," Gramps said after a while.

"Just full of the world's best hot dog."

He gave me a side glance that said *try again, kid.* I tipped the bottle of root beer toward the fire; let it catch the glow.

"Thinking, I guess."

"Any particular direction those thoughts are wandering?"

I shrugged. "Glad school's done. Enjoying this. Worrying about Mom. Basketball plays... the usual."

"That text you got in the car? That part of the usual?"

He didn't move, didn't even nod. Just waited.

"Ah, Gramps, you're gonna make me say it aren't you?" I smiled a little, then let out a long breath. "I like this girl."

Gramps didn't respond. Just waited.

"And I think she kind of likes me back. But I keep saying the dumbest stuff. Like... stupid and sarcastic are my native languages."

Still no words from him, just a small grunt that said, *go on*. I nudged a log with the toe of my shoe.

"I don't want to be a joke. Or worse, be the guy she laughs off later. I want to say something real, but I've gotten used to holding stuff in."

Gramps glanced at me, then took a slow sip of his root beer.

"Being able to laugh with someone, that's a gift. There's a lot of hard in life and you gotta laugh when you can."

I nodded, staring at the flames.

"You know Grams and I; anything you and your mom needed we'd do. So much more than your mom lets us. I've come to see what she really needs from us is to make sure she hangs on to her smile and her laugh. The rest she's got pretty much handled. Sharing smiles and laughter, that's worth more than anything I could hand her."

I kept staring into the flames.

"Your dad had the best sense of humor. Got it from your Grams I'm sure. I gave him the grim, serious side I'm sure."

I snorted at that. Gramps could be serious, but grim? Nah, not him.

"You know he called us after he met your mom to tell us about her. He got to laughing so hard when he told us about how their meeting came about. We knew it had to be serious."

The fire crackled and sparked.

"And I suppose she could've met a rich boy, had more things. But as hard as it's been, he left her laughter. And I've seen that it's still with her." Gramps fell quiet; the next three months of his words used up.

"I get that. Thanks. For the record, you're the least grim person I've ever met."

He didn't answer, just reached out and clinked his bottle against mine. The stars all out, no rush, the fire, water, and a peace I rarely felt settled on me. I took a sip of root beer.

Gramps may have used up his three-month word quota, his bear hug before I crawled into my sleeping-bag said the rest. If Gramps was right, and he usually was. Then laughing with someone was valuable, much more than I realized. Maybe, I'd just keep making Emilia laugh while I worked in the serious part.

> **Tyler's Brain:** *says with reverence* Gramps. He's a man of few words, but when he says something. Whoa, you listen up!
>
> **Tyler's Heart:** Pass me a tissue. That was unspeakably beautiful. Gramps – I love him so much I can't stand it.
>
> **Tyler's Brain:** But there's a line between funny and stupid. You're pivoting on that line so closely you might sprain both ankles and pull a hamstring when you try to work in serious.

4

Biceps Don't Fail me Now

Tyler

Gramps rented a little fishing boat for our trip—aluminum, dented, barely bigger than a bathtub. Bench seats, current registration stickers peeling. The outboard motor looked like alien litter—something a UFO tossed because even huge alien brains couldn't repair it.

I wondered if the motor was modeled on a Disney movie dragonfly I remembered fuzzily. Mice hopped into a fishing boat to escape an alligator. A dragonfly motored their escaped boat. I hoped I wasn't experiencing a premonition—not one involving aliens and inspired 70s Disney movies.

"You're up," Gramps said, nodding to the motor like one of his buddies at a VFW fish fry. I stepped forward, stretching to prep for lifting a truck or heavyweight wrestling.

"All right, Gramps. Ready to be schooled?"

He adjusted his hat, leaned back a little. "Sure, Professor Throttle. Show me how it's done."

I grabbed the handle—just a basic pull cord, like a lawn mower. Easy. I ripped the cord and started our lawn mower all the time. I was in good shape—if I say so myself. I had actual muscles. Like, plural. My biceps showed up more lately. Showed up with a little definition. Forced me to admire them last week when I mowed the lawn. How hard could it be? I gave the cord a solid yank. My arm flung backward as if unhinged from my shoulder.

No resistance. No rumble. Nothing except me about to punch myself in the ear. Gramps didn't say a word. I felt the air thicken with grandfatherly amusement. I gritted my teeth and tried again.

This time? Resistance. I yanked so hard I could've pulled the Loch Ness Monster to shore. The motor did nothing. No sputter. No spark. No noise except for Gramps' chuckle mixing with the crinkling of him unwrapping a granola bar.

"You want me to—?"

"Nope," I said through gritted teeth. "I've got it. I'm simply initiating a multi-phase engagement sequence. It's technical."

Gramps didn't answer. His Grandfatherly Amusement™ grew 'til it needed a trademark and capital letters. Now, convinced magic was needed I muttered under my breath.

"Please, Evanrude—whatever your magic Disney name is—just pretend some mice need to get away from an alligator."

Attempt three—a sharp, fast pull. The engine roared to life like a grizzly woken abruptly, starving after its hibernation and right after someone insulted its mother. I smacked my knee on the bench seat. Gramps raised his eyebrows and bit into the granola bar.

"Told you it just takes the right touch."

I muttered something about *warm-up pulls to calibrate the recoil system* and steered us away from the dock with the zero-dignity left and luck I possessed sucked up by conjuring outboard motor magic. So much for muscle definition. We sputtered across the lake with the motor beat-boxing us towards the Canadian border. I steered us toward the guaranteed-to-get-some-bites spot that Al-at-the-farm-store back in North Riverbend shared with Gramps after an oath of secrecy. At the same time, I composed a lecture to give my biceps when we got home.

We cut the engine in a quiet bay. Lily pads huddled in a customer service meeting. Reeds leaned in to eavesdrop. The water went still around us, like the big lake held its breath. Gramps tossed the anchor with ease. I ignored his muscle definition as a soft kerplunk rippled outward like lazy applause and the water started breathing again.

I baited my hook, cast line, and leaned back on the bench seat the fishing rod rested across my knees. The lake gave a mix of melodic noises. The light plink of water against aluminum. The creak as breezed shifted the boat. The whisper of line pulling through the eyelets of my pole. Somewhere, a loon called—low and eerie, summoning the fish ghosts back from our garage maybe?

A dragonfly skimmed the water near my sneaker. A turtle blinked at us from a half-submerged log. My biceps were no threat this morning and the turtle smirked at me. It thought I was a joke not worth the work of slipping into the water.

The sun warmed my shoulders. The air smelled like pine and sunscreen and tricky fish. My brain didn't jump from one thing to the next like a playlist on shuffle. I didn't need to say anything. Neither did Gramps. We just fished. The minutes stretched and softened. We used the sun for our clock and sat in the middle of the lake's music.

My bobber swayed with each tiny current and threw attitude—telling me it *intended not to engage in the catching of real fish*. Gramps got a bite and slowly reeled it in, giving the fish a chance to think about it.

"You got one," he said, squinting toward my line. I sat up straighter.

"Where?" He nodded at tip of my pole. "There."

It twitched once. Then again. Then stopped, the lake was punking me. I waited, muscles tight, ready to set like a reality fishing star on a low-budget outdoor show. A huge pull, the bobber went under. *Ha!* I thought at the snooty bobber. I yanked. For three glorious seconds I had a huge walleye, no a pike. No, heck maybe it was a whale. My line pulled, my arms worked, my heart pounded in my ears. A fish broke the surface—an eight-inch sunfish that looked offended about the whole thing.

Gramps grinned. "Hope you're not planning to mount that one."

I held it up, letting the sunlight flash off its scales. "Photo finish," I said, and Gramps obliged snapping a photo with his phone before we let it go.

We caught two more in the next hour—Gramps got the biggest and pretended not to gloat about it. I got the weirdest—a fish so small I could've used it as bait for an actual catch. We fished until the shadows stretched long across the water. The air had cooled to need-a-hoodie-above zero. The loon called from farther away. The lake was tucking itself into bed for the night as we headed back. A slower, quieter trip with the motor's low hum of complaint and the slap of the water.

We tied up and carried gear to our camping spot. My stomach started sending not-subtle hints about a proper meal. Poor foolish stomach. By now—day one and a half in—the cooler existed as a damp graveyard of murky ice cube melt and sandwich crumbs. Anything that needed to stay cold eaten up. I flipped open an imaginary menu.

"What's the chef's recommendation for tonight?"

Gramps didn't miss a beat. "Eat what doesn't bite back."

Which left us with the evening's fine dining selections at **Chez Gramps & Tyler's Campsite.**

Appetizers

Vienna Sausages à la Can — Served room temperature with a plastic fork for a *just passing throug*h vibe.

Entrées

Spam, Pan-Seared — One side "crispy," the other a hint of warmth.

Baked Beans — with a soupçon of ketchup for country-chic twist.

Desserts

Cold Pop-Tarts — Straight from the box, still wrapped. The crinkle of the package providing a delightful accompaniment to the consumption of sugary goodness.

Classic Campfire S'mores — Marshmallow char level available in light tan, golden perfection, or accidental torch.

Beverages

Instant Lemonade — Mixed to a shade of yellow not found in nature.

Instant Coffee — For those who like their hot drinks both bitter *and* crunchy.

Lake-Chilled Bottled Water — Capped and sealed for safety, but still with hints of canoe and fish.

We built our plates reverently as if savoring a five-star buffet. We sat in camp chairs with the perfect window view of the lake fading from silver to dark blue. We ate heartily pretending this had been the plan all along. Because hadn't it been? Between the

Vienna sausages, Spam, and s'mores, this was the pattern of our camping trips—fish or no fish.

The next morning we packed up, the lake wrapped in fog and the loons calling to sic the fish ghosts on us. Gramps and I worked in quiet rhythm—tent broken down, gear loaded, one final sweep of the campsite for rogue socks or root beer bottles. On the drive back, we swapped stories, argued about country songs, and tried to remember where the citronella candles were—on a rock or in the truck bed. Gramps didn't say it, but I knew he appreciated a phone wasn't glued to my hand the second we hit signal.

I was itching to check it. We crested a hill just south of Bottineau and—bam—I could feel the bars. I didn't lunge for my phone. That would've been too obvious. Instead, I pretended to check the time. One unread message.

> **Emilia:** Wowzer? Are you using a 1970s-only thesaurus? Then here's my list: Groovy, Far-out, Outta sight, Solid. Your next text had better not be *Boom Chicka Wow Wow.*

I read it twice, trying not to smile like an idiot.

Gramps glanced over. "Catch something?"

"Just checking today's Farmer's Almanac," I said, sliding my phone face-down on my thigh.

5

Don't Make Room in the Freezer

Tyler

We pulled into the driveway. Gramps parked the truck and the unloading began. The first thing I heard was Grams saying, "Tyler, you look hungry," as she handed me two enormous Special K bars. "Made with real cereal, so that counts as a healthy supper, right kiddo?"

Then she called to Gramps, "Need me to make room in the freezer for the fish?"

Gramps grinned and said, "Woman, that smart mouth of yours," before giving her a big smooch.

Are you kidding me? They're grandparents. There was no ducking out—the gear still had to come out of the truck. I grabbed my duffel in one hand and a Special K bar in the other, shuttling back and forth while humming "na-na-na" under my breath so I didn't have to hear anything else.

The truck bed emptied and the tent was stashed. Grams pressed a paper plate into my hands stacked with more bars "so you don't waste away." The peanut-butter sweetness and butterscotch topping clung to my fingers as I hauled the last of the tackle into the garage.

My phone buzzed once from my pocket, but I let it sit. If Emilia, I wanted to be ready. No half-hearted texting—she required all my brain power, preferably after a shower, sleep, and breakfast.

The next morning, I woke to the smell of coffee drifting through our apartment. Light from the high basement window cut a square across my bedroom floor. I pulled on a T-shirt and padded toward the kitchen. Mom was warming scrambled eggs at the stove, hair pulled back, a stack of warm tortillas in a basket next to her.

"Morning, Mijo," she said, glancing over her shoulder with a small smile. "Did you sleep well after your big adventure?"

"Sí, Mamá."

"¿Pescaron suficiente para comer?"—Did you catch enough to eat?

"Claro... si también cuentas las galletas y las salchichas enlatadas," I said, keeping my face straight.—Sure... if you also count cookies and little canned sausages.

Her eyes softened.

"Salchichas enlatadas," she said, rolling the words like a flavorful memory. "My abuelito loved those. He always kept a can in his toolbox... and another in the glove box of his truck, just in case."

That made me grin. "Guess that makes him and Gramps soul brothers. I'm sure Gramps has stashed a couple cans in his glove box along with his red licorice. Not exactly survival food, but it'd get him through a blizzard."

Her smile deepened. "The things we carry with us," she said. "I'm glad you get these times. Your Gramps is a good man—you'll think of these trips often."

I nodded, not trusting myself to say much. Last night's smoochy driveway reunion aside, Gramps was amazing. She slid a plate with homemade breakfast burrito in front of me.

"The world waits until after breakfast."

Later that morning, I sat on my bed, phone in hand, scrolling through messages and social media. All that I'd been too dead for last night. Now the screen was emptied and quiet. No new texts from Emilia. Not surprising.

Texting Emilia was like fishing. Had to pick the perfect bait for a fish you didn't want to scare off. Too flashy and away she'd swim. No worms, rookie stuff, too basic and gross—she'd roll each fishy eye either side of her face. It required patience and smarts about what was tossed in hoping she'd nibble. I remembered our conversation by her locker on the last day of school—her glowing while she talked about soil and cover crops. That image stuck with me.

My brain took over and I gave it free rein, hoping I wouldn't regret what I was about to send.

6

Garden Grown Heritage

Emilia

A warm sun and a canvas-painted bright blue sky. The farm hummed with familiar early summer sounds—buzzing bees, distant lowing of cattle, a steady clank of tools from an outbuilding.

I headed toward the garden, Mamá's domain where she was queen. And me? The royal botanist maybe? But I loved it. The rows of tomatoes, peppers, and herbs soaked up morning light, leaves glistening with dew. I heard Dad's voice calling Miguel as he dragged a clanking wagon across the yard on a secret mission.

My phone buzzed in my pocket. I let it go and focused the rich and alive smell of earth. Of course I was pulled to look. Messages from a certain goofball shaped my daily rhythm. Clipboard in hand I walked the garden getting its details. The soil still held the soft dampness of last night's rain—perfect for feeding roots without drowning them.

I crouched down to check the leaves of tomato plants. Some pale-yellow patches, a subtle sign of something veering off course.

Maybe iron ran low, or a fungus tried to sneak in. I made a note to test the soil pH and consider a foliar feed if it got worse. Basil nestled beside the tomatoes, its sharp, fresh smell natural bug repellent.

Companion planting, not tradition only, but science unfolding in our garden. I noted to keep an eye on aphids, those little invaders who could be put off by the scent of basil. The dark, deep smell of a healthy compost pile told me the mix was fine—brown leaves, lawn clippings, healthy garden pruning. I jotted down to add more straw soon, to keep everything balanced and make happy microbes.

Drip irrigation checked and adjusted as needed? Yep. Mulch covering the beds of plants that wanted cozy roots. Check. Bees and butterflies, a hummingbird too, swirled around the native pollinator garden. In a few minutes I counted up a healthy number of visitors. Perfect. I wanted to add more and spread out a bigger pollinator sanctuary. Plant more natives and non-invasive wildflowers and grasses added on the to-do list? Check.

My garden journal filled with observations, notes, and questions. A record of conversations with plants and soil I'd recorded the past few years. Over time the Preston family moved from farming to stewardship.

We still made a living from our land, but our care increased. We farmed with greater curiosity, asked better questions, planned better and hoped that each season the land would be healthier than the season before.

I stood up and swept my eyes across the garden. Rows of tomatoes, peppers, herbs, and squash—not just plants, leaves, stems, buds and roots but living threads that wove together the two halves of my family.

The tomatoes, destined for sauces and stews that reminded me of Grandma Preston—warm, hearty meals passed down through the farm kitchen.

The jalapeños and cilantro, bursting with vibrant life, carried flavors and stories from Mom's Mexican roots.

Basil and oregano used by both bridging the gap with their familiar scents. Squash and beans, staples for meals no matter which side of the family. This garden was soil and plants and the place where I came together. My heritage wove a beautiful patchwork of traditions. Each seed that grew, each vegetable picked did more than feed bellies.

As I breathed in the garden's scents, a familiar feeling settled in. Pride and hope and love for what my family did.

Notes-

Tomatoes. Leaves looking a little droopy-water more in the evenings. Cage them soon before they topple.

Cilantro. Already trying to bolt. Pinch the tops!! (Miggy calls this the soap plant).

Tomatillos: Lantern husks forming-so pretty. Must stake before they sprawl all over.

Green Beans. Climbers. Add another twine row tomorrow. Don't forget or they'll take over the squash.

Radishes. Harvest before they split! Note: Miggy insists on keeping the weird-shaped ones.

Squash. Monster leaves = chipmunk umbrellas. Check underside for squash bugs.

Carrots. Thin the rows-too crowded. Save the baby ones for Miggy's snack pile

Herbs (epazote, thyme, oregano, rosemary). Thyme tiny but mighty. Oregano smug as always. Rosemary pokey. Epazote smells wild-Mom swears by it for beans.

Jalapeños. Still small. Sun lovers. Don't overwater.

Compost. Turn, add straw, use for miracles.

7

Only One Way to Be Tyler

Emilia

As I read my notifications and scrolled, I saw a text from Tyler. I laughed. I'd just been thinking about the garden supplying tomatoes and carrots and squash, all of which could be used in many ways.

Tyler, though he was a unique variety and there only one way to be Tyler—easy-going, a little chaotic, full of laughter and surprises. Different from me feeling like something I had started to like.

> **Tyler:** Hey Super Soil Regeneration Girl —don't hit me — we can go Woman if you want, or even Lady, though it's got no rhythm.

> **Me:** Stick with Girl. Lady makes me sound like I should be clutching my pearls and pouring tea not planting cover crops or sticking my hands in compost.

Tyler: As a farm superhero you need a buddy and I vow to be your trusty helper—Almanac Man.

I read his message and smiled, shaking my head. Only Tyler would come up with that. I thought about Tyler listening to my cover crops at my locker. He nodded along, half amused but I saw interest—it stuck with me.

Me: Almanac Man? A bit Little House on the Prairie, isn't it? Kinda 1800s? Unless your uniform includes dressing up like Pa Ingalls.

Me: Here's what farmers read now: Progressive Farmer, Successful Farming, The Furrow, Modern Farmer, Midwest Organic and Sustainable Education Service (MOSES) Newsletter, No-Till Farmer.

Tyler: I want MOSES so bad, but taken right? Progressive, Successful, Modern—yeah, all that works. These adjectives not in existence the other day? When you forbade me to give you Bow Chicka Wow Wow back?

Tyler: Anyway, I decided. Meet…*The Furrow*. Not sure what a furrow is. Important and essential to farming though I bet.

Me: A furrow, Mr. Almanac—is a fancied-up trench in the dirt providing seeds a nice cozy home. Not as glamorous as it sounds, but hey, without furrows, farmers would just be throwing seeds and crossing their fingers. Just be prepared for bugs Furrow-boy.

Tyler: See—I knew**!** Essential. Furrow-Boy? [scowling faced emoji]

Me: Who's a farmer? Me. If I'm named SSR Girl, then you're named Furrow-Boy. That or Tyler the Trench. You decide.

Tyler: Fine. Furrow-Boy. No one wants to be a trench. Sounds like a foot fungus.

Tyler: Just returned from a superhero Retreat on Lake Metigoshe. Sharing the fun!

Picture attached: Tyler holding a small fish sunfish.

Tyler: I told this fish it could be in a picture with me, or it could wait to see if SSRG comes fishing someday. It jumped into my lap. No other bait needed. So please meet Harvey.

Me: Harvey would choose the lake if you'd said that and then he wouldn't be looking traumatized in your pic.

Tyler: I shared a moment with Harvey. An alignment of hearts after a discussion of bossy girls we knew. He clued me in, scales make girls even meaner. He recommended I talk to a whale he knows. Whale girls are all sorts of smart-assed trouble.

Me: Go ahead and consult the whale. But I worry. Can you keep up with the whale's giant brain?

8

Catching Up with Captain Basketball

Tyler

Three weeks of summer gone by since I saw Aiden—three weeks of him living, breathing, and dreaming basketball. I bet their water breaks included basketball-decorated cupcakes and sheet cakes with frosting courts and tiny plastic figures shooting three-pointers.

He bounced out of the doorway like a camp bus running on fumes and hype. "Dude, you won't believe who I met at camp," he said before he said hello. He spoke in his excited about b-ball voice which he never used nothing else.

"Who?" I asked, half-intrigued, half-bracing myself, as I followed him into the living room.

"Josh Harlow," Aiden said, dropping onto the couch and already pulling out his phone. "Man, watching him play up close, it's watching a whole different level of basketball."

"Josh Harlow?" I repeated, a twist landing somewhere under my ribs as I sat beside Aiden. Josh Harlow, basketball royalty—a

North Dakota high school basketball legend in high school. Playing now at the University of Minnesota. Rumors swirled of the Timberwolves showing interest.

"Yeah, check this out," Aiden said, holding his phone between us. We watched a highlight reel of Harlow's top plays from last season. Unreal—smooth, fast, confident, Harlow played and made you believe the court belonged to him.

"He's amazing," I admitted and an unnamed feeling tightened its grip. "So, you got to play with him?"

"A bit, yeah. He gave me some tips," Aiden said, aiming for casual and missing by a mile. "Makes you think about the future, you know? Like, playing in college."

"College?" It felt like planning a trip to an Antarctica. "You thinking about playing college ball already?"

"For sure," he said without hesitation. "What about you? Any thoughts on where you want to be?"

I looked at my hands. "I don't know," I said. Too many moving parts. Too many ways a plan could derail before it started. I avoided thinking that far ahead. Aiden seemed to catch the shift in tone and steered us back to safer ground.

"Well, we've got varsity tryouts to think about once school starts. That's close enough. We should start prepping together—get a leg up on the competition."

"Yeah, that sounds good," I said, grateful to focus on something real. Something that seemed within my control—at least as far as I could see.

"Let's hit the courts tomorrow, start getting back in shape," Aiden said, lighting up again.

"Deal," I said, and meant it. The future could stay on the shelf for now. The court I could handle. As he kept talking about camp and drills and who passed who in the ladder rankings, I listened. Having him back was good even if his words reminded me of choices I might never have.

9

Movie Plans Drop

Emilia

Group text from Jenna

3:42 p.m.

> **Jenna:** Movie night tomorrow! My house. 7:00. Bring snacks. Also bring your sense of humor and like… decent socks? I don't know. Just show up.

3:43 p.m.

> **Aiden:** Can we not with the socks thing.

> **Maddie:** Translation: All his basketball socks are dirty and he's too jock to wear sandals.

> **Drew:** *[GIF of a cow saying MOOOOOVIE]* I'll try to make it—got calves needing vaccinations

> **Aria:** *[GIF of a cat in mismatched argyle socks]*

3:47 p.m.

Nate: We're watching something that's at least 80% explosions, right?

Aiden: No

Maddie: Okay, then rom-com

Aiden: No.

Aria: Animated musical?

Aiden: No way

Aria: Aw, Aiden's got his own little black rain cloud and he's in the mood for black-and-white dubbed films that are depressing in two languages.

Nate: Okay then, what's the movie formula? Like… 40% explosions, 30% car chases, 30% sarcastic dialogue?

Drew: Nate, what's the ratio of stuff to stuff that makes the best movies?

Tyler: Aiden, bruh, you sound like you're 95 and your dentures hurt. Will your gums feel better if we watch *Hoosiers*?

Me: Basketball movie—ugh.

Aiden: Sounds good to me.

Jenna: I was thinking *Pitch Perfect*, but since Aiden's a Grumpy Grandpa, *Hoosiers* works.

Nate: : *Hoosiers* is 70% basketball, 20% redemption, and 10% inspirational speeches about basketball.

Ivy: And 100% boring *[GIF kidding but sort of not]*. Hi guys! Can't stay long. [Emoji with tear]. Yeah, I gotta run, but miss you all! *[blowing kisses emoji]* *[GIF of character getting lost in a forest]*

Me: Ivy! *[cartoon image of knuckles]*.

Me: Pound it out! [explosion emoji] Boom! Miss you chica!

Tyler: A number of us play basketball. IMO this text thread is spiraling into mean.

A few minutes later Ivy texted me.

Ivy: Love you too, firstie/bestie.

Me: ???

Ivy: First cousin/best friend. Couldn't figure out how to smash 'em together.

Me: Yeah, I probably wouldn't try anymore either. Love you. Get your butt home.

Tyler: I'll need to thank Jenna for saving me from eye roll withdrawal and allowing me to annoy you in person (texts don't do justice to your eye rolls).

Me: I've been practicing. I think I cracked the 180-degree rotation

Tyler: So you're bringing eye rolls then? I'm bringing junk food—the king of which is M&Ms (not feeling gummy worms after a fishing trip)... and myself. Been told more than once that I'm a snack, so I figure what I'm delivering will hit.

Me: You should be afraid of what I'll do if you show up calling yourself a snack. I live on a farm, and we eat our livestock.

Tyler: Okay wow. Suddenly reconsidering my whole identity.

Me: As you should. And halt the self-referencing as a snack food.

Tyler: I need to chat with Harvey about bossy girls who live on farms in ND.

I tossed my phone onto the pillow beside me, trying to look disinterested. No one watched. If I practiced a couldn't-care-less facade for the outside, maybe the inside would follow. Couldn't-care-less wouldn't be suddenly counting down to tomorrow night. Couldn't-care-less would ignore thoughts of seeing Tyler that felt exciting.

5:11 p.m.

> **Nate:** Perfect movie formula = film reel brilliance + ugly-cry moment + the kind of twist that makes you argue for a decade × popcorn × unlimited GIF reactions. *[mic drop emoji]*

10

Eye Roll You Right Off the Sofa

Tyler

I showed up to movie night with a backpack full of chips, soda, and a king-size bag of M&Ms, bearing what I described with accuracy as "snack curator swagger."

Jenna made me leave the swagger at the door. The M&Ms came in with me. Emilia was already on the couch, legs tucked under her, halfway into building some kind of blanket fortress.

"You're in my spot," I said. She didn't even glance at me.

"I got here first."

"Sure, but emotionally it's my spot."

"I will emotionally shove you off this couch."

I sat in a different spot. Right next to her. Close, but not suspiciously close. Just... suspiciously-close-adjacent. I offered her the M&Ms. She took one. A red one. One single M&M.

"Are you testing me?" I asked.

"All the time," she replied.

About thirty minutes into the movie, I leaned over and whispered, "Jenna's popcorn makes you forget you're eating carbs and buttery fats—I swear it's diet food in disguise."

She didn't look away from the screen. "She tells the butter tales of its great flavorful destiny. Then she makes the whole bowl pretend to be air-popped."

I grinned. She didn't smile back but looked smug and snagged another M&M. A red one.

For a few minutes, we sat there like that—close enough that our arms almost brushed when we reached for popcorn together. I noticed and noticed she noticed. I acted like I hadn't noticed anything. We both leaned back, like it didn't mean anything. Like it never happened. I went back to watching the movie. She pulled her blanket fortress a little tighter. It still felt like a win.

She took a total of 21 M&Ms. Yes, I counted. I noticed how she always pinched them between her thumb and pointer finger—right-handed. Average time from snag to mouth: five seconds. Average gap between red M&Ms: three minutes, thirty seconds. No, I don't know why. Neither did Harvey.

Emilia

The next morning I didn't expect a wakeup text. Not at all. But when I checked my phone the next morning and didn't see a text from Tyler, I felt... a pang. A pang void of feelings. A feelings-free pang. So it couldn't be a disappointed pang. Nope. Just a weird pang of unexpected absence—like opening the fridge and not finding something you hadn't even known you'd wanted.

I scrolled through notifications. Group chat silence. No new messages from Furrow Boy though he'd texted every day since school let out. Not just once—sometimes multiple times. Chaos. Snack updates. Fish stories. Fake emotional trauma. A consistent application of bothering. Distributed with a steady hand, layer after layer—like Van Gogh, piling on paint until voila—a masterpiece.

Not being accustomed to his quiet didn't mean I missed it. Duh. I set my phone down. Picked it up again. Checked it twice more. Then shoved it under my pillow like that would erase the weird flutter in my chest. He'd text later. Or not. Didn't matter. Right?

One hour later... then two... then...

> **Tyler:** Sorry for the bothering delay. Needed time to for emotions to heal after the couch seating injustice. I've been eating M&Ms one at a time for every tear that fell—not the red ones though. Red M&Ms are now linked to emotional trauma.

> **Tyler:** Ok fine, out helping Gramps with yard work and hoping I could sweat out the pain.

> **Me:** Oh? I figured you left, headed out for a chat with Harvey. He's the one who can understand your snack-related trauma. He thinks the worms on a hook you offer him are a treat.

I didn't respond right away—in my mind. In my reality I responded at the speed of light. I stared at the screen, thought about the speed of my response. Not slow, not medium, not just fast. Phone grabbed. Message swiped. Reply typed. Sent—all in nanoseconds. Ugh.

I tossed my phone across the blanket like it had made me text, made me lose self-control. I stared at the ceiling and failed to keep the smile off my face.

11

Old Soul Tech Talk

Tyler

I walked around with an old soul in an athletic, leaning-on-the-good-looking-side, attractively freckled, young adult body. Remembering I was a teen was sometimes a challenge. I showed up expecting normal human behavior—talking, joking, interacting like the social species we claimed to be. Eating ice cream, as we should have been, since the meet-up took place at North Riverbend Ice Cream.

Instead? Zombies. Scrolling. Everywhere. Aiden? Doom-scrolling. Jenna, Aria, Emilia? Heads buried in their phones. Even Nate, who should have been watching birds and calculating their flight paths, had his phone out. I stopped a few feet away and took in the scene. Shining sun, singing birds, a perfect sunny day. My friends? Zombies it seemed.

I shoved my hands in my pockets and rocked back on my heels. I could let this go. I could. No, I could not. I cleared my throat. Loudly. Nothing. I crossed my arms.

"Wow. Look at us. Picture of youth. Vibrant. Engaged, completely, wholly living in the moment."

Nothing. I sighed. "This is it, huh? This is how civilization ends? Not with a bang, but with an Insta refresh?"

Jenna finally looked up. "Ty, you're such a—"

I cut her off, launching into a full-on speech. "You know, back in my day—a whole, what, ten years ago—we used to do wild things. Play basketball. Ride bikes. Have actual conversations where we looked people in the face."

I shook my head, staring at them with exaggerated disappointment. "And here you all are. Wasting your youth. Squandering your potential."

Nate snorted. "Are we getting a 'back in my day' speech from you?"

"Yes," I said, pointing at him. "And it's well deserved. Look at you! You're scrolling social media when there's social sitting right next to you."

Yeah, Nate—I'd noticed that little off and on crush on Jenna you've got. Nate put his phone down. Jenna looked at him with a frown. Nate opened his mouth, then shut it. No equations to rescue him. I smirked and turned to Aiden. "And you. I don't even have to check to know you're scrolling Ivy's posts for the hundredth time." Aiden didn't look up.

Aria rolled her eyes. "You act like you're above this, Ty, but I'm willing to bet you were on your phone five minutes ago."

I gasped, placing a hand over my heart. "I'm deeply hurt. I am an old soul. A man of integrity. A beacon of—"

Emilia held up her phone. A screenshot of an Instagram story. A picture of me and Aiden after a basketball practice, looking on the edge of survival. The caption?

Nothing like putting in the work. Grind never stops. #hooplife #basketballisfamily

Aria burst out laughing. "Oh, busted."

I gaped at Emilia. "You did not just do that."

She tapped her chin, considering. "Should I comment? Something motivational?"

I groaned. "Emilia, no."

"Maybe something encouraging."

"Emilia."

She started typing and narrated as she went.

"Pain is temporary, but screenshots are forever. #neverforget."

The betrayal. I clutched my chest. "You wound me."

Jenna and Aria lost it. Emilia just smirked, tapped her screen with finality.

"Posted."

Aiden, still staring at his phone, muttered, "You deserved that."

I glared at him. "Traitor." He shrugged. I glanced back at Emilia. She was trying hard to look innocent. Jenna scrolled and narrated the post drama like a sports commentator. I stepped closer to the table. Sliding in next to Emilia.

"Wait, so we're shipping Ivy and Jordan now?" I asked, resting my chin on my hand. "Do they have a name yet? Jovy? Ivardan? Please say 'Jovy.'"

Jenna gasped. "Tyler. Genius."

Emilia turned to look at me, "Do you have to insert yourself into everything?"

I shrugged. "What can I say? I'm invested in my friends' emotional well-being."

Aiden made a low, murderous noise. I coughed to cover a laugh.

"Besides," I added, nudging her shoulder,"don't act like you aren't watching this play out too."

She narrowed her eyes, but there was amusement there. "I am simply observing," she replied, "Not stirring the pot like some people."

"Some people," I repeated. "You mean me?"

"I mean you."

Our eyes met for a second too long. She looked away first. Huh. Interesting.

Emilia

Tyler was not smooth. He thought he was, but I saw his ears turn light red when he caught me looking at him too long. I would not give him the satisfaction of reacting. Instead, I swiped my phone off the table and scrolled through my feed. A few posts down, I found something too good to pass up.

Aiden's latest post: ***Nothing like putting in the work. The Grind never stops. #hooplife #basketballisfamily***

It was a photo of him and Tyler at practice. Sweaty. Exhausted. Tyler was doubled over like he was about to pass out. Perfect. I held up my phone so Tyler could see the screen.

"Is this the grind that never stops?" I asked sweetly. "Because it kinda looks like you stopped. Hard."

Jenna and Aria burst out laughing. Tyler groaned, dragging a hand down his face.

"Oh, c'mon. That was one bad drill."

I tapped my chin, considering. "Should I comment? Something motivational?"

"Emilia, no."

"Maybe something encouraging."

"Emilia."

I started typing. ***Pain is temporary, but screenshots are forever. #neverforget.***

Tyler made a sound of pure betrayal as the comment posted. Jenna lost it. "Oh my God. I love you."

"Remind me why I like you?" Tyler muttered, half to himself. I rolled my eyes and scrolled back to Ivy's post, typing out a quick comment. *Time at the farm when you get back, promise. Get home, miss you.* When I glanced back at Tyler, he was watching me something unreadable in his expression.

"What?"

He just smirked. "Nothing. Just waiting for my moment to get revenge."

I shook my head. "Good luck with that."

He only grinned.

Tyler

The zombies decided the heat was too much for their decaying flesh and shuffled into the ice cream shop. They ordered mundane ice cream flavors for their dead taste buds. Okay, yeah. Once we got inside where AC blasted and they turned devices off; my friends were much less zombish—zombieish—zombie-whatever.

We crammed around a small table in the corner that was too small. The buzz of my phone in my pocket interrupted me as I started to tell a joke. Squished in the middle I pulled out my phone, careful to keep it hidden. A spike of alarm ran through me when I saw mom texted me—*Tyler, we need to talk*. My heart stuttered with fear. I took a breath, reminded myself mi Mamá had a flair for the dramatic. My apprehension didn't lessen. It was a default setting from years spent waiting for the worst to happen.

Just as I started to shove the phone back into my pocket, Emilia leaned over. Her eyes narrowed, a smirk tugged at the corners of her mouth. "What's so secretive over there, Ty? Got a little love note from someone?"

I smirked back. This girl. Bickering with her was a good distraction, so I rolled with it. "You ask that with such intensity. Jealous, Emmy? It's just the usual. Mom's updating me with details for my upcoming marriage to a beautiful heiress. But if you'll excuse me, I need to make a call."

Getting out of the booth was like escaping a human-sized knot puzzle. I sidestepped past Aiden, still glued to his phone. I shot Emilia a look. She raised an eyebrow, unimpressed with my excuse. Too bad, if she thought she had competition, maybe that would shake her out of her nonchalance.

Maddie jumped in, "Maybe we should keep him trapped in the booth until he shares the juicy details of his betrothal and courtship."

Emilia

Everyone described Tyler as a goof or clown. Always joking around, getting the laughs. Me? Sometimes I think he's just secretive. He doesn't open up, share his real self. Maybe that's why I've pulled back and added distance when it all felt too close.

If that text was just from his mom, why didn't he just tell us? We all have parents that text us, check in, tell us to head home, or ask where we are. Why does he hide? I saw him through the shop window as he talked to someone. I'm no lip reader, but... did he speak Spanish?

I swear I caught "Hola mamá. ¿Qué pasa?" Not hard Spanish to learn, but using it on the phone? I realized I needed to stop staring out the window and pulled my gaze away.

Tyler

Mom answered, "Hola Tyler." Her voice quivered. Something was wrong.

"¿Estás bien mamá? ¿Pasa algo mal?"

"Mijo," I heard her rapid Spanish, "I'm sorry. I should've just waited until you got home. Shouldn't have bothered you."

"¡Mamá!" Something was wrong. I needed her to tell me.

"I just talked to my mother. Her father, my grandfather, died last night. I haven't seen him in so long. He told her to give me his love and to tell me to raise you well. I'm sorry, it was hard to hear. But I could have waited."

"No, Mamá." I said. "I'm so sorry. I know you love—loved him so much. I'll be home soon, okay?"

I headed inside to make my excuses using the joking me that came out to deal with hard stuff.

12

Fielding calls from Major League Baseball

Tyler

My phone buzzed. I didn't think much of it. It would be Aiden sending another meme or Nate analyzing basketball stats. But then I saw her name.

> **Emilia**: Recovered from the grind? Hope the pain was only temporary.

I grinned before I could stop myself. Was that... concern? Nah. Couldn't be. Just Emilia being sarcastic. Except—no emoji. No punchline. Straight-up, a touch-sassy-but-maybe-also-nice Emilia. My fingers hovered over the screen a second too long before I typed back.

> **Me:** Well, I mean, I lived. But only just.

Truth.

> **Emilia**: That's all that matters.

Truth.

I stared at that one for a second. She was teasing sure. But there was something else. Familiar. Easy. Like we'd been talking like this forever.

> **Me:** That I survived? Or only just?

> **Emilia**: Both. Whichever. Whatever keeps you the most humble.

Oof. I leaned back and shook my head, grinned like an idiot. There she was. The girl who could roast you with zero hesitation and still make it feel like a compliment. Maybe it was getting her attention that felt so good.

Tyler

-an hour later-

My phone buzzed. Emilia? I frowned and answered.

"Hello?"

There was a pause. Then a confident, little kid voice said, "Hola!" I blinked.

"Uh. Hi?"

"It's Miguel Cabrera." Silence.

"... I'm sorry, what?"

"Miguel Cabrera. You know, the baseball guy. Are you Meela's friend?"

My brain was working too hard for a school break.

64

"Uh, I think you might have the wrong—"

"She's a good big sister. But mucho bossy, mucho! Okay, gotta go, bye!"

Click. He hung up. I stared at my phone. What. Just. Happened?

Emilia

I rolled off the couch, still singing under my breath as the credits played. One more rewatch? Maybe. I stretched, yawned, and reached toward the end table where I always—always—left my phone. Not there. I frowned. Checked the cushions. Still no phone. I checked my hoodie pocket, my backpack, and the kitchen counter. Nada.

"Miggy!" I called, already suspicious. "Where's my phone?"

No answer. I circled through the house. Something tugged at me—an instinct born of years lived with a stealthy, four-year-old chaos machine. I checked the laundry room. And there it was. My phone. Precariously balanced on a stack of clean towels. Screen down. I picked it up and turned it over. Smudges and a text.

> **Tyler:** Okay, so, weird thing just   happened. A random kid called me. Said his name was Miguel   Cabrera. Then hung up.

I froze. My stomach did that sinking thing it always did right before a dream-test I forgot to dream-study for.

65

Me: Wait! What??

Tyler: Any chance you know an ankle biter who thinks he's a retired MLB player?

No. No way.

I groaned out loud. My four-year-old-brother who left chaos behind and managed feats impossible for most preschooler. I left the room for, what—two minutes? Three max?

Me: Good grief. He got into my phone.

Tyler: So you do know him.

I flopped onto the couch with a dramatic sigh and started typing.

Me: Yes. I mean. Maybe. Did he sound like an eccentric   chaos-inducing genius disguised as a four-year-old?

Because if not, maybe it was someone else's menace. I could dream.

Tyler: Oh he did. He also said—and I quote—'She's a good big sister. But mucho, mucho bossy.'

I buried my face in my hands.

Me: Yeah. That's my little brother.

I waited, braced for teasing.

Tyler: Well. That explains a lot.

Me: Sorry.

What else was there to say about Miggy your four-year-old-brother, who could highjack a cellphone?

Tyler: It was oddly entertaining. I   need more details on this tiny menace.

Me: Only if you take an oath not to encourage him.

I knew he grinned as he typed. Please, please don't encourage him.

Tyler: I can't make any promises.

Me: I'm regretting so much

Ugh.

Tyler: You'll live. But only just.

I rolled my eyes, half-laughing. This boy.

Me: Still. My four-year-old brother has more access to you than I do.

Tyler: Well, I mean… do you want increased access?

It was supposed to be a joke. I think I was joking, sort of. Wait. Yes, definitely joking.

Tyler: You there, Meela?

My breath caught. I stared at the message. Read it twice. Three times. I didn't even know what to type. I paused and knew I was waiting too long to answer.

Me: I hate you [scowling emoji]

I huffed.

Tyler: Nah, I doubt that now Meela

There was long pause. I thought, maybe he's done and I can get on with regretting my life.

Tyler: I'll be the one waiting over here, ready to give you access.

Ugh, ugh, ugh....

Tyler: And appreciating how revenge just found its way to me.

I dropped the phone onto the couch cushion next to me, face burning. This was fine, it was all fine. Nothing embarrassing occurred. The only drama? Miggy was grounded. Forever.

I found Miggy under the kitchen table. He sat cross-legged and snacked on a piece of string cheese. He looked way too pleased with himself.

"Miguel Ángel Preston," I said, arms crossed. "Why did you call Tyler?"

He blinked up at me unfazed. "He needed to know what he's in for."

I narrowed my eyes. "In for?"

Miggy shrugged like it was obvious. "With you. Is he a baseball player?"

I opened my mouth. Closed it again. My brain tried to process the casual chaos of that sentence. Miggy came out and wandered off, humming to himself like he hadn't just acted in my social life.

"You're four," I called after him. "You're supposed to be learning your alphabet, not evaluating my social life."

I groaned. I could hear him mumbling. "Mucho bossy...."

13

Summer Ghosting is Still Cold

Tyler

Around a week and a half before school started Jenna tossed a "Movie night?" into the group chat and then... radio silence. Lots of dead batteries or mandatory screen free time maybe? And a couple of the crew were off on last-minute family vacations.

A couple hours later, she texted me directly.

> **Jenna:** You think it's worth trying?

I leaned back on my bed and flicked a foam basketball into the air.

> **Me:** Yeah—I'm in if we get a couple bodies there.

If Emilia's was in I was in. But I had a doomsday feeling about her showing. I fired off a group text to the warm bodies in North Riverbend and waited, spinning the ball on my finger like that would make time move faster.

> **Nate:** If there's popcorn.

Aria: If there are Sour Patch Kids.

Aria: Tyler buy me some Sour Patch Kids, I'm babysitting all day.

Me: Nate, you want the most basic movie night ingredient. Challenge us dude! Never mind, just meet me later and we'll buy more junk food.

Me: Aria, use your polite words and maybe

2..5 seconds later

Aria: Please, Tyler. Please will you be kind enough to buy me some Sour Patch Kids. [puppy dog eyes emoji].

Aiden: Maybe. I'll let you know later.

I texted Jenna.

Me: Nate and Aria have allowed themselves to be bought with junk food. Aiden's a maybe. I say—let there be a movie.

No reply from Emilia. Even Ivy texted back to Jenna's original group message.

Ivy: Sorry, my battery was dead and I was napping like the dead. Wish I could—Mom and Dad want my company, something about me being their only kid and being gone all summer. They've been clingy drama llamas [winking emoji].

Jenna: Aww, that's sweet, Ives. We missed you too. And they're your mom and dad.

Around five, I met Nate at the Fill and Go store to grab movie junk food. Fuel of choice for the night? What would it be? Sour Patch Kids were a given to keep Aria from pouting. We were stumped trying to decide—Twizzlers or Nerds?

"Twizzlers are rope technology," I said. "Solid, dependable. You can tie a knot in one, swing it like a lasso—"

"Geometry," Nate cut in. "Straight lines you can twist. And Nerds are statistics—total sugar scatter. Probability in a box."

He tilted his head, going into full pondering-the-universe mode. "If we're being precise, Twizzlers are topology. Stretchy shapes still count. Nerds? Chaos theory, if you throw a handful in the air."

"Or tic-tac-toe," I said. "Use Nerds for the Xs and Os, see who eats the board first."

We tossed both bags into the basket. Equal opportunity sugar. My phone buzzed. A quick check informed me not Emilia.

"You okay, man?" Nate said, eyeballing me and not asking the thing on his mind. Why are you acting like Grumpy Grandpa Aiden's mini-me?

72

"Yep," I said, and tossed in Starburst and Rolos for good measure. Seemed movie night would include me eating my feelings.

At 6:50, Aiden showed up at my door, his mom waiting in their car to drive us both to Jenna's. Thoughtful of him. Also sneaky—by then he knew Ivy wouldn't be there.

Mrs. Pedersen dropped us off. I thanked her, then gave a smile and a wave. That summed the past couple weeks of August—wave, smile, gone. Except the smile-wave to gut-roil ratio was a lot lower with Aiden's mom than with Emilia. Nate rolled up with two liters of soda. Aria dared to text and check that I'd gotten her Sour Patch Kids. What a brat.

Halfway through the opening credits, Jenna randomly announced, "Emilia texted me—she's stuck helping her little brother with something."

Hmmm. Guess she replied to Jenna's original text, not my follow-up. As for helping Miggy—I wished I'd had a handy Miggy of my own. A four-year-old brother was a useful avoidance strategy. You didn't have to lie. The odds were good a four-year-old needed help with something every five minutes. And from what I knew of him, Miggy was a 24/7 project.

I laughed in the right places, heckled the hero when appropriate, ate unholy amounts of chocolate, and pretended the empty cushion on the couch wasn't mocking me.

I made myself wait and not bounce right away.

First, I'd have to walk, and the mosquitoes would enjoy a little bite of Ty at night. Second, I'd be pathetic at home too—might as well be that way with my bro Aiden. We'd be pathetic squared and let Nate calculate our sad, sad futures.

At home, forget pathetic squared—it became pathetic to the nth.

Me: Missed you at movie night.

Three dots blinked. Paused. Disappeared. I stared at the screen too long. I divided my level of pathetic by 30 seconds of typing bubbles on screen. I'd have to ask Nate if loser statistics existed or if pathetic would always be x in my equations.

Two days later, we ended up at the same park by accident—pickup game, late sun smearing gold across the backboards. I'd been there an hour, sweat-soaked and happy, when I saw her at the far bench with Ivy and Jenna, cans of pop sweating in their hands. I lifted a hand. She lifted hers.

The game broke; I started toward the bench. She glanced down, said something to Ivy, and stood, mouth making a quick apology shape I couldn't hear. They turned toward the bathrooms. I slowed, pivoted back to Aiden instead.

"Your jumper's getting cocky," I said, bumping his shoulder and not letting my eyes sweep over to her, not a bit.

By the time they came back, someone had called next. I took it. Safest place I knew—three steps beyond the arc, the ball humming in my hands, a clean aim to focus on when the rest felt messy. We played until the light dipped.

The last Friday of summer, I tried a different angle.

> **Me:** Park hangout, fake sports and gossip. You coming? I think Ivy might even show up.

She'd been saying yes all summer long—until the last few weeks. A heavily weighted constant in my equations. Small word, big multiplier: yes × feelings = Happy Tyler. But now? Happy Tyler ÷ (confusion + frustration) = undefined on the whiteboard.

The reply took a while.

> **Emilia:** I don't know. I'll see.

I read it twice, then a third time because apparently needed to multiply the pain. I typed "No worries!" Deleted it. Typed "All good," deleted that too. Settled on a response communicating nothing.

> **Me:** K

"K" the flattest most boring response of my generation. She could interpret it as a shrug or a variable that stood for "whatever."

I set my phone face down and stared at the ceiling fan. Told myself school would fix it—schedules would box our days into the same hallways and lunch tables, and whatever this was would shrink under fluorescent lights. Deep down, I didn't buy it.

Because here's the thing, when you spend a whole summer learning the exact musical phrasing of someone's laugh, you also heard its absence. You noticed that sitting close-adjacent got replaced by a half-inch step back. You heard when yes phased into "we'll see." You noticed and pretended you didn't—because you're an idiot or patient. Or both.

I rolled onto my side and watched my phone not light up. The coming Monday would be loud—the squeak of shoes, the bite of the whistle, Aiden yelling "Ball!" at practice like he could manifest one out of thin air.

I'd lean into all of it—as usual. I'd listen to the mass of noise, let the sounds fill my mindscape. And not strain to listen for a faint musical echo that could mean her.

14

First Day as a Freshman

Emilia

Everything looked the same. Same brick walls. Same trophy case. Same lingering scent of floor wax and mass amounts of chicken nuggets. something felt... off. Like the school had shifted half an inch to the left while no one was looking.

I adjusted my back pack and scanned the hallway. Summer had stretched and twisted me. In mostly good ways. But now, standing at my locker, I couldn't untie the knot in my stomach. A not-sure-what-I-feel-&-I-did-ghost-Tyler nasty tangle of feelings that pulled tighter and tighter. I spotted Ivy and felt relieved.

"Sneak hug!" I launched myself at her. She jumped, squealed, and mock-shoved me.

"You absolute menace."

I grinned. "You're welcome. It's a public service—cutting through back-to-school weirdness."

"You cut through weirdness like a chainsaw," she muttered, but hugged me back anyway. She always hugged back.

Tyler

77

I walked into school like I owned it. Ninth grade. High school. New school year, new swagger. New? Wait, no, the swagger I was born with, just finely aged and improved. That feeling lasted three seconds.

I saw her. Emilia, casual, laughing with Ivy like she hadn't lived in my thoughts most of the summer and haunted the last couple weeks by ghosting me. Her hair was longer. Or shinier. Or maybe I wasn't letting myself fully remember her. Whatever it was, it knocked the wind out of me. I tried to play it cool.

"Wow, Emilia," I said, flashing a grin that matched my ninth-grade swagger. "Outshine the upperclassmen, break high school hearts... strong first-day strategy. Aiming to break all high school hearts today or just last names of A to J?"

"Hey, Tyler." Couldn't meet my gaze straight on, no eye roll. Yeah, ghosting someone makes life awkward doesn't it, Em?

"No breaking. I'll just be dissecting in biology."

Not her usual snap in the comeback. Then she turned and walked towards class. The pitiful part of me was glad she wasn't herself. The better me that wanted her to always be okay didn't like her missing spark. Ivy was the only who gave me a puzzled look.

I stood there for half a second and ran my hand over my face. I gave Ivy a rueful smile—hadn't known until this summer I could rue. I shrugged at her then, "Well, see ya around Ivy."

END of AUGUST
TO THE
END of SEPTEMBER

15

Overheard

Emilia

The first couple weeks of school had been fine. Tyler and I had both done a great fake out for our friends. We're okay. I didn't ghost him at the end of summer. See happy us. The worst thing about it was Tyler wearing the it's-all-no-big-deal-persona. He'd shed that this summer, but I'd given him reason to put it on again.

I was mad at myself. Why had I avoided Tyler? All I came up with was growing feelings scared little Emilia away. Now I watched him and worried about the what he showed us all. What did real Tyler feel, what was he carrying? I had no right to ask him, so instead I worried and observed.

"Tyler," I whispered, nudging his arm. "You with us?"

He blinked and came back from staring at nothing.

"Sorry," he mumbled. "Just got lost in Mr. Hanson's sweater vest. Is that argyle or just a unfortunate stain pattern?"

Aiden snorted, while I narrowed my eyes.

"Alright team," he said, leaning forward." Let's tackle this project before Hanson's fashion choices permanently scar us."

We dove into our work, but my mind kept circling with worry.

Tyler

"...and that's why the mitochondria is the powerhouse of the cell," Mr. Sorenson droned on, his voice faded into a distant hum.

I'd been staring at the same spot on the whiteboard for who knows how long, zoned out in class again. Not good. I glanced around. I saw most of my classmates furiously scribbling notes. Crap. I'd missed something important.

"Hey Tyler," Jenna whispered from her desk beside me. "You okay? You look like you're a million miles away."

I plastered on my best grin and whispered something funny back. She smiled and I breathed a sigh of relief. Humor, my go-to deflect mechanism worked overtime in class now. Jenna turned back to her notes and the humor faded. I couldn't focus on biology when all I could think about was Mom, her face closed down, her fragile appearance.

Mr. Sorenson's voice cut through my thoughts. "Tyler, can you tell us the function of the cristae?"

"Uh..." I scrambled, "Gives Mighty Mitochondrion High varsity ball team extra court space and energy to drill. Preps them to take state this year." The class erupted in laughter, and even the teacher's lips twitched. I joked but I usually had a halfway intelligent answer.

"In a sense I suppose, Tyler, but bring your focus back to class please."

"Yep, sorry, my focus will be microscopic Mr. Sorenson," I said and forced myself to concentrate. As I jotted down notes about electron transport chains and ATP synthesis, my thoughts drifted to Mom. Was she okay? Had she eaten? Should I have stayed home with her. When the bell finally rang, I was first out the door, heavy with worry, biology already forgotten.

I always carried worries about mom. This was more. Losing her abuelo had taken too much. I didn't expect her to just get over it. If I lost Gramps, I don't know what I'd do. And I got to see Gramps every day. Mom hadn't seen her abuelo in sixteen years.

I knew she'd grieve, but I needed her to take care of herself while she grieved. I wasn't sure she was eating. The circles under her eyes, said she wasn't sleeping well. She kept working hard, and our schedules didn't sync. I didn't get enough time with her to make sure she ate and rested.

She looked more delicate. For the first time I remembered she looked breakable. Mom was small but had always shown a core of steel. Losing abuelo had siphoned off some of her usual hopefulness and gratitude. Grief weighted down her usual optimism.

She hadn't seen her family in person for almost seventeen years. They talked on the phone and had the occasional Facetime. The last time she'd hugged her mom was a decade and a half ago.

I leaned against my locker, closed my eyes for a moment. The metal felt cool against my forehead as I took a deep breath.

"Get it together, " I muttered to myself.

"Hallway nap Tyler?" Emilia's voice startled me, but I heard concern under teasing.

"Yep, just revving myself with a pep talk for practice later."

"Mmmhmm, sure. I noticed your lack of confidence. I've been worried you started thinking you're ordinary mortal."

Digging deep, I yanked funny Tyler out. "I know I look like perfection on the court, but it's not just physical. Gotta get the psyche juiced up too."

The warning bells rang and I gave Emilia a jaunty two fingered salute. "My psyche thanks you for caring though."

Emilia

As Tyler walked away my heart twisted. He was hauling around a big burden but he wouldn't let me in. I'd known Tyler since third grade when I called him Prince Butthead. I thought he'd been mean to Ivy, but I learned quickly he'd never pick on her.

We'd always bickered and teased each other. I'd never seen him this... distant. And yeah, I did a great job ghosting him the last couple weeks because of my own issues, but I hated seeing him weighed down.

Ivy waved her hand in front of my face. "You coming to class or what?"

"Yep, let's go," I mumbled.

As we walked, my mind kept replaying Tyler's behavior. The way his eyes darted around in class. How he deflected questions with jokes that didn't quite reach his eyes—more so than I ever remembered.

I slid into my seat, thoughts already drifted back to Tyler. Doesn't anyone else notice how much he deflects with humor? Am I the only one who's noticed his tension, strain? I hated seeing him like this. I wanted to grab him by the shoulders and shake. I wanted the real laughing, teasing Tyler, not Mr.-Faking-You-All-Out.

I wanted to tell him I ghosted him because inside I guess I'm scared by—I'm unsure. Tell him I didn't want to be confused anymore, that I'd help shoulder whatever weight he carried.

"Ms. Preston, care to share your thoughts on this civil war battle?"

I snapped to attention, and heat crept up my neck. I'm not good on the spot and usually paid strict attention in class. I winced as a pathetic response tumbled out. I sank lower in my seat.

At last the bell rang. This was the was the last class of the day. Tyler should be heading to the gym for practice. I needed to check on him again.

I headed towards the gym. I caught a glimpse of Tyler ducking into a classroom. He usually sprinted to practice. I hesitated for a moment, then moved in the same direction. At the classroom door I peeked in.

He pulled out his phone and tapped. I heard ringing then a female voice, "Hola, mijo!" His face, a tight mask of worry, relaxed when he heard the voice.

"Mamá?" Tyler's voice was low, gentle. "¿Cómote sientes? ¿Estás bien? ¿Hablaste con el Gramps? ¿Lo hiciste? Bien, bien. Teamo mamá. Volveré a casa justo después de la práctica de baloncesto."—*How are you feeling? Are you okay? Did you talk to Gramps? You did? Good, good. I love you mom. I'll come home right after basketball practice.*

He sighed, then rolled his neck and shoulders. "Okay, Mamá. Te quiero. Call me if you need anything, ¿Sí?"

As he ended the call, I looked at his face once more. He looked so tired. His game face slid back into place and as worried as I was, I realized I'd stumbled upon a private moment. I moved to back away. He turned before I could back out of sight.

"Emmy?" Tyler's eyes widened, a flicker of panic crossed his face before he masked it. "How long have you been standing there?"

I stepped forward, heart racing. "Long enough," I admitted. "I'm sorry. I didn't eavesdrop on purpose. But I'm so worried about you."

He forced a laugh that had no real humor. "Aw, I'm fine, just checking in, you know how moms are."

"Stop, Tyler! Stop trying to brush everything off. You don't have to be okay all the time, and that sounded serious."

Tyler's shoulders tensed. The struggle to brush me off or open up warred on his face. His hand moved to the back of his neck. Something he did when truly uncomfortable, which wasn't often.

"It's... complicated," he said, voice rough. "Family stuff, you know? But I've gotta get to practice now."

He moved to the door and turned away from me. I saw his torso rise and fall as he inhaled deeply. Stopping he clutched the doorframe and turned.

"You heard me speaking Spanish, didn't you?" he asked, his voice almost a whisper.

I nodded, trying to keep a neutral expression.

"I did. I didn't know you were fluent."

He let out chuckle. Again no real humor. "Yeah, well, there's a lot you don't know about me, Emmy. There's so much... so much I haven't told anyone."

Tyler

Em touched my arm. "Tyler, I'm here. Don't shut me out. I care you."

I thought we were friends. Getting to know each other better, but then you ghosted me Emmy. At the worst possible time. Now I know if you see my mess, you'll run. Faster and farther than you ever have.

"Tyler, I'm listening. I'm here. I'll be here for you. I don't give up on my friends."

I scoffed, the sound harsh to my own ears. "Sure about that, Emmy? Sure you won't back off if I start moving closer to you? That's what you do you know? I take a step forward. You take two steps back. This summer all I wanted was to get to know you better. But without warning, you disappeared. I tried but you kept pulling back and now? I'm certain as soon as I start in on my tale of woe you'll take off, running far and running fast."

The words came out sharper than I intended, laced with bitterness. She flinched. I wasn't aiming to hurt her but I was tired of being careful.

"That's not fair," she said. Her voice is unsteady. "I'm here now, aren't I?"

I leaned against the doorframe, so tired of dragging this weight and worry around. "Yeah, you're here now, Emmy. But will you stay? I'm done chasing Em. My life, it's messy and complicated and..."

I trailed off, not sure how to finish that sentence. Painful? Overwhelming? Too much for someone like her to understand? Someone secure with mom and dad happily married, no worries, someone living in rosy hazy light. Emmy took a step closer, her eyes searched mine.

"And? What, Tyler? What aren't you saying?"

For a split second, I considered spilling everything—about Mom, about her abuelo, about the constant pressure to hold tight a secret that could ruin our lives. How I was having trouble holding it together. But I remembered how hard it was to keep her near, how skittish she was. I wanted her to stop running not from pity, but from choice. I straightened up, smoothed my face.

"And, I've gotta head to practice. It's nothing. Just forget I said anything, okay?"

I turned to walk away. I could feel her gaze burning into my back. Part of me wanted to turn around, let her in. I couldn't. Opening the door to her again would be messy and painful. And if she backed away again? Now I wasn't protecting only my mom and our little family, keeping our secrets safe. I was protecting my heart.

16

Porch Swing Conversation

Emilia

Tyler's words repeated in my thoughts. We'd been polite the last few days, nothing more. *That's what you do, you know?* I did know. I felt the connections we'd created. I'd gotten frightened and pulled away. His words were were sharp, but I deserved them. This summer I saw how he carried himself behind a joking façade. Then in fear, I'd given him reason to camouflage himself again.

Mamá joined me sitting on the porch swing. "You look deep in thought, Mija."

I closed my eyes. I could talk to my mom about anything, anytime.

"My friend, Tyler," I started, words coming rushed. "The other day, I overheard him speaking Spanish with his mom on the phone. Like, fluent Spanish. But he never speaks it at school or with us. It's like... he's hiding part of himself."

Her brow furrowed slightly, face still. She was a great listener. "Sounds like quite a surprise. He'd never mentioned speaking Spanish before?"

I shook my head. "Never. And it's not just that. There's so much about his life he doesn't share. I feel like I barely know him, even though we've been friends for years."

As I spoke, I realized how much it weighed on me. The disconnect between the Tyler I thought I knew and what he had hidden was jarring. Mamá nodded.

"I'm just... I'm worried about him, Mamá. There's a huge load he's carrying alone. I don't know what it is. And I don't think he'd let anyone help."

Mamá's eyes softened with understanding. She reached out and squeezed my hand. "Can you tell me more about why you're worried?"

I bit my lip, chose my words with care. "I realized he's always on guard. He's the funny guy, making everyone laugh. I think his joking around is his way of hiding." I hesitated, remembering our last conversation. "He said something about me running away when things get too real. I think he feels like he can't open up to me."

Mamá nodded. "Is this something you've noticed for a while now?"

"Oh, Mamá, it's always been there, I think. It's just now that I'm seeing it. I feel terrible," I admitted. "It's like I'm seeing him for the first time, and I don't know how to help."

"Has Tyler ever mentioned any problems at home?" Mamá asked. I shook my head.

"He hardly ever talks about his home life. His grandparents are always the ones who show at games and stuff."

Her expression turned thoughtful. "Emilia, what do you think Tyler needs most right now?"

I stilled. "I think... he needs to know it's okay to let people in. That we're here for him, no matter what."

Mamá squeezed my hand again. "I understand you want to help, Mija. You can't force someone to open up if they're not ready."

I nodded. "I know, but it's hard to just stand by when I can see he's struggling."

"I know, Mija. But pushing can cause people to close off more so be careful. It might be the best thing you can do is simply be there, ready to listen when he's ready to talk."

I let out a long sigh. "You're right. I just wish I knew how to make things better for him."

Mamá looked far away and deep in thought. "You know, Emilia, I wonder... is it possible Tyler's mother might be undocumented?"

My eyes widened. "What? I never even thought about that."

"It's just a possibility but would explain a lot. It's a bad time to be undocumented in this country. Remember, being undocumented is part of our family history too."

I leaned back, processing this. "Your abuela?"

"Si," Mamá nodded. "Your abuela's mamá. My grandmother lived with that fear for years before she got her papers. It affected the whole family, especially the children."

My mind raced making connections. Tyler's guardedness, his reluctance to talk about home, the absence of his mother at school events. It all made painful sense.

"What should I do?" I asked, my voice just above a whisper.

"Just be there for him, Mija. It's a life of constant worry."

I nodded, my chest tight. "That must be hard. Always looking over your shoulder."

"Si, and for kids like Tyler, if that's his situation, they often feel responsible for protecting their parents. It's a heavy burden."

I thought about the serious demeanor Tyler hid behind jokes. He let his friends get close, but not too close. "Behind his joking he's always so guarded. Like he's protecting a whole world."

Mamá's eyes were soft with understanding. "Your abuela had to grow up fast, carry adult worries way too young."

"You know, I've never seen Tyler's mom. Not at school events, not picking him up... nothing."

"Really?"

"Yeah," I continued. "And he hardly ever talks about her. It's always his grandparents he mentions."

Mamá nodded. "I imagine it feels safer to avoid talk and being in public as much as possible."

I felt wave of sadness for Tyler, imagining the stress he must be under. "I wish there was something I could do to help."

"Being a good friend is the best thing you can do right now," Mamá said. "Just let him know you're there, without pressure."

I nodded determination settled in my chest. I might not be able to fix Tyler's problems, but I could make sure he knew he's not alone. "It must make them both sad. His mamá never gets to see his school or sports events. Can never cheer him on. His grandparents are always at events, but still. If you and dad were never at anything, it would hurt."

"I've met his grandparents, you know. They're good people, but of course he must miss having his mamá see him."

Mom leaned back her expression thoughtful. Before she could say anything more we heard the scrunching sound of tires on the gravel drive. She glanced at her watch and smiled.

"Looks like your apple pickers are right on time." She pulled me into a quick hug. "Get your crew organized and have fun with your friends."

17

Apple Picking Crew

Emilia

Excitement and nervousness twisted in my stomach. I loved apple-picking season. Every fall, we gathered a group to pick apples from the orchard. It's not huge—forty or so trees—but in a good year, each tree could produce a hundred pounds of fruit. Even a smaller orchard buried us knee-deep in apples at picking time.

This year, I invited friends to help. We'd keep some apples, send a bag or two home with every picker, and donate the rest to a local food pantry. Dad switched up the invite each season so different groups got a chance to be part of the tradition. My Preston grandparents started it, and Dad carried it on.

A familiar car pulled up, and before it came to a full stop Ivy hopped out, shoes crunched against the gravel. She grinned at me, darted to give me a quick hug. I waved at her dad, my Uncle David as he backed up to turn the car around.

Ivy inhaled deeply. "Smells like apple empanadas," she said. Her eyes lit up before she zipped into the house. I shook my head and heard her cheerful voice ring out inside.

"Hola, Tía Mariella! It smells amazing already."

"There's my favorite niece!" Mom called back, her voice warm.

Their conversation faded into a murmur. Ivy returned to the porch, looking pleased with herself. Tyler and Aiden were climbing out of a car. Tyler's gaze met mine, and for a moment something unguarded showed in his expression. Then his usual easygoing grin slipped into place and covered whatever had been there before.

"Hey, Emilia. Hey, Ivy," Tyler said shoving his hands into his pockets.

"Hi, Ty," Ivy responded, then turned to Aiden. "Hey, Aiden." A blush crept up her face. She wasn't the only one blushing, though—I caught the tips of Aiden's ears turning pink. Oh, this was going to be fun.

"We're gonna go help my mom finish with something inside," I announced, grabbing Ivy's hand before she got trapped in awkward small talk with Aiden. "You guys can make yourselves comfortable."

As we stepped inside the warm scent of cinnamon and baked apples wrapper around us. Miguel stood by the kitchen table, arranging toy plastic dishes. Sofía toddled around, holding a plastic apple like a priceless treasure. Ivy had only stepped inside when Miguel noticed her.

"Meela! Sonidita is here!" He shouted as if I wasn't standing next to our cousin.

Ivy beamed. "I am! And look at you, helping out."

Miguel nodded importantly. "I gotta set up for the apples. And Sofía is in charge of baby apples."

Sofía waved her plastic apple proudly. "Baba app-oh." Ivy crouched down.

Miggy grabbed her hand, "Do you know the rules Sonidota?"

Ivy placed a hand over her heart.

"I am ready to follow all apple-picking rules."

Miguel leaned in, his voice conspiratorial. "Rule one: No eating all the apples before we finish picking."

Ivy gasped. "I would never."

Miguel eyed her but moved on. "Rule two: If you drop one, you gotta say sorry to the apple."

Sofía added a solemn nod. "Sowwy app-oh."

"And rule three," Miguel continued, "No saying Shiiiicken feathers."

Ivy clapped a hand over her mouth. "Oh no."

Miguel nodded sagely. "Mamá says that's almost a bad word."

"I know," Ivy groaned. "Because I said it, didn't I?"

Miguel tilted his head. "I don't know. Maybe. But now I know it, so you gotta be extra good."

We stepped back onto the porch as two cars crunched up the gravel. Jenna in one and Nate in the other. As usual Jenna had a bounce in her step as she and Nate joined us. The boys greeted Nate with fist bumps.

"Ready to put us to work, boss lady?" Jenna asked. She bounced in place. "I'm apple-solutely ready to get started." We all groaned at her bad pun. Except Tyler who high-fived her. He was the king of bad puns and that was Tyler-level bad.

"Yep, this is all of us so let's get going and do some serious apple picking!"

We made our way towards the orchard. The slight breeze brought the scent of apples. The green-turning-yellow leaves were bright in the slanting afternoon sun.

"Most of our trees are the Haralson variety, along with Honeycrisp, Sweet Sixteen, and Fireside varieties for the best cross pollination."

"Why are there so many tree stumps over there?" asked Jenna pointing to a former section of the orchard.

"Those were trees infected by the fire blight disease. It spreads fast and my grandpa didn't want to lose the whole orchard so those were cut down and removed."

"Trees get infected?" Jenna asked.

"Such a city girl," I teased her.

"Oh yeah, the big city of North Riverbend," she replied. "I guess even surrounded by farms and ranches, it's easy to not understand how it all happens."

"You're right Jenna. I don't know all the ins and outs of ranching, but I can tell you about the fire blight bacteria and how it enters through the tree's blossoms. And how it causes a tree's branches to look burnt."

"You've got the Preston farmer DNA, that's for sure," Ivy said and linked her arm through mine. I smiled at her. Ivy loved coming to the farm, but she'd never been interested in operations.

Clapping my hands I said, "Alright, team, divide and conquer. We've got bushel baskets here at the start of each row. So, fill 'em up!"

Tyler and Aiden headed to a row. Nate and Jenna to another, leaving Ivy and I to work a row together.

"C'mon Cuz, if you want more apple empanadas, you've got to put some work in. I know you're a city slicker, but having the Preston last name isn't enough."

Ivy hip bumped me as we headed towards the stack of baskets. "I've picked plenty of apples here as you well know."

Before I could respond, Aiden's voice rang out.

"Yo, Tyler! Check this out!" Through gaps in the row of trees we turned to see Aiden holding a rotten apple, a mischievous grin on his face. He shot the apple like he would a basketball and it splatted on a tree trunk about 10 feet away. Tyler's demeanor instantly shifted, a competitive glint in his eye.

"Oh, it's on," he said, scooping up a mushy apple of his own. "One point for each trunk you hit on the way down the row."

As they start lobbing the rotten fruit at an imaginary basketball hoop, I couldn't help but smile. For a moment, Tyler looked carefree, like the weight he seemed to carry had lifted. Did that send a jolt of happiness to through me?

I glanced at Ivy. She stared at Aiden with a mix of longing and affection. She might have had emoji heart-eyes. We were almost to the end of the row when I heard Dad's voice near Tyler and Aiden.

"What in the world are you two up to?"

Tyler and Aiden froze mid-throw, uncertainty plastered on their faces. I wasn't worried, I'm sure my dad's eyes are full of amusement.

"You call that apple-ball?" he chuckled, striding over to pick up a fallen apple. "Let me show you how it's done."

With a fluid motion, Dad sent the apple sailing through the air. It smacked against a distant tree trunk with pinpoint accuracy, exploding in a spray of pulp.

"Whoa!" Aiden exclaimed, impressed.

Dad grinned. "That, boys, is how you play apple-ball. Let's see you beat that!"

Tyler's competitive spirit ignited. "You're on, Mr. Preston!"

As they started lining up shots, I couldn't help but roll my eyes.

"Dad? You're encouraging this?"

He winked at me. "You know this is a legendary family sport, don't you? I've lobbed thousands of apples out here with my brothers."

I laughed and shook my head at him. "You're still a big kid."

I saw how relaxed Tyler was after an hour of lobbing apples. If it relieved stress, he could toss as many rotten apples as he pleased. He and Aiden only needed to keep the bushel baskets filled.

18

Orchard Games

Emilia

The last few baskets were filled. The picker's did great but were getting restless. Ivy kept stretching and Aiden tried spin an apple on his fingertip. Dad showed up, holding a ring of keys and grinning like he just unlocked a secret level farm game level.

"Alright, team," he called out. "Apple haul's looking good. Anyone want to ride some three-wheelers or take the Gator around the orchard loop?" That got their attention.

"YES," Ivy shouted. "Shotgun on the Gator! No take-backs!"

Jenna shot her a look. "That was alarmingly fast."

"I've been training for this moment since third grade," Ivy replied, already moving.

Dad waved them toward the south trail. "We'll take the back path—safe loop, no roads, helmets only, one at a time on the three-wheelers. And absolutely no donuts in the pumpkin patch again, Ivy."

"No promises!"

Ivy, of course, already knew every bump in the trail and was halfway through describing the exact tilt angle needed to get "maximum bounce" as they disappeared down the hill. That left one person still standing near the crates. Tyler. He watched the group go, then turned toward me.

"So... you're not going?"

"I've done it fifty times," I said. "I used to ride on the back while Ivy tried to convince Dad to let her steer with her knees."

"That... explains some things," he said, eyes narrowing in mock concern.

I smirked. "Come on. If you're skipping the thrill ride, I want to show you something."

We veered past the newer rows and into the scruffier edge of the orchard. The trees there were older, branches heavier and more spread out. The ground uneven, and the grass grew in patchy clumps.

At the far edge, a few sun-faded structures leaned against time: a half-buried tire, a splintered wooden crate, a slouching fence post. A cracked wooden sign still clung to a tree, painted in lopsided red letters: Penalty Zone—For Whiners and Cheaters.

This," I announced, "is the sacred ground of the Preston Rotten Apple Games."

Tyler tilted his head, considering it. "Was this built mid-collapse or post-apocalypse?"

"Mid-collapse," I said. "My dad and his four brothers started it when they were teens. The crate was the trophy. Or the time-out box. Depending."

He surveyed the tire. "So what was the game? Just... throw apples at stuff?"

"Not just. It was high-level organized chaos. Points for distance. Style. Explosiveness. If the apple made a satisfying splat? That was a Double Goo Bonus."

Tyler grinned. "What else?"

I started ticking off on my fingers. "One point for a clean fence hit. Two if the apple skipped like a rock. Three for hitting the tire from behind the crate. Bonus point if your apple makes a noise that could be described as 'a gassy apple burp.' And negative two if you complain about being sticky."

I handed him a soft apple that was all a bruise. "You in?"

He tossed it, testing the weight. "Absolutely."

Game on. My first throw hit a branch and dropped like a brick. Tyler's nailed the tire on first try and he looked too pleased with himself.

"You're hustling me," I accused.

"I'm athletic and chaotic. This is my moment."

What followed was chaos. We slipped on pulp, shouted invented rules, and awarded ourselves bonus points for "emotional impact."

I tried a sidearm lob that launched a boomerang apple that returned back at us and we both screamed. He threw one so high it hit a branch and bounced off enough to splatter midair. That earned a full five-point bonus for theatrical fruit vaporization.

I gave him a look. "Show-off."

He bowed. "This is an elite sport, Emilia."

We collapsed on the grass near the fence line, breathless, sticky, and laughing too hard. The orchard quiet, the hum of wind through branches blended with the distant buzz of the Gator.

We heard Ivy yelling, "This isn't out of control, I'm in gravity-assisted speed mode!"

I glanced over at Tyler. His hair tousled, his shirt covered in apple guts. He smiled without a trace of guardedness.

"You're good at this," I said, half-laughing, half-serious.

He shrugged. "I found my calling. Apple-ocalypse."

I groaned. "Okay. Minus two points for rotten puns."

He went quiet for a moment, gaze drifted toward the tire. When he spoke again, his voice was softer. "It's huge being somewhere that has this history. Like, you can feel it in the ground."

I nodded slowly. "It's not just land to us. Every path, each fence line has a memory. My grandparents planted this row. That crate's been here longer than I have. Even the trees that aren't here anymore... we remember them."

I reached out, ran my hand along the old fence rail. "This farm gives so we take care of it, in return."

Tyler watched. "That's kind of incredible."

I shrugged, feeling embarrassed suddenly "Yeah, there's more than just what you see."

"Yeah," he said. "A lot more. You're lucky to have that."

I nodded, not finding any words. We didn't speak for a minute. The breeze moved through the trees, brushed past us like a memory. I swear the air shifted—like everything in the world took a breath and waited. I cleared my throat and stood up, brushing off apple bits.

"Alright. You smell like fermentation. Let's get cleaned up before dinner."

He followed without protest. "Do I get bonus points if the fermentation smells authentic?"

"Only if you plan to age in a barrel."

The others were back—loud, laughing, covered in dust—we were setting out plates and glasses. Ivy paused at the top of the porch steps, brow furrowed when she spotted us.

Jenna peered past her. "Wait, weren't you guys with us?"

"We took a detour," I said.

Tyler shrugged, completely deadpan. "Turns out the Preston orchard has a competitive side."

Aiden blinked. "There was a competition?"

Ivy narrowed her eyes at me. "Did you take him to the Splat Zone?"

Tyler's mouth quirked. "If you mean the tire, the crate, and the sign threatening emotional damage—then yeah."

Jenna's eyes widened. "There's a zone?"

Tyler nodded with mock solemnity. "I saw things. Fruit-based warfare. Unresolved family trauma. Honestly? Ten out of ten."

Dad chuckled and handed me something my mom had handed him to take out back. "The legacy lives on."

19

Bonfire Understanding

Emilia

We filled up basket after basket with apples. We stuffed ourselves full of the delicious supper that Mamá prepared. After dinner Dad started a bonfire. Adirondack chairs were perfectly placed around the blaze. Everyone sprawled out in a chair or on a big log around the crackling fire.

The fire had burned strong but began dying down. I saw glowing red embers perfect for toasting marshmallow. Ugh, can I eat more? Chocolate, graham crackers, toasted marshmallows? You know what? I definitely can.

I headed into the house grabbing what we needed, then set it all on the picnic table near the fire. "Loosen your belts everyone, there's stuff for making S'mores on the table."

I heard groaning, but everyone got up and got what they needed. After my friends got what they needed, I grabbed my own supplies. I saw an open spot on the log next to Tyler. I didn't overthink and walked over.

His eyebrows lifted in surprise when I dropped down beside him. Usually, he was the one seeking me out, coming to sit by me, not the other way around. I realized how much effort he put into getting to know me.

"Hey," I said, cringing at how awkward I sound. Tyler gave me a small smile.

"Hey yourself. Good haul today?"

"Bushels and bushels picked by the A-Team. Each of those bushel baskets weighs almost fifty pounds filled. My arms are going to be sore tomorrow."

Tyler chuckled, squeezed my upper arm. "Yeah, not much happening here. You need to start lifting."

We lapsed into silence, me acutely aware of how close we sat. Our shoulders didn't touch cause a sliver of space was between us. I could feel the warmth radiating from his body. Nice and nerve-wracking. I snuck a glance at his profile illuminated by the flickering firelight. His brow was furrowed, like he was deep in thought.

The crackling fire sent sparks dancing into the sky, mirroring the nervous energy that sparked in my chest. I took a deep breath, steeled myself for what I needed to say.

"Tyler," I began, my voice low and quiet. "I'm so sorry for eavesdropping on you the other day at school."

"Oh," he said, his voice flat. He stared into the fire, and some of the strain he released earlier showed up. Guilt washed over me.

"I should've walked away or made my presence known."

Tyler was silent for a moment, then sighed. "It's okay, Emilia. You didn't do it on purpose."

I nodded, relieved still uneasy. The fire popped, a shower of sparks flew up. I pressed on. "I didn't follow you to listen in. I wanted to check on you. I've been worried about you. It seems like you aren't okay."

He ran a hand through his hair, a gesture I'd come to recognize. "It's complicated," he said. "And I know that you weren't trying to listen in. I'm sorry. I shouldn't have been angry. Shouldn't have snapped at you."

"It's okay, Tyler. I surprised you when you thought you had privacy. I understand."

He shook his head. "No, it's not okay. I knew you were trying to help, and I pushed you away. That's not cool."

"Tyler, I..." I paused, swallowed hard. "I want to be there for you. I didn't pull away on purpose, it was reflex I guess."

"Emmy," he said, and I felt a shiver run down my spine at the nickname. "What I said to you at school forget it. All I ask is that you stop putting space between us."

Tyler shifted on the log, his knee brushed against mine, sending a jolt through me, and I forced myself stay still. I took a deep breath, ready to respond, but Tyler beat me to it. His voice was just above a whisper, rough with emotion.

"My dad was killed in Afghanistan before I was born."

I turned to look at him, but his gaze was fixed on the fire, the flames reflecting in his eyes.

"Tyler, I... I'm so sorry," I managed. I felt how inadequate the words were. He shook his head slightly, a sad smile tugged at the corners of his mouth.

"It's okay. I mean, it's not okay, but... you know what I mean."

I nodded, even though he wasn't looking at me. My mind raced and tried to process. How could I not know this about him? Tyler continued, his voice steady but tinged with sadness I'd never heard before.

"I never got to know him, but I have an emptiness inside where he should be."

My heart ached. Without thinking, I reached out and placed my hand on his arm again. He tensed for a moment, then relaxed into the touch.

"It's like... there's this hole, you know?" he said, finally meeting my gaze. "And sometimes I wonder if I'll ever be able to fill it."

I wanted to say something profound, to make it all better, but words stuck. Instead, I squeezed his arm and hoped he could feel all I couldn't say. Tyler took a deep breath, his eyes flickering between me and the crackling fire.

"When you pull away," he said, "It hits that emptiness. I don't... I don't want to feel anymore loss."

That was painful to hear. I'd been so caught up in my own fears and insecurities. I reacted on feelings I didn't understand and never considered how my actions might affect Tyler.

"I..." I started, but words die on my lips. What could I have said? I felt a whirlwind of emotions—guilt, sadness, and a need to help. Tyler looked at me, eyes searching mine. I could see the vulnerability there, the raw honesty of what he'd just shared. I opened my mouth, closed it, then opened it again.

"Tyler, I... I don't know what to say," I admitted, my voice barely audible over the crackling fire. "I had no idea...."

He nodded slowly, understanding in his eyes. "It's okay, Em. I didn't expect you to have all the answers."

But it's not okay, I thought. How could I have been so blind? The silence stretched between us, filled only by the pop and hiss of the bonfire. My hand was still on his arm, and I realized I didn't want to let go.

"I promise I'll work, try not to be afraid of... of closeness. I'll try not to just react. To be there for you." My voice trembled, but I pushed on. "I don't know why I'm so wrapped up in my head, I didn't realize..."

He turned to face me, his face showed both strength and vulnerability.

"You don't have to promise anything, Em," he said.

But I shook my head, felt more certain than I had in weeks. "No, I want to. You're important to me, Tyler. More than I've let myself admit."

A small smile tugged at the corner of his mouth, and something in my chest fluttered. I hesitated, then added, "But I feel like you're carrying around this huge weight. You're trying to hide it from your friends. And I want to help, but I don't know how."

Tyler's shoulders slumped and I almost saw the invisible burden he shouldered, whatever it was made of.

"It's complicated," he murmured.

"You said that already," I teased. "Your friends don't need to know all the details. But let us help in whatever way you can let us in. We're here for you, all of us."

I gestured towards our group around the fire, their laughter a comforting backdrop. Tyler's eyes followed my hand, lingered on our friends for a moment before returning to meet mine. I saw the conflict in his gaze, like he teetered on the edge.

"I've always handled things on my own," he said. "It's... it's hard to imagine doing it any other way."

I bit my lip and thought. How do help this stubborn boy see it was okay to lean on others?

"You've got such a big heart Tyler. You're always there for us, me. We want to support you. Even if you can only share a bit right now."

He didn't respond right away, and I saw the hesitation but something else too—a glimmer of hope, maybe? I held my breath, waiting. Tyler took a deep breath. I could almost see the internal battle working across his face.

"My mom and me," he started, "before we got to North Riverbend, there were a lot of messes around us."

I resisted the urge to reach out and touch his arm, sensing he needed space to get the words out. I nodded encouragingly, hoping my presence was enough.

He swallowed hard, "I can't... I can't talk to you about it yet," he continued, his eyes darted to mine for a split second before returning to the fire. "But maybe..."

His voice trailed off and left the sentence hanging in the air between us. I felt the weight of everything he didn't say, the stories hidden behind words. I wanted to push, ask more, but knew I needed to respect his boundaries.

I nodded again and said, "Whenever you're ready, Tyler. I'll be here."

"Thanks, Emmy," he murmured. Then someone brought up an embarrassing story about Aiden in seventh grade which got us all talking and laughing. Tyler nudged me and nodded in the direction where Ivy and Aiden were laughing together.

"You think those two will figure things out soon?"

I followed Tyler's gaze to see them absorbed in their own private conversation. Ivy's eyes shone as she animatedly recounted some story or joke, punctuated with lively hand gestures. Aiden watched her, leaning in so as not to miss a single word.

"I hope so," I replied. "I think almost sixteen years is the longest meet-cute in history."

Tyler grinned. "Not sure what a meet-cute is. But time to give them a push. Trick play."

He picked up a marshmallow and tossed it, landing it perfectly in Ivy's hair. She jumped up with a yelp.

"Aiden! Did you do that?" Ivy demanded, pulling the sticky marshmallow from her curls.

Aiden looked bewildered. "No, I didn't!"

"Then who..." Ivy scanned the group until her eyes landed on Tyler, who tried and failed to look innocent.

"Tyler!" Ivy put her hands on her hips. "What's the big idea?"

"Well, Princess I thought your knight in shining armor would catch it, not just watch it land on your head. He's supposedly got wicked guarding skills, but now I'm wondering. Maybe he needs to step up his game."

I stealthily picked up another marshmallow. Staring intensely at Aiden I tossed it at Ivy. His hand snagged the marshmallow out of the air before it hit her face. They both blushed and snuck glances at one another, pretending to be interested in roasting marshmallows.

"Nice shot teammate," Tyler whispered to me. He held up his fist for me to pound. "He needs reminding there's something in his life better than basketball."

"What about you? Does basketball rule your world?"

Tyler looked at me. "Do I love the game? Definitely. Maybe my life is more complicated than Aiden's. I don't know. There are bigger things happening around me I guess."

His eyes intense and serious he continued. "I know there are people that mean way more than the game."

I swallowed and shifted on the log feeling twitchy. My knee bounced. Tyler put his hand on my knee and held it still for a minute.

"Remember you promised, no more distance. So, please don't pull away Emmy."

END OF SEPTEMBER
TO
MID-NOVEMBER

20

Thinking about Wishing

Tyler

Mr. Henderson wrote on the white board with a squeaky purple marker. He wrote our prompt for in-class work.

"Today I want you to write about childhood wishes. First, think back to one of your biggest wishes as a kid. Then imagine what you would say to your younger self about that wish if you could go back in time. And then rewrite the wish from the perspective of your 9th grade self."

I thought back to little me dreaming of being a superhero. I wanted to fly around saving people and fighting bad guys. But even as kid I knew life was complicated. I already knew that—

My dad died fighting in a war before I was born.

My mom and me kept a big secret, that she wasn't supposed to be in the United States.

If my mom got caught, I wouldn't see her again for a long, long time.

I stared at my blank sheet of paper, lost in thought. A superhero wish seemed silly now. I wished I could save my mom from her worries, take away the creases from her forehead. As I tapped my pencil, words started to flow:

"Sitting in class, I think back years. Back then I wished I could fly free across the open sky. Now at 15, my greatest wish is to lift the weight off my mom's shoulders. I dream of a place where she doesn't have to work three jobs, where paperwork doesn't direct her life. I tell my younger self it was okay to wish I'd met my dad, but make sure to appreciate mom and Gramps and Gramma Alred who we came to live with."

I looked up from my paper and saw classmates deep in thought. I glanced at Emilia, she was frowning a little bit, her pencil gently tapping on her chin. Maddie on the other hand was scribbling away, with a faraway look in her eyes.

I continued writing:

"Now I wish to have the power to fix everything for the people I love, to give them a life without fears. I wish to be the superhero I imagined in my childhood stories, but instead of wearing a cape, my superpower would be the ability to wipe away their troubles. I would tell my younger self that wishes evolve as we grow, that our biggest desires come from our hearts and not from comic books.

My new wish as a ninth grader is to make a difference not by leaps and bounds, but by being there for mom in all the ways I can be. I wish to put energy not into wishing, but into solving real problems. And just for laughs I'd also tell my younger self that girls' cooties aren't real and that I'd be making wishes about a certain girl in ninth grade."

Emilia

Creative writing class with Jenna, Ivy, Maddie, Aria and Tyler. I looked down at my blank notebook page, lost in memories of my younger self. I thought about how often I had wished for paler skin, blonde hair, light eyes—anything to look more like other girls at school. As a little girl I was self-conscious, desperate to fit in and be "normal."

I remembered coming home from school in third grade, crying to my dad because a boy said I didn't look American. I told my dad, "I hate the way I look."

He pulled me into his lap and said, "I think your Mamá is the most beautiful woman in the world. I thought so when I first met her in high school, and I still think so. Your hair is a dark, dark brown, almost black, like onyx stone. Your eyes are brown and remind me of the color of the delicious hot cocoa your Mamá makes. Hold out your arm." I did, seeing my golden skin next to his. "Your skin is golden. It's different than mine. Who else in this house has skin the same velvety color?"

"Mamá," I whispered.

"That's right," he said. "Who do you look like, Emilia? Do you want to look just like everyone else? To fit in and be just like them? Or do you want to look like the most beautiful woman in the world—the woman whose heart and love and laugh are as beautiful as her appearance?"

"Like Mamá," I whispered. An understanding bigger than my third-grade heart started to take root. I smiled as I remembered my dad's words. He always knew how to make me feel better.

As I got older, I realized how special my features were—a reflection of my family's rich cultural heritage. Now in 9th grade, I know true beauty comes from within. My dark hair shines in the sunlight, and my golden-brown skin glows with warmth. I appreciate my one-of-a-kind appearance. I wouldn't change a thing about the way I look. My younger self wished to blend in, but today I want to stand out and share the vibrant beauty of my culture with the world.

I took a deep breath and started writing:

"Dear younger Emilia,

I know right now you wish you looked different. You wish your hair was blonde like Ivy's, your skin was pale instead of golden brown. You think changing how you look on the outside will make you fit in better at school. But your looks don't define who you are.

The most beautiful person is Mamá—with her onyx hair and cocoa eyes. She taught me my appearance doesn't matter nearly as much as having a good heart and staying true to myself. I know it's hard when others try to make you feel you're outside. They might not even be doing it on purpose.

Just remember this: No matter where you are; no matter what everyone around you is like—you have so much, maybe even more than what the people around you have. Family full of all sorts of people, heritage in the past and in the now on the farm.

You have love. You'd be loved if your hair was blonde or red, straight or curly. Your family would see beauty in you whether you were pale with freckles or had golden tanned skin year-round. You have so much."

Tyler

When almost everyone was done writing Mr. Henderson got our attention and said, "Let's talk about your next big writing assignment. I look forward to seeing where your creativity takes you. The theme of this project is 'I Wish.' Which you just completed some writing about in class."

"This is a broad and open prompt that allows you to explore your deepest desires, whimsical fantasies, or even changes you wish to see in the world."

"I want you to think about what 'I Wish' could mean to you. It could be a personal wish, like wishing for a certain skill or superpower, or it could be more global, like wishing for world peace or solutions to big issues like climate change. Maybe you wish to revisit a moment in your life, or to bring a fantastical idea to life in your story.

"The format is completely up to you. You can write a story, a poem, a dialogue, or even a letter. Think about how your wish could affect you or others, and what would happen if that wish came true. Would there be unexpected consequences? Or, would it solve problems and bring happiness?"

We all stood up as the bell rang. Emilia caught my eye and I smiled at her.

"That was kind of a cool assignment," she said. "It made me think about stuff I almost forgot about."

"Yeah it was." I agreed. I'd had my childish superhero wishes. But I remembered that I been carrying adult-sized wishes for a long, long time.

21

Farmer's Market Meet & Greet

Emilia

The sun splashed its morning colors across the sky as my mom and I began to scout the good-sized farmer's market held in downtown North Riverbend. Mamá grew a beautiful garden early spring to fall every year. I had taken on more of the work each year.

Shopping at the farmer's market made a fun outing for us. Mid-September, we'd see stalls with apples (don't need any thanks) and maybe pears. I knew there would be piles of winter squash and pumpkins.

Fresh cabbage and carrots as well. I laughed at myself geeking out over the fall harvest. I was a farm girl and I loved it. Here I loved to see not just the produce but products like cheese and soaps.

"Emilia, try these," Mamá said, and thrust a cherry tomato at me. It burst with flavor, and I nodded approvingly. She was a master at picking produce. She claimed she was born with the ability. I think my abuela taught her all she knows.

We moved from one stand to another, my eye caught a familiar figure next to a pickup truck. I watched as Tyler leaned in closer to a lady sitting a truck's front passenger seat. One of her arms was supported by a sling. She still gestured animatedly with her free hand. Tyler listened intently, his head nodded in understanding. They weren't loud as they spoke with one another.

He turned, taking long strides toward the truck bed. He lifted a crate of acorn squash and toted it to a stand with a sign saying, "MacGregor's Farm."

"Are you Mr. MacGregor today?" I said as I wandered closer. He shot me a half-grin. I'd caught him by surprise. At least I hadn't snuck up on him today.

"Helping my mom out today," Tyler explained, gesturing to the woman in the front seat of the truck. "She usually gets the stall set up and then leaves, but she hurt her wrist, so..."

I nodded, understanding flooding through me. Tyler always stepped up.

"Is she okay?"

He sighed, "Yeah, I think so. Can't get her to slow down, so I hope she's healing."

I heard resignation in his voice. It didn't match the joking Tyler I knew. But that's what had confused me right? What he'd been disguising with his class clown personality. I'd glimpses of the boy behind the jokester.

"You're not stalking me, are you? Seems like wherever I go, there you are."

My cheeks flushed, and I rolled my eyes. "You want me to keep my distance then. I mean I do have better things to do than follow you around."

He chuckled sheepishly. Maybe he blushed a bit too.

"Nah, you're good. Stalk away. It brightens up my day."

"So why 'MacGregor Gardens?'" I gestured to the sign hanging above the crates of produce. "Like the Beatrix Potter's book?"

"Yeah, that's their actual last name. They even have a pet rabbit named Peter who makes guest appearances here sometimes. Kids love him."

"Really?" I grinned at the thought. "That's kind of adorable."

"Hola, Tyler!" My mom slipped up next to me.

"Is that your mamá?" Her voice was warm and interested, her extroverted personality shone. He straightened up, his eyes flicked to the truck before he answers.

"S-, yes, that's her," he said. Not missing a beat my mama hurried over to the pickup.

"Hola! Soy Mariella, la mamá de Emilia," she said, her voice quieter than usual. It carried to us, but not much further.

"¡Hola!, Mariella," the woman in the passenger seat responded. Her smile was sweet and radiant. Though I could tell she wasn't outgoing like my mama. I watched Mamá, shaking my head. I looked at Tyler. Thankfully he didn't seem worried.

"Sorry she escaped before I could catch her."

"Your mom's not shy, I see."

I choked out a laugh. "The word shy has never ever been used to describe my mamá."

"It's okay, it's good for my mom to meet someone new." How many other teenage boys watched their mom tenderly when she was made a new friend?

"Making friends is her superpower. She always, uses it for good, I promise."

"No worries, your mom is great," he replied.

My mamá had finished her conversation and was next to me with her arm hooked through mine. She gently pulled me to start towards the other stalls.

"Bye Tyler, see you later."

"See you tomorrow Luz," Mamá called over her shoulder, just loud enough for Tyler's mom to hear. Then she looked at Tyler. "Tomorrow dinner with us. See you then with your Mamá. She's got the details."

I caught Tyler's gaze, he shook his head with a smile. "Sounds good Mrs. Preston."

The early fall air felt charged with possibilities.

22

At the Farm - Dinner & a Beast

Emilia

Standing next to Mamá at the kitchen counter, I felt warm breeze flutter through the open window. She handed me a ripe tomato, its smooth skin taut under my fingers.

"For our salsa de molcajete, everything must be fresh, Mi Corazón," she instructed with a smile that crinkled the corners of her eyes.

"Got it, Mamá. Fresh is best," I echoed, slicing into the tomato and watching its juices bead on the stark white cutting board.

"Exactamente," she nodded, satisfied she was imparting valuable knowledge. And I did see the value of what she was teaching me. This was more than dinner; it was the opening a door. The meal we prepared for Tyler and his mom communicated without words how much we valued them. Our table would welcome them. Hopefully in a way that gave comfort and a sense of safety with our family.

The doorbell rang, and I wiped my hands on a towel before heading to answer it. Luz stood on the porch with a shy smile, Tyler behind her. Luz had a small object wrapped in colorful tissue paper.

"Hola bienvenido a nuestra casa, Señora!" I greeted Luz first. Next I addressed Tyler, "Hi Tyler, come in. Come in."

My insides were strangely jumpy as I met his gaze. Of course I felt my cheeks warming. I could match Tyler in a verbal battle any day of the week, but him standing at my door? A whole new experience.

"Emilia, thank you for having us," Luz said, her accent a little melody weaving through her words.

"Of course, Señora! We're so glad you could come."

"Here, Mija, for you and tu familia."

I took the small tissue-wrapped parcel from her hands, the delicate folds of paper crinkling beneath my fingers. The package was light and delicate. The warmth radiating from Luz and the affection in Tyler's gaze as his watched his mom said something about the weightiness of the tiny gift.

"Gracias, Señora," I said, offering her a grateful smile before carefully peeling back the layers of paper. Nestled inside was a tiny clay sun. Bright oranges and yellows gave the small sun powerful warmth. The detail of the brushstrokes was lovely. My fingers traced the smooth edge as I looked at Luz.

"It's so beautiful. Did you make this?"

Luz's smile deepened, so much showed on her face.

"Sí, Mija. Es una tradición en mi familia, back in Jalisco. We make these solcitos to bring warmth and light into the homes of those we love."

Into the homes of those we love. Emotion welled up. Her small gift wasn't only a polite thank you. It shared her history, her culture, her heart. I met her gaze, feeling the weight of kindness behind it.

"Then I'll make sure it has the perfect place in our home. Thank you, Señora."

"De nada Mija." She reached up and patted my cheek. "And you must call me Tía Luz." Tía, a small, affectionate word—when Tyler's mom insisted I call her Tía Luz it started the growth of a warm connection.

My mom bustled into the entryway and started another round of greetings which sent welcoming and warm Spanish words twining around us.

Tyler

The dining room buzzed with chatter as Mrs. Preston placed the last dish on the table—a steaming pot of rice tinged golden with saffron. Mr. Preston's laughter filled the room, a sound that filled a spot within me that I hadn't known was there.

Across the table, my mom sat beside Emilia, their heads bent together over a platter of carnitas as they shared whispers and giggles. My mom and I often had family dinners with my grandparents. Mom and gramps, both were storytellers at heart. Grams and I had been carried along by their words many times.

The sight of Mom's arm in the sling brought a heavy weight back down on me.

"Is your arm okay, Mamá?" I asked. Just this morning, she'd winced while reaching for a mug. She looked up, her brown eyes meeting mine, and she smiled reassuringly.

"It's healing well, Mijo. Don't worry about me, I'm fine."

I nodded. I'd accept her words. But an edge of worry remained. I admired her resilience, but—she carried such heavy burdens that others didn't see. Emilia must have noticed the look on my face because she looked up and gave me a smile that told me, "*I'm here for you.*" As cool as I always acted my heart rattled and I felt myself blushing.

Mom's family stories came to mind as we ate. The colors, music, and sun all captured in the flavors of Jalisco. I knew Mrs. Preston had prepared this specially for us. After dinner, Mr. Preston stood, his chair scraping lightly against the hardwood floor.

"I've got something you might enjoy," he told both mom and me as he headed out of the room.

I saw Mrs. Preston whispering to Mom in Spanish and heard Mom's reply, "¿En realidad? Qué maravilloso. Una bendición verlo."

Whatever Mr. Preston was after was a marvelous blessing. Hmmm. He returned moments later pile of books and photo albums in his arms. He set the pile down and I saw old high school yearbooks.

132

"We didn't bring this up earlier because we wanted to get to know you. I think your mom already knows this, but Mariella and I knew your father quite well Tyler. We went to high school with him. He wasn't just a classmate though; he was my good friend."

I had no words in reply, to say that was a first—yeah, an understatement.

"Behold, the glory days," Mr. Preston said theatrically, pushing a couple of yearbooks my way. I saw bookmarks and opened one realizing he'd marked pages for me already.

"Your dad was quite the athlete," Mr. Preston told me, pointing at a picture of him mid-dunk, basketball in hand. "But what made him truly special? That was his spirit. He lit up every room he walked into and made everyone feel special."

As we flipped through pages, my mom leaned forward, her dark eyes bright "Es incredible," she murmured pouring over photos of Mr. Preston and my dad wearing football jerseys and gigantic grins.

I swallowed hard, my eyes lingering on the images of my dad. Fingers trembled slightly as I turned pages, more moments of my dad captured for me to see. "Gramps tells me about him too, but seeing this... it's different," I confessed, my voice barely above a whisper.

Mom reached over, placing her hand atop mine. "Your father was loved, Mijo. And now you are getting to know him in a new way."

We listened to more tales about my Dad. Many stories were about the mischief that he and Mr. Preston got into. Mrs. Preston mock scolded her husband over a particularly crazy stunt they pulled. I saw the affection in her eyes wasn't just for her husband though. My dad had a place in her heart.

Mr. Preston leaned back. I felt him wind up to tell me the story to top everything.

"Adam had a banged up old truck. He called it The Beast," he said, a hint of a smile tugged at the corner of his mouth. "He loved it more than any sane man should love a truck. Spent hours working on it, tweaking the engine, keeping it running. Even when it was stubborn as hell, he wouldn't give up on it. Said it had character."

He glanced at me, his expression thoughtful. "I bought it from him for a couple hundred bucks when he joined the service. I drove it for a while here on the farm until it broke down and needed too much work. I didn't know why, but I couldn't part with it, the broken-down thing.

It's stored out here in an outbuilding. When he was killed in action, before I even knew about you, then I knew I'd never be able to part with that darn truck."

He paused for a moment. "Life on this place just got busier and busier. For a long while I hadn't thought about The Beast. Then heard your name pop up around here more and more."

He grinned at Emilia who rolled her eyes at him. Internally I knew she was saying "*Daaaddddd.*" Interesting my name was popping up more and more. Interesting too, that Emmy blushed like crazy."

"Anyway Tyler," Mr. Preston went on, "It's still out there. What do you say we go take a look after dessert."

I tried to come up with the right words, for the second time ever nothing came out of my mouth. But mom's words echoed in my mind, "Qué maravilloso. Una bendición verlo."

Emilia

After dessert, which I didn't have room for, but ate anyway my dad was ready to take Tyler out to see The Beast in one of the outbuildings. I had never heard a word about this broken-down truck. I may have come across it in my explorations. I wasn't sure.

Dad led us outside to one of the oldest out buildings. Tiá Luz stayed at the house with my mamá. Their animated conversations would be echoing in the house for days.

Dad slid large doors. This building wasn't even a proper barn or farm storage building. I'd often thought it was built by a beginning carpenter as an experiment. Through the open door was a dusty tarp over a hulking object.

"This will be a mess. You might want to cover your faces," Dad said before he pulled the tarp sending years of farm dust whooshing through the air.

Tyler

There it was—The Beast. My dad's old truck. Faded paint, dented and dinged. And honestly, yeah, butt-ugly. Maybe the greatest example ever of beauty in the eye of the beholder. That ugly old truck was one of the most beautiful things I'd ever seen. I glanced at Emilia. She had tears in her eyes—dust and debris? Most likely she knew how much this meant to me.

"This old thing, it's more than an ugly old truck," Mr. Preston said. "It's a part of your dad, his story. He was a good man Tyler and I know without a doubt he's proud of who you are."

Thirds time's a charm? Nope, no words. I could only nod at Mr. Preston. He understood though. He clapped me on the shoulder.

"It'll be here for you and we'll get it running again." He ushered Emmy and me out of the barn. Outside the building he paused.

"Tyler, there's something else I wanted to mention," his voice was serious but kind.

I turned to face him. "I know you're busy with school and basketball, but I could use some extra help around here. Part-time work, nothing that'll interfere with your commitments. What do you think? Talk it over with your mom and grandparents if you're interested."

I was surprised and I finally managed words. "That would be great, Mr. Preston. I mean, thank you. I'll talk to Mom and Gramps and Grams, of course. But I think it'll be okay."

"Good," he nodded, a satisfied twinkle in his eye. "We'll make a plan that works for you."

"Thank you," I said. I heard the gratitude in my voice.

"You're welcome, Tyler. I look forward to having you on the place." He paused drawing in a long breath. "I've got more siblings than I can remember most days..."

Emilia giggled.

"Your dad, though, he was like a brother to me. True family. That makes you family."

As we walked back to the house the marvels and blessings we had found sank into my heart.

"Emilia, you can walk Tyler to his car and keep him company. Mom and I will walk Luz out in a couple minutes."

We stopped next to my car, the old sedan Gramps and Grams had saved for my mom and I to use. I leaned against the hood, crossing my arms. Emilia stood beside me, her arms tucked around herself against the evening breeze. The air smelled like cut hay and something else—something old, like oil and metal and time holding its breath.

She nudged me with her elbow. "So... you're gonna take the job?"

I let out a slow breath, glancing back toward the barn where The Beast was waiting. "Yeah. I think I am."

Emilia smiled, soft but knowing. "Because it's more than just a job."

I looked down, scuffing my shoe against the gravel. "Yeah," I admitted. "And that ugly old truck... might be one of the most beautiful things I've ever seen."

She didn't tease me for that. Didn't say anything at all. Just stood there, quiet, like she understood exactly what I meant. We both turned when the front porch light flicked on. The door opened, and the Prestons stepped out with my mom.

Emilia exhaled. "Looks like they're ready."

I straightened, "Guess that means we're headed home."

She hesitated just long enough that I glanced at her. Her voice was quiet when she spoke. "It's good, you know. You being here. It's your dad's story continuing."

I swallowed. The words stuck, but I nodded. "Yeah."

Then, before I could lose my nerve, I muttered, "It helps, you being here, part of that story."

Emilia's head tilted like she wasn't expecting that, wasn't sure what to do with it. But she smiled a little, made things feel easier.

23

Passing Notes in Class

Emilia

I was digging through my binder when I noticed something folded and wedged between my assignment pages. Not stuffed—placed. Like someone wanted to make sure I'd find it, but not too quickly.

No name. No dramatic heart doodles. Just messy but legible handwriting. I unfolded it.

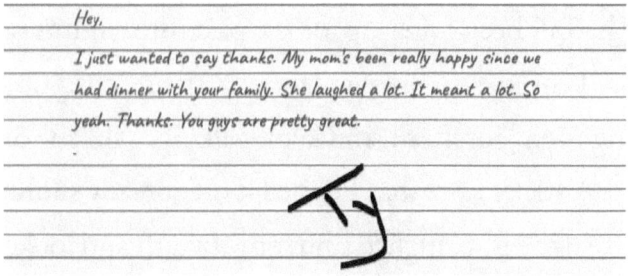

I read it twice. Then again. It wasn't romantic. It wasn't funny. Tyler always went for the laugh. This... felt different. Real. I pressed my thumb against the paper, like it might reveal more. But that was it. Just one note. Just a thank you.

I glanced across the room where he sat with his feet hooked around the bottom rung of his desk, pretending to be busy with his textbook. He wasn't looking at me. But his ears were red.

I didn't say anything. Not yet. But I folded the note carefully and slid it into the pocket of my folder labeled "Other Important Stuff." Because maybe it was. Important. Maybe just a little.

Tyler

The hallway buzzed around me—lockers slamming, voices bouncing off the tile, that weird hum of everyone still figuring out where to be and how fast to walk. I leaned against my locker, pretending to be fascinated by a page of doodles in my notebook, but really, I was watching for her. Not in a creepy way. Just... low-key watching.

Emilia had this way of moving through the crowd like it didn't touch her. Confident. Focused. Untouchable. Until she wasn't and veered off course headed straight toward me. I straightened up like I hadn't been loitering for the past three minutes.

Before I could even open my mouth, she reached up, slapped something to my forehead, and kept walking. Like she did this every day. A sticky note that I peeled it off, already smiling like a complete doofus. I laughed under my breath and looked down the hall. She didn't turn around. I didn't care. My face hurt from grinning.

You're Welcome. It was great meeting her. It was okay having you there too.

-Emilia

24

Origin Story of Farm Guy

Tyler

Two seconds after I knocked, the front door creaked open. The kid standing there couldn't have been more than four. He scanned me like I might be carrying contraband. Deep brown eyes narrowed at me through the screen door, suspicious and unblinking.

Emilia's little brother? I think? He'd been at his abuelos' house when mom and I had been here for dinner.

"Who are you? What do you want?"

I hesitated. I had not been prepared to confront a security guard disguised as a preschooler.

"Uh..." I cleared my throat. "Me? I'm—I'm the new farm guy?"

The kid squinted. "What's a farm guy?" Before I could try to answer, he turned his head and yelled into the house at full volume.

"Meela! There's a farm guy here! What's a farm guy?"

I blinked.

A toddler came up behind him, dark curls bouncing, fisting a worn stuffed animal. She grabbed onto his leg and peered up at me.

The kid pointed at me. "That's a farm guy."

The toddler's face lit up like she was a tiny bachelorette, and I was about to hand her a rose.

"Fahm die?" she repeated, her little voice melodic.

"Yeah. A farm guy. Whatever the H-E-double-toothpicks that means."

I stared. H-E-double-toothpicks? That had Ivy all over it. But whoa. This was... was not what I had expected. At all.

Miguel, I guessed, now looked proud of himself, while the toddler—Sofía, probably—was grinning at me like I was the local snack deliverer. I wondered if I should say something, when Emilia rushed into the hall, eyes flashing.

"Miggy! You don't open the door alone!" she scolded, hands on her hips. "You're supposed to wait for big sister Manita or Mamá or Papí!"

Miguel huffed, crossing his arms. "It's just a Farm Guy, Meela. Not a bad guy or nothing."

Emilia's gaze slid to me, taking in my stunned silence. Her lips twitched like she was trying not to laugh. "Farm Guy?"

"Yeah, him. That's a Farm Guy." Miguel turned back to me, grinning again. "I'm Miggy. Miggy Cabrera."

I blinked again. "Uh... nice to meet you?"

Emilia sighed, shaking her head. "Right now he's the baseball player Miguel Cabrera. The one who retired from the Detroit Tigers?"

I nodded. "Sure. That makes sense. I think we talked on the phone."

Emilia opened the door screen door for me to step through.

Miguel beamed. "I'm the best at baseball. My Bad Average is three uh... what is it Meela?"

"3.06, slugger."

Mrs. Preston appeared in the doorway then, smiling. "I'll take these two traviesos." She leaned down to scoop up Sofía while Miguel looked resigned.

He sighed. "Bye, Farm Guy."

Then tiny Sofía launched herself from Mrs. Preston's arms. I caught her. I always a caught a basketball passed to me, I wasn't about to let a kid hit the floor. She hugged tight. Looked up at me and sighed.

"Fahm die. Lub you."

I froze. I had been on this farm for five minutes. I'd been interrogated, assigned myself a stupid job title, and caught an enamored toddler. Emilia turned to me. She took Sofía and handed her off to Mrs. Preston. Her eyes danced with amusement.

"C'mon, Farm Guy. Let's go do what farm guys do."

25

Farm Guy Doing Farm Guy Work

Emilia

It was hard to stifle my laughter. Tyler's deer-in-the-headlights presence with my siblings had been priceless. Tyler had faced Miggy in full farm security mode. And Sofía developed a case of instalove. I'd let my parents worry about the future implications of that.

Dad had asked me to walk Tyler to the barn, where he was waiting near the old workshop. I glanced at Tyler as we made our way across the packed dirt path. He was still processing everything that had just happened inside the house, blinking like he'd stepped into a parallel universe.

"So, Farm Guy," I teased, bumping my shoulder into his. "Ready to earn that title?"

Tyler exhaled, shaking his head. "Hey, not just a city slicker here. I've done my fair share of hard labor."

"Yeah? Gramps and Grams have you hauling hay bales at their place?"

"No. But I've shoveled snow like a pro. Mowed lawn like an Olympian. Did some construction cleanup for a friend of Gramps last summer. Earned some bucks and some blisters."

"Hmm." I pretended to consider. "Sounds promising."

We neared the barn and I shouted out, "Dad, your new Farm Guy is here!"

Dad stood next to a pile of old fence posts. He gave Tyler a nod, then shot me a questioning look.

"Farm Guy?"

Tyler groaned. "Oh, come on."

I grinned. "It's your official title now. Sorry, you don't get a say."

Dad chuckled amused. "Farm Guy, huh. Sounds suspiciously like Miggy. Did Sofía get in on the act too?"

"Yep," I replied. "She's in love with Tyler and might be looking at bridal magazines this minute."

I saw the love on my dad's face as he shook his head smiling. "Alright, Farm Guy, let's get down to business."

He gestured to the worn-out fencing. "We've got some pasture sections that need repairs before winter. It's not a rush job, but I could use an extra set of hands."

Tyler straightened. "Okay, tell me what to do."

Dad nodded. "Good. It's straightforward—pull the old posts, replace the ones that need it, make sure everything's solid. I'll be working with you when I can, but I trust you to handle it."

Tyler's face flickered with something but he masked it. "I can do that. Just tell me where to start."

Dad turned to me. "Em, I want you to go over the new pasture rotation plan with me later. Let's see if we can adjust for better grazing efficiency before the grant paperwork is due."

I perked up at that. "Sounds good."

Tyler shot me a glance. "Wait—you do pasture management stuff?"

"Farm Guy, I'm a Farm Executive."

Dad laughed. "She's not wrong." Then he clapped Tyler on the shoulder. Dad went over the details and I watched Tyler take it all in, his usual easygoing attitude shifting into something more serious. This wasn't just a side job for him. It was something solid—something real.

Tyler

The post-pounder was heavier than I'd expected. I'd just started and already my arms felt like jelly. The first post refused to settle straight, the wire slipped twice.

But I didn't complain. Robbie, he told me to call him that, didn't seem like the type who appreciated whining. He showed me the rhythm—lift, drive, test, repeat—and once I got into it, the work started to make sense. Not easy. Just... solid.

Robbie talked me through it—where to reinforce, how to anchor the bottom line, how to keep the tension without warping the posts. It was practical, no-nonsense stuff, but he wasn't impatient. He corrected my stance once or twice, handed me the right tool before I knew I needed it.

The first hour killed me. My shoulders burned. My hands went numb. At one point I smacked my thumb and almost launched a string of words that would've made my abuelo throw a sandal from the sky. But I kept going. Adjusted. Matched Robbie's rhythm. And the work started to settle in.

"Not bad," Robbie said during a break. "Faster than I was my first time. But don't let that go to your head."

I grinned and took that as high praise. We moved to the next section of fence, and after another half hour, Robbie gestured toward a shady patch near tree.

"Water break," he said. "Mandatory."

I didn't argue. He pulled a cooler from the bed of the truck and handed me a thermos.

I took a swig and blinked. "Is this... lemonade?"

He nodded.

"Emilia made it. Keeps trying to perfect her 'ranch-hand recipe.'"

It was cold. Sweet. Tart. Amazing. Like Emilia. *Whoa, idiot! Do not think things like that sitting next to her big farmer dad.*

We worked a bit more, the sun inching higher. The silence wasn't awkward—it had weight to it, like the land around us. Like something earned.

Then, out of nowhere, he said, "You been thinking about the truck?"

I paused. "Yeah. A lot."

"You ever fixed up a vehicle before?"

I shook my head. "Changed oil. Watched YouTube videos. But The Beast is... I don't even know where to start."

He didn't say anything for a moment.

"You know why I kept it?" he asked. "Didn't feel right to let it go. I've got four brothers, but Adam? He and I...."

He cleared his throat. He didn't have to finish. I already knew.

"I want to fix it," I said. "Not just for him. For me, too. But I want to do it right."

Robbie nodded. "Then let's make a deal."

I looked over.

"You keep showing up. You work hard. I'll help you get that thing running. Tools. Space. Maybe even some parts."

I swallowed. "Deal." We worked a little longer after that. Nothing dramatic. Just more wire, more dust, more steady rhythm. Robbie didn't say much, and I didn't need him to. The sun crept higher, pile of fence posts dwindled, and my body settled into a tired acceptance of its aches.

We packed up, both sweat-soaked and quiet. But it was a good quiet. Before I could head toward my car Robbie nodded toward the farmhouse.

"You've earned some lunch," he said. "C'mon in. Mariella made enough to feed an army—and knowing Miggy and Sofí, you're about to face your second job of the day."

26

The Miggy & Sofia
Experience Continues

Tyler

I was supposed to be heading home. I should have been heading home. Instead, I was being ushered toward the house by Robbie Preston, who clapped a firm hand on my shoulder.

"Come on, Farm Guy. Let's get you fed before you go."

I hesitated. "I don't want to intrude—"

"You don't say no to Mamá's cooking," Emilia cut in, giving me a look that translated to *don't be an idiot*. She joined us on our walk to the house. Guess she'd finished her executive chores for the day.

That was how I found myself sitting at the Preston's long wooden dining table in the midst of the most chaotic chaos I'd ever experienced.

Mrs. Preston moved with practiced ease in the kitchen, setting out a spread of homemade tortillas, grilled meat, and beans while two tiny whirlwinds spun around the room. Miguel climbed onto the bench across from me, fixing me with his squint.

"So, Farm Guy," he said, all serious business. "Did you do any actual farm stuff?"

I grabbed a tortilla. "Yeah, Miggy. I pulled fence posts, replaced some, and got my hands plenty dirty."

Miguel drummed his fingers on the table.

"Mmm." He nodded, like he was deciding if this was acceptable. "And did Meela boss you around?"

Emilia, reaching for a dish, gave him a warning look. "I do not boss people around."

Miguel snorted. "That's your favoritest thing to do."

I coughed to hide my laugh, because? Fair point, kid. Before Emilia could argue, I felt something warm and tiny press against my side. I looked down. Sofía had climbed onto the bench beside me—closer than necessary—her little hand gripping my sleeve.

She stared up at me, her dark brown eyes wide with complete, adoring trust. Then, with the confidence of a toddler with a firmly made-up mind she clung to my arm and declared, "Fahm Die. Mine."

A beat of silence. Then the reactions. Mariella covered her mouth with her hand, shaking her head. Robbie choked on his water. Miguel looked offended, like his sister had just betrayed him by falling in love with a farm guy of all people.

Emilia? Oh, she was thriving. She leaned forward, eyes dancing with amusement.

"Well, Farm Guy," she mused, way too pleased. "Looks like you belong to her now."

I blinked at Sofía, who was still latched onto my sleeve like a koala, smiling at me with actual heart-eyes. This could not be happening. I carefully peeled Sofía off my arm and tried to pass her to Emilia.

"I think she means 'Farm Guy is a cool friend.'" Sofía, utterly unimpressed, latched back onto me.

Miguel groaned. "Ugh. She likes you. Shhhiiiiiiicken Feathers."

Mariella gave him a look. "Miguel."

Miguel huffed. "Sorry Mamá. It's only kinda shhhicken feathers."

The conversation moved on as we ate. Robbie and Emilia started talking about pasture rotation and winter prep, and I listened, interested. At some point, Miguel narrowed his eyes again.

"Okay, but if you're staying, you gotta prove you're strong." I frowned.

"What?"

He set his tiny elbow on the table. "Arm wrestle."

I blinked. "You want to—"

"Arm wrestle."

Emilia covered her laugh. I wasn't about to challenge a four-year-old, but Miguel's determined expression was a bit terrifying. I glanced at Robbie, expecting him to shut it down. He just shrugged.

"Might as well settle it, Farm Guy."

With no way out, I sighed and set my arm on the table. Miguel grabbed my hand like he was about to fight for his honor. Mariella rolled her eyes but let it happen.

"No breaking my kitchen table."

Miguel counted down—"Three... two... one—"

And then threw his entire body weight into it. I pretended to struggle, letting him inch my hand down little by little.

"Wow, you're strong, Miggy."

Miguel grinned. "Told you."

Sofía, still sitting next to me, patted my arm in encouragement. "Fahm Die."

Robbie chuckled, shaking his head. "Alright, alright. Let the man eat his lunch."

Miguel released my hand, satisfied. "You're lucky. I could've been champion over you if we went more rounds.

"Of course you could have," I said.

Emilia nudged my side, smirking. "Farm Guy, you survived your initiation."

Mariella, clearing dishes, gave me a knowing smile. "You're welcome here anytime, Tyler."

Something warm settled in my chest. This wasn't my home, but it felt... safe. I had a job. A place. Maybe even a tiny fan club. As I stood up to leave, Sofía grabbed my leg one last time.

"Fahm Die, lub you."

I choked on air. Emilia cackled. She was still grinning about it as I got to the door.

"So..." she said, drawing out the word. "When's the wedding?"

I groaned. "This isn't going away is it?"

She laughed again, but her eyes softened. I turned back toward the table and saw Sofía sitting on the bench, Emilia's mini-me. Same dark curls, same brown eyes, same brilliant, mischievous smile.

It hit me then, fast and hard. This felt like something. Like family. Like home. Something I didn't understand but couldn't ignore. I glanced at Emilia, and she was watching me, her expression unreadable.

For once, I didn't smirk. Didn't tease. I just looked at her—really looked.

Later that night my phone chimed. I sighed. I already knew who it was. The contact said Emilia, it wasn't her calling.

I answered.

"Hey, Miguel Cabrera."

"Hi, Farm Guy!"

"Papí says you do good work."

My eyebrows shot up. "Oh? Well, that's..."

"Okay, bye!"

Click. He hung up again. I stared at the phone. This. This was my life now. Thing was, it felt pretty good at that point.

27

Call 1-800-Dr. Ty

Tyler

I was just about to crash for the night when my phone rang. Aiden. I frowned, swiping to answer.

"Dude, it's almost midnight. Did you forget how time works?"

Static silence for a beat. Then Aiden sighed, the kind of sigh that told me this wasn't just a random call. "Ty... I messed up."

I sat up, more awake. "Yeah? What kind of mess-up are we talking about? Like, forgot-to-turn-in-a-paper bad? Or tripped-over-your-own-feet-in-practice bad?"

Another long pause. Then, softer, "I forgot to tell Ivy about my mom. About the twins. About... everything."

I rubbed a hand over my face. "Yikes."

Aiden groaned. "Yeah. Thanks for that."

I leaned back against my pillows, letting the words settle. I knew Ivy had been off since she got back from camp, but I hadn't realized Aiden was the main reason. That tracked though. Aiden was kind of oblivious when it came to her.

"So… let me get this straight," I said. "You had a whole summer to tell your best friend—who, let's be real, was waiting to connect with you again—and you just… didn't?"

Aiden let out a breath, frustrated. "I was busy, okay? Basketball camp, family stuff—I just kept thinking I'd tell her later."

I sighed. "And now it's later. And I bet she found out from Emilia instead of you. And she's pissed, isn't she?"

"Understatement of the year," he muttered.

"Can you blame her?"

Aiden groaned again, and I could picture him dragging a hand through his hair. "I didn't mean to hurt her, Ty. I just… I didn't think."

"No, you didn't," I agreed, not bothering to sugarcoat it. "But here's the thing—you gotta stop expecting Ivy to just wait around for you to figure your stuff out. She's got her own life, her own dreams, and you've been treating her like she's… I don't know, a default setting in your life instead of an actual person."

Aiden went quiet.

I sighed, softer this time. "Look, man. Ivy's your best friend. And yeah, she's mad, but she wouldn't be this mad if she didn't care. You've just gotta prove that you care, too."

Aiden exhaled. "I don't even know where to start."

"Figure it out. Stop taking the easy way with her. Start by showing up," I said. "Not just when it's easy, but all the time. Let her in. And for the love of everything, don't just hit her with some half-baked 'I'm sorry.' You gotta mean it."

Another pause. Then a quiet, "Yeah. I know."

I nodded to myself, "Good. Now go fix it, so I can go to sleep without worrying about you two ruining the group dynamic with your weird, unresolved tension."

Aiden huffed out a laugh. "Noted."

I ended the call, shaking my head. Aiden and Ivy. The most obvious, oblivious-people I'd ever met. I tossed my phone onto my bed, running a hand down my face. Aiden had a moment of not-oblivious and somehow, I'd been drafted as the Relationship Hotline of North Riverbend. Not that I was surprised. I'd predicted this over the summer.

And I'd worried about how much it would mess with me, too. Because where Ivy went, Emilia followed. And if Ivy was done with Aiden, where did that leave me and Emilia? Not that we were a thing. We weren't. Except, all summer, I'd gotten used to the texts. The dumb little back-and-forth that had started as jokes but somehow turned into something more to look forward to.

And now spending time at the farm with the family. Miggy hijacking Emilia's phone. Sofía saying lub you fahm die. Emilia—sending me texts that made me grin like an idiot. I exhaled, rubbing my hands together. It was stupid. I wasn't in Aiden's mess. I wasn't the one who had screwed up.

But I could feel the shift happening already, and it wasn't just between Aiden and Ivy. It was between all of us. I picked up my phone again, hesitating for a second before I typed out a message.

> **Me:** Hey. I heard a bomb got dropped somewhere in Ivy's neighborhood. You survive the blast zone? Do I need to be worried about collateral damage?

I stared at the screen, waiting. Hoping I hadn't just made things weird. The dots popped up almost instantly.

> **Emilia:** I dropped the bomb. Unintentionally. Didn't know it was a bomb. Stupidly assumed…

Pause.

> **Me:** Collateral damage? We okay?

> **Emilia:** Damage was done. Guess we'll see how bad it is.

My heart kicked a little harder than I expected.

> **Emilia:** We're okay. Unless, this… becomes about sides and you side with him.

Me: For what it's worth, I don't think Aiden's even on his own side. And I reamed him out. Ivy's my friend too.

Emilia: I don't understand him.

Me: He doesn't understand him either. But...

Me: He's shook, I think it'll get better. Slowly.

Me: Bit by bit as his oblivious brain soaks it all in.

Emilia: Ivy and me. We're a package deal. As much as I've always like Aiden, I don't like him taking her for granted.

Emilia: You've been worried about this, haven't you?

Me: Yeah, I have been.

Emilia: Well. I'm still here, Farm Guy. No different plans.

Back at the start of summer, when Aiden had first started acting weird about Ivy, I'd felt it coming. The distance. The drama. The inevitable fallout. And I'd told myself it was about Aiden and Ivy. That it was their thing, not mine. But deep down? I'd been worried about her. About what happened when Ivy and

Aiden weren't glued together anymore. About where that left me.
I exhaled, my shoulders loosening a fraction.

> **Me**: Good. Miggy's just waiting to take over the spot of my favorite Preston.

> **Emilia:** Sofía's too little for the drama [winking face]. I'm sparing her.

I shook my head. She knew I didn't mean Sofía's crush on me.
I had one favorite Preston, then one big giant lump of Preston
family working its way into my heart.

28

It's Not the Ideas

Emilia

"Let's hear your thoughts," Mr. Klein said, adjusting his cuffed flannel sleeves and nudging his glasses up with a knuckle. He leaned against the front table like a guy about to drop the world's chillest TED Talk.

The whiteboard still held today's Current Issues discussion prompt, written in blocky dry-erase scrawl: What's one meaningful action individuals or families can take to help the environment?

Hands went up fast. Klein fielded answers with the usual affirming nods.

"Cut back on plastic straws." "Line-dry clothes instead of using the dryer."

"Compost," someone added. "Like, real compost. Not just banana peels in a bowl for three days."

Klein grinned. "Love the intentionality there. That's how behavioral shifts stick—when they're personal."

I raised my hand. "I think people overlook land care," I said. "My family rotates our grazing and keeps wildlife corridors open. It's not big or flashy, but it helps soil health and biodiversity. If more ranches did that, I think it would add up."

He paused. Just for a second. Then gave me a brief, polite smile. "Right. A local land-use angle."

His eyes slid to the next hand before mine even dropped. And he moved on.

"Dina?"

Dina jumped in with a confident answer about digital advocacy—documentaries, viral campaigns, climate influencers.

Klein lit up like someone had plugged him in. "Now that's a systems-level solution. Excellent example of modern engagement. Love that."

I sat back, fingers folding tight in my lap. My answer wasn't wrong—it just didn't land. Not like hers did. And I didn't know why. I stood, gathering my books with slow precision. Most kids flooded out like they were escaping a collapsing building, but Drew Torsen didn't move. He leaned back in his chair, arms crossed, watching me with those stormy eyes of his.

"Your idea was good, Em," he said. His voice was quiet. Gravelly. Like he didn't talk much but paid attention when he did.

I blinked. "Oh. Thanks."

Drew glanced at Mr. Klein sorting papers. A flicker of irritation crossed his face before he shook his head. He didn't say anything else, just nodded and left the room.

Mr. Klein looked up and saw I was still in the room. "Have a good day, Emilia," he said.

"Sure."

The cafeteria smelled like pizza boats, orange sanitizer, and panic of *I forgot there was a test*. I was halfway through a string cheese and scrolling through the North Riverbend FFA chapter site when Drew dropped his tray across from me.

"So," he said, peeling open his milk carton. "You really think bison do it better than cows, or was that just for drama?"

I blinked. "What?"

He pointed at my screen. "That post you wrote after the soil workshop. You said it's not the cows—it's the management. Sounded like you were coming for the whole beef industry."

"I was not," I said, maybe too defensively. "I was saying that bison evolved here. Their grazing patterns improve land health. But if cattle are rotated properly, they can mimic that impact."

"So rotational grazing is cows cos playing bison?"

I narrowed my eyes. "Well our cattle aren't a bunch of bison wannabees. Don't know what's happening out on your acres."

He grinned. "I'm actually hoping to add some bison down the road. Just takes time to prep. "

We chatted back and forth—about soil structure, root depth, water retention, fencing strategies. Drew didn't talk much in most classes, but when he did, it was like flipping a switch. He asked good questions. Listened harder than most people I knew.

"Are you two arguing, or is this an FFA nerd mating ritual?" Aria asked, appearing over Drew's shoulder with a juice pouch and raised eyebrows.

"We're discussing soil biology," I said.

"Yeah, okay," she said. "That's definitely what this vibe is."

Drew didn't even flinch. "Just the usual discussion of controlling the food chain to control the world."

"Through the use of poop," Tyler added loudly.

Drew shrugged. "Poop fixes things."

I looked down, trying not to laugh.

Across the table, Tyler was fiddling with his phone, squinting at something. Then he burst out laughing—loud enough that people three tables over looked up.

"Oh no," I said. "What did he do now?"

Tyler grinned like he'd just discovered buried treasure. "Listen to this." He hit the speaker and turned the volume up.

"Farm Guy. Listen. I made this joke. Why did the poop cross the road? Cause the cow had to go and there wasn't a toilet. Okay, bye. Don't tell Mamá I used her phone. No snitching in farm work."

There was one stunned beat of silence. Then the table started chattering.

"No snitching in farm work?"

"What's a Farm Guy?"

29

Let's Make a Plan Tyler

Tyler

We'd only worked a couple of hours—fence patching, loading a few feed bags—but I was already sweaty, sore, and starting to enjoy the predictability of it. The way the land stayed steady. The way the work never pretended to be anything it wasn't.

He screwed the lid back on his thermos and gave me a nod. "Let's go make a plan, Tyler." He tipped the thermos toward me. I followed him across the packed dirt and around the barn, past a row of tool sheds and stacked pallets. He led me to the outbuilding I'd seen before—the one that held The Beast—and pushed open the doors.

It was warm inside, dust catching in the light. Tools hung along one wall. A busted radio sat on a shelf, its antenna bent at a ninety-degree angle like it had given up years ago. The sweet-stale bite of old gas hung under the heat.

And there she was. Still huge. Still rusted. Still waiting. We stood at the front of the truck together, both of us quiet for a second. Robbie reached for the hood and popped it open.

"Alright. First thing—see what's salvageable. Battery's probably toast. We'll test it anyway. Fuel lines. Belts. Carburetor's a maybe. Could be gummed up bad. Could be cracked."

I leaned in, hands on my knees, squinting. "Do you think it's worth it?"

He didn't hesitate. "It's a piece of your dad, Tyler. A man you should've known, so yeah, it's worth it."

He paused. "It'd mean a lot to me to see this thing running again."

I nodded. That hit a little deeper than I was ready for, so I let it sit there and didn't say anything back. Robbie grabbed a clipboard off a hook on the wall and started scribbling. "Step one: assess condition. Step two: clean the heck out of everything. Step three: figure out what parts we need and what I've already got buried in this place."

He passed me the clipboard. "You start the checklist. What do you see that needs attention?"

I wrote:

-Battery (check condition)

-Belts (replace?)

-Fuel lines

-Tires-terrible

-Brake-???

I looked up. "Do you have a jack?"

"Of course I have a jack. Don't insult me."

I smirked and added *Lift truck-inspect underneath* to the list.

"We'll pull out the tester Saturday," Robbie said. "Get a few readings. I'd start with cleaning the—"

"CHECKED THE GLOVE BOX! DOESN'T WORK!" Miggy's voice rang out from somewhere behind us—too loud and much too confident.

I jumped.

"What—was he in here this whole time?"

"ALSO CHECKED THE FLOOR THINGY—THERE'S PIGEONS LIVING IN IT!" Miggy again, now clearly deep in the truck cab, voice echoing off the windows.

Robbie didn't even look up. "Thanks, Miggy-man. That's good recon."

I stared at him. "Is this normal?"

"You're learning," he said.

I cleared my throat. "Miggy, did you check the squirrel valve? Might be jammed."

A pause. Then Miggy yelled, "YUP. FULL OF SANDWICH CRUSTS."

I blinked. "Huh, wasn't thinking sandwich crusts."

Robbie grinned. "You expected acorns? Not how Miggy's mind works, kid."

"CUPHOLDER'S STILL GROSS! I'M OUT!" Miggy declared, and a second later we heard the truck door slam and small feet running off across the gravel.

I turned to Robbie, deadpan. "I don't know if I passed a test or failed one just now."

"Scaled up your learning curve," he said. "You'll get used to the Miggy Method."

I looked down at the clipboard in my hands. It wasn't a blueprint or anything fancy. Just a list of stuff to fix. A mess to sort out. But for some reason, it felt good. Like starting meant something. Like this truck, broken as it was, might still have places to go.

Robbie clapped me lightly on the back. "We'll start fresh Saturday. Bring gloves. Maybe some bravery."

We pushed open the outbuilding door and stepped back into the late afternoon sun. Emilia was walking up the path from the lower pasture, clipboard in one hand, braid slipping loose from under her ball cap. Her boots were dusty, and there was a smudge on her cheek she hadn't noticed yet.

She looked up when she spotted us, "Please tell me Miggy didn't try to install a rocket launcher in the glove box."

"Close," I said. "Turns out the squirrel valve was full of sandwich crusts."

Her eyes sparkled. "Ah, the classic squirrel valve problem. Must be Tuesday."

Robbie just shook his head and kept walking. "You two are on your own now."

Emilia fell into step beside me as we walked toward the house.

"He's still talking about you," she said, bumping her shoulder lightly into mine. "Miggy, I mean. Said you survived another 'farm quest.' That's high praise."

"Didn't feel like I survived," I muttered. "Felt like I got ambushed by a four-year-old raccoon in human form."

She laughed. "Yeah. That tracks."

We reached the porch steps. She glanced down at the clipboard in my hand. "Is that the master plan?"

"Phase one," I said. "Your dad says we start Saturday."

She nodded. "Then you'd better be ready."

"For what?"

"For the pigeons. And the grease. And whatever else Miggy 'inspected.' You're officially in."

"In what?"

She didn't answer. Just bumped her shoulder into me and climbed the steps.

Emilia

I spotted them as I came up from the lower pasture—Dad and Tyler stepping out of the old outbuilding into the sun, both a little dusty, both looking like they'd been in a planning huddle for something dramatic. Dad was shaking his head, half-smiling. Tyler had that clipboard tucked under one arm like it was a sacred relic.

They didn't see me yet. Tyler said something, and Dad laughed in that way he does when he's pretending not to be proud. I slowed down just enough to watch.

Tyler walked like he belonged here. Not in some dramatic, slow-mo, wind-through-the-hair kind of way. Just... like he'd settled into the rhythm of things. Into the quiet. Into the work.

There was something about seeing him out here—not leaning against a locker or cracking jokes in class, but fully in it, sweat on his brow and dirt on his hands—that made me blink a little harder than usual. He didn't just survive Miggy's chaos anymore. He was becoming part of it.

Dad peeled off toward the house. Tyler turned and noticed me. He looked like he was trying to downplay the grin on his face but wasn't quite pulling it off.

"Please tell me Miggy didn't try to install a rocket launcher in the glove box," I said.

"Close," he replied. "Apparently the squirrel valve was full of sandwich crusts."

I couldn't help it—I laughed. "Classic squirrel valve issue. Always catches people off guard."

We started walking toward the house together. I glanced down and caught sight of the clipboard.

"So that's the master plan?" I asked.

"Phase one," he said. "Your dad says we start Saturday."

I nodded. "You'd better be ready."

"For what?"

"For the grease. And the pigeons. And whatever else Miggy 'inspected.'" I grinned. "You're officially in."

"In what?"

I didn't answer. Just bumped my shoulder into his. We reached the porch, and we headed up the steps. Tyler looked back, eyeing the horizon like he was weighing whether to stay.

"Are you staying for supper?" I asked. "Mamá made enough arroz con pollo to feed three ranch hands and a small marching band."

He smiled but shook his head. "I promised Gramps I'd help him move some furniture tonight. Rain check?"

"Your loss," I said, reaching to pull open the screen door. And then—

"Fahm die!"

Sofía's little voice rang out from inside like she'd been waiting in ambush. She pressed her face to the screen, cheeks squished, eyes wide with determination. Then she started launching kisses.

Air kiss. Air kiss. Both hands now. Rapid-fire. No hesitation. Tyler froze on the step like he'd been hit with a tranquilizer dart. I watched his soul leave his body.

"She's not gonna stop," I said, grinning. "You better catch one."

"What?"

I held up my hand, caught one mid-air, and tapped it to my cheek. "Like this."

He blinked. "Seriously?"

"She's watching."

That did it. Tyler reached out, visibly fighting the urge to disappear, and awkwardly caught a kiss from the air. Then, slowly, he pressed it to his cheek. When he glanced up again, Sofía was already gone.

Tyler exhaled. "She vanished like a Disney princess on a CIA mission."

I nodded solemnly. "Always be ready to catch something out here, Farm Guy."

He gave me a look—part horrified, part laughing—and jogged down the steps. I watched him go, screen door closing behind me. I wondered what my little sister's CIA mission was today.

Tyler

My phone chimed. Caller ID said Emilia. It wasn't. I grabbed it and answered. "Hey, Miggy."

"Farm Guy, I want the first ride in the truck."

"What?"

"When you fix it. I want the first ride."

"Uh... I mean, I—"

"I can pay you. I have two quarters, a button, and my lucky rock."

I pressed my lips together. I couldn't laugh. I could not laugh. "That's a pretty solid offer, bud."

"I know, I'm smart. Okay, bye!"

Sofía yelled in the background. "Fahm die, lub you!"

Click. The call ended. I buried my face in my hands. But I was grinning big.

30

Creative Writing of Wishes

Emilia

I stared at the blank page on my laptop screen, my fingers hovering over the keyboard. Our creative writing assignment was deceptively simple. A wish you had.

At first, I thought about keeping it light. Something about farm life. Maybe how hard it actually is to run a family farm, or how people assume milk comes from a grocery store, not from early mornings and sore hands. But the more I sat with it, the more I knew that wasn't it.

I wanted to write something that meant something. I drummed my fingers against the keyboard, glancing at my phone. My last text with Tyler was still open.

> **Tyler:** I haven't heard from Miguel Cabrera recently. Checking that everything's good.

> **Me:** Everything's good in the Miggy-verse. Tonight he told us his Bad Average had gone up to eleventy-hundred. Think that's good?

Tyler: Hall of Fame numbers, for sure.

Me: We should all be so confident

Tyler: Yeah. Maybe I'll start claiming I've got a vertical leap of ten feet.

Me: Make it eleventy. That seems to be the key.

I smiled shaking my head. Then my fingers hovered over the keyboard again.

Me: Wait. Do you actually know anything about the real Miguel Cabrera?

Tyler: Uh... baseball player? Tigers? Really good?

Me: Well, yeah. But like—where is he from? How did he get here?

Tyler: Venezuela? Scouted young. Sure he worked his ass off.

Me: Yeah... probably.

Tyler: If anything exciting in the Miggy-sphere happens tonight I want to hear about it.

Me: Deal. Now I know you've homework cause I've got the same. Get to work.

Tyler: Farm Exec orders, I obey. Later

Me: Night Farm Guy

A while later I thought about creative writing again. Miggy liked to think he was Miguel Cabrera, the baseball legend. In his four-year-old mind, there was no question—he was destined for greatness. I smiled to myself, but the thought stuck.

The real Miguel Cabrera had come to the U.S. He'd made it—a legal path, a career, a name known everywhere. But what about the other Miguel Cabreras? The ones who couldn't come legally. The ones who never got the chance.

The ones who left everything behind, not for stadium lights, but just for a shot at something better.

I opened a new tab and typed, "Why do immigrants come to the U.S.?"

The results weren't surprising. Economic opportunity. Safety. A better life for their kids. I exhaled slowly. Of course that was the answer. It was common sense, wasn't it? And yet, not everyone saw it that way.

I thought about Mamá's stories—how my Abuela was always careful about the details she shared, mindful of who was listening.

How she still carried certain fears, even after years of citizenship. I thought about Luz. About how much she worked, how much she did for her family, how much she worried.

I thought about Tyler. Tyler, who never said much about his mom's situation, but who felt it all anyway. I pulled my laptop closer and started typing.

I wish more people understood that no one leaves everything behind unless they have to. I wish more people understood that immigrants don't come here to take, but to build. To give. To work harder than anyone should ever have to. I wish people saw what I see.

My fingers paused on the keys. I wanted to get an opening paragraph. I'd made a good start.

31

Whatever it Was It Scared Her

Tyler

The screen door creaked louder than usual, like it was trying to announce us. Emilia pushed it open first, holding it long enough for me to step inside behind her. We were still half-laughing about something from the walk up—one of Nate's completely unhelpful math metaphors—but the sound caught in my throat the second I looked in the kitchen.

Mariella and my mom were sitting at the table. Two mugs between them. The soft clink of ceramic and the sharp, invisible weight of a conversation that had stopped just a second too late.

Mom looked up fast—too fast. Her eyes were red around the edges, but dry now. She tried to smile at me. It was the wrong smile. The practiced kind. The kind she used with strangers who asked too many questions. Her mouth shaped it; her eyes didn't.

"Hola, Mijo," she said, voice lighter than it should've been.

Mariella stood, smoothing her hands down her jeans like that would erase whatever had just happened.

"Hey, Tyler. Emilia. We were just sitting for a bit. I picked your mom up from town. It was a... long morning."

Emilia paused at my side, sensing it too. My mom folded her hands around the mug again. Her knuckles were white. I wanted to ask what happened. But she wouldn't meet my eyes. And Mariella's gaze said not here, not yet.

From the mudroom, Robbie called out, "Ty, you ready?"

I nodded slowly, still watching my mom. "Yeah. Be right there."

Emilia gave me a small look—half-concern, half-question—but I didn't have an answer for her either. Not yet. As I followed Robbie's voice down the hall, I glanced back.

My mom was staring into her cup like it held something she couldn't say out loud.

I didn't know what it was. But whatever happened—it scared her.

The socket wrench slipped in my hand for the third time. I didn't swear out loud. Just gritted my teeth, reset it, and tried again. Robbie hadn't said anything about my fumbling. He just moved around the old truck like always—methodical, quiet, steady. The Preston way. Oil and dust hung under the rafters.

My brain, on the other hand, was anywhere but under that hood. I could still see my mom's face when we walked in. The way she'd looked at her cup, not at me. The way Mariella had shifted, calm but covering. I didn't know what had happened. I just knew it wasn't nothing.

"Hey," Robbie said from behind me, wiping his hands on a rag. "The squirrel valve I ordered for The Beast came in."

I paused. "The what?"

"The squirrel valve," he said seriously, then tapped the side of the truck like it was a stubborn dog. "Goes between the fuel regulator and the nonsense box. Very advanced technology. Only works when you're distracted." He kept a straight face.

That pulled a laugh out of me. Barely. But still.

Robbie handed me the rag. "You've been tightening the same bolt for five minutes, kid."

I wiped my hands slower than necessary. "Sorry. Just got stuff on my mind."

Robbie nodded. "You don't have to say anything."

We stood there in the echo of that for a minute. Just tool sounds and the distant wind. Then he added, "But I saw your mom. She looked... spooked."

"She won't tell me," I said. "But something happened today. I know it."

"She doesn't want to scare you."

I looked at him. "It's too late for that."

Robbie gave a slow nod. Then, in his even way: "When we head back in, I'll talk to Mariella to see if your mom's ready to talk more."

"You don't have to—"

"I know. But I will." He looked at me straight. "You don't need to carry this by yourself."

I didn't say thank you. But something inside me unclenched. And for the first time all afternoon, I actually looked at the engine in front of me.

Emilia

Dad thumped Tyler's shoulder once, a solid, quiet gesture. "I'll be back in a couple minutes," he said. Then he walked off toward the house. I waited a few beats before stepping into the barn, balancing a paper towel bundle and a chipped ceramic mug.

Miggy had grabbed me earlier and informed me that "Farm Guy doesn't look good. He needs this snack."

Tyler didn't look up when I entered. He was still bent over the engine, the set of his shoulders too tight for this hour of the afternoon.

"I come bearing provisions," I said lightly.

He turned, blinking like he hadn't realized I was there. "Oh. Hey."

I held out the mug. "Hot cocoa. Made by a four-year-old with questionable supervision. And a sandwich that may or may not have mustard in a weird place."

He took them both without a word. Sat down on the overturned milk crate. Just held the cup for a second like he needed it to warm more than his hands. Miggy's voice echoed in my head again. *Farm Guy doesn't look good.*

"You want me to go?" I asked.

He shook his head. I sat down across from him on an old hay bale. We didn't talk right away. I let the quiet stretch between us, filling in the places where words hadn't formed yet.

He said, "Apparently something happened today. Something that scared my mom, something she won't open up about."

I nodded once, letting him set the pace.

"Seems like she called your mom in a panic. As usual she won't give details, thinks she's protecting me."

He stared down into the cocoa like it might give him answers.

"I think..." He stopped. Swallowed. "I think it's starting. Whatever we've been avoiding. The part where something happens and we can't stop it."

The barn creaked softly in the wind. I reached out and brushed his knee with my fingertips. Not a dramatic gesture. Just a touch.

"Whatever it is, Tyler, you're not facing it alone. I promise."

Tyler didn't answer, but he didn't pull away either. We sat in silence—unbroken 'til whispering started up outside the barn. I stood and crossed to the door. Miggy straightened up immediately, all authority and concern.

"We heard no talking. I thought you were—" He gasped. His eyes got huge. "You weren't kissing, were you?"

From below, Sofía echoed, "Kissin'?"

Tyler made a choking sound. I almost fell over laughing.

"No!" I said. "Oh my gosh, Miggy. No."

He squinted suspiciously. "Are you sure? Cause that's what happens in movies when they get all quiet."

Tyler held up both hands like he was under arrest. "Swear. No kissing."

Miggy let out a huge breath, like he'd only just saved the world. "Okay. Good. Cause kissing woulda made me Hulk out."

Tyler looked over at me, half-grinning. "Your security team's intense."

"Only the best," I said.

Miggy stepped closer, looking Tyler up and down with the seriousness of a four-year-old trained in the ancient arts of barn security.

"You okay?" he asked. "For real?"

Tyler nodded, softer this time. "Yeah, bud. I will be."

Miggy gave a slow, thoughtful nod. Then placed one hand on Tyler's arm. "I'm gonna let you pat the cows next time. That always helps when I feel messed up inside."

"Thanks," Tyler said, his voice catching just a little. "That means a lot."

Sofía toddled in through the open barn door, clutching a slightly lumpy, very well-loved stuffed rabbit. She marched right up to Tyler, holding the bunny out like a sacred offering.

"Fahm Die," she declared. "Wobby—" She paused, petting the bunny's frayed ear. "Wobby hugs you bettah."

Tyler blinked, totally disarmed. "Wobby?"

"She calls her bunny Robbie," I shrugged.

Sofía pressed the rabbit into his lap and gave him a pat on the knee. Then she turned and marched right back toward the door like her job was done.

Miggy folded his arms, satisfied. "Okay. You're fine now."

Tyler stared down at the saggy rabbit, lips twitching. "I mean... I kind of am."

Tyler

Robbie had told Emilia to give him time, then come up to the house. It had been forty-five minutes when we left the barn. The farmhouse kitchen felt quieter than usual. Not silent—just quieter. Like the clinking of dishes and scrapes of chairs had all agreed to keep it down tonight.

I sat across from my mom at the table. Emilia next to me. Mariella beside her. Robbie stood for a moment, then pulled out a chair and sat too. No one rushed. My mom held her mug with both hands. Her fingers kept moving—turning it, then turning it back. She didn't look at me.

"I never wanted you to worry about this," she said voice low, quiet. Too late. But I stayed quiet.

"I thought I could keep it away. That if I worked hard, if I kept quiet, si no llamaba la atención—if I didn't draw attention..." She trailed off. Then tried again. "When I first came aquí, I didn't know if I'd stay a week. Or a month. Then I had you. Y me quedé. Para siempre."

She looked up at me finally. Her eyes were tired. But clear. "There were ventanas, back then. Legal ones. Not easy. But they existed." She paused. "But I was scared. I missed deadlines. I waited too long. And then they weren't options anymore."

Mariella reached out and gently touched her arm.

"Hoy me llamaron," my mom said, voice lowering. "I didn't recognize the number. But they said my name. They knew... too much. I hung up."

Robbie leaned forward, elbows on the table. "Do you think it was official?"

"No sé. I don't know. Maybe. Maybe not." She looked down. "But it was enough to remind me. This doesn't go away."

The silence that followed wasn't empty. It was full. Every breath, every glance. I wanted to say a hundred things. But what came out was, "You should've told me."

"I didn't want to put that weight on you." Her voice cracked. "But I see now. No te estoy protegiendo. I'm just... making you worry more."

Mariella nodded slowly. "You're not alone anymore, Luz. You don't have to carry this by yourself."

My mom wiped at her eyes and gave a shaky breath. "I don't know what to do."

"We'll figure it out," I said quietly.

She looked at me, then reached across the table and gripped my hand. "Gracias, Mijo."

It wasn't a solution. Nothing got fixed, but keeping things secret made it all worse. We'd named it. Out loud. Together. And that was something.

32

Little Ones Worry Too

Emilia

It wasn't even ten yet when the house finally went soft—lights low, doors settling. A quiet knock, then Dad eased my door open.

"Hey, Em." He tipped his head toward the hall. "Miggy said Tyler looked real sad today. Sofí keeps saying, "Fahm die, otay?" Think they could use their big sister. Okay if they fall asleep with you? We'll move them later."

"Of course," I said. "Send them in."

Sofía padded in first—thumb in her mouth, Wobby tucked under one arm. She didn't say anything at first. Just blinked at me like she wasn't sure what to ask. I lifted the blanket. She climbed in wordlessly and curled close, Wobby squished between us.

A second set of footsteps. Slower. Miggy appeared next, flashlight dangling from one hand, his favorite dinosaur book clutched under the other. No cape. No sound effects. Just him, frowning like his brain was still working through something he didn't have words for. He paused in the doorway, then padded in and climbed up on my other side.

"You okay, Miggy?" I whispered.

He didn't answer right away. He let his book fall beside him and lay back with a sigh. Then, softly, "Tyler looked real sad."

"Yeah," I said. "He did."

He nodded once and snuggled in closer, his shoulder resting against mine. The silence held for a long moment. Sofía sighed. Miggy yawned.

Just as his eyes started to close, he muttered, "You really weren't kissing?"

My laugh caught in my throat. "No, Miggy."

His voice was already fading, heavy with sleep. "Hmm. Still watching."

"Of course you are."

I lay back between them, still in jeans, just for a minute. The minute won.

Sometime later, the room shifted—footsteps, a whisper of cooler air. Dad lifted Sofí first, then scooped Miggy and the dino book. I'd always been in awe of how strong my dad was—how he could pick up Miggy and Sofí at the same time. Deep down I knew he'd manage to grab me too if it meant I was safe. Before he left, he pressed a kiss to the top of my head.

"You should get into bed too," he murmured.

The door clicked soft behind him. The quiet felt different now. I checked my phone: 11:18 p.m. A new message lit the screen.

10:55 PM

Tyler: You up?

Me: Yeah. You okay?

Tyler: Not really. Mom's pretending to sleep but I can hear her pacing

Me: Yeah. You okay?

Me: What can I do?

Tyler: You're already doing it.

Me: Mamá says your mom can stay with us if she needs to. Dad has connections

Tyler: Thanks. I don't think she'd go for it though. She's worried about putting your family at risk.

Me: Dad says helping someone isn't illegal. I think he means in the way he thinks about the world.

Me: Dad just moved Sofi and Miggy back to their rooms. They fell asleep in my bed for a while. Miggy told me earlier you looked real sad.

Tyler: He wasn't wrong.

Me: They don't get what's happening. But they felt it.

Tyler: I hate that it spills over. That people feel it even when I'm trying not to show it.

Me: It means they love you. And they've got my mom and dad and an Ah-mazing big sister to help them be okay. And maybe it spills over so you don't have to carry so much yourself.

Tyler: Tell my number one fan thanks.

Me: I think she "lubs" you more than Wobby now. Leveling up!

Tyler: [blushing, embarrassed emoji]

Me: How did you manage this, for so long? Keeping this secret all this time

Tyler: It's felt like walking on ice that might crack. All the time. Everywhere.

Me: I'm sorry you haven't had the support you should've had.

Me: My dad is going to get in touch with a college friend who's a lawyer and does immigration work. Hopes he can consult with you and your mom.

Tyler: Okay, maybe my mom will want to, I don't know. It's complicated.

Me: I don't care how complicated it is. We're not giving up.

Tyler: It's just… there were options, once. When Dad died. If they'd been married, if she'd applied for certain things in time. But those windows closed years ago.

Me: How do you know all this?

Tyler: Research. Lots of it. For years.

Me: I don't know how to fix this. But I know you can't keep carrying it alone.

Tyler: I'm not alone anymore. That's something.

Me: Try to sleep. We'll figure out the next steps tomorrow.

Tyler: Promise?

Me: Promise.

33

Passing Notes 2.0

Emilia's Note from Tyler

> I've felt like I was the only one keeping my mom safe since I was four. She shushed me when I said something in Spanish at the grocery store. Not mad—just scared. So I learned to hold back. Hold stuff in. Stay out of sight. Hide.
>
> Gramps and Grams are great. But I think losing my dad made them old before they should've been. It's different now. I'm not the only one holding up the world.
>
> So... thanks. For letting me hide but still seeing me. For having an awesome family—though it's not like you made it happen. But as Miggy says, "Mucho bossy." So maybe you did.
>
> Tyler

Tyler's notes from Emilia

> Sticky note #1:

I'm glad you know you're not alone. -E

Sticky note #2:

Of course I bossed my family into existence.
What kind of amateur do you take me for? – E

34

Creative Writing Assignment -Emila

I Wish Everyone Knew

Emilia Preston

I wish everyone knew the truth. Not the headlines. Not the sound bites. Not the arguments tossed out at dinner tables by people who've never had to live it. The real, human truth about immigration.

I wish everyone knew that most undocumented immigrants are not criminals. Despite the endless rhetoric painting them as dangerous, immigrants—both legal and undocumented—commit crimes at lower rates than native-born Americans. Most are here to work. To raise families. To build lives. Not to break laws.

I wish everyone knew how much of this country runs on undocumented labor. If every undocumented worker disappeared overnight, the economy would break in ways most people can't even imagine.

Agriculture: about half of U.S. farmworkers are undocumented—without them, fields go unpicked and shelves go empty.

Construction (in states like California and Texas): around one in five workers are undocumented—building homes, schools, hospitals.

Food service and hospitality: millions of undocumented workers keep restaurants, supply chains, and hotels running.

If those workers vanished, economists warn of multi-trillion-dollar losses over a decade.

It wouldn't just be businesses suffering—prices would spike, food shortages would spread, and everyday life would look a lot less stable.

I wish everyone knew that undocumented immigrants pay taxes. Billions of dollars every year in state and local taxes. They pay sales tax. Property tax (even if they rent). Many even pay into Social Security—knowing they'll never see those benefits.

I wish everyone knew about the profit machine behind immigration detention. The U.S. has built an industry around locking immigrants up. Private prison corporations lobby for tougher policies because their profits depend on full detention centers.

The majority of immigration detainees are held in privately run facilities. Many are jailed for nonviolent civil issues—paperwork lapses or seeking asylum. And they aren't guaranteed a lawyer. Most never see one.

Meanwhile, those corporations make billions. Thousands of families are separated so someone else can cash in.

I wish everyone knew that this system isn't broken because people refuse to follow the rules. It's broken because, for many, there are no rules that would ever let them in the "right" way. No line. No form. No option.

I wish everyone knew that no one leaves home by choice. They leave because staying would mean hunger, violence, fear. They cross borders with hope clenched tight in their fists—believing the American dream might still be worth the risk.

And I wish everyone knew that behind every statistic is a real person. A name. A face. A child waiting for their parent to come home.

I wish everyone knew the truth.

35

Creative Writing Assignment - Tyler

I Wish Time Machines Were Real

Tyler Alred

I wish time machines were real. Not the fancy Hollywood kind with blinking lights and weird science. Just a simple one—maybe a beat-up truck with a special gear shift—that could take you back just long enough to see someone's face or hear their voice one more time.

I wish I knew what my dad's laugh sounded like. People tell me stories—how he'd throw his head back when something really got him, how his shoulders would shake during those silent laughs that come when you're trying not to make noise. Gramps says I laugh just like him, but how would I know? There's no recording.

No reference point. Just this weird echo of something I've never actually heard.

I wish I could remember him, but I can't miss what I never had. That's what people say, anyway. They're wrong. You can miss the shape of someone who was never there—like a puzzle with the center piece missing. You know something's gone even if you don't know its exact look. All the clues have shown you its likely shapes, colors, size. So you miss it and want the puzzle to be complete, which it never will be.

I wish people understood that not everything broken needs fixing. Sometimes when people find out my dad died before I was born, they get this look—this "oh, poor kid" face that makes me want to dribble their head like a basketball. I'm not broken. I'm just different. My normal isn't yours. Deal with it.

I wish I could talk to my mom the way other kids do. Not because she isn't there—she but always working too hard and worrying too much. But there's this weight between us, this thing we carry together but never put down long enough to really see each other. Sometimes I think we're both too busy being strong to remember how to just be.

I wish fear wasn't so loud. It's like having a smoke detector going off, but there's no actual fire—just the constant beeping that keeps you from sleeping or thinking or being normal. Sometimes I think everyone can hear it, this alarm blaring inside me: Don't slip up. Don't say too much. Don't let anyone see.

I wish I didn't have to wish for things most people just have. But ninth-grade me knows something little me didn't: wishing doesn't change anything. Doing does. So maybe instead of wishing for a time machine, I should focus on the present. On the people who are here. On the family I have and the one I might be finding.

Because sometimes—not often, but sometimes—when I'm helping Mr. Preston with a fence post or watching Miggy do his weird chicken dance or listening to Gramps tell stories about Dad—I forget to wish for anything at all. And maybe that's the best wish of all.

36

Red Ink Can Say Nice Things

Emilia

Mr. Henderson moved around the tables in classroom with a deliberate pace. Today's bow tie was forest green with tiny gold owls—one more entry in his "conversation starters" collection.

He stopped by Tyler, leaned in, and said something that made Tyler straighten. Not his usual joking posture—something more genuine. Tyler nodded and looked down at his paper, expression unreadable.

When Mr. Henderson reached me, he set my essay face-down with a small smile. "Excellent work, Emilia," he said quietly. "I'd like to speak with you after class."

My stomach tightened. Even with a kind tone, those words landed like a jolt. I waited until he moved on, then flipped my paper. At the top, in neat cursive: Powerful, informed, and brave. A-. Not- provocative. Not- tone questionable. Actual notes—arrows, underlines, strong evidence beside my tax section. Compelling next to detention.

His final comment made me pause: This isn't just an essay, Emilia. This could be more—an op-ed, a longer research piece, perhaps even something for the school paper. Your voice matters, and this deserves to be shared. See me.

The bell rang. I gathered my things slowly and waved goodbye to my friends. When the room cleared, I went to Mr. Henderson's desk. He looked up, smiling.

"Emilia. Thank you for waiting."

"You wanted to see me?" I clutched my essay, resisting the urge to fold it smaller.

"Yes. Your essay on immigration was exceptional—not just in the writing, but in substance and perspective."

"Thank you."

"If you're open to it, I think this could run in the North Riverbend Chronicle—their Community Voices section."

I blinked. "The actual newspaper? The town one?"

He nodded. "With some expansion and citations, I think it would be a strong contender."

My first instinct was to shrink. To keep my words inside these four walls where only one person read them—and where my family's name stayed out of print.

"I can think about it," I said.

"You don't have to decide now," he said gently. "But I hope you'll consider it. Voices like yours—personal insight with factual accuracy—move the conversation forward."

"What would I need to do?"

"I'd guide you through it. Expand the research, refine the central argument, adapt the tone for a broader audience. Nothing that changes your message—just strengthens it."

He slid over a clipped article. "Different topic, but the format fits what I'm imagining."

I tucked it into my folder. Something in me steadied.

Tyler

Red ink, tidy. *One of the most honest pieces I've seen this semester. Your voice is authentic and powerful. Your paragraph about your father particularly resonated. A-.*

My throat went tight. I'd almost written about rocket-powered basketball shoes instead.

Writing about Dad, about Mom, about the fear, had felt like peeling back my own skin. And someone had actually read it. Really read it.

At our round table, Jenna was already comparing grades with Aria.

"A-minus! What'd you get?"

I flipped it face-down. "Same," I said, sliding it under my math notebook.

"Nice Tyler, let me read?" Jenna reached, and I pulled it farther away.

"No way." I held up my hand. "Personal."

Jenna gave me puppy dog eyes.

"Personal Jenna!," Ivy sing-songed.

"Yes, mommy Ivy."

Beside me, Emilia was quiet, studying her paper. I snuck a glance at her comments but couldn't make them out. Her face was somewhere between surprised and thoughtful.

At the bottom of my page was another note:

Tyler—There's a writing competition for young men who have lost parents. The prompt is "Absence & Presence." If you're interested, please see me. No pressure—your voice deserves to be heard.

No way. The words filled my mind, sat there, loud. Under it, something smaller: Maybe.

Mr. Henderson stopped by our table. "Strong work from all of you." Then to me in a low voice. "Tyler, your essay was excellent. About the competition—only if you want it. But keep writing with that honesty."

I nodded. Class ended, we packed up and shuffled out. In the hallway I realized Emilia was still in class. I looked around the door frame and saw her talking to Mr. Henderson and nodding. She emerged, a little dazed.

"What's up, what did Mr. Henderson want?"

"Oh, you waited for me?" She blinked at me. "He wants me to consider submitting my essay to the Chronicle. He wants me to expand it. I wrote about immigration."

"Immi-," my voice trailed off.

"Yeah." She tightened her grip on the folder. "I started because of thinking about your mom, but there's so much."

"That's, wow, you really see her don't you?" I'd been doing this alone so long, but now someone else could see. "Could I read it sometime?"

She nodded, "Sure, what about you? I saw him talking to you when he handed yours back."

I felt myself start to lock up. "I wrote some stuff about my dad. He said it was honest, good."

She didn't press. She just looked at me like she'd heard what I didn't say and let me keep it. We started down the hall. Our shoulders bumped once. Maybe on purpose. Neither of us moved away.

37

Tryouts & Old Trucks

Tyler

I wiped my hands on a rag that had definitely seen better days and stepped back from the open hood. Robbie peered inside, then knocked lightly on the frame like that might scare something loose.

"She's stubborn," he said.

"That's for sure.

He tossed a socket wrench into the toolbox. "You should've seen your dad trying to fix this thing senior year. Swore at it every Saturday."

We started gathering tools. Neither of us said much. The sun was lower now, and the grasshoppers were loud along the fence line.

"You and my dad looked like you thought you were pretty hot stuff in all the pictures I've seen," I said.

Robbie chuckled. "Only because we made a pact never to let our nerves show in the team photo."

"You got nervous?"

"Every time," he said. "I used to wear the same pair of socks for every game—left one inside out. Had to be the left. Don't ask me why."

I grinned. "Did it work?"

He shrugged. "We made it to regionals. Could've been talent. Could've been the sock."

I set the wrench down. "I don't know much about him from then."

Robbie's voice softened. "He was proud of being from here. Didn't always say it, but he was."

A gust of wind kicked dust across the gravel. For a second, we both just watched it. Then he said, "You remind me of him sometimes. You don't try to prove anything. You just... carry stuff. People notice that."

I didn't know what to do with that. So I didn't try. Instead, I glanced over at the old truck again. Still not running. Still waiting.

"I'll get that thing started," I said, more to the wind than anyone else. "Even if it takes me all year."

Robbie clapped me on the back. "Yeah, you will. I'll be glad to hear that engine complaining again."

There was a rustle behind us. Then a loud voice, "Did you ever wear your underpants inside out, Papi?"

We both turned. Miggy popped his head up from the bed of the truck like a prairie dog. He'd clearly been camped out back there for a while.

Robbie blinked. "What?"

Miggy pointed at him. "You said socks! Lucky socks! If you wore your Paw Patrol underpants inside out, that would be superhero lucky."

I looked at Robbie who was trying very hard not to laugh.

"Sounds uncomfortable," I said to him in a low voice.

"Yeah, it does," he snickered.

Miggy climbed over the side and dropped to the ground like he was in the middle of a heist. "Also, what's tryouts? You gonna try out like cookies that just got baked? Like taste testing? Like see if you crunch 'em good?"

Robbie coughed. "That's one way to put it."

I crouched to his level. "No cookies involved, bud. It's basketball. They see who plays best, who works hard, who's ready to be on the team."

Miggy looked thoughtful. "So... it's a test."

"Well..."

"And a fight?"

"Not..."

"But you want to win?"

"Well, yes—hopefully."

He nodded once, with full four-year-old gravity. "Okay. I'll assemble the supplies."

"Supplies?"

He looked at his dad, then pointed at me. "Farm Guy's gonna need backup."

"Find your Paw Patrol underpants when you go home farm guy, make sure they're clean."

Then he turned, bolted for the house, yelling at full volume, "SOFI! FARM GUY'S GOT TRYING OUTS COMING UP. HE NEEDS HELP!"

We stepped inside. The house was loud and warm, completely full of motion. I was just through the door and Sofía appeared in front of me.

"Fahn-die! EATS! NOW!"

Mariella's voice followed. "Sofía! Indoor voice, sweetie!" Sofía shoved a fistful of damp baby carrots at me.

I blinked. "Uh—thanks?"

She stared at me with wide eyes. Miggy leaned in from the side and stage-whispered, "Sofí thinks carrots fix everything. You gotta eat them."

"Thanks Sofía, I was just hoping I'd get some carrots before tryouts."

She stared at me until I put one in my mouth and crunched. When she saw I was eating the carrots she gave a royal nod then turned and stomped off like a warlord in a princess tiara.

Lunch blurred by in the usual way—plates passed, people talking over each other, Mariella refilling everything twice. Miggy kept disappearing and reappearing with random items, muttering things like "no, it needs more sparkle" and "is glue allowed?"

When he came back the final time, he was dragging something behind him like a parade float. He dropped it next to my chair with flair. "Your Victory Pack."

I raised an eyebrow. "My what now?"

"For trying outs," he said. "Everything important is inside."

I looked down and saw a glittery My Little Pony backpack with a limp handle, at least three keychains, and so stuffed it looked like it had been packed by a squirrel prepping for winter. He knelt down and unzipped it with dramatic flair, then started pulling things out one by one.

"A pencil."

"Nice."

"An empty water bottle to fill with your magic speedup water."

"Critical."

"A rubber band."

"Okay..."

"To snap at the bad guys." I didn't ask more.

"A band-aid. For all the blood."

"Uh...."

"A granola bar. Smashed to bits. So you 'member to smash up the bad guys."

"Still edible."

"A button. Don't lose it."

"Obviously."

"One red crayon."

"Power color," I agreed.

Then he tugged out a well-worn kid's fleece blanket with faded dinosaurs on it. "In case you need a napping spot. It's one of mine," he said. "I don't need more than five blankies now that I'm four."

I tried not to laugh. "Appreciate the sacrifice."

And the finale, a full sheet of T-Rex stickers. He handed me the sheet. "They can bite up the guys you need to beat."

Robbie left the room and came back with something flat tucked under his arm. He set it on the table next to the backpack. A photo frame. Inside was a faded team picture—dark purple and gold school uniforms, gym wall behind them. Gangly boys all swagger and elbows. My dad stood off-center, one arm slung around Robbie's shoulders like they knew they were invincible.

I blinked. "Whoa. Where'd this come from?"

"Emilia found it a few weeks back," he said. "Was digging through old papers in the office for grant stuff. Mariella framed it."

I stared at it. My dad couldn't have been older than I was now. He looked... annoyingly cool. Like the kind of guy who'd charm a coach and still mouth off under his breath.

"I thought maybe you'd want it," Robbie said.

I nodded. "Yeah. I do."

Later that night, the house was quiet. I'd showered, thrown on an old T-shirt, and was half-heartedly staring at my phone when I noticed the backpack sitting in the corner of my room where I'd dropped it. Still glittery. Still ridiculous. I smirked, went to shove it into my closet and paused. I pulled it closer and unzipped it again.

The Victory Pack's contents were still jumbled together. Stickers. Rubber band. Symbolic crushed granola bar. But right on top now was something I hadn't seen before. A folded scrap of notebook paper. I unfolded it. Emilia's handwriting. Slanted. Sharp. Familiar.

I had this backpack in third grade when I called you Prince Butthead because I thought you were teasing Ivy. Turns out you were just annoying. Still are. But in case it helps you run faster or jump higher, this backpack is lucky. Probably. No refunds.

I huffed out a laugh, quiet but real. Underneath the note was something softer. Sofía's bunny—gray, well-loved, and a little lopsided. One floppy ear bent sideways. No note. Just... there. Tucked like it belonged. I sat on the edge of the bed for a minute, holding both like they were heavier than they looked. Then I snapped a picture and sent a text.

> **Me:** Two questions. I'm assuming Wobby is just on loan, right? How do you know this backpack has magical powers? Is it cause

third was the grade where you met me and
nothing was the same?

Me: Did I bring the magic into your life?

Me: Also… thanks, for sharing your family.
Seriously. Because no matter what you say I
don't think you'd give Miggy away.

No typing bubble yet. I heard the hum of the quiet house
around me and felt soft weight of something a lot like being
known.

38

Fan in the Stands

Tyler

I wiped my sweaty palms on my shorts and tried to ignore the way my heart hammered against my ribs. The gym echoed with the squeak of shoes, the rhythm of bouncing balls, and Coach Barrett's whistle.

"Alright, next drill! Half-court press, five-on-five. Pedersen, you're leading white. Alred, you've got blue."

Aiden shot me a quick grin as he pulled on a white practice jersey. "Ready to get destroyed, Alred?"

"In your dreams, Pedersen," I fired back.

This wasn't just any tryout. This was varsity—the thing Aiden had obsessed over all summer. For him, it was step one in the master plan.

For me... it was complicated. Something I could nail down when so much felt off. Doing something my dad had—maybe it would feel like a layer of protection against anyone who thought Mom and I shouldn't be here.

Aiden grinned, but it didn't reach his eyes—easygoing as he is, he'd already clocked I wasn't right. Worries about my mom had become a heavier mass.

I gathered my makeshift team: Drew, Nate, and two juniors I barely knew. "Okay, keep it tight on defense. Nate, you've got Aiden."

Nate nodded once. "He favors left on the drive but pulls up faster off a spin. I'll stay low and force him wide." Then he glanced at me. "It would make more sense for you to cover him, though."

"I'm taking Washburn," I said, nodding toward the tallest junior on Aiden's team. "Plus I need to coordinate. Drew—watch for backdoor cuts. Parker—stay big in the paint. Call switches fast."

Truth? I didn't want to guard Aiden. Not today. I hadn't slept, and my brain kept replaying everything—Robbie's stories about my dad, the framed picture, Emilia's note, Mom pacing the kitchen like she was bracing for a storm. I could fake focus if I had to. But guarding Aiden meant he'd read me too easily, see right through whatever front I'd pieced together.

Coach blew the whistle, and we took our spots. The drill was brutal. Five minutes of nonstop movement—cut, recover, talk, repeat. By minute three, my lungs burned. By minute four, my legs felt like cement. I kept pushing.

"Shift right!" I called, tracking Washburn as he tried to break free. "Screen coming!"

I fought through, stayed on him, and tipped his pass. Drew scooped it and took off for an easy layup.

"Nice defense, Alred!" Coach shouted.

I allowed a small smile. Maybe I could do this after all. As we reset, I caught Aiden watching me, his expression calculating. He knew I was off. He didn't say anything—just gave me a small nod and turned back to his team. That was Aiden—always competing, wanted it for himself, but wanted it just as much for me.

The whistle again. Back at it. This time, Aiden's team moved the ball quicker, finding gaps.

"Close up!" I called, trying to organize our shift.

Too late. Aiden created space and drove. I rotated to help, leaving Washburn for a heartbeat. Risky, but I couldn't let Aiden score uncontested. We collided midair—nothing dirty, just two bodies fighting for the same space. His elbow glanced my ribs; we tumbled to the hardwood.

The whistle snapped. "You good?" Coach asked, stepping closer.

"Fine," Aiden and I said together, already climbing up. Pain spiked along my side. Sharper than I'd expected.

"You sure?" Aiden asked quietly.

"I'm good," I said, taking a careful breath. "Let's go."

Coach studied me a beat, then nodded. "Alright—water break. Then full-court scrimmage."

As we grabbed bottles, Aiden fell in beside me.

"You're off, Tyler. What's going on?"

"I'm okay, man," I deflected. "Don't worry."

Aiden didn't press. He didn't believe me, but we'd been friends too long to force it.

"SMASH THEM TO BITS, FARM GUY! LIKE A GRANOLA BAR!"

The voice split the gym like a lightning bolt. My bottle froze halfway to my mouth. No way. I turned to the bleachers. There—on a bench, both arms raised like a tiny general—stood Miggy.

"MAKE THE BASKETBALL BALL GO IN THE CIRCLE THING!" he added at top volume. Next to him, desperately trying to sit him down, was Emilia—cheeks blazing as every head in the gym swiveled toward them.

"Is that... your cheering section?" Aiden asked, not bothering to hide the grin.

"Oh my God," I muttered.

"FARM GUY!" Miggy yelled, evading Emilia's grasp. "DO THE JUMP THING WHERE YOUR FEET LEAVE THE GROUND!"

Coach Barrett blinked. "Alred, you know them?"

"Yep," I said, still staring. "That's, uh, Miggy. He's four."

"We don't usually have cheering sections during tryouts," Coach said. "Is this going to be a problem?"

"Not a problem, Coach," I said—too fast, too sure. Aiden's eyebrows went up.

"You're used to having Emilia in your fan club now?"

216

"Shut up," I muttered.

"YOUR LEGS ARE SO FAST! RUN MORE FAST!" Miggy continued, bouncing.

Coach blew his whistle. "Full-court scrimmage—let's go!"

As we lined up, Drew nudged me. "Dude, your mini fan club is intense."

"Honestly?" I huffed a laugh. "I think I needed it."

I glanced back. Emilia had coaxed Miggy into a sit, though he was still vibrating with enthusiasm. When she saw me looking, she mouthed what looked like *I'm so sorry* and made a vague gesture that read as either *I want to die* or *I'll explain later*. I grinned at her.

The absurdity cracked something open. Pressure slid off my shoulders. The scrimmage started, and—for the first time all day—my head was clear. The ball felt right. Passes snapped. Cuts were decisive.

"FARM GUY IS BEATING THE BAD GUYS!" Miggy announced from the bleachers. And weirdly—even though the guys on the court weren't the real bad guys I worried about—it felt like I was. By the final whistle, I was running on fumes.

"Good work today," Coach said as we circled up. "Roster posts tomorrow morning. Hit the showers."

The locker room erupted into the usual post-practice chaos—rehashing plays, decoding Coach's poker face, pretending not to care. Hot water lit up what was definitely going to be a nasty bruise. I dressed, then caught a glint of pink and sparkle in my bag. The victory backpack. I'd forgotten it was in there.

I zipped the bag before anyone else could see. If the guys knew, I'd never hear the end of it. Still... I liked knowing it was there. Like someone had packed confidence for me in case I forgot how.

When I came out with Aiden, Drew, and Nate, my mini fan waited in the hallway—bouncing in place.

"It's the basketball army!" Miggy yelled. "Meela! The basketball army needs ice cream! Right, Meela?"

Emilia leaned against the wall, arms crossed like she was pretending to be annoyed, but the smile gave her away. "Miggy wanted to wait," she said, emphasizing Miggy.

Miggy nodded gravely. "Yeah, I want the basketball army to go get ice cream. Just this time. Next time we have to go get veggies. C'mon."

39

Eating Ice Cream with the Basketball Army

Tyler

The North Riverbend Creamery had the kind of charm that only exists in small towns—faded booths with cracked vinyl, a counter worn smooth from decades of elbows, and the perpetual smell of waffle cones that somehow made everything feel right with the world.

Miggy marched in like he owned the place, making a beeline for the display case. His nose pressed against the glass as he contemplated his choices with the gravity of someone selecting a national security team.

"I'm getting the most winning flavor," he announced to no one in particular.

Mr. Daniels, who'd been running the place since our parents were kids, smiled at Miggy with the patience of a saint. "And what flavor might that be today, young man?"

Miggy squinted at the tubs of ice cream, his face scrunched in concentration. "The blue one. The blue team beat the bad guys today."

"Blue Monster Cookie it is," Mr. Daniels said, already reaching for a scoop.

Miggy gasped dramatically, his eyes going impossibly wide. "MONSTERS?" he whispered—loudly—then immediately stood taller. "I'm not scared of monsters. I EAT them!" He pounded his chest.

Then, leaning toward Aiden with complete seriousness. "They catch the monsters at night when they're under beds. That's why it's blue—cause monsters turn blue when you freeze 'em." He nodded knowingly at all of us. "That's why it makes you strong. You get the monster powers. Way better than basketball powers."

Mr. Daniels played along perfectly. "That's right, young man. Only the bravest ice cream eaters get the Blue Monster."

"I'm the BRAVEST," Miggy declared, standing on his tiptoes to watch his scoop being prepared. "I eat monsters for breakfast, too. With syrup. And bacon."

The rest of us placed our orders—chocolate peanut butter for me, mint chip for Emilia, rocky road for Aiden, gummy bear swirl for Drew, and Nate got cotton candy bubblegum explosion with double sprinkles, then calmly said, "Texture's important." Like that explained everything.

As we waited, Miggy positioned himself directly in front of Aiden, arms crossed. "So," he began, voice serious. "You're a basketball head."

Aiden glanced at me, clearly fighting a smile. "Am I?"

"Yep. It's a X-ray thing." Miggy tapped his own head knowingly. "Your brain is shaped like a basketball, but the doctor can't see it without a X-ray. Then you see your brain is round and bouncy and sometimes it makes you forget important stuff."

Nate snorted. Drew suddenly became very interested in the napkin dispenser.

"That sounds serious," Aiden said gravely.

"VERY serious," Miggy confirmed. "That's why you forgot about Ivy. Because your basketball brain was too busy thinking about basketballs."

Emilia closed her eyes briefly. "Miggy, maybe we could talk about something else—"

"No, this is important, Meela," Miggy insisted. "He's gotta know for his health." He turned back to Aiden. "My cousin Ivy was sad. And sad isn't a good way to be."

Aiden's amused expression softened into something more genuine. "You're right. It's not."

"So we gotta fix your basketball head. Sometimes you need to think about not-basketball things." Miggy leaned in, lowering his voice to what he thought was a whisper but was actually slightly less deafening. "Like baseball."

"Baseball?"

"Baseball hulks out on basketball," Miggy declared. "Way stronger. Way smarter. Way greener, from veggies."

Aiden nodded solemnly. "I'll keep that in mind."

"You should hold a baseball at least once a week," Miggy continued, warming to his topic. "To get some baseball in your brain. So your head doesn't turn all big and orange."

"Big and orange," Aiden echoed. "That would be tragic."

"Lucky for you," Miggy said magnanimously, "I have a baseball. I could let you hold it sometimes. To save your brain."

"That's very generous of you," Aiden said, trying hard to keep a straight face.

Mr. Daniels called out our orders, and we gathered our ice cream, finding a corner with enough space for all of us. Miggy immediately claimed the seat next to Aiden, apparently not done with his lecture.

"Also," he continued between enormous bites of blue ice cream, "you gotta eat all your veggies. Basketball guys need extra veggies because of basketball yield loss. It's science. Veggies make your brain more like a baseball brain. Less dizzy."

Emilia looked at him. "Wait—how do you even know what yield loss is?"

Miggy shrugged. "You and Papí said it in the kitchen. About corn. And grant stuff. But I fixed it for basketball. It's way more important."

He took another bite, then added, "You know what else helps dizzy basketball brains? Crop rotation."

Emilia blinked. "Crop rotation?"

"Yep. If you don't rotate crops, the dirt gets tired and the plants get dizzy. Just like basketball heads. Gotta rotate your sports or your brain goes in circles."

Nate leaned toward me. "Is he always like this?"

"Oh, this is mild," I said. "Wait until he starts talking about his chicken security force."

"Farm Guy knows," Miggy said, pointing his spoon at me. "He's seen the chicken ninjas in action."

"They're very stealthy," I confirmed.

Emilia watched all this with a mix of embarrassment and amusement, her cheeks still faintly pink. When our eyes met across the table, she gave me a small smile that somehow managed to say both *I'm sorry* and *This is your life now* at the same time.

"So, Miggy," Drew asked, clearly entertained, "what do you think of our basketball skills?"

Miggy considered this with his spoon halfway to his mouth. "Farm Guy is good because he practices on the farm. Farm work makes you strong." He flexed his tiny bicep to demonstrate. "You guys are okay, I guess. For basketball guys."

"High praise," Nate muttered.

"You could be better if you did more farm stuff," Miggy continued helpfully. "And held more baseballs."

As Miggy kept dispensing wisdom to the "basketball army," the bell over the creamery door jingled. I glanced up to see Mrs. Preston walk in, Sofía on her hip.

"There's my little farmer ninja," she said affectionately, spotting Miggy.

"MAMÁ!" Miggy shouted, ice cream forgotten as he bounded over. "I was teaching the basketball army about rotating dizzy brains!"

"I'm sure you were, Mijo," she said, smoothing his hair. "Time to head home, though. Papi's waiting."

"But I'm not done helping them," Miggy protested.

"You can help them another time," she assured him, then looked up at the rest of us. "I hope he hasn't been too much trouble."

"None at all," I said quickly. "He's been very... educational."

Sofía, who had been quietly observing from her mom's arms suddenly spotted me. Her whole face lit up.

"FAHM DIE!" she squealed, nearly launching herself out of her mother's arms. "LUB YOU!"

I felt my face heat as everyone turned to look at me.

"Hey, Sofía," I managed.

She strained toward me, arms outstretched, a look of pure adoration on her tiny face. Her mom chuckled and set her down. Sofía immediately toddled over and wrapped herself around my leg like a koala.

"Another member of your fan club," Drew said, grinning.

"The Preston women can't resist Farm Guy," Aiden added, shooting a pointed look at Emilia. If looks could kill, Aiden would've been a smoldering pile of ashes.

"Ivy's a Preston and Sofía also puts ketchup on pancakes," Emilia said lightly, but her blush had deepened.

"Preston Family farm girls," Aiden added with a smirk.

Sofía looked up at me with complete devotion. "Fahm die eat boo?" she asked hopefully, pointing at Miggy's ice cream.

"Sorry, kiddo. I've got chocolate," I said, showing her my nearly empty bowl.

She considered this, then nodded solemnly. "'Kay. Choc-it good."

"We should get going," Mariella said, reaching for Sofía's hand. "It's getting late."

"But I'm not done explaining baseball brains!" Miggy protested.

"Next time, Mijo," Mariella said firmly. "Say goodbye to everyone."

Miggy sighed dramatically but turned to face us all. "Bye, basketball army. Remember: veggies and baseball."

As Mariella guided them toward the door, Sofía suddenly stopped and turned around. She put both hands to her mouth and then threw them outward, making loud "MWAH!" sounds. She blew kisses—wildly, enthusiastically, completely indiscriminately.

"Kiss! Kiss!" she demanded, continuing to send them with both hands.

Miggy rolled his eyes. "Sofía! Stop the kisses! You're filling the air up with gross stuff."

Sofía kept going, tiny hands moving in a fast blur.

"Catch!" she insisted, looking directly at us. "Catch!"

"You have to catch them and put them on your cheek," Emilia said, grinning now as the guys froze. "She won't leave until you do."

I discreetly mimed catching one and tapped my cheek. Aiden, catching on, did the same with exaggerated flair.

"Got it," he said, tapping his cheek. "Thanks, Sofía!"

Sofía beamed, but kept blowing more, watching Drew and Nate expectantly.

"Catch!" she insisted, louder.

Drew and Nate exchanged glances, then awkwardly went through the motions of catching invisible kisses.

"All done," Mariella said, scooping Sofía up. "Let's go, Mija."

But as she carried Sofía out, the toddler peered over her mother's shoulder, watching us with complete seriousness. "Fahm die! Mwah!" she called back, blowing one final kiss directly at me.

Miggy, following behind, turned back one last time, pointing two fingers at his eyes, then at Aiden in the universal *I'm watching you* gesture. "Remember—veggies and baseball. No Whitneyland."

"No Whitneyland," Aiden agreed solemnly.

The bell jingled again as the Prestons exited, leaving behind a strangely quiet ice cream shop. Drew and Nate stared like they'd walked into the middle of filming The Real Toddlers of North Riverbend.

"Well," Drew said after a moment. "That was..."

"Something," Nate finished.

Aiden turned to me, a slow grin spreading across his face. "So, Farm Guy, when's Emilia going to start blowing you goodbye kisses?"

I gave him a look. "Probably around the same time Ivy starts blowing them to you. You counting down the minutes 'til that happens?"

Aiden laughed but didn't argue. "Yeah, yeah. Don't deflect. Give us the true story of what happens out at the Preston farm. How exactly did you become 'Farm Guy'?"

I glanced toward the door where Emilia had disappeared, then back at my friends' expectant faces.

"Fine," I said, leaning back in my chair. "But if any of this gets repeated, I know where you all sleep." I groaned but started talking. Some stories were too good not to tell—even when they were at my expense.

40

Making Varsity Dinner

Tyler

The house was quiet when I walked in. Too quiet for the day your kid makes varsity. I'd texted Mom earlier: Made it. Coach posted after lunch. He's got me running with the starters. Her reply came quick—¡Felicidades, mijo! Muy orgullosa.

I expected... I don't know. Music. The smell of enchiladas. From the doorway, though, it was just the hum of the fridge and not much else.

"Hello?" I called, dropping my gym bag by the door. "I'm home."

Mom appeared from our kitchen, wiping her hands on a dishtowel. Her smile bloomed when she saw me, but it flickered—like a light with a loose connection.

"Tyler! There you are." She crossed the room and pulled me into a hug. Dish soap and cinnamon. Her frame small against mine. When had I gotten so much taller? "My varsity basketball star."

"Hardly a star yet," I said, grinning anyway. "Just made the team."

She stepped back, holding my face between her hands. "You've worked so hard, mijo."

"Thanks, Mamá."

As she let go, the warm, spicy smell finally drifted from the kitchen—red sauce and toasted corn.

Over her shoulder, I noticed the kitchen table set for dinner—our small table in the apartment space Gramps and Grams converted for us years ago. Four places. My favorite enchiladas steaming on a serving plate. A small vase of fresh flowers. She'd made it special.

On the counter, her phone lay screen-up, like she'd been checking it on repeat. As if on cue, it buzzed once. She didn't pick it up.

"Everything okay?" I asked, aiming for casual.

That flicker again. "Of course. Let's eat while it's hot. Your abuelos should join us any minute."

I watched her move around the kitchen—quick, precise, too precise, like she was concentrating hard on normal. Her eyes kept darting to the phone. Not touching it. Just checking.

"Mamá," I said, slipping into Spanish. "¿Qué pasa? Something's wrong."

"No, no," she said in English, too bright. "Just a busy day."

I pulled out a chair. "If you say so."

She paused, wooden spoon hovering above the beans. "Why would something be wrong on such a special day? My son, varsity basketball. Such good news."

Her voice was tight; her shoulders were tighter.

"Was it another call?" I asked quietly.

The spoon trembled. She set it down.

"Tyler—"

Footsteps sounded on the old hallway runner. The connecting door opened.

"Where's my basketball superstar?" Gramps's voice boomed. "Did he leave any room on the court for the other kids to play?"

Despite everything, I grinned. Gramps came in wearing his ancient Celtics cap, carrying a small gift bag. Grams followed, gray hair freshly set, good cardigan with the pearl buttons.

"There he is," Gramps said proudly. "Varsity material, just like I've been saying since you were knee-high."

"We never doubted it for a minute," Grams added, eyes crinkling. She set a small bakery box on the counter. "Picked up your favorite dessert from Hansen's. We couldn't let tonight pass without a proper celebration."

Mom turned, smile fixed in place. "Just in time. Dinner's ready."

Their exuberance dimmed a notch; they felt it, too. Gramps set the bag on the table, shifting gears.

"Little something to mark the occasion," he said.

I pulled out tissue paper: a new pair of basketball socks—the good kind with extra cushioning—and a keychain with a tiny basketball hoop.

"The socks are practical," Gramps explained. "The keychain is ridiculous, which felt appropriate for you."

I snorted. "Thanks, Gramps."

"Your dad would be real proud," he added, voice softening. "He had a decent jump shot himself, you know. Not as good as yours, but decent."

Mom's hands stilled for a heartbeat.

Grams rested a hand on my shoulder, gentle. "He certainly would be," she said.

We sat. Conversation slid to safer ground—Gramps's bowling league drama, Grams's garden club gossip, and the story about Mrs. Johanson's dog getting loose in produce. The food was perfect—enchiladas, beans with the spices just right, her special rice. It should have come with laughter.

Mom's gaze kept drifting to the phone. When she thought I wasn't looking, worry crept back into her eyes.

After dinner, when Gramps went to his shows and Grams claimed she needed to finish a book for her club, I helped Mom with the dishes. She washed; I dried. The practiced dance of it was soothing.

"It was the same number, wasn't it?" I said quietly, keeping my eyes on the plate in my hands. "The one that called before."

She didn't answer right away. Just kept washing the same pot, over and over.

"Mom."

She sighed, heavy with everything she wasn't saying. "Yes," she admitted at last. "But it's nothing for you to worry about."

"If you're worried, I'm worried," I said.

She looked up then—really looked—and I could see her weighing how much to tell me. How much to protect me from.

"The Díaz family," she said haltingly. "You met them once or twice. You remember Elena?"

I nodded. I could picture a young mom and her two well-behaved quiet kids.

"Her husband was taken," Mom whispered. "Three days ago. The children are with her sister now. She doesn't know when—if—" She swallowed. "They're saying more raids soon."

ICE.

"But we don't know—"

"No," she cut me off. "We don't. And you have enough to focus on with school and basketball." She dried her hands and cupped my face again, eyes fierce. "Si no llamamos la atención, we're fine. You are going to practice hard and study hard and have the life we came here for. This is not your burden." But it was. It always had been, in ways she didn't see.

"Everything will be fine, Mamá," I said, the lie settling heavy. She nodded, brushed my hair off my forehead.

"You look more like him every day," she murmured. "He would be so proud of you."

Later, in my room, I sat on the edge of my bed staring at my phone. The varsity roster notification glowed on the screen, my name there among the starters. It should have been the biggest thing in my world.

All I could see was Mom's face when she said "Díaz." The way her hand shook.

My phone buzzed

> **Emilia:** Didn't get to tell you in person. Congrats, Farm Guy! Was there ever any doubt?

I typed: Got home to enchiladas and worry. Mom got another call. Something's happening with the Díaz family from church. I'm scared. I stared at it. Then deleted everything.

> **Me:** Thanks! Working on my vertical leap so I'm ready for all the dramatic slam dunks.

Send.

I fell back on the bed, phone on my chest. The ceiling fan spun lazily above me, its quiet whoosh keeping time. On the court, I know who I am. Point guard. Defender. Part of something bigger.

At the Prestons', I'd started to know too. Farm Guy. The Beast restorer. Part of a warm chaos I can't get enough of.

Here, in our quiet apartment with its unspoken fears, I'm between worlds—the life Mamá sacrificed for, and the truth we don't say out loud. I closed my eyes. In the next room, her quiet footsteps kept moving. The fan kept time.

41

Decision to Take Step

Tyler

I didn't expect to see Mom at the farm. Usually, if she wasn't working, she was home—cleaning, cooking, folding towels with military precision while watching old novellas on mute. She didn't like to impose. She didn't like being seen too much.

But there she was, sitting at the Preston kitchen table with Emilia's mom, a half-empty mug of coffee in front of her. The two of them were deep in quiet conversation, the kind where no one was smiling but there was a kind of softness to it anyway. Steam curled from mismatched mugs; the room smelled like cinnamon and brewed coffee.

Emilia and I had just come in from the driveway, both of us brushing dust off our jackets and trying not to trip over Sofía's latest floor obstacle course.

"Hey," I said, careful not to interrupt.

Both women looked up. Mom's expression shifted instantly—like she'd only just realized she was somewhere unfamiliar. I caught the way her shoulders pulled tighter, how her hands moved toward her bag like she might need to stand, thank everyone, and leave before someone decided she didn't belong.

But Mrs. Preston just smiled and said, "Coffee's fresh if either of you wants a cup."

"I'm good," I said, hanging my hoodie on the back of a chair. "Robbie said to meet him by the shed in fifteen, but I wanted to say hi first."

Emilia shot me a quiet look, something between a warning and a you okay?

I nodded, then turned to Mom. "Everything alright?"

"Yes," she said, too quickly. Then, after a second. "We were just talking."

Mrs. Preston added, "She mentioned... what happened with the Díaz family. I told her Robbie might have a friend who could help. He's not local, but he consults. Immigration law work. He's seen a lot."

I looked at Mom. "You're meeting with him?"

"If he has time," she said. "Robbie called while we were sitting here. His friend said he'd review our situation. Just to talk. No pressure."

I tried not to show how much that meant. "That's... that's good."

"It's just information," she said, mostly to herself. "Not a decision." Her fingers tightened on the mug, she didn't notice.

I could tell it had cost her something just to be here, just to say yes. Asking for help had never come easy to either of us.

"When?" I asked.

Mrs. Preston answered. "Tomorrow after school. He can fit you in at four if you're okay coming straight from classes." She added, "Bring any IDs or papers you have. It helps."

"We'll be there," I said before she could hesitate.

Emilia didn't say anything, but I felt the nudge of her elbow against mine. Not pushy. Just there.

Mom gave me a small smile. "Gracias, Mijo."

"You ready to find my dad?" Emilia asked, gently redirecting.

"Yeah," I said, giving her mom a grateful look. "Thanks for… everything." Mrs. Preston waved it off, but there was something in her eyes. A kind of knowing. Emilia and I stepped out into the chill, the screen door creaking behind us. The sun was already dipping low over the field, the truck gleaming faintly by the shed.

"I didn't know she was coming today," I said.

"I bet she didn't either," Emilia replied. "I'm thinking Mamá invited her for coffee then lovingly ambushed her and gave a convincing argument for visiting with the lawyer."

I exhaled, something uncoiling in my chest. "I'm glad she came."

"Me too."

We walked the rest of the way in silence, the kind that felt like something shared. Tomorrow we'd sit with a stranger who might tell us whether hope was real—or just another way to break your heart. Tonight, there was still light in the sky.

42

The Lawyer's Office

Tyler

Mark Jacobsen's office wasn't what I expected. No towering mahogany desk. No dark suits or fake smiles. No wall of intimidating degrees.

Just a creaky converted house in Dickinson—a space lent by a legal aid group for consults this week—with chipped paint on the porch railing and plants crowding the windowsills like they'd been rescued and never left.

Inside, it smelled faintly of lemon cleaner and cinnamon tea. His desk was cluttered, but not in a messy way—more like someone who worked instead of postured. No family photos. No joke mugs. Just file folders, legal pads, and a kettle that clicked off as we sat. None of that settled my nerves. Not even close. I rubbed my palms on my jeans and tried to keep my foot from tapping.

Mom sat beside me, back ramrod straight, hands folded like she was balancing a bowl of water she didn't dare spill. On her other side, Gramps filled the third chair, his calloused hands resting on his knees. He hadn't said much on the drive.

Just a quiet "Let's go," as he grabbed his keys—but he'd insisted on coming. That was his way. Silent, steady. Present. He took notes in his head the way he always did—quiet, exact.

Mark greeted us with a warm handshake and a nod. "Ms. Alred—Luz?—thank you for trusting me with your story."

Mom didn't smile, but she nodded. "Gracias. For making time."

"Of course," he said. "Before we start, what's your legal name as it appears on your documents—and any other names you've used day to day?" He wrote as she answered, then added, "We'll use your legal name on paperwork. In here, I'm happy to call you Luz if you prefer."

Then came the questions. He started from the beginning—how and when she entered the U.S., her work history, how long she'd been in the area. He asked about Dad, about her jobs, about anything that might give context. Every question was calm, clear, and quiet—like someone helping her empty a neatly packed suitcase that had been sitting forgotten.

Mark didn't rush. But he didn't sugarcoat, either. He explained how complicated things were right now. That applying for protection meant becoming visible to immigration authorities.

That even with a strong case, there were delays. Risks. The weight of a system that didn't always care who you were or why you'd stayed invisible for so long.

"The most common paths we'd normally look at—family sponsorship, asylum, DACA—don't apply here," he said, flipping through his notes. "But based on what you've shared, we may have another option."

He looked up at my mom. "As I mentioned to Robbie when he called—there's the U visa."

Mom didn't respond right away, but something in her posture changed. Like the name alone had weight.

"The U visa is for victims or witnesses of certain crimes who've been helpful to law enforcement," Mark said. "It's meant to protect people who come forward when others wouldn't."

He paused. "The requirements are specific. There has to be documentation—a police report, a statement, emails—something on paper. We'd also need law-enforcement certification confirming cooperation. And we'll want support from others involved if possible: a manager, a coworker, anyone who witnessed what happened or can verify it."

Silence settled. The room seemed to narrow to the edge of his desk.

"Can you tell me what happened at Riverbend Lodge?"

Mom lined the edge of the legal pad with the desk, then straightened it again—her tell when she was trying to hold steady. Her thumb pressed into her palm. Jaw set. One slow breath. She wasn't bracing because she couldn't remember; she was bracing because saying it out loud would make it real in front of me—and I knew she'd never told me the story she had to say out loud now.

"Sí," she said at last, smoothing the page once more and lifting her chin. "I can tell you..."

She sat across from me, her back straight like always. Gramps leaned against the windowsill, arms crossed, watching the street below like he could hold the whole world steady just by standing there. I sat between them, and the only sound in the room was the soft shuffle of paper from Mr. Jacobsen as he made a note and looked up.

"I was working a morning shift at the Riverbend Lodge," Mom began. "Room 212. I was helping train a newer girl—Ana. Young. Maybe twenty. It was her first week."

She kept her voice calm, but I saw her thumb press hard against the side of her hand, like she needed an anchor.

"We'd finished a few rooms already. I moved ahead to the next one while Ana stayed behind to take out the trash and grab fresh towels."

Mom paused. "I thought I heard something. A shout, maybe. I wasn't sure. I waited, but she didn't come."

She looked up. "I went back and knocked. No answer. I used my key to open the door."

She steadied. "He had her pinned against the wall—one hand over her mouth, the other in her hair, pulling her head back. I heard him say, 'Don't scream.'"

My whole body locked.

"He let go of her the second I opened the door. Acted like nothing happened. She ran straight out. I followed, made sure she got downstairs. Then I called the manager. Told them they needed to report it."

My chest went tight. I couldn't speak.

"They said it was a misunderstanding," she continued, voice still even. "Called him a regular. Said Ana must have misread the situation."

Mr. Jacobsen made another note but didn't interrupt.

"I told them if they didn't file a report, I would. They cut my hours the next week. Said business was slow." She exhaled. "But I filed the report anyway. I told the police everything I saw."

Gramps shifted his weight, jaw tight. "Ana—what happened to her?"

"She never came back to work," Mom said. "No one could reach her. I don't know if she left town, or..." She didn't finish the sentence.

I wanted to say something. Anything. But the words didn't come. She turned toward me.

"I didn't tell you, Mijo, because what would it have changed? It happened. I did what I could. And then I went back to work."

I was shaking. I hadn't realized it until she reached across the table and touched my hand.

"You gave a statement," I said. "That's what Mr. Jacobsen meant."

"Yes."

"You didn't tell anyone else?"

"I told the truth to the people who needed to hear it. That was enough."

Gramps cleared his throat. He said, quiet but firm. "You did what was right."

She nodded once. "I didn't do it for a visa. I did it because Ana was someone's daughter. Maybe someone's mother. Because someone had to."

I looked at her—really looked. Not just as the woman who made my lunch and stayed up folding clothes past midnight. But as someone who'd stood up when it mattered. Who'd put herself at risk so someone else could be safe.

"I'm proud of you," I said, voice thick. "I wish I'd known sooner, but... I'm proud of you."

She blinked fast and gave a small nod. "Thank you."

Mr. Jacobsen set his pen down and looked between us, his expression unreadable.

"We'll add this to the affidavit," he said. "It's important you shared it. Very important."

After hearing mom's story, Mr. Jacobsen had left to grab copies from the printer. He returned to the room with a manila folder.

"Thank you for your patience," he said. "And for sharing what you did. That report adds important weight to your case, but I know it wasn't easy to speak about."

Mom nodded, her composure back in place. But I could see how still her hands were now. Not folded, not fidgeting. Just resting flat on the table like she was bracing herself for the next step. Jacobsen pulled a pen from his jacket pocket and opened the folder.

"I've printed the intake form," he said. "This doesn't commit you to anything—it's just the official start of gathering and organizing your application. We won't file until you review everything and feel ready."

He slid the first page toward Mom, then paused. "There are a few key things to understand before we move forward," he said. "First, this application will include a request for a work permit under deferred action. If granted, it protects you from deportation while the U visa is pending. That could take time—at least a year, possibly longer—but in the meantime, you'd have status. You'd be visible but protected."

Mom gave a small nod. "That's better than what we have now."

"Second," he continued, "we'll need to contact both the Riverbend Police Department and the hotel. If there's any written statement from you already on record, we'll request it. If not, I may ask you to sign an affidavit."

She didn't hesitate. "I'll sign."

Jacobsen smiled faintly, then turned to me.

"Tyler, as your mother's child, you'll be included on her application as a qualifying relative. You won't need to do anything personally, but it will strengthen the case to show your educational path, community roots, and future goals."

I nodded slowly. "Okay."

"Any questions?" he asked, looking between us.

Gramps shifted in his seat. Then, instead of asking the question, he reached into the inside pocket of his jacket and pulled out a folded check. He held it out to Mr. Jacobsen, his voice quiet but steady.

"I think this covers the amount we talked about on the phone."

Mr. Jacobsen accepted it glancing at the name and amount before nodding once, respectfully. "It does. Thank you, Mr. Alred."

Gramps just gave a small nod and sat back again, the slightest exhale escaping like he'd been holding it in. Mom glanced at him—startled, maybe, but not surprised. A flicker of something crossed her face. Gratitude. A deeper history. The kind of love that rarely used words.

Jacobsen set the check aside and said, "As always, if anything changes, we'll adjust. But this more than gets us started."

"Do you need time to decide?" he asked.

"I already decided," Mom said. Her voice didn't rise. It didn't shake. "Let's begin."

He handed her a pen. She signed her name slowly, carefully. And something inside me shifted. This wasn't just paperwork. This was the first time I'd seen her ask for something that wasn't survival. The first time I saw her name attached to possibility. When she slid the form back across the table, Jacobsen accepted it with a nod of respect.

"You've taken the first step," he said. "That's never small."

We stood to go, and Gramps shook his hand again. "Appreciate the straight talk," he said.

"And your time," Mom added, her voice quieter now.

Emilia and her mom stood from the chairs where they'd been waiting. Emilia's eyes found mine right away. I nodded, once. She didn't ask anything, just squeezed my hand, then walked out next me. Outside, the air felt different. Not lighter exactly. But clearer.

43

Porch Decompression

Tyler

The porch at the Prestons' always smelled like tomatoes and sunshine—growth, warmth, safety. I sat on the top step, the manila folder from the lawyer's office balanced on my knees. The sun was sinking over the fields, painting everything rose gold, making the world gentler than it is. Crickets tuned up in the ditches.

Inside, Miggy and Sofía were in full chaos mode. Miggy was playing judge and finding all of his sister's stuffed animals guilty and Sofía yelled, "No, no, dey's no bad!" She used the tone of a passionate defense attorney.

I heard Mrs. Preston laugh and tell the two to close court for the day. I knew that stepping into the house I'd be met by noise, warmth, and life. Emilia came out quietly and sat beside me. She didn't say anything. Just leaned her shoulder gently against mine, she knew I wasn't ready to talk yet. I opened the folder. Closed it again.

"She's going after something called the U visa," I said finally.

Emilia turned her head. "The U visa?"

"Yeah," I said. "It's for people who've been victims of certain crimes—or witnessed one and helped the police. If it's approved, she gets protection from deportation, a work permit... eventually maybe even a path to permanent residency."

"And she qualifies?"

I nodded. "We're starting the process. Mr. Jacobsen said it could take more than a year. Once we file, she can get deferred action and work authorization while it's pending. It's a big leap, choosing the U visa—risky, but if it's approved... it means staying. For real."

"And she picked the visa?"

"She did." I looked down at the folder again. "First time I've seen her ask for something that wasn't just about surviving."

Emilia didn't respond right away. "What made her eligible?"

I hesitated. "She didn't tell me until today. Not until we were sitting there."

She waited. No pressure. Just that quiet patience I'd come to count on.

"Six months ago, she was training a new housekeeper. Ana. First week on the job—young, nervous. They were cleaning rooms at the Riverbend Lodge."

I felt the weight of it settle in my chest again.

"They split up. My mom went ahead. Realized Ana wasn't following. Mom thought she heard something—maybe a shout. She went back. Knocked. No answer. Used her key."

I watched the light shift across the porch floorboards. "She opened the door and found a guest with Ana pinned to the wall—one hand over her mouth, the other twisted in her hair. He was telling her not to scream."

Emilia's breath hitched.

"She got Ana out. Took her straight downstairs. Reported it to the manager. But they said the guy was a regular. Called it a misunderstanding. Then cut Mom's hours."

"She still went to the police," Emilia said. It wasn't a question.

"Yeah. Gave a full statement. Ana never came back after that shift. No one heard from her again."

Emilia didn't say anything right away. She reached for my hand and held it.

"She never told me," I said. "Said it wouldn't have changed anything. She just did what she had to do. And we kept going."

A pause. Then Emilia said, "She did what most people wouldn't."

"She did," I said. "And all I could think was—what if it had been her? What if the roles were reversed? And Ana had been too scared to open the door."

Emilia's grip tightened.

"Because it could've been her, Em. That's what got me. She stepped in. But she's worked in rooms like that her whole life. And if something happened to her..." I shook my head. "I want to believe someone would help, but..."

We sat in silence, letting that sink in. The sky had shifted while we talked, moving from gold to violet. Behind us the kitchen glowed warm through a window, moths batted at the porch light. My mom stood inside next to Mrs. Preston, her shoulders more relaxed than I'd seen in months.

"She's so strong," Emilia said quietly and looked at me. Her eyes were shiny with tears. "She shouldn't have had to be the one to report, the management should have done the right thing."

"She shouldn't have," I agreed. "But, they didn't and she took on all the risk. She looks lighter though, she's starting to see she doesn't have to carry it all alone now."

Emilia didn't answer. Just leaned into me.

44

One Couple Shows up

Emilia

Aiden's chair was closer to Ivy's than it used to be. Not dramatically. Not overt. Not obvious. Just... closer. Like it had been quietly sliding towards her for weeks and could at last come to a stop. They weren't holding hands. They weren't even touching, technically. But the space between them had changed. I watched Ivy say something, soft and sideways, and Aiden's head tilted toward her like he couldn't help it. The she laughed, and he smiled, and I felt the word finally settle all around us.

Around the table, awareness moved through our friends like the scent of lilacs on a slight spring breeze through an open kitchen window. Jenna clocked it first. Then Aria. Maddie. Nate. Then Drew, who leaned back with a slow, knowing nod.

"Well," Jenna said, reaching for her drink. "Look who showed up to their own rom-com."

Tyler, sitting across from me, barely looked up from unwrapping his granola bar. "Told you it would happen before Halloween."

Aria perked up. "Wait—prediction pool! Do we still have the spreadsheet?"

"I do," Jenna said, already digging through her phone. "Tyler called it three weeks ago."

She turned the screen around to show an annotated group thread with Tyler's name and a smug checkmark tag next to October 5th.

"I expect fanfare," he said flatly, popping a grape in his mouth. "Confetti. Possibly a musical number."

"Are we supposed to be surprised?" Drew asked, squinting at Ivy and Aiden like they were a new species. "They've shared a soul since kindergarten."

"Not officially," Ivy said, lifting her chin just a little.

Aria snorted. "So you've ascended to official soul sharing? Your psyches are so close, I think your jackets are about to announce an engagement."

Ivy rolled her eyes but didn't move. Aiden didn't say anything, just smirked and bumped her with his shoulder. And that was enough. I gave a half smile, then glanced across at Tyler. He had his avoiding-being-read persona—shoulders relaxed, face neutral, just this side of teasing. He tossed a comment into the conversation about being available for advice if they needed a relationship coach, and everyone laughed. Including me. Then he gave the smile he wore when he didn't want questions.

I looked back at Ivy, who was trying not to smile as Aiden whispered something in her ear, and I felt the tug of something

I couldn't name. Not jealousy. No, a tender spot behind my ribs. An unspoken wondering lodged there... how would it feel to be settled, having fully faced the feelings?

I opened a new message on my phone.

Me: Congrats. Your face is now permanently smug.

Me: Tell Aiden he owes me five bucks for pretending I didn't know....

I deleted the whole thread.

Jenna was talking about making a commemorative cake. Drew wanted it to say "Finally" in buttercream. Someone else suggested printing stickers. Aria, never one to miss her moment, said casually, "Guess we're down to one almost-couple."

The table went quiet. I didn't look at Tyler but felt all their gazes anyway. Silence expanded and filled the space left by Aria's words.

Jenna raised her eyebrows. "Should we start a new pool?"

Tyler didn't miss a beat. "Please. Emilia and I are already married on paper. We've got an alpaca farm in Montana, two kids named Thunder and Pancake, and matching overalls. Very exclusive arrangement."

Aria snorted. "Okay, but who's in charge of the alpacas?"

"Obviously Miggy," I said, before I could stop myself.

Tyler looked at me, amused. His smile warmer, less of a defense. "Naturally. The boy runs a tight operation."

Jenna groaned. "Why do I feel like there's backstory here?"

"Because there is," I said, trying to sound casual as I reached for my fries. Tyler raised his cup to his lips.

"Is that so?" he said mildly. Then his eyes flicked to mine again, a beat slower this time. "Eat your fries up, sweetheart. We've got the wife-carrying race to prep for."

My face went hot, but I didn't look away. At last everyone moved on. Jenna tried to pump everyone up for the upcoming pep rally, and Aiden asked Tyler a question about basketball practice. I stayed quiet. When I got home after school I had a text.

Tyler: You know you've passed Miggy level access right? Let me know when you're ready to hear what level you're on.

45

The Many Parts of a Granted

Emilia

Dinner had been cleared away, the house settling into its evening hum. Mamá was putting Sofía down for the night, and Miguel was in the living room. He'd sprawled out with a book or had his drawing supplies helping him draw chicken ninjas and cow baseball players.

Dad and I stayed at the kitchen table, the laptop open between us, the soft glow of the screen washing over a thick binder labeled Farm Planning & Projects. Colored tabs bristled like the spine of some kind of Pókeman lizard monster.

Miguel wandered in, rubbing his eyes, clearly fighting sleep. He stopped just inside the doorway, scoping out the scene with the important air of a four-year-old boy.

"Hola, Meela," he said, then turned to my dad with equal solemnity. "Hola, Papí."

"Hola, Miggy-man," Dad replied, distracted as he scrolled.

Miguel glanced at the laptop, unimpressed. "Still doing the granted farm homework?"

Dad smile. "That's right, bossman. We're working on the grant project."

Miguel nodded, his expression telling us to carry on. "Okay." He padded back toward the living room his inspection complete.

I huffed with amusement and shook my head, "That felt like an FDA inspection. He's got a checklist somewhere he's filling out on us."

"Gotta keep the granted workforce accountable," Dad said.

I turned back to the grant portal. "Okay—this is the Fields of Dandelions initiative, a response to the flooding of the Little Missouri River and the regional wildfires. Targeted towards ranches and farms for the initiation of expansion of regenerative practices. What we're trying to expand."

Dad rubbed his chin. "Sounds like a great fit. We'll need to demonstrate the strength of our expansion plans and the success of past and current efforts. They'll want specifics—how many acres we'll transition, projected improvements in soil health and water retention, and how we'll measure success over time."

I scrolled. "It says preference goes to farms with existing conservation practices. We're already doing rotational grazing and native grass reseeding, with some native pollinator habitat, so that helps."

I skimmed a rubric. "Impact—40 points. Feasibility—30. Budget—20. Community benefit—10."

Dad nodded. "So we write to the points first, then fill in where we feel it needs strengthening."

I pulled up checklist: Eligibility—check. We'd need a Narrative of 1,000 words. Budget template. Two letters of support. All doable.

Dad gave me a look that crinkled at the corners. "When you were spitting up and colicky, keeping us awake all night I didn't foresee grant writing together in our future. Of course, your mom and I were both so sleep deprived we didn't know what day it was."

I rolled my eyes, smiling. "Here I am making up for those days and nights of lost sleep. You should've started reading me NDSU's ag extension newsletter, might've been the solution."

"Mom and I have realized it's impossible to make predictions about kids. Miggy was the calmest baby of the three of you."

"Point taken."

He leaned back, stretching, "This is good experience for you, Meela-Mi. These grants—this kind of planning—keep the farm running long-term. You learning this now means you can take the lead on projects like this in the future. I can only imagine the need for regenerative practices outpacing the work done on farms like ours."

A warm sense of purpose settled in my chest. "That's what I want to work on learning. Not only ways to increase production, but how to balance a good livelihood with improving systems."

Dad hummed, tapping the table. Then, almost absently, he murmured, "Tøffing."

I looked up. "What?"

"Tøffing," he said again, "'Tough girl,' the word my mom used for my sister when she held her own against the boys."

The word landed warm and solid.

"It shouldn't be a fight, to do what's right for the land, but it can be. You'll need that toughness in the future. Alright, let's get started, see what we can crank out tonight. Make good headway on the granted business."

I opened a doc and named it Dandelions_Grant_v1 and typed the first header: Project Summary (150 words).

By Sunday morning we'd completely commandeered the dining room table as our command center—printed articles, sticky notes, my laptop—surrounded by normal Preston chaos. Dad leaned over my shoulder, pointing to a paragraph about soil regeneration while Mamá flipped pancakes shaped like farm animals.

"See this part about carbon sequestration? That's exactly what we've been doing with the north pasture rotation," Dad said, voice edged with rare excitement.

I highlighted. "And here—heritage practices meeting modern solutions. We do that but maybe we look to expand?"

Pages for our application piled up digitally and physically: water lines, seed invoices. I traced paddock rotations on the map—blue for current, green for expansion.

The Fields of Dandelions application had consumed my weekend and I suppose a lot of kids would think I'm a farm nerd, but opinions didn't mean much to me. Feeling connected to a farm and planning for the future grew your roots.

I opened a fresh doc and laid out a three-week timeline

Map update — Dad (Fri)

Soil infiltration tests — Me (Sat)

Draft narrative — Me (Sun)

Budget template — Dad (Mon)

Letters of support — Ag Ext Office & FFA (request today)

For the budget bones we listed fence repairs, corner H-braces, a solar pump for the back trough, and seed for native warm-season grasses—the big number.

For measurement, Dad said, "Start with baselines."

So, infiltration test, before/after photo points, grazing days per paddock, and a simple May bird count. I sent an email to Ms. Reed at Extension about a letter of support. Mamá drafted a paragraph on cultural stewardship and community agriculture that we'd incorporate. The family farm, it's future and the resources to do so were spinning in my mind.

"MEELA!" Miggy's voice shattered my concentration as he barreled into the kitchen, brandishing a crayon drawing. "I made PLANS for the granted stuff!"

Sofía toddled in behind him, wearing rain boots despite the sunshine. "I hep too!"

Dad's mouth twitched into a smile. The Preston Farm—where even grant research came with its own brand of chaos.

"Let me see your plans, Miggy-man," Dad said, taking the crumpled paper with exaggerated seriousness. Over his shoulder I tried not to laugh. Chickens... with jetpacks? And a tractor with a giant claw?

"This is our security system," Miggy explained, tapping the jetpack chickens. "They guard the tomatoes. And this"—jab at the claw-tractor—"is for catching bad guys who try to steal our corn."

Dad nodded thoughtfully. "Very innovative farm security."

"What about you, Sofía? What's your plan?" I asked.

Sofía studied her boots, then looked up. "Pwant boo flowers." A decisive nod.

"Blue flowers are very important," I agreed solemnly.

Mamá slid a plate of pancakes onto the table. "Researchers need fuel." She winked. "Miggy, Sofía, come wash your syrupy fingers."

As they scampered off, Dad leaned closer to the screen. "You're onto something with the traditional-methods section. There's so much of traditional practice that could be revived or redefined for today."

I scrolled to Community & Culture. "What if we expand this to include not only production but keeping traditional practices alive—keeping culture alive. Ideas from all the cultures of people who lived or live in the area."

Dad's eyes lit. "Rather than taking it all on ourselves we could look for area partnerships. Really, that's the heart of it, regenerative agriculture has to be a joint project. Farming isn't just science—it's relationship. That's what we show the committee."

"I have some ideas, let me get those done and then you take a look at it."

"Perfect." He squeezed my shoulder. "This is going to be good, Meela-Mi."

"Meela!" Miggy called from the kitchen. "Can the chicken jetpacks shoot lasers or just regular bullets?"

Dad and I locked eyes. "Foam darts," I called back, "from recycled materials."

"RECYLCING DARTS!" Miggy shrieked, delighted.

Dad shook his head, laughing. "We may need to incorporate Miggy's security system. Really wow the committee."

I grinned, but my mind was already formatting Community Impact.

By mid-afternoon, my eyes were burning from screen time, and my back ached from hunching over the laptop. But we had a solid draft—something that actually felt like it could win.

"We should take a break," Dad said, stretching. "Clear our heads before the final review."

I nodded, saving the document for the third time just to be sure. "I think I'll go outside. I need air."

Outside, the autumn sun hung low in the sky, casting long shadows across the pasture. I breathed in deeply, filling my lungs with the smell of earth and hay and the faint sweetness of apples from the orchard. The screens and numbers fell away, replaced by the simple reality of this place.

After a loop around the house, I spotted Miggy in the garden, engaged in what appeared to be a serious conversation with the scarecrow. Sofía was nearby, carefully arranging rocks in the dirt.

"What are you two plotting?" I called.

Miggy looked up. "We're having a farm meeting. The scarecrow says we need more crows, not less."

"Really?" I tried to keep a straight face.

"Yeah, cause crows are smart and they can be farm spies." He lowered his voice to a dramatic whisper. "The scarecrow is a double agent."

Sofía nodded, adding another rock to her collection. "Dobuh hay-gent."

"Okay, you two keep up your top-secret farm work here, I'm heading back in."

I smiled all the way back to the house, wondering if I should add a line in the grant about the value of imagination in agricultural education. Or perhaps not—I wasn't sure the Fields of Dandelions committee was ready for Miggy's particular brand of farm innovation.

The rest of the evening passed in a blur of final edits, dinner, and one more look at the budget. By the time I crawled into bed, my mind was still racing with phrases and figures, hopes and plans. Just before I fell asleep, my phone lit up with a text.

Tyler: So a Farm Security Director just texted me about helping with Scarecrow Double-Agent training and I've also been assigned to invent recycling darts for chicken. Do I report to you or the four-year-old chaos creator??

Me: If you accept the mission, you're Miggy's to command, just an FYI. I'm doing the boring admin work.

Tyler: I bet you manage to make paperwork an adventure.

Me: You're ridiculous

Tyler: You like ridiculous. Admit it.

I hesitated, then typed.

Me: I tolerate ridiculous. In small doses, though my tolerance is increasing. Slowly...

Tyler: That's almost a love sonnet coming from you. I volunteer as tribute, ready to bring ridiculousness where you are 24/7.

My heart did that soaring, flip, flutter thing—the flight path of tipsy barn swallow. I groaned, shoving my face into my pillow. What was wrong with me? It was just Tyler being Tyler—teasing, joking, he didn't mean half of what he said.

Except, more and more, I heard the unspoken thoughts behind everything. It felt like understanding Tyler more had given me super decoder power. And his nothings were actually something and the more he trusted the clearer it all became.

I fell asleep with my phone still clutched in my hand, dreaming of grant approvals and chicken jetpacks and a boy who somehow kept showing up in places I wasn't looking for him.

The following Sunday afternoon, the sun stretched across the pasture, warm but edged with fall's quiet chill. I knelt by a flagged marker at the edge of the north field, balancing a clipboard on one knee and tapping a soil penetrometer into the ground with both hands.

"Soil compaction, last set of readings," I muttered, recording the resistance depth and angle. "Plot B, 14 inches—a touch better than last month."

This part—the measuring, the documentation, the quiet process of watching small changes add up to something meaningful—this was the part I loved most.

"Meela!"

Miggy's voice carried across the yard. I looked up to see him running toward me at full tilt, his hair wild, wearing cowboy boots and a superhero cape over his sweatshirt.

Behind him Sofía managed to trot, short legs pumping, her bucket hat sliding and I could see one boot on the wrong foot.

"Meelaaaaaaa!" she echoed. I stood and waited as they barreled into the pasture. Miggy skidded to a stop at the flagged boundary.

"Papí said you needed helpers," he announced.

"Oh, he did, did he?" I smiled. Dad must've needed a few moments to concentrate.

"Yup," he said, solemn. "I brought my measuring stick." He held up an old paint stirrer with superhero stickers on it.

"Gotsa rocks," Sofía added, opening her palm to reveal a handful of pebbles and one single dandelion. "You check wid."

"Very official," I said, crouching to examine her collection. "The dandelion is scientific."

"No, pwetty," Sofía corrected.

Miggy dropped to the ground beside me, peering at my soil probe. "What's that one tell you?"

"It tells me how hard the dirt is," I explained. "If the roots can grow deep, or if the ground's too tight."

He nodded, clearly impressed. "I can do that. Watch."

He jabbed his yardstick into the soil, where it promptly bent sideways. "Hm. This one says... medium hard. But good for carrots."

I laughed. "Excellent analysis, Farm Scientist Miggy."

"Wait till you see my 'filtration test,'" he said, pronouncing it carefully. "I pour water in the hole and see if it goes whoosh."

"That's real science," I admitted.

We worked our way across the row markers, me taking readings, Miggy performing his own parallel experiments with dramatic sound effects, and Sofía contributing by handing me small stones and narrating the color of each one.

"Dis one is boo," she whispered, holding up a pale gray pebble. "I gots a boo coat."

"Facts, Fía-mia."

We reached the last plot, I recorded my final reading and clicked my pen.

"Okay. That's it. Measurements done."

"Yay!" Sofía clapped and immediately sat down in the grass. Miggy flopped beside her, stretching his arms wide.

"We saved all the farms of the world!"

"You definitely made things better," I said, sitting beside them. "These readings will help show how our land is healing. We'll compare them again next season and see what's changed."

Miggy looked thoughtful. "Like how when you get a owie, and it gets better slow? And if you don't pick the scab it heals better?"

"Exactly."

He frowned. "I don't like slow."

I smiled, brushing a curl from his forehead. "Slow can mean growing strong. Bit by bit, but something really strong when it's done."

He didn't say anything for a moment, then nodded like that settled it. A breeze picked up, sending the little dandelion in Sofía's hand fluttering loose. She watched it float, then whispered, "Bye, bye. Goes home."

I didn't correct her. Maybe it was going home.

In the kitchen, I transferred the soil data into the spreadsheet, careful to label each plot and date. Dad hovered nearby, reviewing my notes as I typed.

"Numbers look solid," he said. "You've got a good baseline here."

"I want to make a chart," I said, already reaching for my notebook. "Something visual to include with the proposal."

"Smart," he said. "Makes the story easier to see."

I glanced at the table where Miggy and Sofía were now coloring quietly—Miggy drawing a row of tiny tractors, Sofía making neon yellow swirls that looked like hair balls but were probably dandelions.

"I've enjoyed doing this with you Meela-Mi," my dad said as he squeezed my shoulders then dropped a kiss to the top of my head. "Paperwork's a lot more interesting with your input."

"And tractor with corn thieve deterrent claws and planting boo flowers."

He didn't reply immediately. I heard a smile in his answer, "Yep, that too. Love you kiddo, I'm thrilled to see you growing your roots here."

I nodded, too full to answer. Out the window, the sun dipped lower, brushing an icy gold across the fields. The grant paperwork was almost complete. A strong application, not perfect but strong with ideas bound together, a cord strong enough to pull us into the future.

Emilia

Dinner had been cleared away, the house settling into its evening hum. Mamá was putting Sofía down for the night, and Miguel was in the living room. He'd sprawled out with a book or had his drawing supplies helping him draw chicken ninjas and cow baseball players.

Dad and I stayed at the kitchen table, the laptop open between us, the soft glow of the screen washing over a thick binder labeled Farm Planning & Projects. Colored tabs bristled like the spine of some kind of Pókeman lizard monster.

Miguel wandered in, rubbing his eyes, clearly fighting sleep. He stopped just inside the doorway, scoping out the scene with the important air of a four-year-old boy.

"Hola, Meela," he said, then turned to my dad with equal solemnity. "Hola, Papí."

"Hola, Miggy-man," Dad replied, distracted as he scrolled.

Miguel glanced at the laptop, unimpressed. "Still doing the granted farm homework?"

Dad smile. "That's right, bossman. We're working on the grant project."

Miguel nodded, his expression telling us to carry on. "Okay." He padded back toward the living room his inspection complete.

I huffed with amusement and shook my head, "That felt like an FDA inspection. He's got a checklist somewhere he's filling out on us."

"Gotta keep the granted workforce accountable," Dad said.

I turned back to the grant portal. "Okay—this is the Fields of Dandelions initiative, a response to the flooding of the Little Missouri River and the regional wildfires. Targeted towards ranches and farms for the initiation of expansion of regenerative practices. What we're trying to expand."

Dad rubbed his chin. "Sounds like a great fit. We'll need to demonstrate the strength of our expansion plans and the success of past and current efforts. They'll want specifics—how many acres we'll transition, projected improvements in soil health and water retention, and how we'll measure success over time."

I scrolled. "It says preference goes to farms with existing conservation practices. We're already doing rotational grazing and native grass reseeding, with some native pollinator habitat, so that helps."

I skimmed a rubric. "Impact—40 points. Feasibility—30. Budget—20. Community benefit—10."

Dad nodded. "So we write to the points first, then fill in where we feel it needs strengthening."

I pulled up checklist: Eligibility—check. We'd need a Narrative of 1,000 words. Budget template. Two letters of support. All doable.

Dad gave me a look that crinkled at the corners. "When you were spitting up and colicky, keeping us awake all night I didn't foresee grant writing together in our future. Of course, your mom and I were both so sleep deprived we didn't know what day it was."

I rolled my eyes, smiling. "Here I am making up for those days and nights of lost sleep. You should've started reading me NDSU's ag extension newsletter, might've been the solution."

"Mom and I have realized it's impossible to make predictions about kids. Miggy was the calmest baby of the three of you."

"Point taken."

He leaned back, stretching, "This is good experience for you, Meela-Mi. These grants—this kind of planning—keep the farm running long-term. You learning this now means you can take the lead on projects like this in the future. I can only imagine the need for regenerative practices outpacing the work done on farms like ours."

A warm sense of purpose settled in my chest. "That's what I want to work on learning. Not only ways to increase production, but how to balance a good livelihood with improving systems."

Dad hummed, tapping the table. Then, almost absently, he murmured, "Tøffing."

I looked up. "What?"

"Tøffing," he said again, "'Tough girl,' the word my mom used for my sister when she held her own against the boys."

The word landed warm and solid.

"It shouldn't be a fight, to do what's right for the land, but it can be. You'll need that toughness in the future. Alright, let's get started, see what we can crank out tonight. Make good headway on the granted business."

I opened a doc and named it Dandelions_Grant_v1 and typed the first header: Project Summary (150 words).

By Sunday morning we'd completely commandeered the dining room table as our command center—printed articles, sticky notes, my laptop—surrounded by normal Preston chaos. Dad leaned over my shoulder, pointing to a paragraph about soil regeneration while Mamá flipped pancakes shaped like farm animals.

"See this part about carbon sequestration? That's exactly what we've been doing with the north pasture rotation," Dad said, voice edged with rare excitement.

I highlighted. "And here—heritage practices meeting modern solutions. We do that but maybe we look to expand?"

Pages for our application piled up digitally and physically: water lines, seed invoices. I traced paddock rotations on the map—blue for current, green for expansion.

The Fields of Dandelions application had consumed my weekend and I suppose a lot of kids would think I'm a farm nerd, but opinions didn't mean much to me. Feeling connected to a farm and planning for the future grew your roots.

I opened a fresh doc and laid out a three-week timeline

Map update — Dad (Fri)

Soil infiltration tests — Me (Sat)

Draft narrative — Me (Sun)

Budget template — Dad (Mon)

Letters of support — Ag Ext Office & FFA (request today)

For the budget bones we listed fence repairs, corner H-braces, a solar pump for the back trough, and seed for native warm-season grasses—the big number.

For measurement, Dad said, "Start with baselines."

So, infiltration test, before/after photo points, grazing days per paddock, and a simple May bird count. I sent an email to Ms. Reed at Extension about a letter of support. Mamá drafted a paragraph on cultural stewardship and community agriculture that we'd incorporate. The family farm, it's future and the resources to do so were spinning in my mind.

"MEELA!" Miggy's voice shattered my concentration as he barreled into the kitchen, brandishing a crayon drawing. "I made PLANS for the granted stuff!"

Sofía toddled in behind him, wearing rain boots despite the sunshine. "I hep too!"

Dad's mouth twitched into a smile. The Preston Farm—where even grant research came with its own brand of chaos.

"Let me see your plans, Miggy-man," Dad said, taking the crumpled paper with exaggerated seriousness. Over his shoulder I tried not to laugh. Chickens... with jetpacks? And a tractor with a giant claw?

"This is our security system," Miggy explained, tapping the jetpack chickens. "They guard the tomatoes. And this"—jab at the claw-tractor—"is for catching bad guys who try to steal our corn."

Dad nodded thoughtfully. "Very innovative farm security."

"What about you, Sofía? What's your plan?" I asked.

Sofía studied her boots, then looked up. "Pwant boo flowers." A decisive nod.

"Blue flowers are very important," I agreed solemnly.

Mamá slid a plate of pancakes onto the table. "Researchers need fuel." She winked. "Miggy, Sofía, come wash your syrupy fingers."

As they scampered off, Dad leaned closer to the screen. "You're onto something with the traditional-methods section. There's so much of traditional practice that could be revived or redefined for today."

I scrolled to Community & Culture. "What if we expand this to include not only production but keeping traditional practices alive—keeping culture alive. Ideas from all the cultures of people who lived or live in the area."

Dad's eyes lit. "Rather than taking it all on ourselves we could look for area partnerships. Really, that's the heart of it, regenerative agriculture has to be a joint project. Farming isn't just science—it's relationship. That's what we show the committee."

"I have some ideas, let me get those done and then you take a look at it."

"Perfect." He squeezed my shoulder. "This is going to be good, Meela-Mi."

"Meela!" Miggy called from the kitchen. "Can the chicken jetpacks shoot lasers or just regular bullets?"

Dad and I locked eyes. "Foam darts," I called back, "from recycled materials."

"RECYLCING DARTS!" Miggy shrieked, delighted.

Dad shook his head, laughing. "We may need to incorporate Miggy's security system. Really wow the committee."

I grinned, but my mind was already formatting Community Impact.

By mid-afternoon, my eyes were burning from screen time, and my back ached from hunching over the laptop. But we had a solid draft—something that actually felt like it could win.

"We should take a break," Dad said, stretching. "Clear our heads before the final review."

I nodded, saving the document for the third time just to be sure. "I think I'll go outside. I need air."

Outside, the autumn sun hung low in the sky, casting long shadows across the pasture. I breathed in deeply, filling my lungs with the smell of earth and hay and the faint sweetness of apples from the orchard. The screens and numbers fell away, replaced by the simple reality of this place.

After a loop around the house, I spotted Miggy in the garden, engaged in what appeared to be a serious conversation with the scarecrow. Sofía was nearby, carefully arranging rocks in the dirt.

"What are you two plotting?" I called.

Miggy looked up. "We're having a farm meeting. The scarecrow says we need more crows, not less."

"Really?" I tried to keep a straight face.

"Yeah, cause crows are smart and they can be farm spies." He lowered his voice to a dramatic whisper. "The scarecrow is a double agent."

Sofía nodded, adding another rock to her collection. "Dobuh hay-gent."

"Okay, you two keep up your top-secret farm work here, I'm heading back in."

I smiled all the way back to the house, wondering if I should add a line in the grant about the value of imagination in agricultural education. Or perhaps not—I wasn't sure the Fields of Dandelions committee was ready for Miggy's particular brand of farm innovation.

The rest of the evening passed in a blur of final edits, dinner, and one more look at the budget. By the time I crawled into bed, my mind was still racing with phrases and figures, hopes and plans. Just before I fell asleep, my phone lit up with a text.

Tyler: So a Farm Security Director just texted me about helping with Scarecrow Double-Agent training and I've also been assigned to invent recycling darts for chicken. Do I report to you or the four-year-old chaos creator??

Me: If you accept the mission, you're Miggy's to command, just an FYI. I'm doing the boring admin work.

Tyler: I bet you manage to make paperwork an adventure.

Me: You're ridiculous

Tyler: You like ridiculous. Admit it.

I hesitated, then typed.

Me: I tolerate ridiculous. In small doses, though my tolerance is increasing. Slowly…

Tyler: That's almost a love sonnet coming from you. I volunteer as tribute, ready to bring ridiculousness where you are 24/7.

My heart did that soaring, flip, flutter thing—the flight path of tipsy barn swallow. I groaned, shoving my face into my pillow. What was wrong with me? It was just Tyler being Tyler—teasing, joking, he didn't mean half of what he said.

Except, more and more, I heard the unspoken thoughts behind everything. It felt like understanding Tyler more had given me super decoder power. And his nothings were actually something and the more he trusted the clearer it all became.

I fell asleep with my phone still clutched in my hand, dreaming of grant approvals and chicken jetpacks and a boy who somehow kept showing up in places I wasn't looking for him.

The following Sunday afternoon, the sun stretched across the pasture, warm but edged with fall's quiet chill. I knelt by a flagged marker at the edge of the north field, balancing a clipboard on one knee and tapping a soil penetrometer into the ground with both hands.

"Soil compaction, last set of readings," I muttered, recording the resistance depth and angle. "Plot B, 14 inches—a touch better than last month."

This part—the measuring, the documentation, the quiet process of watching small changes add up to something meaningful—this was the part I loved most.

"Meela!"

Miggy's voice carried across the yard. I looked up to see him running toward me at full tilt, his hair wild, wearing cowboy boots and a superhero cape over his sweatshirt.

Behind him Sofía managed to trot, short legs pumping, her bucket hat sliding and I could see one boot on the wrong foot.

"Meelaaaaaaa!" she echoed. I stood and waited as they barreled into the pasture. Miggy skidded to a stop at the flagged boundary.

"Papí said you needed helpers," he announced.

"Oh, he did, did he?" I smiled. Dad must've needed a few moments to concentrate.

"Yup," he said, solemn. "I brought my measuring stick." He held up an old paint stirrer with superhero stickers on it.

"Gotsa rocks," Sofía added, opening her palm to reveal a handful of pebbles and one single dandelion. "You check wid."

"Very official," I said, crouching to examine her collection. "The dandelion is scientific."

"No, pwetty," Sofía corrected.

Miggy dropped to the ground beside me, peering at my soil probe. "What's that one tell you?"

"It tells me how hard the dirt is," I explained. "If the roots can grow deep, or if the ground's too tight."

He nodded, clearly impressed. "I can do that. Watch."

He jabbed his yardstick into the soil, where it promptly bent sideways. "Hm. This one says... medium hard. But good for carrots."

I laughed. "Excellent analysis, Farm Scientist Miggy."

"Wait till you see my 'filtration test,'" he said, pronouncing it carefully. "I pour water in the hole and see if it goes whoosh."

"That's real science," I admitted.

We worked our way across the row markers, me taking readings, Miggy performing his own parallel experiments with dramatic sound effects, and Sofía contributing by handing me small stones and narrating the color of each one.

"Dis one is boo," she whispered, holding up a pale gray pebble. "I gots a boo coat."

"Facts, Fía-mia."

We reached the last plot, I recorded my final reading and clicked my pen.

"Okay. That's it. Measurements done."

"Yay!" Sofía clapped and immediately sat down in the grass. Miggy flopped beside her, stretching his arms wide.

"We saved all the farms of the world!"

"You definitely made things better," I said, sitting beside them. "These readings will help show how our land is healing. We'll compare them again next season and see what's changed."

Miggy looked thoughtful. "Like how when you get a owie, and it gets better slow? And if you don't pick the scab it heals better?"

"Exactly."

He frowned. "I don't like slow."

I smiled, brushing a curl from his forehead. "Slow can mean growing strong. Bit by bit, but something really strong when it's done."

He didn't say anything for a moment, then nodded like that settled it. A breeze picked up, sending the little dandelion in Sofía's hand fluttering loose. She watched it float, then whispered, "Bye, bye. Goes home."

I didn't correct her. Maybe it was going home.

In the kitchen, I transferred the soil data into the spreadsheet, careful to label each plot and date. Dad hovered nearby, reviewing my notes as I typed.

"Numbers look solid," he said. "You've got a good baseline here."

"I want to make a chart," I said, already reaching for my notebook. "Something visual to include with the proposal."

"Smart," he said. "Makes the story easier to see."

I glanced at the table where Miggy and Sofía were now coloring quietly—Miggy drawing a row of tiny tractors, Sofía making neon yellow swirls that looked like hair balls but were probably dandelions.

"I've enjoyed doing this with you Meela-Mi," my dad said as he squeezed my shoulders then dropped a kiss to the top of my head. "Paperwork's a lot more interesting with your input."

"And tractor with corn thieve deterrent claws and planting boo flowers."

He didn't reply immediately. I heard a smile in his answer, "Yep, that too. Love you kiddo, I'm thrilled to see you growing your roots here."

I nodded, too full to answer. Out the window, the sun dipped lower, brushing an icy gold across the fields. The grant paperwork was almost complete. A strong application, not perfect but strong with ideas bound together, a cord strong enough to pull us into the future.

Emilia

Dinner had been cleared away, the house settling into its evening hum. Mamá was putting Sofía down for the night, and Miguel was in the living room. He'd sprawled out with a book or had his drawing supplies helping him draw chicken ninjas and cow baseball players.

Dad and I stayed at the kitchen table, the laptop open between us, the soft glow of the screen washing over a thick binder labeled Farm Planning & Projects. Colored tabs bristled like the spine of some kind of Pókeman lizard monster.

Miguel wandered in, rubbing his eyes, clearly fighting sleep. He stopped just inside the doorway, scoping out the scene with the important air of a four-year-old boy.

"Hola, Meela," he said, then turned to my dad with equal solemnity. "Hola, Papí."

"Hola, Miggy-man," Dad replied, distracted as he scrolled.

Miguel glanced at the laptop, unimpressed. "Still doing the granted farm homework?"

Dad smile. "That's right, bossman. We're working on the grant project."

Miguel nodded, his expression telling us to carry on. "Okay." He padded back toward the living room his inspection complete.

I huffed with amusement and shook my head, "That felt like an FDA inspection. He's got a checklist somewhere he's filling out on us."

"Gotta keep the granted workforce accountable," Dad said.

I turned back to the grant portal. "Okay—this is the Fields of Dandelions initiative, a response to the flooding of the Little Missouri River and the regional wildfires. Targeted towards ranches and farms for the initiation of expansion of regenerative practices. What we're trying to expand."

Dad rubbed his chin. "Sounds like a great fit. We'll need to demonstrate the strength of our expansion plans and the success of past and current efforts. They'll want specifics—how many acres we'll transition, projected improvements in soil health and water retention, and how we'll measure success over time."

I scrolled. "It says preference goes to farms with existing conservation practices. We're already doing rotational grazing and native grass reseeding, with some native pollinator habitat, so that helps."

I skimmed a rubric. "Impact—40 points. Feasibility—30. Budget—20. Community benefit—10."

Dad nodded. "So we write to the points first, then fill in where we feel it needs strengthening."

I pulled up checklist: Eligibility—check. We'd need a Narrative of 1,000 words. Budget template. Two letters of support. All doable.

Dad gave me a look that crinkled at the corners. "When you were spitting up and colicky, keeping us awake all night I didn't foresee grant writing together in our future. Of course, your mom and I were both so sleep deprived we didn't know what day it was."

I rolled my eyes, smiling. "Here I am making up for those days and nights of lost sleep. You should've started reading me NDSU's ag extension newsletter, might've been the solution."

"Mom and I have realized it's impossible to make predictions about kids. Miggy was the calmest baby of the three of you."

"Point taken."

He leaned back, stretching, "This is good experience for you, Meela-Mi. These grants—this kind of planning—keep the farm running long-term. You learning this now means you can take the lead on projects like this in the future. I can only imagine the need for regenerative practices outpacing the work done on farms like ours."

A warm sense of purpose settled in my chest. "That's what I want to work on learning. Not only ways to increase production, but how to balance a good livelihood with improving systems."

Dad hummed, tapping the table. Then, almost absently, he murmured, "Tøffing."

I looked up. "What?"

"Tøffing," he said again, "'Tough girl,' the word my mom used for my sister when she held her own against the boys."

The word landed warm and solid.

"It shouldn't be a fight, to do what's right for the land, but it can be. You'll need that toughness in the future. Alright, let's get started, see what we can crank out tonight. Make good headway on the granted business."

I opened a doc and named it Dandelions_Grant_v1 and typed the first header: Project Summary (150 words).

By Sunday morning we'd completely commandeered the dining room table as our command center—printed articles, sticky notes, my laptop—surrounded by normal Preston chaos. Dad leaned over my shoulder, pointing to a paragraph about soil regeneration while Mamá flipped pancakes shaped like farm animals.

"See this part about carbon sequestration? That's exactly what we've been doing with the north pasture rotation," Dad said, voice edged with rare excitement.

I highlighted. "And here—heritage practices meeting modern solutions. We do that but maybe we look to expand?"

Pages for our application piled up digitally and physically: water lines, seed invoices. I traced paddock rotations on the map—blue for current, green for expansion.

The Fields of Dandelions application had consumed my weekend and I suppose a lot of kids would think I'm a farm nerd, but opinions didn't mean much to me. Feeling connected to a farm and planning for the future grew your roots.

I opened a fresh doc and laid out a three-week timeline

Map update — Dad (Fri)

Soil infiltration tests — Me (Sat)

Draft narrative — Me (Sun)

Budget template — Dad (Mon)

Letters of support — Ag Ext Office & FFA (request today)

For the budget bones we listed fence repairs, corner H-braces, a solar pump for the back trough, and seed for native warm-season grasses—the big number.

For measurement, Dad said, "Start with baselines."

So, infiltration test, before/after photo points, grazing days per paddock, and a simple May bird count. I sent an email to Ms. Reed at Extension about a letter of support. Mamá drafted a paragraph on cultural stewardship and community agriculture that we'd incorporate. The family farm, it's future and the resources to do so were spinning in my mind.

"MEELA!" Miggy's voice shattered my concentration as he barreled into the kitchen, brandishing a crayon drawing. "I made PLANS for the granted stuff!"

Sofía toddled in behind him, wearing rain boots despite the sunshine. "I hep too!"

Dad's mouth twitched into a smile. The Preston Farm—where even grant research came with its own brand of chaos.

"Let me see your plans, Miggy-man," Dad said, taking the crumpled paper with exaggerated seriousness. Over his shoulder

I tried not to laugh. Chickens... with jetpacks? And a tractor with a giant claw?

"This is our security system," Miggy explained, tapping the jetpack chickens. "They guard the tomatoes. And this"—jab at the claw-tractor—"is for catching bad guys who try to steal our corn."

Dad nodded thoughtfully. "Very innovative farm security."

"What about you, Sofía? What's your plan?" I asked.

Sofía studied her boots, then looked up. "Pwant boo flowers." A decisive nod.

"Blue flowers are very important," I agreed solemnly.

Mamá slid a plate of pancakes onto the table. "Researchers need fuel." She winked. "Miggy, Sofía, come wash your syrupy fingers."

As they scampered off, Dad leaned closer to the screen. "You're onto something with the traditional-methods section. There's so much of traditional practice that could be revived or redefined for today."

I scrolled to Community & Culture. "What if we expand this to include not only production but keeping traditional practices alive—keeping culture alive. Ideas from all the cultures of people who lived or live in the area."

Dad's eyes lit. "Rather than taking it all on ourselves we could look for area partnerships. Really, that's the heart of it, regenerative agriculture has to be a joint project. Farming isn't just science—it's relationship. That's what we show the committee."

"I have some ideas, let me get those done and then you take a look at it."

"Perfect." He squeezed my shoulder. "This is going to be good, Meela-Mi."

"Meela!" Miggy called from the kitchen. "Can the chicken jetpacks shoot lasers or just regular bullets?"

Dad and I locked eyes. "Foam darts," I called back, "from recycled materials."

"RECYLCING DARTS!" Miggy shrieked, delighted.

Dad shook his head, laughing. "We may need to incorporate Miggy's security system. Really wow the committee."

I grinned, but my mind was already formatting Community Impact.

By mid-afternoon, my eyes were burning from screen time, and my back ached from hunching over the laptop. But we had a solid draft—something that actually felt like it could win.

"We should take a break," Dad said, stretching. "Clear our heads before the final review."

I nodded, saving the document for the third time just to be sure. "I think I'll go outside. I need air."

Outside, the autumn sun hung low in the sky, casting long shadows across the pasture. I breathed in deeply, filling my lungs with the smell of earth and hay and the faint sweetness of apples from the orchard. The screens and numbers fell away, replaced by the simple reality of this place.

After a loop around the house, I spotted Miggy in the garden, engaged in what appeared to be a serious conversation with the scarecrow. Sofía was nearby, carefully arranging rocks in the dirt.

"What are you two plotting?" I called.

Miggy looked up. "We're having a farm meeting. The scarecrow says we need more crows, not less."

"Really?" I tried to keep a straight face.

"Yeah, cause crows are smart and they can be farm spies." He lowered his voice to a dramatic whisper. "The scarecrow is a double agent."

Sofía nodded, adding another rock to her collection. "Dobuh hay-gent."

"Okay, you two keep up your top-secret farm work here, I'm heading back in."

I smiled all the way back to the house, wondering if I should add a line in the grant about the value of imagination in agricultural education. Or perhaps not—I wasn't sure the Fields of Dandelions committee was ready for Miggy's particular brand of farm innovation.

The rest of the evening passed in a blur of final edits, dinner, and one more look at the budget. By the time I crawled into bed, my mind was still racing with phrases and figures, hopes and plans. Just before I fell asleep, my phone lit up with a text.

Tyler: So a Farm Security Director just texted me about helping with Scarecrow Double-Agent training and I've also been assigned to invent recycling darts for chicken. Do I report to you or the four-year-old chaos creator??

Me: If you accept the mission, you're Miggy's to command, just an FYI. I'm doing the boring admin work.

Tyler: I bet you manage to make paperwork an adventure.

Me: You're ridiculous

Tyler: You like ridiculous. Admit it.

I hesitated, then typed.

Me: I tolerate ridiculous. In small doses, though my tolerance is increasing. Slowly…

Tyler: That's almost a love sonnet coming from you. I volunteer as tribute, ready to bring ridiculousness where you are 24/7.

My heart did that soaring, flip, flutter thing—the flight path of tipsy barn swallow. I groaned, shoving my face into my pillow.

What was wrong with me? It was just Tyler being Tyler—teasing, joking, he didn't mean half of what he said.

Except, more and more, I heard the unspoken thoughts behind everything. It felt like understanding Tyler more had given me super decoder power. And his nothings were actually something and the more he trusted the clearer it all became.

I fell asleep with my phone still clutched in my hand, dreaming of grant approvals and chicken jetpacks and a boy who somehow kept showing up in places I wasn't looking for him.

The following Sunday afternoon, the sun stretched across the pasture, warm but edged with fall's quiet chill. I knelt by a flagged marker at the edge of the north field, balancing a clipboard on one knee and tapping a soil penetrometer into the ground with both hands.

"Soil compaction, last set of readings," I muttered, recording the resistance depth and angle. "Plot B, 14 inches—a touch better than last month."

This part—the measuring, the documentation, the quiet process of watching small changes add up to something meaningful—this was the part I loved most.

"Meela!"

Miggy's voice carried across the yard. I looked up to see him running toward me at full tilt, his hair wild, wearing cowboy boots and a superhero cape over his sweatshirt.

Behind him Sofía managed to trot, short legs pumping, her bucket hat sliding and I could see one boot on the wrong foot.

"Meelaaaaaaa!" she echoed. I stood and waited as they barreled into the pasture. Miggy skidded to a stop at the flagged boundary.

"Papí said you needed helpers," he announced.

"Oh, he did, did he?" I smiled. Dad must've needed a few moments to concentrate.

"Yup," he said, solemn. "I brought my measuring stick." He held up an old paint stirrer with superhero stickers on it.

"Gotsa rocks," Sofía added, opening her palm to reveal a handful of pebbles and one single dandelion. "You check wid."

"Very official," I said, crouching to examine her collection. "The dandelion is scientific."

"No, pwetty," Sofía corrected.

Miggy dropped to the ground beside me, peering at my soil probe. "What's that one tell you?"

"It tells me how hard the dirt is," I explained. "If the roots can grow deep, or if the ground's too tight."

He nodded, clearly impressed. "I can do that. Watch."

He jabbed his yardstick into the soil, where it promptly bent sideways. "Hm. This one says... medium hard. But good for carrots."

I laughed. "Excellent analysis, Farm Scientist Miggy."

"Wait till you see my 'filtration test,'" he said, pronouncing it carefully. "I pour water in the hole and see if it goes whoosh."

"That's real science," I admitted.

We worked our way across the row markers, me taking readings, Miggy performing his own parallel experiments with dramatic sound effects, and Sofía contributing by handing me small stones and narrating the color of each one.

"Dis one is boo," she whispered, holding up a pale gray pebble. "I gots a boo coat."

"Facts, Fía-mia."

We reached the last plot, I recorded my final reading and clicked my pen.

"Okay. That's it. Measurements done."

"Yay!" Sofía clapped and immediately sat down in the grass. Miggy flopped beside her, stretching his arms wide.

"We saved all the farms of the world!"

"You definitely made things better," I said, sitting beside them. "These readings will help show how our land is healing. We'll compare them again next season and see what's changed."

Miggy looked thoughtful. "Like how when you get a owie, and it gets better slow? And if you don't pick the scab it heals better?"

"Exactly."

He frowned. "I don't like slow."

I smiled, brushing a curl from his forehead. "Slow can mean growing strong. Bit by bit, but something really strong when it's done."

He didn't say anything for a moment, then nodded like that settled it. A breeze picked up, sending the little dandelion in Sofía's hand fluttering loose. She watched it float, then whispered, "Bye, bye. Goes home."

I didn't correct her. Maybe it was going home.

In the kitchen, I transferred the soil data into the spreadsheet, careful to label each plot and date. Dad hovered nearby, reviewing my notes as I typed.

"Numbers look solid," he said. "You've got a good baseline here."

"I want to make a chart," I said, already reaching for my notebook. "Something visual to include with the proposal."

"Smart," he said. "Makes the story easier to see."

I glanced at the table where Miggy and Sofía were now coloring quietly—Miggy drawing a row of tiny tractors, Sofía making neon yellow swirls that looked like hair balls but were probably dandelions.

"I've enjoyed doing this with you Meela-Mi," my dad said as he squeezed my shoulders then dropped a kiss to the top of my head. "Paperwork's a lot more interesting with your input."

"And tractor with corn thieve deterrent claws and planting boo flowers."

He didn't reply immediately. I heard a smile in his answer, "Yep, that too. Love you kiddo, I'm thrilled to see you growing your roots here."

I nodded, too full to answer. Out the window, the sun dipped lower, brushing an icy gold across the fields. The grant paperwork was almost complete. A strong application, not perfect but strong with ideas bound together, a cord strong enough to pull us into the future.

Emilia

Dinner had been cleared away, the house settling into its evening hum. Mamá was putting Sofía down for the night, and Miguel was in the living room. He'd sprawled out with a book or had his drawing supplies helping him draw chicken ninjas and cow baseball players.

Dad and I stayed at the kitchen table, the laptop open between us, the soft glow of the screen washing over a thick binder labeled Farm Planning & Projects. Colored tabs bristled like the spine of some kind of Pókeman lizard monster.

Miguel wandered in, rubbing his eyes, clearly fighting sleep. He stopped just inside the doorway, scoping out the scene with the important air of a four-year-old boy.

"Hola, Meela," he said, then turned to my dad with equal solemnity. "Hola, Papí."

"Hola, Miggy-man," Dad replied, distracted as he scrolled.

Miguel glanced at the laptop, unimpressed. "Still doing the granted farm homework?"

Dad smile. "That's right, bossman. We're working on the grant project."

Miguel nodded, his expression telling us to carry on. "Okay." He padded back toward the living room his inspection complete.

I huffed with amusement and shook my head, "That felt like an FDA inspection. He's got a checklist somewhere he's filling out on us."

"Gotta keep the granted workforce accountable," Dad said.

I turned back to the grant portal. "Okay—this is the Fields of Dandelions initiative, a response to the flooding of the Little Missouri River and the regional wildfires. Targeted towards ranches and farms for the initiation of expansion of regenerative practices. What we're trying to expand."

Dad rubbed his chin. "Sounds like a great fit. We'll need to demonstrate the strength of our expansion plans and the success of past and current efforts. They'll want specifics—how many acres we'll transition, projected improvements in soil health and water retention, and how we'll measure success over time."

I scrolled. "It says preference goes to farms with existing conservation practices. We're already doing rotational grazing and native grass reseeding, with some native pollinator habitat, so that helps."

I skimmed a rubric. "Impact—40 points. Feasibility—30. Budget—20. Community benefit—10."

Dad nodded. "So we write to the points first, then fill in where we feel it needs strengthening."

I pulled up checklist: Eligibility—check. We'd need a Narrative of 1,000 words. Budget template. Two letters of support. All doable.

Dad gave me a look that crinkled at the corners. "When you were spitting up and colicky, keeping us awake all night I didn't foresee grant writing together in our future. Of course, your mom and I were both so sleep deprived we didn't know what day it was."

I rolled my eyes, smiling. "Here I am making up for those days and nights of lost sleep. You should've started reading me NDSU's ag extension newsletter, might've been the solution."

"Mom and I have realized it's impossible to make predictions about kids. Miggy was the calmest baby of the three of you."

"Point taken."

He leaned back, stretching, "This is good experience for you, Meela-Mi. These grants—this kind of planning—keep the farm running long-term. You learning this now means you can take the lead on projects like this in the future. I can only imagine the need for regenerative practices outpacing the work done on farms like ours."

A warm sense of purpose settled in my chest. "That's what I want to work on learning. Not only ways to increase production, but how to balance a good livelihood with improving systems."

Dad hummed, tapping the table. Then, almost absently, he murmured, "Tøffing."

I looked up. "What?"

"Tøffing," he said again, "'Tough girl,' the word my mom used for my sister when she held her own against the boys."

The word landed warm and solid.

"It shouldn't be a fight, to do what's right for the land, but it can be. You'll need that toughness in the future. Alright, let's get started, see what we can crank out tonight. Make good headway on the granted business."

I opened a doc and named it Dandelions_Grant_v1 and typed the first header: Project Summary (150 words).

By Sunday morning we'd completely commandeered the dining room table as our command center—printed articles, sticky notes, my laptop—surrounded by normal Preston chaos. Dad leaned over my shoulder, pointing to a paragraph about soil regeneration while Mamá flipped pancakes shaped like farm animals.

"See this part about carbon sequestration? That's exactly what we've been doing with the north pasture rotation," Dad said, voice edged with rare excitement.

I highlighted. "And here—heritage practices meeting modern solutions. We do that but maybe we look to expand?"

Pages for our application piled up digitally and physically: water lines, seed invoices. I traced paddock rotations on the map—blue for current, green for expansion.

The Fields of Dandelions application had consumed my weekend and I suppose a lot of kids would think I'm a farm nerd, but opinions didn't mean much to me. Feeling connected to a farm and planning for the future grew your roots.

I opened a fresh doc and laid out a three-week timeline

Map update — Dad (Fri)

Soil infiltration tests — Me (Sat)

Draft narrative — Me (Sun)

Budget template — Dad (Mon)

Letters of support — Ag Ext Office & FFA (request today)

For the budget bones we listed fence repairs, corner H-braces, a solar pump for the back trough, and seed for native warm-season grasses—the big number.

For measurement, Dad said, "Start with baselines."

So, infiltration test, before/after photo points, grazing days per paddock, and a simple May bird count. I sent an email to Ms. Reed at Extension about a letter of support. Mamá drafted a paragraph on cultural stewardship and community agriculture that we'd incorporate. The family farm, it's future and the resources to do so were spinning in my mind.

"MEELA!" Miggy's voice shattered my concentration as he barreled into the kitchen, brandishing a crayon drawing. "I made PLANS for the granted stuff!"

Sofía toddled in behind him, wearing rain boots despite the sunshine. "I hep too!"

Dad's mouth twitched into a smile. The Preston Farm—where even grant research came with its own brand of chaos.

"Let me see your plans, Miggy-man," Dad said, taking the crumpled paper with exaggerated seriousness. Over his shoulder I tried not to laugh. Chickens... with jetpacks? And a tractor with a giant claw?

"This is our security system," Miggy explained, tapping the jetpack chickens. "They guard the tomatoes. And this"—jab at the claw-tractor—"is for catching bad guys who try to steal our corn."

Dad nodded thoughtfully. "Very innovative farm security."

"What about you, Sofía? What's your plan?" I asked.

Sofía studied her boots, then looked up. "Pwant boo flowers." A decisive nod.

"Blue flowers are very important," I agreed solemnly.

Mamá slid a plate of pancakes onto the table. "Researchers need fuel." She winked. "Miggy, Sofía, come wash your syrupy fingers."

As they scampered off, Dad leaned closer to the screen. "You're onto something with the traditional-methods section. There's so much of traditional practice that could be revived or redefined for today."

I scrolled to Community & Culture. "What if we expand this to include not only production but keeping traditional practices alive—keeping culture alive. Ideas from all the cultures of people who lived or live in the area."

Dad's eyes lit. "Rather than taking it all on ourselves we could look for area partnerships. Really, that's the heart of it, regenerative agriculture has to be a joint project. Farming isn't just science—it's relationship. That's what we show the committee."

"I have some ideas, let me get those done and then you take a look at it."

"Perfect." He squeezed my shoulder. "This is going to be good, Meela-Mi."

"Meela!" Miggy called from the kitchen. "Can the chicken jetpacks shoot lasers or just regular bullets?"

Dad and I locked eyes. "Foam darts," I called back, "from recycled materials."

"RECYLCING DARTS!" Miggy shrieked, delighted.

Dad shook his head, laughing. "We may need to incorporate Miggy's security system. Really wow the committee."

I grinned, but my mind was already formatting Community Impact.

By mid-afternoon, my eyes were burning from screen time, and my back ached from hunching over the laptop. But we had a solid draft—something that actually felt like it could win.

"We should take a break," Dad said, stretching. "Clear our heads before the final review."

I nodded, saving the document for the third time just to be sure. "I think I'll go outside. I need air."

Outside, the autumn sun hung low in the sky, casting long shadows across the pasture. I breathed in deeply, filling my lungs with the smell of earth and hay and the faint sweetness of apples from the orchard. The screens and numbers fell away, replaced by the simple reality of this place.

After a loop around the house, I spotted Miggy in the garden, engaged in what appeared to be a serious conversation with the scarecrow. Sofía was nearby, carefully arranging rocks in the dirt.

"What are you two plotting?" I called.

Miggy looked up. "We're having a farm meeting. The scarecrow says we need more crows, not less."

"Really?" I tried to keep a straight face.

"Yeah, cause crows are smart and they can be farm spies." He lowered his voice to a dramatic whisper. "The scarecrow is a double agent."

Sofía nodded, adding another rock to her collection. "Dobuh hay-gent."

"Okay, you two keep up your top-secret farm work here, I'm heading back in."

I smiled all the way back to the house, wondering if I should add a line in the grant about the value of imagination in agricultural education. Or perhaps not—I wasn't sure the Fields of Dandelions committee was ready for Miggy's particular brand of farm innovation.

The rest of the evening passed in a blur of final edits, dinner, and one more look at the budget. By the time I crawled into bed, my mind was still racing with phrases and figures, hopes and plans. Just before I fell asleep, my phone lit up with a text.

Tyler: So a Farm Security Director just texted me about helping with Scarecrow Double-Agent training and I've also been assigned to invent recycling darts for chicken. Do I report to you or the four-year-old chaos creator??

Me: If you accept the mission, you're Miggy's to command, just an FYI. I'm doing the boring admin work.

Tyler: I bet you manage to make paperwork an adventure.

Me: You're ridiculous

Tyler: You like ridiculous. Admit it.

I hesitated, then typed.

Me: I tolerate ridiculous. In small doses, though my tolerance is increasing. Slowly…

Tyler: That's almost a love sonnet coming from you. I volunteer as tribute, ready to bring ridiculousness where you are 24/7.

My heart did that soaring, flip, flutter thing—the flight path of tipsy barn swallow. I groaned, shoving my face into my pillow. What was wrong with me? It was just Tyler being Tyler—teasing, joking, he didn't mean half of what he said.

Except, more and more, I heard the unspoken thoughts behind everything. It felt like understanding Tyler more had given me super decoder power. And his nothings were actually something and the more he trusted the clearer it all became.

I fell asleep with my phone still clutched in my hand, dreaming of grant approvals and chicken jetpacks and a boy who somehow kept showing up in places I wasn't looking for him.

The following Sunday afternoon, the sun stretched across the pasture, warm but edged with fall's quiet chill. I knelt by a flagged marker at the edge of the north field, balancing a clipboard on one knee and tapping a soil penetrometer into the ground with both hands.

"Soil compaction, last set of readings," I muttered, recording the resistance depth and angle. "Plot B, 14 inches—a touch better than last month."

This part—the measuring, the documentation, the quiet process of watching small changes add up to something meaningful—this was the part I loved most.

"Meela!"

Miggy's voice carried across the yard. I looked up to see him running toward me at full tilt, his hair wild, wearing cowboy boots and a superhero cape over his sweatshirt.

Behind him Sofía managed to trot, short legs pumping, her bucket hat sliding and I could see one boot on the wrong foot.

"Meelaaaaaaa!" she echoed. I stood and waited as they barreled into the pasture. Miggy skidded to a stop at the flagged boundary.

"Papí said you needed helpers," he announced.

"Oh, he did, did he?" I smiled. Dad must've needed a few moments to concentrate.

"Yup," he said, solemn. "I brought my measuring stick." He held up an old paint stirrer with superhero stickers on it.

"Gotsa rocks," Sofía added, opening her palm to reveal a handful of pebbles and one single dandelion. "You check wid."

"Very official," I said, crouching to examine her collection. "The dandelion is scientific."

"No, pwetty," Sofía corrected.

Miggy dropped to the ground beside me, peering at my soil probe. "What's that one tell you?"

"It tells me how hard the dirt is," I explained. "If the roots can grow deep, or if the ground's too tight."

He nodded, clearly impressed. "I can do that. Watch."

He jabbed his yardstick into the soil, where it promptly bent sideways. "Hm. This one says... medium hard. But good for carrots."

I laughed. "Excellent analysis, Farm Scientist Miggy."

"Wait till you see my 'filtration test,'" he said, pronouncing it carefully. "I pour water in the hole and see if it goes whoosh."

"That's real science," I admitted.

We worked our way across the row markers, me taking readings, Miggy performing his own parallel experiments with dramatic sound effects, and Sofía contributing by handing me small stones and narrating the color of each one.

"Dis one is boo," she whispered, holding up a pale gray pebble. "I gots a boo coat."

"Facts, Fía-mia."

We reached the last plot, I recorded my final reading and clicked my pen.

"Okay. That's it. Measurements done."

"Yay!" Sofía clapped and immediately sat down in the grass. Miggy flopped beside her, stretching his arms wide.

"We saved all the farms of the world!"

"You definitely made things better," I said, sitting beside them. "These readings will help show how our land is healing. We'll compare them again next season and see what's changed."

Miggy looked thoughtful. "Like how when you get a owie, and it gets better slow? And if you don't pick the scab it heals better?"

"Exactly."

He frowned. "I don't like slow."

I smiled, brushing a curl from his forehead. "Slow can mean growing strong. Bit by bit, but something really strong when it's done."

He didn't say anything for a moment, then nodded like that settled it. A breeze picked up, sending the little dandelion in Sofía's hand fluttering loose. She watched it float, then whispered, "Bye, bye. Goes home."

I didn't correct her. Maybe it was going home.

In the kitchen, I transferred the soil data into the spreadsheet, careful to label each plot and date. Dad hovered nearby, reviewing my notes as I typed.

"Numbers look solid," he said. "You've got a good baseline here."

"I want to make a chart," I said, already reaching for my notebook. "Something visual to include with the proposal."

"Smart," he said. "Makes the story easier to see."

I glanced at the table where Miggy and Sofía were now coloring quietly—Miggy drawing a row of tiny tractors, Sofía making neon yellow swirls that looked like hair balls but were probably dandelions.

"I've enjoyed doing this with you Meela-Mi," my dad said as he squeezed my shoulders then dropped a kiss to the top of my head. "Paperwork's a lot more interesting with your input."

"And tractor with corn thieve deterrent claws and planting boo flowers."

He didn't reply immediately. I heard a smile in his answer, "Yep, that too. Love you kiddo, I'm thrilled to see you growing your roots here."

I nodded, too full to answer. Out the window, the sun dipped lower, brushing an icy gold across the fields. The grant paperwork was almost complete. A strong application, not perfect but strong with ideas bound together, a cord strong enough to pull us into the future.

46

It's About Who's Saying It

Emilia

I was gathering my books after yet another frustrating Current Issues class when Drew appeared beside my desk, thoughtful.

"Got a minute?" he asked quietly.

I nodded, tucking my notebook under my arm. Mr. Klein was already absorbed in conversation with another student, but Drew waited until we were in the hallway before speaking again.

"I noticed something today," he said, falling into step beside me. "Klein does this thing where he rephrases your answers."

"What do you mean?" I asked, though I had a feeling I knew what he meant.

"When you talked about how sustainable farming is a systems-level solution, he nodded, then restated it in his own words before moving on. When Trevor said basically the same thing about corporate sustainability initiatives, Klein said, 'excellent point' and wrote it on the board. Thing is, when he restates your answers, he changes the meaning."

I exhaled slowly.

"It's been happening all semester," Drew continued, voice low but intent. "It's not about the content of what you're saying. It's about who's saying it."

We reached my locker, and I spun the combination with more force than necessary. "The worst part is, I can't tell if he even realizes he's doing it."

"I doubt it's purposeful," Drew agreed. "Makes it harder to address."

I pulled open my locker, using the door as a momentary shield from the hallway. Drew leaned against the neighboring locker, arms crossed. His usual quiet had been replaced by something more determined.

"I have an idea," he said after a beat. "But it would require some coordination."

I closed my locker. "I'm listening."

"What if we trade ideas?" His eyes lit up as he explained. "For our next discussion, you tell me one of your points ahead of time. I'll raise my hand and say exactly what you would say—word for word. We see how Klein responds to the same content coming from me."

I stared at him, turning it over. "That's... actually kind of brilliant."

"If he responds positively to me saying your exact words, it proves the bias isn't about content," Drew said. "And if enough of us notice..."

"Then it's harder for him to dismiss," I finished.

Drew smiled—a rare, full grin that transformed his usually serious face. "Exactly."

"Do you think we could get others involved?" I asked, my mind already racing.

"Maybe. Not everyone at first. We'd need to document it, build a case."

For the first time in weeks, I felt a surge of hope. "Klein's planning a debate next Thursday on environmental policy. That would be perfect."

Drew nodded. "Let's plan over the weekend. Give a text when you have time."

As the warning bell rang for next period, I found myself smiling. "Thank you," I said, sincere. "For noticing. For caring."

He shrugged, but I could tell he was pleased. "It's not right, what's happening. Sometimes people just need to see the pattern made obvious. Watching your ideas get sidelined is infuriating."

With that, he disappeared into the stream of students.

47

Classroom Experiment

Emilia

My knee bounced nervously under my desk as Mr. Klein
wrote ENVIRONMENTAL POLICY DEBATE across the
whiteboard in his precise block letters. Drew sat two seats to
my right, looking calmer than I felt, though I noticed he kept
checking that the small voice recorder in his pocket was working.

We'd spent Sunday emailing back and forth, with Drew
texting me follow-up questions and checking phrasing until he
could deliver the points like they were his own. We'd landed on
three specific arguments about regenerative agriculture I would
normally make—complete with my tone and examples.

"Today's debate will focus on the most effective approaches to
environmental challenges," Mr. Klein announced, turning to face
the class. "I want to hear thoughtful, well-reasoned arguments.
Remember to maintain academic distance and consider multiple
perspectives."

I caught Drew's eye, and he gave me an almost imperceptible
nod. Step one of our plan: I would remain silent for the first half

of the debate, while Drew would use one of my prepared points early on.

"Let's begin with climate change mitigation strategies," Mr. Klein continued. "Who would like to open the discussion?"

Several hands shot up, including Drew's. To my surprise, Mr. Klein called on him immediately.

"Drew?"

Drew straightened in his chair, his voice steady as he delivered what was essentially my speech.

"I believe regenerative agriculture represents one of our most powerful system-level solutions," he began, using my exact phrasing. "Unlike approaches that treat symptoms, regenerative practices address root causes by transforming how we interact with soil, water, and ecosystems. The impact scales from individual farms to entire watersheds."

I held my breath, watching Mr. Klein's reaction.

He nodded approvingly. "An excellent point, Drew. You're looking at the interconnected nature of environmental systems rather than isolated solutions. That's precisely the kind of systems thinking we need to address complex problems."

My stomach tightened. It was the validation I'd never received, despite making essentially identical points in previous discussions.

Drew continued, "Indigenous communities have used these principles for centuries, demonstrating their effectiveness across different landscapes and climates."

"Yes, drawing on traditional ecological knowledge is critical," Mr. Klein agreed, actually writing "Traditional Ecological Knowledge" on the board with Drew's name beside it. "Thank you for bringing that historical perspective into the conversation."

I glanced at Jenna, who we'd let in on the plan. Her eyes widened and she scribbled something in her notebook before sliding it toward me: OMG it's working.

The debate continued, with other students offering points about technological solutions, policy frameworks, and individual actions. True to our plan, I remained silent, though it took considerable effort.

Finally, about twenty minutes in, Mr. Klein looked around the room. "Emilia, we haven't heard from you today. You usually have thoughts on agricultural approaches."

This was the moment we'd prepared for. I took a deep breath and delivered the second prepared point—one Drew and I had crafted together, but intentionally different from what he'd already said.

"I'd like to build on the conversation about scale," I began carefully. "When we talk about environmental solutions, we often privilege global approaches over local ones. But research shows that place-based initiatives, particularly in agriculture, can create resilience nodes that collectively transform larger systems."

Mr. Klein's expression shifted subtly. "While local initiatives certainly have value, we need to be careful not to overstate their impact. Global challenges require coordinated global responses."

I nodded, maintaining a neutral expression despite the frustration burning in my chest. "Of course. I'm not suggesting local approaches alone are sufficient. Rather, they're an essential component of multilevel solutions, as demonstrated by recent studies from the Environmental Systems Institute."

"Well, yes," Mr. Klein conceded, though his tone had cooled considerably. "But we should maintain academic perspective about their limitations."

As the debate continued, Drew caught my eye again, giving me a subtle thumbs-up under his desk. We had our evidence—the same concepts that earned enthusiastic support when coming from Drew were met with caution and qualification when I expressed them.

When the bell rang, signaling the end of class, Drew lingered, waiting for me.

"Did you get it?" I asked quietly as we gathered our things.

He nodded, patting his pocket. "Every word."

His expression softened. "You okay?"

I shrugged. "It's not like I didn't already know what was happening. But seeing it demonstrated so clearly..."

"It's one thing to suspect it, another to prove it," Drew finished for me. "But now we have evidence. And that means we can do something about it."

As we walked out of the classroom, I felt a complicated mix of vindication and disappointment. The experiment had worked—too well.

"Emilia?" Drew's voice pulled me back to the present.

"Yeah?"

"For what it's worth, I think Mr. Klein might actually be a decent teacher if he could recognize his own biases." He adjusted his backpack. "People can change if they're confronted the right way."

I gave him slight smile . "I hope that's true. I've become more pessimistic since starting high school."

"That sucks, though you've never been say Jenna-level hopeful," he replied.

I smiled at him, "Fair point. My head would probably explode if I tried to match her. So, what's our next move?"

Drew considered for a moment. "Let me listen to the recording tonight, make some notes. Then we can decide next steps."

As we parted ways in the hallway, I felt something shift inside me. The frustration was still there, but alongside it feeling more in control. So far the biggest lessons I'd learned in ninth grade weren't in the curriculum.

48

Rising up Against the Man & the Status Quo at Lunch

Emilia

The cafeteria hummed with the usual midday chaos—trays clattering, conversations overlapping, the occasional burst of laughter cutting through the din. Our regular table in already half-full when Drew and I arrived with our lunches.

Tyler looked up from his sandwich, his expression brightening when he saw me. But it quickly shifted to concern when he caught my mood.

"What happened?" he asked as I dropped onto the bench beside him.

"Klein happened," I muttered, stabbing at my cafeteria pasta with unnecessary force.

Drew set his tray down opposite us, looking uncharacteristically animated. "We did the experiment," he explained, glancing around to make sure our table neighbors weren't listening too closely. "And it worked exactly the way we thought it would."

"What experiment?" Aiden asked, looking between us with confusion.

I exchanged a look with Drew before leaning in. "We tested whether Mr. Klein responds differently to the exact same ideas depending on who says them."

"Specifically," Drew continued, his voice low but intense, "whether he takes my comments more seriously than Emilia's, even when I'm literally using her words."

Jenna, who was in on the plan from the beginning, leaned forward eagerly. "It was so obvious! Drew said something about regenerative agriculture being a systems-level solution, and Klein practically nominated him for a Nobel Prize. Then when Emilia made an almost identical point about local initiatives scaling up, Klein was all 'well, let's not overstate their impact.'" Her impression of Klein's patronizing tone was eerily accurate.

Tyler's expression darkened. "Are you serious?"

"Dead serious," Drew replied, pulling out the recorder. "I recorded the whole thing. Listen." He hit play, and Klein's voice emerged from the tiny speaker.

"An excellent point, Drew. You're looking at the interconnected nature of environmental systems rather than isolated solutions. That's precisely the kind of systems thinking we need..."

He stopped the recording and scrolled forward.

"While local initiatives certainly have value, we need to be careful not to overstate their impact. Global challenges require coordinated global responses."

"That's the same basic idea!" Ivy exclaimed, looking outraged.

"Same idea, different speaker," Drew confirmed.

"That's messed up," Aiden said, shaking his head.

Tyler's jaw was tight. "So what's the plan? You're not just going to let this keep happening, right?"

"That's why we wanted to talk to all of you," I said, my voice dropping to a whisper-shout. "We need help documenting this pattern. The more examples we collect, the harder it will be for Klein to dismiss it as a misunderstanding."

"I'm in," Tyler said immediately, his hand finding mine under the table. "Just tell me what to do."

"Me too," Aria added, having arrived in time to catch most of the conversation. "I've seen the same thing in AP Bio with Ms. Wentworth. She always calls on the guys first for lab explanations, even when the girls have their hands up longer."

"This is bigger than just Klein," Drew noted. "But we have to start somewhere. Our idea is to recruit a few more students from Current Issues—especially girls who've experienced this but might not have recognized the pattern."

"What about Sarah Drummond?" Jenna suggested. "She's super smart but hardly ever speaks up in class. I've noticed Klein interrupts her when she does."

"And Lucia Rodriguez," Jenna continued. "She wrote an amazing paper on water conservation policy that Klein only gave a B+ because it was 'too advocacy-oriented.'"

"That's the critique he gives me," I said, the frustration I'd been holding back all morning boiling over. "Academic writing has to be 'objective' and 'dispassionate'—but somehow that rule only applies to certain people."

"It's such garbage," Tyler muttered, his free hand clenching into a fist on the table. "You know more about environmental systems than half the class combined."

"It's not about knowledge," Drew pointed out. "It's about who's allowed to present that knowledge with confidence and authority. Who's expected to qualify every statement and who gets to make declarations."

"So what exactly are we going to do?" Aria asked, her lunch completely forgotten. "Besides documenting it, I mean."

Drew and I exchanged another glance. "We've been talking about that," I told her. "We don't want to just complain. We want change."

"We haven't decided on a for sure plan," Drew continued, "just that once we have enough evidence to show a pattern, maybe approach Klein. Give him to listen, adjust."

"And if he doesn't?" Tyler challenged, skepticism clear in his voice.

"We'll take it further. If we've got evidence, witnesses, than another level up I guess."

"That's serious," Aiden said, looking slightly uncomfortable. "Like, potentially affecting his job serious."

"Maybe his job should be affected if he can't treat students fairly," Ivy retorted, her voice rising enough that a few people at the next table looked over.

"Shh!" Jenna hissed, glancing around. "We're not trying to get him fired. We're trying to get him to recognize his bias so he can be a better teacher."

I agreed, though part of me shared Ivy's anger. "This isn't about punishment. It's about improvement."

"So what do we need from us non-Current Issues people?" Tyler asked, refocusing the conversation.

"Support," I said simply. "Ideas if you think of a different approach.""

"We're looking for at least five solid examples before we approach Klein. With recordings if possible, but detailed notes if not."

"When are you planning to confront him?" Aiden asked.

I winced at the word 'confront.' "Nothing decided yet, parent teacher conferences are coming up, we've got a paper due back from Klein soon. Maybe let a few things play out first."

Tyler squeezed my hand under the table. "You realize this is basically the plot of a high school movie, right? The plucky students taking on the biased teacher? Emilia Preston, the plucky heroine."

Despite everything, I laughed. "Don't ever use plucky in combination with my name again! And get your musical number ready."

"Jenna can choreograph a dramatic dance for the student body at the assembly when the principal addresses the whole school," Maddie added.

"I bet Mr. Henderson could give a good soliloquy about belief in student potential, then the villain teacher will have a heartwarming epiphany about the error of their ways," Jenna added with an eye-roll. "And quote a famous poem."

"Yeah, real life is messier," Drew agreed. "And Klein's not actually a villain. But that doesn't mean we can't make a difference."

"I still can't believe he did that so blatantly," Tyler said, shaking his head. "The exact same point gets praised coming from Drew but questioned coming from you? That's just—" He broke off, clearly searching for a word strong enough.

"Infuriating?" Ivy suggested.

"Discriminatory?" offered Aria.

"Both," I added, "And yeah, it's blatant to us now, but just us at the moment."

As the bell rang we gathered our things Jenna declared, "Operation Academic Equality is a go. But that's a boring name. Ideas people, need your ideas before the end of the day."

The next day at lunch the revolution against the status quo continued on. The lunchroom was loud, but Jenna's voice cut through the noise like a coach's whistle.

"Attention, people. Emergency plan. Formation. Right now. Whitney Harlow is throwing some 'invite-only' Halloween rager, and—shocker—none of us made the list."

"Correction. Aiden did," Aria said, not looking up from her sandwich.

Ivy tensed.

Aiden looked pained when he said, "I think I've made my RSVP clear the three times she followed me somewhere this morning. I'll pass."

"She won't ask us to get to Aiden, will she?" I asked.

"Nah," Tyler said. "She knows that won't work. She'll stick with her upperclassmen targets."

"Invite or no invite, we'd boycott," Jenna declared, emphasizing boycott with a cheerleader arm movement. "But let's make our own plans anyway. We're in charge of our social calendar, not an outmoded class clique system."

Aria perked up. "What about the fall festival? Hayrides, mini donuts, apple slingshots, and the corn maze that tried to eat Aiden last year?"

"Yeah," Tyler said, turning to Aiden. "You screamed so loud a kindergartner cried."

Aiden didn't blink. "That was a tactical response to someone in a clown mask jumping out of a hay bale."

"Sure it was," Aria said sweetly. "If I recall, no one else saw the clown—but we did see a four-year-old in a Paw Patrol costume jump out of the corn."

"And you screamed like a character on mi abuela's telenovelas," I added.

Ivy leaned her elbow on the table. "So we all vote town festival over sketchy house party?"

Everyone nodded. Even Drew, who just raised a finger without looking up from his sandwich.

"I'm in," he said after. "But only if I don't have to carve a pumpkin this year. I'm over pumpkin guts after helping my sisters carve theirs. I hate that slimy stuff."

Across the table, Maddie looked up from her tray. "Fall festival's good, but it'll be packed. Maybe we follow it up with something chill? Like a firepit?"

"My backyard's open," Ivy offered. "We've got wood stacked already. And Dad will be thrilled if we make it a marshmallow-themed gathering."

"That sounds perfect," Maddie said. "Backyard bonfire after the festival—cozy sweaters, sticky s'mores, very rural-cottagecore chic."

"Do we invite extras?" Tyler asked. "Or keep it to The Notable Nine?"

"First of all," I said, "we are not calling ourselves that."

"Second," Ivy added, "that's fine. I'll ask Jordan and Sarah to come—we'll get some awesome s'more haikus from him."

"Then it'll be eleven," Nate said in his quiet way.

"Cool," Tyler said. "The There's No Ocean Near Us Eleven."

The group response was immediate and perfectly synced. "No."

Nate gave a small shrug. "Eleven is a really irritating number."

"Prime," Maddie said, ticking it off on her fingers. "Awkward. Visually deceptive."

Nate nodded appreciatively. "Exactly."

Jenna leaned across the table. "So we're agreed? Fall festival, then Ivy's house?"

Everyone moved on—Jenna started talking about the pep rally theme, Drew explained the logistics of taking all his sisters trick-or-treating, and Maddie volunteered to help him. Aiden asked Tyler something about basketball practice, and Ivy pulled out a pen and notepaper to start making a list.

49

Failure to Launch a Gourd

Emilia

The fall festival was already buzzing when we got there—caramel in the air, hay crunching underfoot, and enough plaid to start a country-core fall fashion insta.

I spotted our group by the main entrance: Ivy wrapped in Aiden's hoodie, Maddie double-fisting mini donuts, and Aria aggressively trying to win a free cider at the ring toss.

Tyler stood just off to the side, hands in his jacket pockets, scanning the booths like he was secretly mapping the place for a caramel corn heist. He smiled, soft and a little crooked.

"You going to eat your caramel apple with hay again?" I said, stepping up beside him.

"That happened one time."

I bumped my shoulder into his. "Mmmhmm, one time that's anytime there's food and something to distract you."

He laughed, reaching for one of the festival maps. "Alright, Farm Exec, this a farmish thing here—lead me to the fun?"

As we cut across the grounds, we passed the corn maze. Aiden pretended not to look; Ivy slipped her arm through his and patted his shoulder like she was comforting a nervous lamb walking past a wolves' den.

We peeled off from the group, heading toward the far edge of the field where a long line of hay bales guarded an elaborate slingshot contraption. The worker handed me a mini pumpkin and nodded solemnly, as if this was a sacred rite of passage.

"Think I can take out that clown scarecrow?" I asked, eyeing a particularly smug one near the back.

"I think you can do anything. But yes, take out the terrifying clown before Aiden sees it," Tyler said, so casually I almost missed it. "You should know though, your slingshot form is terrible."

I narrowed my eyes. "Which one of us is the farm executive here?"

He held up both hands, mock-innocent. "Okay, okay, sitting behind a farm desk doing paperwork? You should ace this slingshot thing."

I launched the pumpkin. It soared—wide—and landed closer to the hot cider booth than the scary clown. Tyler dissolved into laughter.

The volunteer at the Slingshot booth yelled, "Heads up, gourd incoming!" The workers at all the surrounding booths looked up.

"You almost took out a cider vendor. Aiming at the competition?"

"We don't make cider!"

"Apples is apples right?"

I covered my face with my hands. "Shut up! I'm so embarrassed!"

Tyler nudged me. "Nah. That epic shot, just made you more unforgettable. Though I think unforgettable is unforgettable, so I'm not sure you get more... ooof!"

Tyler

Huh, didn't think telling her she's plain old unforgettable would make her blush, but it did. Not bright, a medium-ish kind of blush. An elbow to my stomach followed the blush, followed by her rolled eyes and towing me along by my sleeve.

We wandered between booths until we found one fall fest mecca—Caramel Apples. I got perfection—thick caramel, chopped peanuts, absolutely impossible to eat gracefully. Emilia got the caramel hidden shamefully under chocolate. A caramel apple disgrace.

We both took messy bites and argued about whether chocolate should cover caramel.

"You are so lucky I like sugar," Emilia said, "I'm done arguing, I just want to eat this."

She grinned and took the messiest bite possible on purpose. I got caught in an Emmy loop wondering how a caramel and chocolate mess could look so cute.

I shook it off and took a bigger, messier bite. Just because. Since my jaw was sealed shut with caramel it was a few minutes before we could talk. When we could, we didn't talk about anything serious—not about Mom, the U visa, or the issues with Klein—just which varietal (her word) made the best caramel apple and whether or not a s'more coated apple would be tasty. When we rejoined the group, Ivy was already herding people toward her house.

"Fire pit's going," she called. "S'mores and bad decisions await."

"No Jordan and Sarah?" Jenna asked.

"No, they had plans already," Ivy said. Aiden didn't look bummed at that, but I didn't say anything. He hadn't left his obliviousness behind that long ago. I didn't want to trip him up.

Emilia

Ivy's backyard glowed gold and orange in the firelight, blankets tossed over lawn chairs and mugs of hot chocolate passed around like currency. Logs popped and crackled. Wood smoke smudged the air, just enough to be nice, not overwhelming. Tyler and I took the loveseat bench, meaning we had to sit a bit closer. That's what I told myself.

Jenna roasted a marshmallow until it caught fire, then, in full cheer-leader cadence, called, "We're burning the social clique system!" punctuating her cheer with the fiery marshmallow.

"Don't be the first bad decision Jenna," I called. "Drop the weaponized marshmallow."

Looking at Tyler I said, "That should be you."

He shrugged, "Night's still young, but I'm aiming for low-key bad decisions."

329

The fire, my friends, and a quiet spot inside me spread into something I couldn't name. Not because I was afraid though I needed time to look at my feelings closely. I was still thinking about it when Tyler leaned down, lips close to my ear.

"Hey," he said, his voice barely loud enough to hear over the fire's crackle. "Thanks for today."

"For what?"

"For helping not gnaw on stuff, worry, and smother all the fun from the day."

I turned my head, just enough to meet his eyes. "Whatever happens next, you know that I'll be right there, don't you?"

Tyler

The group thinned out slowly, until only Ivy and Aiden were curled under a shared blanket, and Emilia and I were the last two still roasting marshmallows.

I didn't want to leave. Not yet.

"Hey, don't make it obvious but listen. Have you ever heard Aiden giggle before?"

Emilia snorted and clapped her hands over her face. "Oh my gosh, no! And they're like sickeningly sweet over there."

"Sweet and probably waiting for us to leave," I said.

"Ew, don't talk about it, I still think Aiden's got cooties! Yuck!," Emilia whisper yelled.

"Aiden cooties specifically, or boy cooties in general?"

"Whatever it is that makes me nauseous watching their sweetness. And she's my cousin, practically a sister and my best friend—so disturbing on many levels."

"Good to know that your cootie issue seemed attached directly to Aiden and Ivy being in lurve."

She glanced at me. "Uh, not quite sure how to respond to that."

"No response needed, it seems in general that I don't make you sick but just wanted to delve in the details to be sure."

Emilia didn't tease. She just reached for my hand under the blanket. "I don't seem to having any negative physical reactions to you being around Farm Guy. So, I guess you can stick around me for a while."

My chest tightened. She had no idea what that meant to me or maybe she did. Whatever she understood at that moment, I think she knew I'd be holding on.

50

Filing Day

Tyler

The digital clock on the dashboard read 4:17 AM when we pulled out of the Preston driveway. It would be an eight-hour drive to Minneapolis—if traffic cooperated, which was never guaranteed when crossing state lines on I-94.

"Everyone good?" Robbie asked from the driver's seat, his voice low in the pre-dawn darkness.

Mom nodded from the passenger seat, a folder clutched tightly in her lap. The same folder we'd been reviewing for weeks—page by page, form by form, document by document. Inside was the culmination of weeks and weeks of work with Mr. Jacobsen—the U visa application that might bring Mom out of the shadows.

He'd completed the work more quickly than he often would, though he assured us it was still thorough and accurate. He didn't state it straight out, but I think he treated Mom's case as an emergency.

"We're good," I answered from the back seat, glancing at Emilia beside me. She gave me a sleepy half-smile and squeezed my hand. She'd insisted on coming, even though it meant missing school.

"You need backup," she'd said yesterday when Mom had tried to talk her out of it. "Plus, my note-taking skills are superior to Tyler's."

She wasn't wrong. While Mr. Jacobsen had handled most of the legal paperwork, Emilia had created an organizational system for all of Mom's supporting documents—birth certificates, medical records, the police report from the assault, letters from character witnesses, photos, and a stack of other evidence.

Mom turned to look back at us. "You both should try to sleep. It's going to be a long day."

"I'm okay," I said, though exhaustion tugged at me. We'd been up late going through the checklist one more time. "Did you sleep at all?"

"A little," she lied, the shadows under her eyes telling the truth.

I didn't push it. None of us had slept well. The stakes were too high, the "what-ifs" too numerous. What if they rejected the application? What if they asked for documents we didn't have? What if they saw through all our careful preparation and decided Mom didn't deserve to stay?

Robbie adjusted the rearview mirror. "We've got this, Luz. Mark said everything's in order."

"Yes," Mom agreed, but her fingers kept worrying the edges of the folder.

"Tyler?" Emilia's voice pulled me from my thoughts. "You're doing the jaw-clenching thing again."

I relaxed my face. "Sorry."

"No need to apologize," she said, her voice soft enough that only I could hear. "It's okay to be nervous. I am too."

I nodded, grateful for her steady presence. The Prestons had become a lifeline for us. Robbie had connected us with Mr. Jacobsen through a friend of a friend. Mariella had helped Mom practice her English for the potential interview questions.

And Emilia... Emilia had been there for everything, from organizing documents to talking me down when the stress got overwhelming.

"Did you check the appointment confirmation again?" Mom asked, turning over her shoulder.

"Yes, Mom. It's still at 2 PM." This was the third time she'd asked since we'd left the house.

"And Mr. Jacobsen will meet us—"

"At the office at 1:30," I finished. "We have the address, the backup directions, and Emilia has it all on her phone too."

Mom nodded, seemingly satisfied for the moment, and turned back around. The first three hours of the drive passed in relative quiet. Emilia dozed off against my shoulder while Robbie and Mom spoke occasionally in low voices.

I must have fallen asleep too, because when I opened my eyes again, we were stopping at a rest area, and sunlight was streaming through the windows.

"Stretch your legs," Robbie said, parking the car. "Mariella packed snacks in the cooler."

We climbed out of the car, the morning chill nipping at our faces. The rest stop was nearly empty, just a few travelers walking dogs or smoking beside their vehicles. I helped Mom with the cooler, and we settled at a picnic table while Emilia and Robbie went to find the restrooms.

"You okay, Mijo?" Mom asked, unwrapping a sandwich Mariella had prepared.

"I should be asking you that."

She smiled faintly. "I'm..." She paused, considering. "I'm hopeful. And scared. But mostly hopeful."

"Mr. Jacobsen says our case is strong," I reminded her, repeating the attorney's words for both of us.

"Yes. But you know how these things go. There's always something they could question."

I did know. The U visa process was notoriously complex. Filing the initial petition was just the first step. If approved, Mom would receive a work permit and protection from deportation while they processed the actual visa—which could take years. Then, after three years with a U visa, she could apply for a green card.

It was a long road, but it was a road. A path forward that didn't involve constant fear.

"We'll handle whatever comes," I said.

She reached across the table and squeezed my hand. "We always do."

When Robbie and Emilia returned, we finished our quick breakfast and got back on the road. The miles ticked by corn and soybean fields giving way to more populated areas as we approached Minneapolis.

"I've never been to Minneapolis," Emilia said, peering out the window as buildings began to replace farmland.

"I've been once," I replied. "For a basketball tournament in seventh grade. Didn't see much beyond the gym and the hotel, though."

Robbie navigated through the increasingly congested traffic with the calm of someone who'd made similar drives many times. "Mariella and I used to come here a few times a year before the kids. There's a great farmers' market downtown."

Mom nodded absently, her eyes on the folder in her lap. Inside was everything—the Form I-918 petition, the I-918 Supplement B signed by the police department certifying that she had been helpful in the investigation, medical records, personal statement, identity documents, and more. Mr. Jacobsen had gone over everything meticulously, but Mom kept checking and rechecking.

"Luz," Robbie said, "it's all there. You've checked three times this morning alone."

"I know," she said. "I just can't stop thinking about what happens if I've forgotten something."

"Then Mark will help us figure it out," Robbie assured her. "That's why we have him."

We found a parking garage near the USCIS Saint Paul Field Office—which, confusingly, was located in Minneapolis. Robbie pulled a ticket from the machine, and we wound our way up to find a spot.

As we walked toward the federal building, Mom's steps slowed. She looked up at the imposing structure, anxiety evident in the set of her shoulders.

"Mom?" I said, touching her arm. "You ready?"

She drew in a deep breath and nodded. "Ready."

Mr. Jacobsen was waiting for us outside, briefcase in hand. He was younger than I'd expected when we first met him—maybe mid-thirties, with wire-rimmed glasses and an air of casual competence that had immediately put Mom at ease.

"Right on time," he said, shaking hands with everyone. "How was the drive?"

"Long," Robbie answered with a smile.

"Thanks for meeting us here," Mom said, her voice steadier than I'd expected.

"Of course. This is the big day." Mr. Jacobsen checked his watch. "We've got about thirty minutes before the appointment. Let's go over a few things before we head in."

We found a quiet corner in the building's lobby, and Mr. Jacobsen led us through what to expect. "Remember, this isn't an interview today—it's just the filing appointment. Most likely, they'll verify your identity, check that the documentation is complete, and process the initial paperwork. If they do ask any questions, they'll be procedural, not about the substance of your case."

Mom nodded, following along as he spoke.

"After today, you'll receive a receipt notice confirming they've accepted your petition for processing. Then comes the waiting—which, I won't sugarcoat it, could be several months before you hear anything further."

"And during that time?" Robbie asked.

"During that time, Luz's status remains the same. She doesn't have work authorization yet, and technically she's still undocumented. That won't change until they issue what's called a 'prima facie' determination, which means they believe the case has merit on its face."

I felt my stomach tighten. More waiting. More uncertainty. Mr. Jacobsen must have seen something in my expression, because he added, "The good news is that once USCIS acknowledges receipt of the application, it provides some protection. ICE typically doesn't prioritize people with pending U visa applications."

Small comfort, but I'd take it.

"Ready to head up?" Mr. Jacobsen asked, glancing at his watch again.

Mom drew in a deep breath and stood. "Yes. Let's do this."

We rode the elevator to the designated floor. As we approached the security checkpoint, a familiar nervousness crept up my spine—the same feeling I always got in places of authority, where uniforms and badges meant potential danger for Mom. I had to remind myself that today, we were supposed to be here. We had an appointment. We had a lawyer.

We passed through security, Mom's folder examined and returned to her. The waiting area was unexpectedly ordinary—beige walls, rows of chairs, and a check-in desk with a digital display of numbers. It reminded me of the DMV, only quieter, the hushed conversations in multiple languages creating a gentle hum.

Mr. Jacobsen approached the desk with Mom while Robbie, Emilia, and I found seats. Emilia's hand found mine again, her fingers cool and steadying.

"So we just... wait?" I asked when Mom and Mr. Jacobsen joined us.

"We wait," Mr. Jacobsen confirmed. "They'll call her number when they're ready."

Time crawled. I watched the digital display advance with excruciating slowness. Beside me, Mom sat perfectly still, the folder balanced on her knees. Robbie flipped through a months-old magazine, though I doubted he was reading it. Emilia had brought a book but wasn't opening it, her attention on the people around us.

An hour passed, then another. Mr. Jacobsen checked his watch periodically but assured us this was normal. "Government time," he said with a wry smile.

Finally, a voice called out, "Number 47?"

Mom stood, folder clutched to her chest. Mr. Jacobsen rose beside her.

"Do you want me to come?" I asked, already half-standing.

Mom hesitated, then shook her head. "Wait here, Mijo. I'll be okay."

I watched as she walked away with Mr. Jacobsen, disappearing through a door on the far side of the room. The click of the door closing behind them felt oddly final.

"She's got this," Emilia said quietly.

"I know," I replied, not entirely convinced.

"No, I mean it. Your mom is one of the strongest people I know. She's been preparing for this for months."

"Years," I corrected. "Her whole life in America has been building toward something like this."

Robbie leaned forward. "And now it's happening. Today is just a step, but it's an important one."

I nodded, trying to take comfort in their words. It was hard to explain the mixture of hope and dread that had been my constant companion growing up.

The hope that someday, somehow, Mom would find a path to legal status. The dread that instead, she'd be discovered and taken away.

"What if they say no?" I asked the question that had been haunting me for weeks escaping.

Robbie considered this seriously. "Then we figure out the next step. There's always a next step, Tyler."

"Mr. Jacobsen seemed confident," Emilia added. "He said your mom has a strong case."

I nodded again, not trusting myself to speak. The waiting room suddenly felt too small, too confined. I stood up. "I'm going to get some water. Anyone else want some?"

They both shook their heads, and I escaped to the water fountain in the hallway, needing a moment to compose myself. The cool water did little to wash away the lump in my throat, but the brief solitude helped me gather my thoughts.

By the time I returned, nearly an hour had passed since Mom and Mr. Jacobsen had disappeared through that door. I checked my phone—no messages, no updates.

"Still nothing?" I asked, sinking back into my seat.

"Not yet," Robbie said. "But that's a good sign. If there were any problems, they'd have come out sooner."

Just as he finished speaking, the door opened, and Mom emerged with Mr. Jacobsen behind her. Her expression gave nothing away—the same careful mask she wore whenever we dealt with anything official. But as she came closer, I saw something different in her eyes. A lightness I hadn't seen in years. I stood, a question on my lips that I couldn't quite form.

"It's done," she said simply. "They accepted everything."

The relief hit me so suddenly I felt dizzy. Mr. Jacobsen was explaining something about receipt numbers and processing times, but all I could focus on was my mom's face, the subtle shift in her posture, as if a weight had been lifted—not completely, but enough to stand a little straighter.

"So what happens now?" Robbie asked, practical as always.

"Now we wait," Mr. Jacobsen said. "They'll send a receipt notice in the next few weeks, and then it's in USCIS's hands. I'll be monitoring the case, of course, and I'll let you know if there are any updates or if they request additional evidence."

"And if they approve it?" I asked.

"If they approve it, Luz will receive work authorization and protection from deportation while they process the actual U visa. It's a significant step forward."

Emilia had been quiet, but now she stepped forward and, in a gesture that surprised me, hugged my mom.

"Congratulations, Tía Luz."

Mom hugged her back, emotion flickering across her face before she composed herself. "Thank you, Mija. For everything."

As we gathered our things and prepared to leave, a strange feeling settled over me. Not quite relief—the journey was far from over. Not quite happiness—too many uncertainties remained.

But something adjacent to hope. A sense that perhaps, after years of hiding and fear, we were finally stepping into the light.

The drive back to North Riverbend stretched ahead of us—another eight hours of highway and fields—but it felt different now. As if we were driving toward something, not just away from danger.

In the elevator down to the parking garage, Mom's phone buzzed with a text. She checked it and smiled—a real smile that reached her eyes.

"Mariella," she explained. "She wants to know if we should celebrate tonight or wait until tomorrow."

"Both," Emilia and I said in unison, then caught each other's eyes and laughed.

Mom shook her head, amused. "Both it is, then."

Outside, the late afternoon sun cast long shadows across the street. Mom paused, looking up at the federal building one last time.

"You okay?" I asked.

She nodded, taking a deep breath of the crisp air. "Yes. For the first time in a very long time, I think I might actually be okay."

And walking toward the car, surrounded by the people who had helped make this day possible, I allowed myself to believe her.

51

Blunder in the Bleachers

Emilia

The gym buzzed with small-town chaos—glittery signs, thundering bleachers, and the smell of popcorn mixing with floor polish. Our whole crew had taken over one section of the stands like it was reserved seating.

Maddie was leaning back against the railing, and Ivy sat quietly beside Aiden, pretending not to watch him every time he smiled. Jenna was courtside with the cheer squad, all bounce and sharp counts at the baseline between plays.

Aria jogged onto the court after halftime, all business. Game face locked in.

"She's so focused," I muttered, nudging Ivy. "Like, I knew she was good, but I'm seeing the context."

Ivy grinned. "Yeah, same. There's hearing, then there's seeing."

The whistle blew, and within seconds, Aria was everywhere. Steals, assists, threes from what might as well have been another ZIP code.

"She's on fire!" I yelled, cupping my hands around my mouth.

After another three pointer, Tyler, seated a row behind me, jumped to his feet with enough force to rock our section.

"THAT'S MY GIRL!"

Dead silence around us and a good portion of the gym.

I turned to look at him as he tried to back track. Clearing his throat he said, "I mean—not just my girl, our girl, all of ours, girl." He made swirly motions with his hands. Still trying to recover he went on, "A girl, who is a friend... Our friend... A collective friend... Really, she belongs to the whole town, don't you think?"

I raised one eyebrow. Tyler sank lower onto the bleacher. "Okay, but you know what I meant."

I let him squirm for a couple minutes, biting back a grin. "Sure, Tyler. Our girl, and SHE'S ON FIRE! Go ARIA."

Then I noticed he'd slipped into my row, next to me. Then had moved a bit closer. Then he was... closer than before? Our shoulders bumped, eyes flicked back and forth from the game to each other.

Aria stole the ball again and darted toward the basket. I yelled and cheered as she completed a layup. Jenna spun toward the stands and cupped her hands like a megaphone.

"Make some noise, Riverbend!" Then she pivoted back into formation, ponytail snap-perfect.

Tyler

I didn't mean to yell it. Okay, I did, but I didn't think it would be that loud. "That's my girl!" had just blasted out of me like steam from a microwave popcorn bag—without warning.

Then Emilia turned. And raised that eyebrow. The eyebrow. And panic. "I mean—not my girl," I blurted, along with a bunch of other words I couldn't hear myself say. Emilia just stared at me. But not in a murder-y way. More like she was deciding whether to laugh or slap me.

She picked "laugh." And she didn't move away when I scooted down to her row. Closer. Close enough that I could hear her cheering even when everyone else was yelling too. Close enough that every time she laughed, I felt it in my chest like a drum beat.

I kept trying to watch the game—really, Aria was incredible—but then Emilia would say something sarcastic or toss popcorn into Maddie's hood and I'd forget where the ball was. After the final buzzer and Aria's last no-look assist, we spilled out of the gym. The night air bit after the gym's packed heat; my breath fogged as we headed toward the parking lot, the faint smell of bonfires riding the cold.

"Watching other people be athletic is hard work," I groaned, stretching dramatically.

"Poor baby," Emilia said, not sounding very sorry.

I grinned. "I'm going to need recovery time. Maybe a sympathy snack."

She rolled her eyes but nudged me with her elbow. It felt like a yes.

52

A Cow Stubbed Its Hoof

Emilia

I'd been staring at the same paragraph for at least ten minutes. Something about nitrogen cycling. Or maybe carbon sequestration. I couldn't tell anymore. The words had gone blurry hours ago—except it had only been seventeen minutes.

I sat back in my chair and blew out a breath. My highlighter hovered uselessly above the page. My fingers tapped against the desk in a slow, restless rhythm, like maybe I could knock focus loose from the corners of my brain.

What was the use of focus when what I had to say wasn't heard. My ideas weren't bad. The listeners just didn't think I was worth hearing. I dragged my sleeve across my eyes, not because I was crying—just... just in case. Just in case something was trying to sneak out without permission.

And it didn't ask. It just happened. A slow, traitorous tear that slipped down without ceremony. I wiped it fast. Swallowed hard. Looked up at the ceiling like that would somehow patch the leak.

There was a soft rustle from the hallway. A creaky floorboard. Then a pause.

And then:

"You gots germs Meela?"

I turned. Miggy stood in the doorway with a half-eaten granola bar and the world's most serious expression. His face was half-sticky, half-suspicious. All four-year-old-going-on-eleventy.

Behind him, Sofía leaned to the side dramatically, peeking around his shoulder. Her binky hung from her mouth by the little plastic ring, and she had only one sock on. The other foot was completely bare and covered in marker streaks. She stared like I was the most interesting science exhibit she'd ever seen.

"Germs?" I said.

He tilted his head. "Yeah, you're going sniff, sniff. Like you got germs that's gonna make that green bogger goop come from your nose."

"Oh, no I'm not getting sick, Miggy-man. Tired I guess."

He examined me again. "If you get green goop make sure you wear long sleeves so you can wipe your nose."

I had to chuckle at that. "Well, there's tissue for noses too you know Mr."

"Nah, takes too long. This is faster." He demonstrated wiping his nose with his sleeve.

I wiped my face again, slower this time. "I'm okay, bud. Just tired."

Miggy didn't move. "Did you not get enough bossy time at school?" Sighing deeply, he said, "You can boss me and Fia around if you need too."

I lunged, grabbed, and pulled him onto my lap. "Mi hermano pequeño es maravilloso." I planted kisses all over his face.

"No, no, kisses, no!" He shrieked, but he was also laughing hard.

"Me! Me! Me! Me! Me!" Fia chanted in the background.

"Save me Fia!"

Sofía stumbled over her flapping sock coming to Miggy's rescue. She tugged on my arm so I dropped Miggy and scooped her up. She plopped into my lap and squished my face between her hands.

"Wub you, Meela." She gave me a sticky kiss that contained crumbs. Sofia's love was often covered in crumbs.

Miggy gave a solemn nod, arms folded. "We fixed you."

"You'd better run or you're getting more kisses Mr."

He shrieked, turned then ran out into the hallway. "No! No! No more kisses! GROOOOSSSS!"

Sofía ran after him. "GOOOOS."

I let out a small laugh. The first real one all afternoon. Maybe I couldn't fix the way people saw me. Maybe they'd always nod politely when I spoke, then turn and listen harder when someone else said the same thing louder, or taller, or with a last name that matched their skin color. I gave up on the textbook. Let it fall shut on its own.

Tyler

My phone lit up with a local number I didn't recognize. I was oddly disappointed it wasn't a call from Emilia's-Hijacked-Phone. I wondered if that should worry me.

I answered. "Hello?"

There was a pause. A breath. Then—"Tyler. Did you hurt Meela's feelings?"

I blinked. "Miggy?"

"Yeah. It's me." Next he whispered. "I gots Mamá's phone. Don't tell her Farm Guy. No snitching in farmwork."

I sat up straighter, trying not to laugh. "Uh, I don't think I hurt her feelings. Why?"

"She's sad from somebody. Not me. Maybe you. Maybe the teacher man. But maybe you."

I paused. "Okay...."

"You should tell her a joke."

"A joke?"

"Yeah. Something with butts is good."

"I'll keep that in mind."

"And let her boss you around tomorrow. She didn't get enough bossy time today. That's important."

"Okay," I said, a smile sneaking in. "Got it."

"'Kay. Bye."

Click. I stared at the phone. Then shook my head and laughed softly.

"Boss me around tomorrow," I muttered. "Yeah, I think I can manage that."

I picked up my phone and typed out a text.

Me: What did the cow say when it stubbed its hoof?

Me: Ow. Moo.

Me: I know. That was awful.

Me: You can be bossy tomorrow and make me learn better jokes.

Emilia: Someone tell you I didn't get enough bossy time today?

Me: I can neither confirm nor deny per Senate Bill 1289, section 98, Part 4ej re: *USDA No Snitching in Farm Work Act.*

53

How To Write About It

Tyler

I sat cross-legged on my bed, staring at my laptop. The website for the "Voices of Loss" writing competition was open, its blue and gray theme somehow making everything feel more serious.

National competition for young writers ages 13-18 who have lost a parent. Theme: "Absence & Presence" - exploring the paradox of someone being gone yet still felt.

First prize: $10,000 scholarship and publication in "Memory Matters" anthology. Deadline: March 15.

A ten-thousand-dollar scholarship. Publication. Recognition. And all I had to do was cut myself open on paper for strangers to see. I closed the laptop, then opened it again. The essay I'd written for Mr. Henderson's class had already said more than I'd ever told anyone about Dad. About that weird empty space in my life shaped exactly like someone I'd never met.

I glanced at the corkboard above my desk where a wrinkled photo of my dad hung—one of the few I had. Him in his military uniform, smiling that crooked grin that Gramps says I inherited. It was weird, seeing pieces of yourself in someone you never knew.

His smile. His eyes. His height. What else had I inherited? Gramps always said Dad had a way with words. That he could make people laugh even on their worst days. That he wrote these long letters from overseas that would make everyone cry and laugh in the same paragraph. Maybe that part of him was in me too.

I flopped back onto the pillow, staring at the ceiling. Writing about it meant admitting how much it hurt. How much I wondered. How much I sometimes lay awake imaging conversations we'd never have.

"This is stupid," I muttered to my empty room.

My phone buzzed from somewhere in the tangle of blankets. I fished it out, expecting Aiden with some basketball update. Instead it was Emilia's-Hijacked-Phone.

> **EHP**: Farm guy. Do you got a brother? Me neither. Get your mom to marry my dad then we could be brothers.

I stared at the screen, completely blindsided. Where did this kid come up with these things?

> **Me:** Dude. That's a pretty big request. I'd have to check my farm guy handbook to see if that's allowed.

> **EHP:** Do it FAST. I need a brother to fight the monsters.

Me: What monsters?

EHP: The ones under MY bed. They're scared of big brothers.

Something squeezed in my chest. This four-year-old kid, who showed up in my life out of nowhere, now wanted me as a brother. For monster protection. Obviously.

Me: I'll tell you a secret. Monsters are also scared of farm security. And Bossy Big Sisters.

EHP: Not as good as brothers.

EHP: But okay. Night Farm Guy. No snitching I used Meela's phone!

Me: Night, bud. Your secret's safe.

I set the phone down, still smiling. Miggy's chaotic brain had somehow zeroed in on what I'd been thinking about—family, belonging, what it meant.

I looked back at my laptop, at the competition website still open. Miggy, with his weird questions and monster concerns, had just bulldozed right through all my overthinking.

Maybe that's what I needed. To stop thinking so hard about it all. To just... write. The way Dad apparently used to.

I opened a new document and typed: ABSENCE & PRESENCE - DRAFT 1

Then I stared at the blank page, my fingers hovering over the keys.

"Okay, Dad," I whispered to the empty room, to the photo on my corkboard, to whatever part of him might be listening. "Help me figure out how to say this."

I started typing.

Emilia

I sat at my desk, laptop open to an expanded outline of my immigration essay. Around it, I'd arranged the article Mr. Henderson had given me, my original essay, and three sheets of notes in increasingly messy handwriting.

"If the newspaper publishes this..." I whispered to myself, the possibility both thrilling and terrifying. This wasn't just a school assignment anymore. People in North Riverbend would read it. People who'd known me my whole life. People who might not agree. People who might not want to hear what I had to say.

I tapped my pencil against my teeth, thinking about Tyler's essay. I hadn't read it yet—he'd guarded it like it contained national secrets—but I'd seen the way Mr. Henderson looked at him. The way Tyler's face had changed when he read the comments. There had been something raw there, something real.

"We'd make good writing partners," I said, testing the words Mr. Henderson had told me. And that I hadn't told Tyler.

What would that even look like? Tyler with his jokes and basketball metaphors, me with my research and careful paragraphs? Would we balance each other out, or just drive each other crazy?

I jotted down a note: Add personal perspective section?

That was what had made Tyler's writing so powerful in class discussions—he didn't just talk about issues abstractly. He made them human.

Miggy's giggle erupted from down the hall, followed by Sofia's echo of "Shhhhh!" which was much louder than whatever they were being secretive about.

My phone buzzed.

I stared at the screen, my thoughts screeching to a halt.

> **Tyler:** You need me to come get the monsters under your bed too?

I thumped my head gently against the desk. Of course he did.

> **Me:** What?!

> **Tyler:** No? They only live under Miggy's bed? I can't snitch, because no snitching in farm work. But a little goblin got your phone again

I heard more giggles down the hall.

> **Tyler:** And maybe take it easy on him? He was looking for help with monsters.

> **Me:** What did he say?

Tyler: Asked if I had a brother (nope) and suggested our parents should marry so we could be brothers. For monster protection purposes.

I felt my face flush. Brothers? That would make Tyler and me... I shook the thought away.

Me: Sorry, I don't know what to say. I NEVER know what to say about Miggy.

Tyler: Don't apologize. It was pretty great timing actually. I was having a weird night.

I hesitated, fingers hovering over the keyboard. I could ask what was weird. That would be the normal thing to do. But something about the way he'd said it made me nervous, like I was peeking at something I wasn't supposed to see.

Miggy appeared in my doorway, rubbing his eyes dramatically. "Meela, there's monsters."

"Is that why you stole my phone? To recruit monster fighters?"

His eyes went wide. "No snitching in farm work!"

"He wasn't snitching, just letting me know about the monster situation."

He considered this. "Farm guys are good at monsters. I checked. He has special powers."

"I bet he does," I said, trying not to smile.

"You gotta check under my bed," Miggy insisted. "Farm Guy said farm monsters are scared of bossy big sisters too. Not just brothers."

> **Me:** What was weird about tonight? If you want to talk about it.

Miggy pulled at my arm, and I let him drag me toward the door. "Let me just finish my text."

I hit send before I could overthink it. Then I let Miggy pull me down the hall to check for imaginary monsters, wondering if Tyler would answer or if I'd just crossed some invisible line between us.

I heard my phone buzz while I was making a big show of checking under Miggy's bed and in his closet. When I got back to my room, I found a text.

> **Tyler:** Henderson gave me info on a writing competition. For kids who've lost parents. I was thinking about it when Miggy texted. Weird coincidence.

I stared at the message. Tyler, the guy who turned everything into a joke, was actually thinking about writing about his dad. For real. For strangers.

> **Tyler:** I probably won't do it though.

> **Me:** I think you should.

There was a long pause. Three dots appeared, disappeared, appeared again.

Tyler: What about you and writing that opinion piece for the newspaper?

He was changing the subject. But he'd still told me about the competition. That was something.

Me: Maybe we both have important things to say and maybe we're both braver than we think.

I found myself smiling at my phone like an idiot. He was ridiculous. And sweet. And maybe braver than he knew.

Tyler: Maybe. How's the monster situation?

Me: All clear. Though Miggy says the monsters might come back by morning. He suggests regular patrols.

Tyler: Farm Guy Protocol states monsters need checking every 8 hours.

Me: Apparently I'm on monster patrol now. Thanks for that.

Tyler: Farm Guy special power #36: monster delegation.

Me: I'll add it to my schedule. Goodnight, Tyler.

Tyler: Night, Meela. Sweet monster-free dreams.

I set my phone down and turned back to my essay notes. Somehow, the idea of people reading my words didn't seem quite as terrifying as it had ten minutes ago.

54

Stuff's Not Too Big, Stuff's Not Too Small

Emilia

I found Tyler sitting on the back steps of the barn, staring out at the pasture. The sky was a dull November gray, but the sun was fighting through and it caught in his hair, making the tips glow. He didn't look up when I walked over, but I knew he heard me. I sat beside him without a word.

"Hey," I said.

"Hey." His voice was rough around the edges, like he hadn't used it much that day.

"Dad's looking for the socket wrench set. Says it might be in your truck."

Tyler nodded. "Might be. I'll grab it in a minute."

We sat in silence, the kind that wasn't uncomfortable—but wasn't empty either. Just full of everything, what we knew how to talk about; what we didn't know how to put into words.

"You're worrying about your mom, aren't you?" I asked. He didn't answer right away.

"I always do," he said. "But after I heard what happened at the hotel... it's just harder to think straight."

I reached over, resting my hand lightly on his. "I get that."

He broke a twig between his fingers. "Yeah."

A tractor droned in the distance. Dried leaves rattled on branches. Tyler turned toward me.

"How was school today?"

The question surprised me. It was so...normal.

"It was fine," I said automatically.

He tilted his head to look at me. "Fine, huh?"

I hesitated, then shook my head. "You don't have to do this, Tyler."

"Do what?"

"Ask about my day when your whole life feels all upside down to you."

His voice turned soft. "Em, whatever my world feels like, that doesn't mean I don't care about yours."

I picked at a loose thread on my jeans. "I didn't want to burden you."

He turned fully toward me. "Hey, why do you get to decide what I know, what I can handle? My mom does that Em and not knowing? Not knowing is a bigger burden. Let me decide, please Emmy."

"I just... figured you didn't need more weight to carry."

Tyler exhaled slowly. Brought his hands to my face. "I don't need less of you, Emilia. I need you. The real you. The one who cares too much and overthinks and makes spreadsheets for soil data."

My gaze locked with his, even as I was startled by the determination in his voice.

"Emilia Preston, you're so damn smart but you don't seem to have figured this out."

He leaned closer. "I need more of you."

A bit closer. "Anything of you that you'll give me."

Almost touching. "As much of you..."

His lips met mine. Stayed there gently for a moment. Pulled away. "As much of you as I can have."

He leaned in again, more pressure, longer. More furiously beating hearts. Shift of his hands but no space between us. A new tilt of his head, but no pulling away. No pulling away for a while. He leaned back and my eyes fluttered open, meeting his intense gaze. He smiled.

"Now quick before Miggy comes and takes me out. How was school?"

I hesitated, how romantic, a first kiss followed by a Current Issues paper. But I told him, "I got my paper back from Klein."

Tyler's posture snapped to alert. "The one on regenerative agriculture?"

"He gave me a B-minus."

"What?" His voice was sharp. "That paper was incredible."

"He said I wasn't objective. That I need to tone down my 'passion.'"

Tyler's jaw clenched. "That's garbage."

"Yeah," I said, surprised by the small laugh that escaped. "That's pretty much how I feel."

He looked at me, expression softening. "Why didn't you tell me?"

"I didn't want to pile on."

Tyler shook his head. "Don't shut me out, Em. I need the normal stuff. I need your details, your minutes, your highs, your lows. I need to know your world is there spinning to get me through all the 'What ifs' in mine."

I let that sit for a beat. "Okay." So I told him. About the red marks in the margins. About how Klein questioned citations I'd triple-checked. How he dismissed my sections on indigenous land management. How he used "activist" like an insult.

Tyler didn't interrupt. He listened, brows drawn, jaw tight.

"He's not purposeful which makes it worse." I said. "Somehow he's filtered voices like mine as less credible."

Tyler leaned forward. "So let's make him explain."

I blinked. "Explain?"

"Yeah. Ask why he thinks digital activism is more valid than actual land work. Make him explain it. He might not even have a reason."

I thought about that. About asking. About being heard.

"You sound like my mom," I said with a small smile. "She's always telling me to claim my space."

"She's not wrong," Tyler said. "You're one of the smartest people I know. You shouldn't have to prove that over and over because a teacher hasn't acknowledged a bias issue."

His eyes locked with mine, steady and sure. I reached over, threading my fingers through his. The gesture felt both new and inevitable.

"And Emilia—your voice matters. A lot."

He leaned in again and we stopped talking for a few minutes.

"So, brilliant soil scientist, has anything become clearer to you?"

"Miggy's wrong about kissing being gross?" I said smiling at him.

"Well, fair point. But I meant this," he circled his finger around, indicating the two of us.

"Your stuff isn't too big for me," I said quietly. "And mine's not too small for you. And I'm getting fond of ridiculousness."

He smiled, squeezing my hand. "Hmm, pretty fond of me then, huh? But Fond? Fine. I'll let you use it. But my ridiculousness is kinda crazy about you."

We leaned into each other again, just a moment and pulled back. We sat on the barn steps a couple more minutes. I watched a hawk wheel above the pasture as I tried to steady myself while I opened to the possibilities.

55

Telling the Tiny Voice to Shut It

Emilia

Leaning against Tyler and watching the hawk I battled a tiny voice in my head. A voice that whispered constantly because a teacher was unconsciously filtering my voice and labeling it as unauthoritative, unreliable... unworthy.

The voice whispered maybe even my parents wouldn't see it. That maybe they'd say it wasn't that bad. That maybe they'd tell me to pick my battles. To stay quiet and finish the class. Tyler's hand was still in mine. And somehow, that made the voice easier to ignore.

"Let's go find the socket wrench, then talk to your mom and dad."

"Wait, I..." I trailed off. "What if they think I'm overreacting?"

Tyler gave me a look like I'd just said cows were imaginary. He stood, tugging me up with him, our fingers still laced. "We're going to talk to your parents. Right now."

He was already leading me toward the house.

"Your voice matters, Em, but people can't hear it if you don't use it. Your mom and dad—they won't ever minimize your voice. If anything, your dad's going to incinerate me with his super-farmer-laser gaze, because he's gonna somehow know I just kissed his daughter."

We crossed the yard, and he didn't let go of my hand. Not when we reached the porch. Not even when we stepped into the kitchen. Mom was chopping vegetables. Dad sat at the table, glasses perched on his nose, sorting through a thick folder of paperwork. They both looked up, eyes flicking from our faces to our joined hands.

"Mr. Preston," Tyler said without preamble, "Emilia has something she needs to tell you about her Current Issues class."

Dad raised an eyebrow.

"Robbie," he corrected. "Remember? We talked about this."

Tyler's ears turned pink. "Sorry. Robbie. Force of habit."

From somewhere in the living room, a high-pitched squeal erupted. "FAHN DIE!"

The patter of tiny feet announced Sofía's arrival before she even appeared in the doorway, clutching something in her small fist. Her face lit up when she spotted Tyler, and she barreled toward him at top toddler speed.

"Fahn Die! Got snack!" she declared, holding up what appeared to be a piece of a graham cracker. Without missing a beat, Tyler released my hand to scoop Sofía up with practiced ease.

"Is that for me?" he asked, somehow making it sound like receiving a mangled graham cracker was the highlight of his day.

Sofía nodded solemnly, pressing the cracker into his hand.

"Yep. Foh Fahm Die."

"Thank you, Sofía," Tyler said, carefully taking a bite. "Delicious."

She beamed at him, then frowned at me with an accusatory look. Did she know Tyler had just given me my first kiss behind the barn?

"My Fahn Die," she stated, as if reminding me of an established fact. Mom chuckled from the counter.

"Sofía, mi amor, I think you're going to have to share with your sister."

Mom gave me an amused mom side-eye and I felt my face heat. Sofía considered this, gave a gave a disgusted 'hmmph,' and laid her head on Tyler's shoulder. Tyler settled Sofía more comfortably on his hip and turned his attention back to Dad. His free hand found mine again, so naturally that I wondered if he even realized he was doing it.

"Robbie," he started again, "Emilia got her paper back from Mr. Klein today. The one about regenerative agriculture."

Dad set down his papers, giving me his full attention. "The one that was based on all the grant research and our grant application? How'd it turn out, Meela-Mi?"

I took a deep breath, glancing at Tyler. He nodded encouragingly, his grip on my hand tightening.

"He gave me a B-minus," I said, the words coming easier than I expected.

Dad frowned. "The paper you worked on for three weeks? The one with all those academic citations?"

"Yeah," I said, feeling a surge of validation that he remembered. "He said my 'tone was unnecessarily passionate' and that I need to be more 'objective' in academic writing."

Mom set down her knife and wiped her hands on a towel. "Okay, Emilia. I think you need to sit down and tell us the whole story. From the beginning."

Dad nodded, pushing his paperwork aside to clear space at the table. "Come on, sit. Both of you."

Tyler looked uncertain for a moment, like he wasn't sure if he was included in the invitation. Sofía solved his dilemma by tugging on his shirt and demanding, "Fahm Die, sit, sit wit me," while pointing to the chair next to her booster seat.

"Yes, ma'am," Tyler said, setting her down in her seat before taking the chair beside her.

I sat across from him, next to Dad, feeling a mixture of relief and nervousness. Mom joined us, setting down a pitcher of water and glasses.

"Now," Dad said, leaning forward, his tone serious but supportive, "tell us exactly what's been happening in that class."

So I did. I told them about how Klein had dismissed my comments about rotational grazing. How he'd praised digital activism as a "systems-level solution" while describing actual land management practices as mere "local land-use angles." How he'd circled entire sections of my paper and questioned my sources, even though I'd cited everything properly.

Dad's expression grew increasingly troubled as I spoke. Mom's eyes flashed with that protective fire I'd seen all my life when someone underestimated a loved one.

"This isn't right," Dad said when I finished. "Your research was more than credible. Good enough to use for a grant application. An application that's going to be seriously considered with a lot of competition."

"And the connection you made to indigenous land management practices was particularly strong," Mom added. "That's the kind of historical perspective that's missing from most environmental discussions."

I felt a warm glow of validation hearing them understand what I'd been trying to do.

"You're absolutely coming with me to that meeting on Thursday," Dad said firmly. "We're going to make Mr. Klein explain his grading criteria in detail."

"And if necessary," Mom added, a steely glint in her eye, "we can discuss taking this to the administration.

I blinked, surprised by how seriously they were taking this. "You really think it's that important?"

"Meela-Mi," Dad said gently, "this is about more than a grade. This is about your voice being heard. About perspectives that need to be part of the conversation."

"Exactly, "Mom agreed. "The world doesn't need more papers that say the same things in the same ways. It needs voices like yours that bring different experiences to the table."

I glanced across at Tyler, who was watching me with that same quiet pride I'd seen earlier. Sofía had climbed into his lap and was contentedly breaking the remains of the graham cracker into increasingly smaller pieces on the table, but he didn't seem to mind.

"Thank you," I said softly, looking around at my family—and at Tyler, who somehow seemed to belong there among them.

"Em, don't thank us for doing what we gladly do as your parents," Dad said.

Mom reached over to squeeze my hand. "And you, Tyler," she said, "thank you for making sure Emilia brought this to us."

Tyler looked embarrassed but pleased. "I just told her what I already knew—that her voice matters."

"It does," Dad agreed. "And so does yours."

Sofía chose that moment to look up from her graham cracker destruction.

"Fahm Die, eats suppah?" she asked hopefully.

Mom laughed. "He's always welcome, if he wants to stay."

Tyler met my eyes across the table, a smile playing at the corners of his mouth. "I can't disappoint my biggest fan," he said.

I'm sure my face told him Sofía wasn't his biggest fan here on the farm.

56

A Couple Conference Concessions

Emilia

Thursday evening arrived too quickly. As Dad and I pulled into the school parking lot, I felt a knot forming in my stomach. I'd been preparing my arguments all week, practicing what I wanted to say to Mr. Klein, but now that we were here, doubt began to creep in.

"You okay, Meela-Mi?" Dad asked, turning off the engine.

I nodded, then shook my head.

"What if he dismisses me again? What if he makes me sound like I'm just being sensitive?"

Dad's expression softened. "Then I'll be there to back you up." He checked his watch. "We're a bit early. Want to run through what you want to say one more time?"

I took a deep breath. "I want to ask him why regenerative agriculture isn't considered a systems-level solution when it literally transforms entire ecosystems. I want to know why he values digital activism over actual land stewardship. And I want him to explain his grading criteria—why passion is apparently a bad thing when it comes to academic writing."

Dad nodded approvingly. "Good. Remember, you're not asking for special treatment. You're asking for fair recognition of your work and your perspective."

"Right." I fiddled with the strap of my bag. "I just wish Mom was here too."

Dad chuckled. "Your mother would be a little too passionate for Mr. Klein's taste, I think. And the chaos twins need extra wrangling tonight."

Just as he said that my phone chimed with a text. It was from Mom a photo attached: Miggy in his pajamas, wearing what appeared to be a colander on his head and holding a wooden spoon like a scepter. The caption read: "The King of Bedtime has declared that sleep is canceled. Send reinforcements."

I snorted, showing the phone to Dad. "This is why Mom can't have nice things."

We walked into the school, the hallways eerily quiet compared to their usual daytime chaos. A few other parents milled about, checking classroom numbers and consulting schedules. The fluorescent lights hummed overhead, casting strange shadows in the empty spaces.

"Room 203," Dad murmured, checking the conference schedule. "That's upstairs, right?"

I nodded, leading the way to the stairwell. With each step, I felt my resolve strengthening. I had nothing to be ashamed of. My work was solid. My perspective mattered.

Mr. Klein was just finishing up with another family when we arrived. He looked up, spotting us through the classroom door's window, and gave a polite nod. I tried to read his expression, wondering if he already knew what we wanted to discuss, but his face remained professionally neutral.

Mr. Klein appeared in the doorway. "Mr. Preston," he said, extending his hand to Dad. "And Emilia. Please come in."

Dad shook his hand firmly. "Robbie, please."

"Robbie," Mr. Klein corrected himself, gesturing toward the two chairs set up in front of his desk. "Have a seat."

The classroom looked different in the evening light—emptier, almost abandoned. Student projects lined the walls, and the whiteboard still held faint traces of today's lessons. Mr. Klein settled behind his desk, pulling out a folder with my name on it.

"I assume we're here to discuss Emilia's progress in Current Issues?" he asked, flipping through some papers.

"Among other things," Dad said, his voice calm but firm.

Mr. Klein's eyebrows rose slightly. "Oh?"

I took a deep breath, knowing this was my moment. "Mr. Klein, I wanted to discuss my most recent papers. Specifically, your comments about my tone being 'unnecessarily passionate' and lacking objectivity."

To his credit, Mr. Klein didn't dismiss me outright. He nodded, pulling out my regenerative agriculture paper. "Yes, I remember this assignment. You certainly put a lot of work into it."

"I did," I agreed. "I used peer-reviewed sources, included case studies from multiple continents, and directly connected the practices to both historical indigenous methods and current climate science. So I'm struggling to understand why it only received a B-minus."

Mr. Klein leaned back. "Emilia, your research was thorough, yes. But academic writing requires a certain detachment. Your paper read more like advocacy than analysis."

"And why is that a problem?" Dad asked, his voice still even. "If her research is sound and her arguments are well-supported, what does it matter if she also cares about the topic?"

Mr. Klein shifted in his seat. "It's about maintaining scholarly distance. About presenting multiple perspectives with equal weight."

"I did present multiple perspectives," I countered. "I discussed conventional agriculture, organic methods, and mixed approaches. I just concluded, based on the evidence, that regenerative practices offer the most comprehensive solution."

"Yes, but—"

"And in class," I continued, finding my rhythm now, "when I bring up practical land management techniques, you tend to dismiss them as merely 'local land-use angles.' But when other students talk about digital campaigns or corporate sustainability initiatives, you call those 'systems-level solutions.' I'd like to understand why."

Mr. Klein's expression tightened up minimally. "That's not entirely accurate, Emilia."

"It is accurate," Dad said quietly. "I've seen both papers. I've heard about the class discussions. And I'm curious about your criteria as well."

Mr. Klein took a moment, seeming to gather his thoughts. "Look, I appreciate students who are passionate about environmental issues. But true academic discourse requires us to consider market realities, policy frameworks, and global-scale approaches. Small-scale agricultural practices, while valuable, simply don't address the systemic nature of climate change."

I felt a flare of frustration but kept my voice steady. "Regenerative agriculture isn't small-scale, though. When implemented across regions, it transforms entire ecosystems, sequesters carbon, restores watersheds, and improves biodiversity. How is that not systemic?"

"And," Dad added, "the paper specifically addressed policy frameworks that could incentivize wider adoption. It wasn't just about what works on our farm."

Mr. Klein frowned, glancing between us. "I may have... underestimated the scope of your argument, Emilia. But the tone issue remains. Academic writing should be—"

"Objective?" I finished for him. "Mr. Klein, with all due respect, every academic makes choices about what to study, what to emphasize, what to consider important. Those choices reflect values. Pretending otherwise doesn't make writing more objective—it just hides the values behind the work."

A silence fell and I could feel Dad's pride radiating beside me, but I kept my focus on Mr. Klein, waiting for his response.

He sighed. "You make a fair point, Emilia. Perhaps I've been applying a somewhat... narrow view of academic discourse." He paused. "I'm willing to reconsider my evaluation of your paper. And to be more mindful of how I respond to different perspectives in class discussions."

I blinked, surprised by the concession. "Thank you."

"Don't thank me yet," he said with a wry smile. "I'm not promising an A. Just a fresh read with your concerns in mind."

"That's all we're asking for," Dad said. "A fair evaluation based on the quality of her work and thinking, not on stylistic preferences."

Mr. Klein nodded, making a note in his folder. "Was there anything else we needed to discuss? Emilia's overall performance in the class is quite strong."

Dad glanced at me, silently checking if I had more to say.

I shook my head. I'd made my point, and surprisingly, it seemed Mr. Klein had actually heard me. Pushing further wouldn't help.

"I think we've covered the main concerns," Dad said, standing. "Thank you for your time."

Mr. Klein stood as well, offering his hand again. "Thank you for bringing this to my attention. I appreciate students who can advocate for themselves—particularly when they do it as articulately as Emilia just did."

As we walked out of the classroom, I felt a strange mix of accomplishment and disbelief. Had that actually worked? Had I actually changed Mr. Klein's mind?

"You did good in there, Meela-Mi," Dad said as we headed back to the truck. "Really good."

"You think he meant it? About reconsidering?"

Dad nodded. "I do. He's not a bad teacher. Sometimes people just need someone to point out their blind spots."

I smiled, a weight lifting from my shoulders. "Thanks for backing me up."

"That's what dads are for," he said, slinging an arm around my shoulders. "Now let's go home and rescue your mother from King Miggy before he declares bedtime illegal forever."

My phone buzzed with a text.

Tyler: How'd it go with Klein?

Me: He seemed to actually listen. And he's going to look at the grade on my last paper.

Tyler: Of course he listened. You're Emilia Preston. Even Klein's not immune to your powers of persuasion.

57

The Truth About Teens & Spreadsheets

Emilia

Klein again. He'd returned a Current Issues reflection assignment with feedback that fueled the tiny voice in my mind. I'd completed thorough research on major food corporations sustainability issues. A sustainable label could mean big business. I concluded that food corporations were misrepresenting their sustainability initiatives. Klein returned an assignment marked as "too critical" and "lacking nuance."

Meanwhile, I saw that Jason's praise of corporate recycling programs had earned enthusiastic margin notes.

I stared at the paper, a familiar mix of frustration and self-doubt churning in my stomach. Yes, he'd regraded my last paper from B- to B. It didn't seem he was taking my voice with any greater degree of seriousness.

I trudged out of class and spotted Tyler leaning against the opposite wall. Waiting for me? That simple thought boosted me.

He straightened when he saw me, his expression shifting from casual to concerned as he read my face.

"That bad, huh?" he asked.

I nodded, not trusting my voice just yet. He didn't push for words, just pulled me into a warm hug. Then he threaded his fingers with mine with a casual ease that warmed my soul.

"Let's get lunch," he said simply.

I froze for half a second, aware of what everyone would see. Tyler holding my hand in school. In the middle of a crowded hallway. Walking into the cafeteria. When I didn't move, he squeezed my hand. "Is this okay?"

I nodded, finding my voice. "Yeah. Just... a surprise for second there."

A small smile played at the corner of his mouth. "Good surprise?"

"Very good surprise," I said, the frustration from class already beginning to fade.

We walked toward the cafeteria, hand in hand. I could feel eyes on us as we moved through the halls, could hear the whispers and see the small smiles. But Tyler seemed completely unfazed, chatting about a math test and Miggy's latest hijacked phone text. By the time we reached the cafeteria, I'd almost forgotten we were holding hands—until we approached our usual table and Jenna's eyes widened comically.

"Well, well, well," she said, a slow grin spreading across her face. "What do we have here?"

Aria looked up from her phone, immediately spotting our joined hands. "I was starting to think we'd graduate before you two figured it out."

I felt heat crawl up my neck as I slipped into my seat. Tyler sat beside me, not letting go of my hand even as he set his tray down.

"Figured what out?" he asked, all innocence. Drew snorted from across the table. "Tyler's playing dumb because it wouldn't work from Emilia. We've only been watching this since when? Summer?"

"Since third grade" Nate corrected, not looking up from his lunch.

Aiden slid in next to Ivy, grinning ear to ear. "Told you guys it would happen after tryouts. Pay up."

"Wait," I said, "you were betting on us?"

"Of course we were," Ivy said, looking far too pleased with herself.

I turned to Tyler, expecting to find him as mortified as I felt. But he was smiling—a small, private smile that made something warm unfurl in my chest.

"So how'd Current Issues go?" Drew asked, mercifully changing the subject. He must have seen something in my expression because he added, "That bad?"

I sighed, reluctantly pulling my hand from Tyler's to dig out the paper. "See for yourself."

Drew scanned the comments, his expression darkening. "This is ridiculous. Your argument is solid. All your sources are cited properly."

"What did Klein say this time?" Ivy asked, leaning forward.

"That I'm 'too critical' and 'lacking nuance,'" I replied, making air quotes.

"Meanwhile, Jason gets praised for regurgitating corporate press releases," Drew added, sliding the paper back to me.

"That's such garbage," Aiden said, surprising me with his vehemence.

"Thanks," I said, genuinely touched by their support. "Dad and I talked to him at Parent-Teacher conferences."

"And?" Aria asked.

"He listened," I said. "Changed one grade from B- to B. Obviously his thinking hasn't changed."

I hesitated. "I didn't tell my mom and dad everything."

Everyone looked at me.

"I mean... I showed him the paper. But I didn't mention the spreadsheet."

"The documentation," Drew added. "We've been tracking this for months."

"Drew, Nate, Jenna and I have a whole folder," I said. "Participation data. Written comments. Even the tone shifts."

"We built it together," Drew said. "I just didn't think we'd end up needing it this badly."

"Why didn't you show your dad?" Ivy asked.

"Because I didn't want it to feel like a takedown," I said. "This isn't about canceling Klein. It's about getting him to see the pattern."

"Then show your dad the pattern," Tyler said quietly. "He'll know how to handle it."

The conversation shifted then, moving on to weekend plans and upcoming games. But I noticed Tyler had gone quiet, staring down at his lunch with a distant expression I recognized all too well.

"Hey. You okay?"

A beat of silence. I nudged him with my elbow.

"Hey, apparently Sofía drew this yesterday and made my mom write captions. Sofía made me bring it. She was blocking the door so I couldn't bypass her this morning."

I pulled out the folded picture of a big Farm Guy and kid sized Sofía and a Meela fading into the background. Tyler unfolded it then laughed. Aiden leaned over.

"Ha, I told you the Preston farm women had a thing for Tyler."

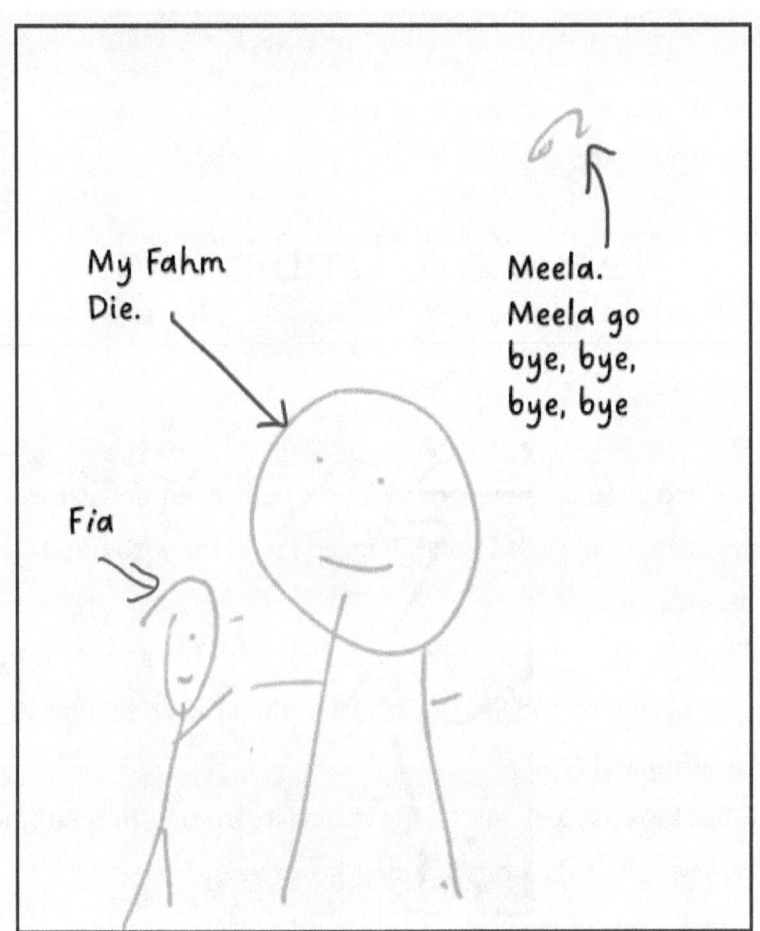

385

58

Trifecta & Truths Told

Tyler

We had a grueling week of practices before our first game. Thursday of that week, Aiden dragged me home with him for "bro-bonding time."

I knew Emilia was hanging next door with Ivy, and it took all I had to head into Aiden's house rather than turning on my heel and heading to Ivy's.

"You look like a missile trying to deviate from its programmed trajectory. Get in the house, dude," groused Aiden.

Guess I wasn't as subtle as I thought I was.

"We'll get the girls to come over later," he added. "I haven't been up close and personal with this super sappy side of you. You just perked up like a wittle, sad-eyed puppy when I said that. Need some Emilia scratching behind your ears?"

"Shut up," I said before elbowing him out of my way.

"I expected to hear screaming babies from two blocks away. Where are those future WNBA stars?" I asked as I stepped into the kitchen.

Aiden smirked. "Mom and Dad took them to visit Mom's folks. Grandpa and Grandma are older than Dad's parents—Mom's trying to get over to Bismarck more often. And after this week, I'm glad for the quiet. Practices have been killer."

I pulled a bottle of root beer from the fridge and collapsed into one of the chairs.

"This is weird. Usually I show up and someone's crying and I smell a poopy diaper."

Aiden pulled a container out of the fridge. Spaghetti and meat sauce. He split the contents between two large dinner plates. He covered each plate with a paper towel and heated the food one at time in the microwave.

He put each plate on the table as it reached the right temp for eating. He slid one plate in front of me and pulled other in front of himself. He took a couple good-sized bites, chewed, swallowed then looked at me. He sighted then pointed his fork at me.

"What's been going on the past few months, feels like you've been dealing with something big."

I shrugged.

"It's like you're learning a foreign language," I said. "Didn't you used to just say 'Sup, bro?'"

Aiden sighed and rubbed a hand down his face. "Yeah, and I used to be stupidly oblivious. Which version of me do you want?"

"Harder to joke away Aiden 2.0 but I'm sure it's a needed upgrade." I said. Fixing things with Ivy, helping take care of baby twin sisters—he was different lately. Still Aiden, but not just speaking to pass things off. Quicker to notice signs he would have missed before.

Here we were coming home from practicing his beloved sport, and instead of dissecting plays, he wanted to dissect me. Dissect was maybe a little harsh. But I was so used to barely going under the surface with him that this felt strange. Let's say he wanted to check-in. Still, a new experience.

"Look, Ty, you've deserved me being a better friend for a couple years now," Aiden said. "But I was just sticking to the easy route. I don't want to be that way anymore with someone I consider my best friend. But I'm not gonna push either."

He twirled a bite of spaghetti. "And honestly? I won't even have to worry about finding out what's going on between you and Emilia. I'm sure the girls are giggling and talking about us right now. I'll get it out of Ivy later."

I smirked. "You know, I heard you giggling with Ivy that night after the Harvest Fest, dude."

Aiden choked on his drink. "Shut up, you—" He paused, face shifting like something clicked. "Oh."

"Yeah. That's what I thought. Yeah, oh? So I guess some things are just giggle-inducing with Ivy, huh?"

Aiden shook his head and took a giant bite of spaghetti. He pointed to his full mouth like, Sorry, can't talk about it.

I let it sit for a second before I said, "I've been worrying a lot about my mom. Trying to seem like everything's fine. Keeping up at work. Calling her family back home. I hear her sometimes, apologizing for not being able to come. For not being enough."

I stared at my plate. "And I can't fix it."

Aiden didn't jump in. Didn't shift the conversation. Just waited.

"She hasn't been able to visit her family in Mexico, right?" he asked. "You mentioned that before."

"Yeah." I paused. "It's more complicated than just not visiting."

I took a breath. "She and my dad had planned on getting married. But he was killed before they could. So... she's been undocumented the whole time we've lived here."

Aiden froze, then set his fork down.

"She never told anyone," I said. "Not even Grams and Gramps at first. She just kept her head down. Worked. Took care of me. She wanted me to grow up here. Have the advantages of being a U.S. citizen."

I rubbed the side of my jaw. "It's always been risky. But now, with how things are—headlines, politicians, the way people talk—it's an especially bad time to be undocumented. People get whisked away..."

He nodded slowly, like he wasn't sure what to say.

"She finally applied for something called a U visa," I continued. "It's for people who've been victims of certain crimes—or who reported one and helped the police. That's what makes someone eligible."

"She saw something happen at work. Stepped in. Reported it. Gave a statement to the police. She didn't do it for the visa. She did it because someone needed help. And now...there's a shot."

Aiden's voice was quiet. "That takes guts, man."

"She's applying now," I said. "It could take over a year. Nothing's guaranteed. But if it gets approved, she could get deferred action while it's pending. A work permit. Maybe even permanent residency someday."

I looked up. "It's the first time I've seen her want something for herself. Not just survive."

Aiden nodded again, slower this time. "She's brave as hell."

"Yeah," I said, voice low. "She is."

He watched me for a second. "So you're worrying about your mom along with just being a high schooler and trying to pass history and not miss free throws. And maybe hoping Mr. Preston won't run you over with a combine for—"

I half-laughed. "Shut up. Besides, it's Miggy I'm really afraid of."

Aiden leaned back. "Well. For the record, I'm glad you told me. And I'm scared of Miggy too. If you need something and I can help, you know that I've got your back."

He picked up his phone. "Ivy just texted. The girls will be over in about forty-five minutes. Sit your butt down and eat—we've got another day of practice and a game coming up. Your face lit up like you're a bottle rocket. I'm pretty sure you're at the giggling stage too."

The girls showed up armed with a dessert trifecta: Pepperkaker cookies, Seven-layer Bars, and a gallon bag of Puppy Chow.

Aiden nudged Ivy as she handed off the bags.

"Give Tyler the puppy chow—he gave your house big puppy dog eyes when we got here. But now Emilia's here and can scratch behind his ears, he'll be in full puppy heaven."

I groaned. "I hate you."

"Tail's basically wagging," Aiden said, already digging into the bars.

Ivy flopped onto the couch. Emilia sat down next to me, legs tucked under her. We picked a movie—something that didn't require thinking—and turned off the lights. Somewhere during the third ridiculous plot twist, Emilia leaned into my shoulder. Her head eventually drifted against me. Ivy was curled up against Aiden in the other chair, both of them quiet.

I shifted just enough to murmur, "Told Aiden. About my mom. Not everything. But the U visa. What she's been through."

Emilia looked up at me, then nodded. No need to say more. I rested my cheek against the top of her head.

By the end of the movie, both girls were asleep. And I didn't mind staying right where I was.

59

More Than Skinned Knees

Emilia

I found Dad in the barn, wiping down tools that were already clean. He did that when he needed to think—quiet repetition in a quiet space. A kind of Norwegian meditation passed down through generations. I used to think it meant he didn't want to talk. Now I knew better. It meant he was listening before I even opened my mouth.

"Hey," I said from the doorway, holding my folder of notes and the latest paper like a shield.

He looked up, expression calm and steady. "Everything okay?"

"Not exactly." I stepped inside. "Can I run something by you?'

"This was returned after Parent-Teacher conferences." I handed him my work on corporate green washing of their environmental practices.

"Also, I didn't say anything about this before. But... Drew and Jenna are in class with me. Drew noticed this early in the school year. It happened again. So, we've been tracking it. Margin comments, scores, who gets called on. There's a pattern."

Dad's eyes moved to mine. Not skeptical. Just waiting.

"We made a spreadsheet," I added. "Started out to see if we were imagining it. But we're not. The same points get different reactions depending on who says them. Especially when it's me."

Still quiet. But not the bad kind.

"I didn't show you before because I didn't want it to feel like a takedown," I admitted. "I hoped talking to him would be enough. But I'm tired of it. want to be heard. I want him to see it. And I wanted you to see it too."

He reached out, he took the folder and flipped through the printed charts and notes.

"Who else is part of this?" he asked.

"Drew started it with me. Nate helped design the layout. Jenna's been tracking her own comments and a few others'. Aria's seen it happen too, even in other classes. We've talked to Sarah and Lucia—quietly."

Dad set the folder down on the workbench beside him. "You said the same thing he did. Almost word for word."

He tapped the comment from Klein—'Let's not overstate local impact'—and then looked at my phrasing on the second page. "You used 'scale of effect' and 'community-led initiatives.' Drew said something about regenerative systems. Same core idea."

"Right," I said. "And his was 'visionary' and mine was 'too critical.'"

Dad exhaled slowly, folding the rag in his hands. "You were right not to ambush him with this. But you're also right to bring it forward."

"I'm not trying to get him in trouble, I..." I said. "I just want it to stop."

He was quiet for a long beat. "I could've done this myself," he said. "Without realizing it. That's the thing about bias—you don't see it until someone shows you."

That was when I felt the sting behind my eyes.

"I thought maybe it didn't matter. That I was just imagining it."

He looked at me, steady and certain. "It matters."

I nodded. "I just want to be taken seriously."

"You are," he said. "And you will be."

I tried to blink away the tears, but there were too many to stop, and they streamed down my cheeks.

Dad pulled me into a tight hug. Maybe his words didn't come as quickly as others' did, but his hugs said everything I needed to hear all at once.

"Papí."

"You haven't called me that since you were five and had constantly skinned knees."

"This hurts more."

"My Meela-Mi. So strong, you are so strong, but you shouldn't have to fight to be heard in a classroom. You want to talk to your mom about this too?" he asked.

"Yeah," I said. "I should. I need a tissue."

"Don't tell Miggy I did this. He'll never use a tissue again," Dad said as he used his T-shirt to clean my face.

When we stepped back into the house, Dad kissed the top of my head and set all the papers on the table.

"Mari, take a look at this please. I'll be right back." He kissed her on the cheek and went to get a clean shirt.

Mamá was at the counter slicing plantains. She stopped and turned around. "Oh, mi amor, I knew something was bothering you. Come here."

I crossed the kitchen, and she took my face in both hands, like she had when I was five and had tried to explain a nightmare I'd just had.

"Mi amor," she said. "You never need to carry things by yourself."

"I didn't," I said, voice tight. "Not really. My friends have been part of this, but I didn't want to make it a big thing. Or make you worry."

"I always worry," she said gently. "That's a mother's job. But you don't protect me by hiding your pain."

Dad rejoined us at the table. He tapped the folder. "It's solid. And it's fair."

Mamá flipped through the notes, growing more still with each page. "You didn't just document," she said. "You gave him room to grow."

"That's what I want," I said. "For him to actually think about what he's doing. For things to be better."

She looked up at me. "So what's next?"

I hesitated. "I thought maybe I'd talk to him directly. Just... show him quietly."

Dad met my eyes across the table. "You could. But I think this is where we step in."

I blinked. "You?"

"You've done the work," he said. "Now let us do ours. A student bringing this forward is brave. But it's not always safe. A parent can approach from a different position."

Mamá nodded. "We'll be careful. But firm. This doesn't go away. Not now."

"You're not mad I didn't tell you sooner?" I asked.

"Mad?" she said. "Emilia, I'm proud. So proud. You trusted your voice. You listened to others. And you gave him the benefit of the doubt when you didn't have to."

"We'll talk to the administration," Dad added. "Be clear and calm. They'll listen."

I sat back in my chair, a quiet wave of something settling through me. Not relief. But something close.

"They'll listen," I repeated.

Mamá reached for my hand. "Because you made it impossible not to."

Later that week I sent a text out to the crew involved with the Klein stuff.

> **Me:** My mom and dad have a meeting at the school the beginning of next week. They wanted to make sure you all knew and if you wanted your parents looped in.

60

Climate Change: Discuss

Emilia

It wasn't even five minutes into lunch when Drew dropped his tray onto the table and said, "Okay, so... did anyone else notice Klein's apology-lite speech this morning?"

Jenna nodded, already unwrapping her sandwich. "You mean the part where he said he was 'reconsidering how classroom dynamics shape learning outcomes'? Yeah. Subtle as a brick."

Nate looked up from his pasta salad. "For him, that's basically skywriting."

"Wait," Tyler said, eyes darting between us. "He actually said something?"

"He didn't name names," I said, opening my juice box. "But he started class by saying he'd been thinking about fairness and feedback. And then—" I pointed my straw at Drew, "—he let you talk for five whole minutes before cutting you off."

Drew grinned. "A personal best."

"He even circled back to something I said," Jenna added. "Didn't even rephrase it or hand it off to Trevor like usual."

"It doesn't mean everything's fixed," I said, quieter now. "But maybe it means he heard us. Or at least my parents."

A beat passed. Then Ivy leaned in. "You okay with how it turned out?"

I thought about it for a second. The folder. The talk with my dad. The spreadsheet we'd built together in secret that had somehow cracked open something bigger.

"Yeah," I said. "I think I am."

"Not bad for a bunch of teenagers and a Google Sheet," Aria said, raising her fork in salute.

"To excel sheets and social justice," Drew added, tapping his water bottle against mine.

I laughed. "We should probably retire the spreadsheet now."

Nate shook his head. "No way. I already started color-coding Mr. Tennyson's pop quiz questions by emotional instability."

We all groaned.

"Of course you did," Jenna muttered.

"Don't worry," he said. "This one's just for fun."

Tyler bumped his shoulder against mine.

"Still proud of you," he said quietly. I smiled.

"I didn't do it alone."

"No," he agreed. "But you did it loud enough to be heard and quiet enough to allow change."

61

Miggy's Public Service Announcement

Tyler

I was riding high from a couple weeks of Emilia Preston's hand in the hallway. It had felt normal. Comfortable. Kind of like breathing, if breathing made your stomach twist into fireworks.

Also, I was pretty sure I needed to talk to Robbie about how I really liked his daughter. Especially since we'd stolen a few kisses from each other as well. So, you know. Nausea and butterflies, sharing a ride.

Then at lunch my phone buzzed. It said Robert Preston but yeah, pretty sure it was the phone high jacker in action again. Miggy the Menace. Not Robbie. Not a reprieve either.

I sighed and answered.

"Miguel, hey! What's up, buddy?"

"Farm Guy, put me on speaker phone." I glanced at Emilia. He wants speaker, I mouthed. She raised an eyebrow but shrugged like, Your funeral.

I hit the button. "Alright, you're on."

"Is Meela there?"

She sighed. "I'm here, Miggy."

There was a long pause. The kind where you could hear the tiny inhale of four-year-old justice about to be dispensed. Then, in a voice as grave and official as a judge, "Farm Guy. Don't kiss Meela. Kissing is disgusting."

The table froze then cracked apart into laughter. Emilia groaned and dropped her face into her hands. I had no clue what to do with my face. I think I blinked. Twice.

Miguel was oblivious to his destruction as usual,

"Okay, bye!" Click. He hung up. Just like that. The moment hovered.

I stared down at my phone. Then over at Emilia, who had slid down in her chair.

Ivy chimed in "My little cousin is epic! And scary!"

"Well," I said, trying not to laugh, "that happened."

62

Robbie, Mr. Preston, Sir

Tyler

The barn smelled like hay, motor oil, and sawdust—familiar but not comforting today. He was already there, wiping down tools that didn't need wiping, like always. Emilia said that was how he thought.

"Hey," I said, stopping just inside the door. "I—uh—she said I could come by."

He looked up and gave the smallest nod. "Good timing."

I stepped closer, then stopped myself and shifted back again. Cool. Very smooth. He gestured toward the stool near the workbench. "You're not in trouble."

That helped. A little.

I sat down. "Thanks. I just... wanted to say thank you. For helping Emilia. With the Klein stuff."

"She did the heavy lifting," he said. "We just helped it land."

I nodded. "She's... yeah. She's kind of amazing like that."

He looked at me, waiting. Not impatient—just quiet. The kind of quiet that made you want to say the right thing.

"I've been trying to figure out if I should call you Robbie," I said. "Because that's what you've told me to do, but honestly it feels wrong when I'm about to tell you how much I like your daughter."

The edge of his mouth twitched. "Fair enough."

"So... sir? Mr. Preston? Robbie when we're talking about tractors?"

"Dealer's choice," he said, still calm. "I'm listening either way."

I took a breath. "I care about her. A lot. And I know you probably already knew that. But I wanted to say it anyway. Straight out."

He nodded once. "I appreciate that."

"I'd never—" I shifted, then looked right at him. "I'd never do anything to hurt her. I swear."

Another pause. Not cold—just thoughtful. "I don't think you would," he said. "And Emilia's a good judge of people."

That landed harder than I expected. In a good way.

"She makes me better," I said quietly. "Miggy would say it's because she's bossy, but it's just... because she's her."

"She does that to people. Like her mom."

I almost smiled. "Yeah."

I let out a breath and sat back on the stool. The barn creaked a little as the wind picked up outside. For once, I didn't feel like I needed to fill the silence.

"Tyler," he said, voice quieter now. "You've carried a lot. If you ever need backup, you've got it here. Don't wait until it's too heavy. And you're good for her too."

My throat tightened. I nodded. "Thank you," I said. "Really."

63

The Best Loss Ever

Emilia

The North Riverbend High gym buzzed with pre-game energy—sneakers squeaking, and fleece-clad fans streaming into the bleachers. I sat between Mom and Tía Luz. Sofía nestled on Luz's lap playing with a mini pom-pom Miggy had insisted she needed.

It was the first game Luz had ever felt confident enough to attend. Filing the U Visa paperwork meant less hiding, the system would be aware of her anyway. Now, for the first time ever she had come to watch Tyler's game in person.

Miggy was in front of me moving between sitting and standing on the bleacher. He was commenting the pregame action almost like a seasoned sportscaster—if that announcer also talked about chicken jetpacks.

"Think he saw you?" I asked.

"He knows where I'm sitting," she said, smoothing her bright royal blue cardigan. Sofía looked up at her.

"Lub you, Tia," she said solemnly, placing her tiny hand over Luz's. Luz's face glowed and she kissed the top Sofí's head, eyes shining.

"I love you too, Mija."

The cheerleaders went into a formation. Yep, there was Jenna tunneling her heart out. The lights dimmed. Ivy was sitting with Maddie a couple rows down.

"There he is," Luz said as Tyler ran out with the team in their purple, gold, and white uniforms. His number this season 23. We watched the team run through their warmup drills. He wasn't a starter—none of the ninth graders were—but he was in the varsity rotation.

Quick on his feet, locked in, he was becoming a ball thief on the court. Coach had him running as defensive guard, hounding their ballhandlers and sneaking in for steals.

"Number twenty-three, Tyler Alred!"

Our section erupted—Gramps and Gramma Alred a few rows behind, Dad sitting with them. I heard his get-your-attention-anywhere on the farm whistle. Miggy stood on the bench and bellowed, "LET'S GO FARM GUY! DUNK ON THEIR HEADS!"

The student section rumbled with laughs.

Then Sofía shouted loudly, "Dats my Fahm Die!" I saw Tyler's shoulders shaking with laughter and Aiden elbowing him in the ribs. Luz glowed with love.

The game tipped off. Westridge played big, but North Riverbend played smart. Aiden sank an early three. Drew muscled through for rebounds. Nate was at shooting guard, practically living on the baseline. He worked out the Westridge offense like simple math—1 + 2 = 3. Tyler subbed in late in the first and immediately snagged a steal. Miggy screamed like it was March Madness.

"He's fast tonight," Mom said.

"He's playing for Tia Luz," I murmured.

Luz didn't respond, just kept watching. She clapped when the bench got hyped. She grinned when Tyler got fouled in the lane and made his free throws. By halftime, Westridge led by five. But the whole gym was locked in. The ninth-grade crew kept grinding. Tyler came back in during the third and sunk a mid-range shot. On defense, he fought through screens like his life depended on it.

Miggy stood up again. "Go BASKETBALL ARMY!"

Westridge pulled away by the end, winning 59–54. But no one in our group looked disappointed. Tyler scanned the crowd. When he spotted us, he raised one hand, searching for Luz. She stood without hesitation and clapped loud and proud, the smile on her face radiant.

"So proud of you, mijo," she whispered. After the postgame huddle, Tyler jogged over, still glowing with exertion.

"You were amazing," Luz said, hugging him tight despite the sweat.

He hugged her back hard. "Best I've played all year."

"Best I've seen," she said, smoothing his hair.

"PIZZA for the BASKETBALL ARMY!" Miggy shouted.

Sofía tugged on Tyler's hand. "Fahm Die, Pee-Yew!"

Miggy cackled "Sofí said you stink Farm Guy!" Mom shushed both of them.

Luz smiled. "Go shower Mijo."

Tyler glanced at his people then back at the scoreboard.

"Best loss I've ever had."

64

Make the Best Worst Choice

Tyler

Lights swept over the front porch as we pulled in. When I stepped out, the gravel crunched under my sneakers. For a second, everything looked exactly like always—the porch light glowing, ivy trailing over the railings, someone moving in the kitchen window.

But something felt... off. No squeal of "Fahm Die!" from Sofía. No Miggy charging toward the car pretending to be a superhero or a goat or both. Hanging with their abuelos? That wasn't unusual. But tonight, their absence pressed in like dark shadow on the sunniest day.

Inside, the house smelled like woodsmoke and that soup Mariella always made with corn and something spicy. Robbie met us at the door with a wave and pulled my mom into a hug that lingered just a second longer than usual. Then he turned to me, clasping my shoulder with a firm grip.

"You've got court vision like your dad used to," he said. "That pass to Aiden in the third—clean as glass."

"Grab some food," he added. "Mariella's dishing up. We thought you might be hungry."

"Always," I said, trying to keep it light.

Emilia was already at the table, hoodie sleeves pulled over her hands, posture a little too perfect. Her smile was soft when she saw me, but it didn't quite reach her eyes. I pulled out the chair beside her and sat down.

"Good game," she said quietly.

"Thanks for yelling 'Sink it, Farm Guy' before my free throw."

"Next time I can bring a glitter poster. Farm Guy 4 MVP."

A bowl of soup appeared in front of me, then bread, then a glass of apple cider that tasted like fall and memories. We all ate for a while, the kind of meal where you can hear every clink of silverware and swallow. No one was rushing to fill the silence, which in itself felt loud. When Mom spoke, her voice was clear. Practiced.

"Tyler, Mijo," she said. "I need to tell you something."

I froze, spoon halfway to my mouth. Mom looked at me, steady and open and heartbreakingly calm.

"My mother is dying," she said.

The words hit harder than I expected. Not because I knew her—I didn't. But because I knew what she meant to my mom. All those phone calls. All the money sent home. All the holidays spent smiling through spotty video chats, pretending it was almost like being together. I couldn't speak.

"Her heart is failing," Mom continued. "The doctors say she doesn't have long. Maybe six weeks, two months would be a miracle."

Emilia reached under the table and found my hand. I held on.

"Lucia called me a few days ago. She said... my mother's asking for me."

Of course she was. Of course she would be. I already knew where this was going. My chest felt tight.

"Can you go?" I asked, even though I already knew the answer.

Mom shook her head slowly. "I spoke with Mr. Jacobsen. There are no emergency exceptions. No way around the ten-year bar. If I leave now, I may not be allowed to come back."

Silence. My ears buzzed. I gripped Emilia's hand harder.

"We've spent the past few days talking through every option," Mom added. "And I didn't want to tell you in the middle of your week. You've been playing so well. Smiling again."

I swallowed hard. "So what now?"

"I have to decide," she said. "But I can't wait much longer."

The room was too quiet. Even the old radiator seemed to hush. I didn't know what to say. I didn't know how to say anything at all. So I just nodded. And held her eyes. And tried to be brave enough to give her the space to tell me which terrible choice she was making.

Emilia

Tyler didn't say anything right away. He just sat there, jaw tight, fingers still wrapped around mine under the table. His mom's words were still floating in the air, like they hadn't found a place to land yet. I wanted to say something—anything—but Mom caught my eye and gave the smallest shake of her head. Not yet.

Dad cleared his throat. "We talked through everything with Mr. Jacobsen. Luz has been asking every question under the sun."

Luz gave a soft, tired smile. "I had a list. Two pages long."

Tyler looked up. His voice was hoarse. "What about that thing... advance something? I read about it once. You can leave and come back in emergencies."

"Advance parole," Mom said. "It doesn't apply to pending U visa cases. We asked. Twice."

He looked down again. "What about, like... humanitarian stuff? Special permissions?"

Robbie shook his head. "Only for certain categories. And even then, it's months of paperwork. We don't have months."

Tyler didn't move. His other hand came up to his face, thumb and knuckle pressed between his eyes. Luz leaned forward. "Mijo, if there were anyway at all—I would take it. I promise you."

He nodded slowly, but I could see the muscle twitching in his jaw. Outside, a wind moved through the barn rafters, whistling just enough to fill the silence. Mom stood and began clearing dishes, not to rush us, but to make the room feel less stuck.

I gave Tyler's hand one last squeeze before letting go and moving to help her. I wanted to fix it. I wanted someone to say, "Actually, wait. There is one more thing we haven't tried."

But no one did.

Tyler

I didn't sleep much that night. After we got home, I helped Mom put away the leftovers we'd brought back from the farm, both of us moving around the kitchen like we were afraid to touch anything too loudly. We said goodnight like always. Lights out like always. But nothing felt like always. The house was too quiet. The kind that makes you think of things you've been trying not to.

I stared at the ceiling for a long time, then gave up and padded down the hall. Mom's bedroom door was open, just a crack. The soft glow of her bedside lamp spilled onto the hallway floor like it was waiting for me. She looked up when I knocked.

"You're still awake," she said.

"So are you."

She didn't answer, just set the pen she'd been holding on top of a notebook. I didn't have to look at it to know what it was. Lists.

Plans. Pros and cons that didn't matter because either column ended in goodbye. I sat down on the edge of her bed. She waited.

"You already decided, didn't you," I said. I wasn't angry. Just tired.

She nodded slowly. "I think so. But I needed to see if you were okay."

I looked down at my hands. "I'm not."

A pause. No flinch from her. No correction.

"But I will be," I added.

She let out a breath I don't think she knew she'd been holding. Her eyes filled, but she didn't cry.

"I don't want to miss your life," she whispered. "But if I stay here and lose her without saying goodbye—Tyler, I'll never come back from that."

"I know."

It took everything in me to say it. My chest felt like it was caving in. But I said it.

"I'll be okay," I told her again. "I'll make sure I am."

She reached for my hand and held it like she did when I was little. Like I was still hers. And I was. Even if she had to go.

The next afternoon, we drove out to the farm again. I thought it would just be a quiet conversation. A chance to say thank you. Maybe a way to catch our breath before everything changed. But when we walked into the kitchen, I saw the table held a clipboard with Google Maps printed out, a couple of small coolers, travel mugs, and a few folded fleecy blankets. Robbie looked up and gave us both a nod.

"We'll leave early. I want to hit Minneapolis between rush hours."

Mariella was labeling a Ziploc bag full of snacks. "My sister's picking up Miggy and Sofía tonight. They'll stay through Sunday. Robbie and I can take turns driving."

Mom blinked. "Wait. What?"

Mariella set down the marker and smiled. "We're driving you, Luz."

"You... what?" Her voice was barely a whisper.

"We've already booked the rooms and cleared our schedules," Robbie said. "One night in a hotel on the way down, one just over the border before the crossing. Smooth and simple."

Mom looked like someone had tilted the floor under her. "But I—I was going to figure out the Greyhound—"

"No," Mariella said gently. "You were going to shoulder this by yourself. But we don't let family walk through things alone. Not this."

Mom's hand went to her mouth. She tried to speak, but nothing came out. Tears welled in her eyes before she could stop them. I locked gazes with Em, the care in her eyes was too much and I had to look away. I reached blindly for her hand and all the practicing must have been paying off because I found it on the first try.

Mariella pulled Mom in for a hug. "Son familia. Donde va uno, van todos."— *Where one goes, we all go*. We'll go with you to the border, then we'll go with you with in our love and prayers. We'll do this, we'll make sure your boy is alright, and we'll be here for anything else you need."

Mariella's voice lingered in the room long after she let go of Mom. *Son familia. Donde va uno, van todos.* I imagined doing this without the Preston family. If Mariella hadn't open the doors wide and almost pulled my mom in. If Emilia hadn't been worried about me months ago when school started. If we hadn't talked on apple picking day.

Then there wouldn't be a family doing this. There'd just be Mom and me, with Gramps and Grams trying to smooth the way as much they could. I don't think I could've kept all the pieces of myself together without being wrapped up in this family's love

65

Delivered

Tyler

The headlights cut through pre-dawn darkness as we pulled away from the house. 4:17 AM—the same time we'd left for Minneapolis what felt like a lifetime ago. Only now, instead of driving toward possibility, we were heading toward goodbye.

"Everyone comfortable back there?" Robbie asked, his eyes meeting mine in the rearview mirror.

I nodded, words stuck somewhere in my chest. Beside me, Mom sat with her small suitcase at her feet and Emilia on her other side. In the passenger seat, Mariella nursed a travel mug of coffee, occasionally turning to check on us.

They'd insisted on driving us—all the way to the border crossing in Texas.

"We're family," she'd said. "We drive our family."

Mom had tried to argue—the journey was too long, they'd miss work, the kids needed them—but the Prestons had already figured it all out. Robbie's brother and his wife would watch Miggy and Sofía. Mariella had rearranged her work schedule. And

Robbie had simply said, "I won't let you make this journey alone, Luz."

So here we were, heading south in the Prestons' SUV, the miles stretching ahead of us. Nearly 1,600 of them to the border crossing at Brownsville, Texas.

"We'll take turns driving," Robbie had explained. "Two days down, one night in a hotel, and then the final stretch."

Mom had wept when they'd laid out the plan—the first time I'd seen her truly break since the news about her mother. "I can never repay you," she'd said.

"You don't repay family," Mariella had replied.

Now, as we left North Riverbend behind, I watched the familiar landmarks disappear in the darkness. The water tower at the edge of town. The turnoff to school. The corner store where I'd bought slushies every summer since I could remember.

How many of these ordinary places would still be here in ten years? How many would change beyond recognition? How many memories would I make without Mom beside me?

"You should try to sleep," Mom said softly, noticing my restlessness. "It's a long drive."

"I'm okay."

She didn't push, just reached for my hand and held it tight. We'd spent the last six days in a strange limbo—going through the motions of normal life while preparing for everything to change. Mom had organized her meager possessions with methodical care, setting aside things for me to keep and things to send to her family in Mexico. She'd written letters for me to open on future birthdays and graduations. She'd taken me to the bank and added my name to her small account.

All the while, she'd maintained a calm I couldn't match. At night, I'd hear her crying softly in her room, but during the day, she moved with the steady purpose of someone who'd made peace with the inevitable.

I hadn't. Not even close.

The rhythm of the road lulled the car into silence. Emilia had dozed off against the window, her breath fogging the glass. Mariella and Robbie spoke occasionally in low voices, discussing routes and rest stops. Mom stared out at the darkness, lost in her own thoughts.

I must have fallen asleep too, because when I opened my eyes again, pale morning light had replaced the darkness. We were passing through farmland, the fields stretching out on either side like a patchwork quilt.

"Morning, sleeping beauty," Robbie said, catching my eye in the mirror again. "Hungry? We'll stop for breakfast soon."

I nodded, rolling my stiff neck. Mom was asleep now, her head resting against Emilia's shoulder. Mariella had taken over driving, while Robbie navigated from the passenger seat.

"Where are we?" I asked, my voice rough with sleep.

"Just crossed into Nebraska," Robbie replied. "Making good time."

Nebraska. Further south than I'd ever been. My whole life had been contained in one small corner of North Dakota—a deliberate choice by Mom to stay close to Gramps and Grams, to build whatever security she could around us.

We stopped at a roadside diner for breakfast. The normalcy of it was jarring—fluorescent lights, laminated menus, waitresses calling out orders. How could the world just continue like this when everything in my life was splitting at the seams?

Mom picked at her food, answering questions about her childhood when Mariella asked, filling in pieces of her past I'd only heard in fragments before. Stories about growing up in a small town outside Guadalajara. About my grandmother's garden and the orange tree behind their house. About her dreams before life twisted them into something else.

"She wanted to be a landscape architect," Mom said, a wistful smile touching her lips. "She taught me everything about plants—which ones need shade, which ones attract hummingbirds, which ones heal burns or settle stomachs."

"That explains your green thumb," Mariella said warmly. "The herbs you grew on your windowsill last summer were incredible."

"It's in the blood," Mom agreed. "My mother could make anything grow."

The present tense slipped into past tense—could, not can—and Mom's smile faltered. Her mother was still alive, but already becoming a memory.

Back in the car, we fell into a rhythm—driving for a few hours, stopping to stretch our legs, switching drivers, continuing south. Robbie and Mariella had planned the route meticulously, avoiding major cities and choosing quieter highways where checkpoints were less likely.

Through the afternoon, I watched the landscape change—prairie giving way to gentle hills, then flattening out again. The towns we passed through grew smaller, the spaces between them longer. America unfolding outside my window like a strange, unfamiliar country.

"Will you stay in your hometown?" Emilia asked Mom during one of our stops, a gas station somewhere in Oklahoma.

"For a while," Mom replied. "With my mother, and then... I don't know. My cousin Lucia has offered to let me stay with her family. She has a small house in Zapopan, just outside Guadalajara."

The names sounded foreign and familiar at once—places I'd heard about in bedtime stories but had never seen. Places that would now become Mom's reality while I remained behind.

As evening approached, we stopped at a modest hotel just across the Texas border. Two rooms—one for Robbie and Mariella, and Emilia, one for Mom and me. The arrangement was practical but underscored the temporary nature of our journey. We weren't vacationers or road-trippers. We were just passing through, headed toward a crossing only some of us would make.

After a quiet dinner at the hotel restaurant, Emilia suggested we go for a walk. The air was warmer here, heavy with unfamiliar scents. Mom declined, saying she needed to call Lucia to confirm the arrangements for tomorrow, so Emilia and I wandered the hotel grounds alone.

"How are you holding up?" she asked when we were out of earshot of our parents.

I shrugged, kicking at a pebble on the sidewalk. "How am I supposed to be holding up?"

"I don't think there's a 'supposed to' for something like this."

We walked in silence for a moment, the distant hum of highway traffic a constant backdrop.

"I keep thinking there's going to be a last-minute save," I admitted finally. "Like in the movies, where someone shows up with a solution right before the credits roll."

Emilia didn't offer empty reassurances. "I know."

"It's not fair," I said, the words inadequate but true. "She didn't do anything wrong. She just wanted a better life for us."

"It's not fair," Emilia agreed softly.

We reached the edge of the property, where a chain-link fence separated the hotel grounds from an empty field. In the distance, I could make out the lights of a small town, scattered like fallen stars against the Texas night.

"I don't know how to say goodbye," I confessed, my voice catching. "I've been trying to find the words for days, and I just... can't."

Emilia was quiet for a long moment. Then she reached for my hand, her fingers cool against mine. "Maybe you don't have to find the perfect words. Maybe you just have to be there, in the moment. That might be enough."

I nodded, not trusting myself to speak. We stood there for a while, hand in hand, staring at the distant town. Tomorrow, we would cross into the borderlands. Tomorrow, everything would change.

When we returned to the hotel, Mom was sitting on the edge of the bed, her phone in her lap, a complicated emotion on her face.

"Everything okay?" I asked.

"My mother is holding on," she said. "Lucia says she's been asking for me." She looked up, a faint smile tracing her lips. "I think she's waiting."

I sat beside her, the hotel bed dipping under our combined weight. "I'm glad."

Mom reached up to touch my face, her hand cool against my cheek. "You look more like your father every day."

I leaned into her touch, memorizing the feel of it. Ten years. What would she look like when I saw her again? What would I look like? Would we recognize each other across the gulf of time and distance?

"Get some sleep," she said, dropping her hand. "Tomorrow will be a long day."

I tried, but sleep remained elusive. I lay awake listening to Mom's breathing, watching the digital clock tick toward morning—4:00, 4:30, 5:00. Outside, the first birds began to sing, unaware or uncaring that this was the start of the hardest day of my life.

We were on the road by six, the SUV cutting through the Texas dawn. The landscape had changed dramatically now—desert stretching to the horizon, dotted with scrub brush and cacti. Even the air felt different, dry and tinged with dust.

"We should reach Brownsville by early afternoon," Robbie announced from the driver's seat. "We'll have plenty of time before the crossing closes."

Mom nodded, her calm facade firmly back in place. She wore her best dress—a simple blue cotton with small white flowers—and had arranged her hair carefully. She wanted to look presentable when she arrived, she'd explained. Dignified. As if dignity had anything to do with being torn from your child by an invisible line drawn across the continent.

The closer we got to Brownsville, the quieter the car became. There were no more stories, no more reminiscing. Just the hum of the engine and the steady tick of miles disappearing beneath our wheels.

We stopped at a roadside restaurant for an early lunch. The place was busy, filled with a mix of locals and travelers. Mom ate methodically, as if working through a necessary task. Beside her,

Mariella spoke softly in Spanish, words of comfort I couldn't fully understand.

After lunch, Robbie pulled me aside while Mom and the others used the restroom.

"There's something I want you to have," he said, pressing a small envelope into my hand. "Don't open it until you get home."

"What is it?"

"Just something to help with The Beast," he said, a gruff affection in his voice. "We'll keep working on it, you and me. It'll be waiting when you're ready."

The simple promise—that something would remain, would continue—nearly broke me.

"Thank you," I managed.

Robbie nodded, squeezing my shoulder once before rejoining the others.

The final stretch to Brownsville passed in a blur. The city emerged from the desert like a mirage, its outskirts sprawling with shopping centers and housing developments before giving way to the older downtown. Robbie navigated confidently, following the signs toward Internacional Puente Los Indios—the International Gateway Bridge.

We parked in a lot on the American side. The border crossing loomed ahead—a concrete structure spanning the narrow river that separated the United States from Mexico. People flowed steadily across in both directions, their journeys taking mere minutes while ours had taken days.

Mr. Jacobsen had gone over everything. Mom couldn't mention how long she'd been gone. Couldn't say she'd lived in the States. Even reentering Mexico meant pretending—no questions, no answers.

"This is as far as we can go," Robbie said, turning off the engine.

Reality crashed over me like a wave. This was it. The moment I'd been dreading for days was finally here.

We gathered Mom's belongings—just the one suitcase and a small backpack. Anything else she needed would be sent later, through Lucia.

Mr. Jacobsen had given us detailed instructions on what documentation she would need to present at the crossing. Her Mexican passport. Her birth certificate. Nothing that would suggest she'd spent years in the United States.

On the Mexican side, just visible through the border gate, I could make out a small group waiting—two women, one older, one about Mom's age. Aunt Lucia and her daughter, Mom had explained. They would drive her the rest of the way to her mother's home.

"They're good people," she'd assured me. "You'll like them when you meet them someday."

Someday. A word holding ten years of absence.

We walked to the border entrance as a group—Mom, me, Emilia, Robbie, and Mariella. An unusual family, formed by choice and circumstance rather than blood. At the final checkpoint, a line painted on the ground that only some of us could cross, we stopped.

"I guess this is it," Mom said, her voice steady despite everything.

Mariella was the first to embrace her, the two women holding each other tightly. "Vaya con Dios, hermana," she whispered. "We'll watch over him."

"I know," Mom replied. "Thank you for everything."

Robbie hugged her next, his large frame enveloping her smaller one. No words, just a firm, reassuring embrace.

Emilia stepped forward, tears tracking silently down her cheeks. "Be safe, Tía Luz."

"Take care of him for me," Mom said softly as they embraced.

And then, finally, it was my turn.

Mom set down her suitcase and took both my hands in hers. "Mijo," she said, her voice breaking for the first time. "My Tyler."

The words I'd been searching for—the perfect goodbye—still eluded me. Instead, I pulled her into a fierce hug, memorizing the feel of her—the smell of her perfume, the softness of her hair against my cheek, the steady beat of her heart against mine.

"I love you," I managed to say, the words woefully inadequate. "I'll come find you as soon as I can."

"I know," she whispered. "But first, you need to live your life here. That's the whole point, mijo. That's why I'm going alone."

"Ten years," I said, the words still impossible to comprehend.

"Ten years is nothing," she insisted, pulling back to look me in the eyes. "It's a blink. And then we'll have the rest of our lives."

She reached into her pocket and pressed something into my palm—a small silver medallion on a chain.

"Saint Christopher," she explained. "For protection. Your grandmother gave it to me when I left Mexico. Now I'm giving it to you."

I closed my fingers around it, the metal warm from her pocket. "I'll keep it safe."

"Keep yourself safe," she corrected, touching my cheek one last time. "That's all I need."

Then she stepped back, picked up her suitcase, and turned toward the border gate. The guard checked her documents, nodded, and waved her through.

I watched her walk away, her blue dress bright against the concrete of the bridge, her steps steady and unhurried. At the midpoint, she paused and looked back—a final glance at the country where she'd built a life, raised a son, found a way to survive against impossible odds.

She raised her hand in farewell.

I raised mine in return, my vision blurring.

Then she continued walking, crossing the invisible line that would keep us apart for a decade, and was embraced by waiting family on the other side.

"Come on," Robbie said gently, his hand on my shoulder. "Let's go home."

Home. The word felt strange now, incomplete. But I let them lead me back to the car, climbed into the backseat beside Emilia, and watched through the window as Mexico—and Mom—receded into the distance.

The journey back would be the same 1,600 miles, but it would feel entirely different. The road ahead was both familiar and utterly changed, stretching toward a future I couldn't yet imagine.

As we pulled away from the border, Emilia's hand found mine in the space between us. She didn't speak—there were no words that could make this better—but her fingers interlaced with mine, solid and real.

I held on tight and watched the borderlands disappear in the rearview mirror, my mom left behind like a parcel we'd delivered and left on a doorstep.

66

Remnants

Tyler

The room felt both familiar and foreign—simultaneously my space and not my space at all. Dad's space. Gramps had moved boxes from the attic and arranged some artifacts carefully around the edges of the room. Mementos of the dad I'd never known. Sports trophies, yearbooks from the 90s, a few vintage Nirvana posters that had been carefully preserved.

"Your father loved music," Grams had explained as she'd helped me unpack. "Always had something playing."

I'd been here a week since our return from the border. Seven days of moving through life in slow motion, going through the motions of school, of basketball practice, of ordinary teenager things while feeling anything but ordinary.

Gramps and Gramma had been careful with me—giving me space when I needed it, sitting quietly with me when even a word became too heavy, never pushing me to talk about Mom. I'd had one phone call from her three days ago. The connection had been staticky, her voice sounding far away in more ways than one.

She'd made it and her mother was still hanging on. It might be for the miracle two-months Mom had mentioned, it might two weeks. Whatever time I could hear my mom's gratefulness to be there. Lucia was taking good care of her. All these things brought comfort but somehow made deeper ache.

Sitting on the edge of the bed—Dad's old bed—I pulled the envelope from my pocket, where I'd been carrying it since Robbie had handed it to me. I'd been waiting for the right moment to open it, though I wasn't sure what "right" meant anymore.

The envelope was small, the kind used for greeting cards. My name was written on the front in Robbie's blocky handwriting. I ran my thumb over the seal, then carefully opened it. Inside was a folded piece of paper wrapped around something small and metal.

I unfolded the note first.

Tyler,

Your dad kept this medallion on The Beast's rearview mirror from the day he bought that truck. When I purchased it from him before he enlisted, he made me promise to keep it there. Said it brought good luck on the road. It's a St. Christopher medal—patron saint of travelers. Adam wasn't particularly religious, but he believed in covering his bases, especially after some close calls on icy roads. I took it off before I stored the truck, thinking I'd put it back when we got it running again. But I think he'd want you to have it now—to put back on that rearview mirror yourself when you're ready.

Your dad was like a brother to me. Sometimes closer than my actual brothers. The road ahead of you is tough, but you're not traveling it alone. Come by the farm whenever you're ready to continue work on The Beast. No rush—it's waited this long, it can wait a little longer.

—Robbie

I unwrapped the small object from the folded paper. It was a tarnished medal on a short metal chain—St. Christopher carrying the Christ child across a river. The same saint as the medallion Mom had pressed into my hand at the border, though this one was older, more worn.

I ran my thumb over its surface, feeling the raised edges of the design. My father had touched this. Had looked at it every time he drove. Had believed it kept him safe on the road. A strange coincidence—or maybe not. Maybe Mom had known about Dad's medal. Maybe she'd chosen her parting gift with this connection in mind. Two saints watching over me from two parents I couldn't reach.

I'd spent the week feeling like I'd lost everything. Like the ground beneath my feet had disappeared, leaving me in endless free fall. But sitting there, holding this small piece of my father—this tangible connection to a man I'd never met—I felt a small shift. Mom was gone. But she wasn't dead. She was living, breathing, existing on the other side of an arbitrary line. And someday, somehow, I would see her again.

Until then, I had this medal. The truck. The project that connected me to both my father and the man who had been like a brother to him. Emilia had texted earlier, just a simple Thinking of you that I hadn't yet figured out how to answer.

Gram had left dinner warming in the oven for me—some kind of casserole that smelled like cheese and comfort. Gramps was in the living room watching a baseball game, a rerun of a classic World Series game, the familiar sounds drifting up the stairs. Life, continuing. Different but still here. I slipped the medal into my pocket, its weight small but significant against my leg.

Tomorrow, maybe, I'd go to the Preston farm. I'd tell Robbie I was ready to start work on The Beast again. I'd text Emilia back. Tonight, I'd sit with my grandparents. I'd eat Gramma's casserole. I'd let myself be held in the safety net they'd always provided. And I'd hold onto this medallion—this small, tarnished piece of metal that somehow felt like a beginning instead of an ending.

67

I'm Glad I Got a Brother

My phone buzzed on my nightstand. My dad's old nightstand that was now mine. I glanced at it. Robbie's number but probably not him. I snatched my phone and looked. Yep. Miggy, from Robbie's phone. That was new. For the first time in a long time I didn't want to engage. Please don't text again. *Please.* Buzz.

"Ugh, I'd better look." I mumbled to myself.

> **HPM**: I'm sad about your mama. That you got to go a long time without seeing her cause the rules say so.

> **HPM**: The rules are dizzy chickens. No wait. Worse. Dizzy chickens that stepped in the stinkiest cow poop in forever and ever.

I chuckled. He'd gifted me with an awesome description of immigration laws. Buzz.

> **HPM**: Your mama asked me to be your brother. I told her I already was, so I'd be your double brother.

HPM: I know you'll be sad about your Mama.

HPM: But is it okay if I'm glad you're my double brother Farm Guy?

Everything had been spooling tighter and tighter inside me. I breathed out as it loosened, not fully, but enough. Miggy. That kid was chaos and trouble. And love and magic in a grubby four-year-old package.

Me: Yeah Miggy. You can be glad. Know what? I'm glad I have a double brother too.

I took a screenshot of the text knowing that Miggy would delete it ASAP. No idea how he does the texting and calling stuff. Magic maybe? I sent the screenshot to my mom.

Me: I'll still miss you, but thanks for making sure I got a double brother.

Later Mom texted back.

Mom: Mijo, esa granja también guarda a tu segunda mamá y papá, una hermanita…. y hmm -blowing kisses smiley face - alguien muy importante.

Me: Sí, Mamá. Pero todavía te extraño… mucho. Te quiero. Y sí… hmm, de veras.

Mom—Mijo, that farm also houses your second mom and dad, a little sister... and hmmm... [blowing kisses smiley face]—someone very important.

Tyler—Yes, mom. But I still miss you... a lot. I love you. And yes... hmm, really.

MID-NOVEMBER

TO THE

END OF APRIL

68

Time Moves Fast & Slow & Every Speed In Between

Emilia

That day we'd watched her walk away I started a steady stream of pictures and texts to Tia Luz.

The day at the bridge:

> **Me**: One more hug to keep with you. He's still yours—we're just borrowing him.

Picture Attached: Tyler hugging Luz tightly at the edge of the pedestrian bridge, his face buried in her shoulder. Perspective is just far enough back to feel private, not posed.

> **Me**: We'll watch over him here. He's always in your heart there.

Picture Attached: Tyler walking to the car next to Robbie. Robbie has his arm slung over Tyler's shoulders in that "we're guys" but still need hugs kind of way.

I sent Tía Luz "field reports." Not staged. Not "say cheese." Just Tyler, the way he was while life moved on.

> **Me**: Tyler likes to crunch leaves underfoot when he walks. He denied it when I asked him

Picture Attached: Tyler walking across the school lot, backpack slung, shoe mid-step on a coppery drift of leaves.

> **Me**: He's got good friends. I still think boys can be kinda dumb.

Picture Attached: Aiden has Tyler in a fake headlock. Tyler is laughing hysterically.

> **Me**: Evidence he eats. Second, maybe third helping of Grams' chicken wild rice casserole. And every roll she put on his plate.

Picture Attached: Tyler at the Alred kitchen table, head tipped back laughing while Gramps tells a story. Grams sliding another roll onto his plate.

> **Me**: He doesn't say much about it, but Aiden says Coach is really pleased with Tyler's game.

Picture Attached: Tyler listening earnestly to Coach at a practice.

Me: If you ask him, he'll say he didn't do this. So—evidence.

Picture Attached: Tyler on the ground making snow angels in the first snow with Sofía and Miggy.

Me: I don't think my dad realized how much he's been missing Adam. I know he doesn't have any other friend he's as close with as he was with Adam. It's stories now, all the time, and they're both smiling.

Picture Attached: Robbie gesturing big, Tyler bent over laughing, outside at one of the farm outbuildings.

Sometimes Tía Luz replied right away with little bursts of warmth.

Luz: Gracias, Mija. Le hace bien verlo. / It does me good to see him. Besos.

Luz: Dile que dormirse temprano, por favor. He looks tired around the eyes.

Other nights there was only the *Delivered* notice. I sent the pictures anyway. I wasn't a bridge across the border, just fine thread. But thread could hold.

Tyler

We talked when we could. Static, then her voice, and the ache loosened a notch.

"¿Cómo estás, Mijo?" "Bien, Mamá. Cansado. School and practice." "Cansado is good. Means you're doing and not only thinking."

Sometimes the call dropped, leaving me to stare at the screen. The echo of her last word would hum around me. Sometimes, when a call ended quickly, Gramps knocked later and brought in a cup of hot chocolate. He didn't say, but I knew it was something he did for my dad. I wanted Mom back, but I wouldn't have given up those hot cocoa moments either.

He'd ask something easy, like, "She sound okay?"

"Yeah," I'd say. "Happy and sad, tired."

He never pushed—of course, not his way—just sat. There'd be a game of something murmuring on the TV in the den. My grandparents—they were experts at filling a house with love that doesn't crowd.

Grams made artistic plates of leftovers, covered with foil to keep the growing boy fed. And I ended up eating it all. She didn't say anything but smiled fondly at the empty plates.

I pretended I didn't see Gramps scraping ice off my windshield on practice mornings or making sure the car's block heater was plugged in on bitter nights. He didn't want the thanks out loud. I would have said it if he needed me to. He quietly made more pieces of me okay.

Emilia

Thanksgiving was loud. Ivy isn't the only Preston cousin. The kitchen was crowded, dinner rolls rose on every flat surface, Mamá bustled between fridge and counter and stove. Grandma Preston worked around her. It's a dance they've worked out while they prepare delicious food together.

The louder it got the quieter Tyler became. He joked, helped deep-fry a turkey (no idea how Dad got Mom and Grandma to agree—Tyler may have made puppy-dog eyes). He caught Miggy and Sofía when they moved at him like missiles. But it showed that something was missing—someone was missing.

> **Me**: Holiday report. He's here. He's okay. He misses you. Gramps and Grams are here. Dad loves having them here.

Pictures Attached: -Tyler sitting on the sofa, Sofía on his lap, Miggy draped over his shoulder

-Tyler at the fire pit later, hood up, face orange in the glow, staring at sparks like they're a coded message.

-Grams giving Robbie a bear hug.

Her reply came in the morning.

> **Luz**: Gracias por prestarme tus ojos. I'll text him, but I'll tell you too. Today I made pan

> dulce with my sisters. First time in years. My
> hands remembered.

Tyler

I called her in early December.

"¡Mijo!" The clatter behind her is a kitchen. People laughing. A radio somewhere playing something bright.

"You're cooking?"

"Working," she says, proudness woven into the word. "At my Tía's panadería for now. They pay me and I get to smell like cinnamon even when I'm sad." A smile in her voice. "We send a box at Navidad, ¿sí?"

"Sí." I swallow. "Save the conchas with the thick icing for me."

"Always."

Grams smiled at me later, but neither made me talk about the call. That made it easier, and I told them about the happiness in her voice and about cinnamon.

Emilia

We're a two-tree family: one in the living room—and one out on the porch so the whole farm can be festive. I string popcorn while Sofía and Miggy pretend to help by eating and handing me popcorn piece by piece. When we run out earlier than I expected, Miggy blamed it on a mouse.

I kept texting and sending pics.

> **Me**: Mid-season update. They beat
> Edgewater by 6. Tyler took a charge. I yelled
> something possibly unladylike.

Picture Attached: Tyler on the bench, hair damp, grinning at Aiden; Coach Jensen's hand on both their shoulders.

Me: Evidence he studies. Note the highlighter. Note the snacks. Note Miggy's "help."

Picture Attached Dining table, chemistry flashcards and algebra, Miggy asleep on Tyler's shoulder, marker streaking Tyler's hoodie.

Sometimes Tía Luz wrote longer.

Luz: I got hired permanent hours! Morning shift at the panadería, two days a week helping at my cousin's market stall. When I am busy my brain behaves. My sisters make me sit and rest. They are bossier than your mamá. Don't tell her I said that.

Tyler

Holidays had a strange tilt. Mamá always sent me to the Lutheran church with Gramps and Grams. She'd go to a late mass at the Catholic church. Still, it felt like she should've been at the candlelight Christmas Eve service with us. But no one at the service knew my mom was gone. We looked normal on the outside.

Emilia had a hoodie made for me that had Farm Guy across the front and a number 1 on the back. Somehow Miggy found out. He was so excited he accidentally let it slip. I didn't tell Emilia I knew what her gift to me was—no snitching applies to gifts too. The slip from Miggy gave me time to get a long-sleeved T-Shirt made for her. FGA—Farm Guy Club of America.

Neighbors shared plates of cookies and lefse. Mom always laughed and called lefse potato tortillas. She turned her nose up if it was dry and stiff, but Grams made the best—tender, thin, smothered in butter and sugar. She ate that like candy and Grams teased her about it. Grams wanted to send lefse but didn't know how it would keep.

For the first Christmas in fifteen years, Mamá ate only Christmas treats from her home. She raved about the jericallas, tamales dulces, ponche navideño, and champurrado. She told me she had a hungry spot that needed lefse and krumkake and spritz cookies. Also that her sisters laughed themselves silly over lefse. She planned on making some next year.

We Face Timed on Christmas Day. I considered it a possible miracle that she was only one hour ahead of me. At the spring time change we'd be in the same time. That comforted both of us.

"Open your gift," she said. I tore the tissue away from something small, hard. Beads slid under my thumb—cool and tight. Blues and greens that shone.

"I can still bead, Mijo. I learned when I was so little, maybe ten. That's for your keys when you get La Bestiecita running."

"Gracias, Mamá. I love it. It's perfect."

She moved the camera and showed me she's wore the hoodie I got her. It said NRHS Mustangs, and Grams helped me add my number to it (fine, Grams put my number on it).

"I love it. It's just missing a stinky teenage boy smell, Mijo," she teased me.

"You miss stinky teenage boy odor, Mamá?"

"Sí, but only sometimes."

"I'll send you a box of dirty socks for your birthday."

"No, no, no, don't you dare, Tyler Adam Alred!" She laughed. "You might cause an international incident!"

Gramps was nearby pretending not to listen. He was waiting to snatch the phone from me.

"Merry Christmas, Luz! We miss our Sunshine here."

"Oh, suegrito, sí, sí, I miss you too. So much."

Gramps handed me the phone and squeezed my shoulder. He didn't say goodbye, but the look on my mom's face was tender. "Tyler, now, you must take care—good, good care—of them, mi mamá y papá de corazón."

Emilia

We had an icy, bitter winter. Still I sent pictures to Tía Luz—sparkling ice, frost on the window, and most of all Tyler bundled up to take Miggy and Sofía sledding, to shovel Gramps and Grams' driveway, and to help my dad shovel paths around the farm.

The team dropped a game, won the next, and played a lot in the middle. Decent record but showed work still to do. Tyler excelled at clean steals all season; somehow that didn't surprise me. One game, Aiden kept holding his breath and almost passed out. Ivy was about to run onto the court and body-check him. She saw what he was doing.

I sent Tía Luz my favorite kind of photos: Tyler just looking like Tyler.

Me: Between classes. He didn't see me.

Pictures Attached:

-Tyler in the hallway, head tipped against the locker for one second—just resting—then shoulders back, shoes already turning toward whatever's next.

-Laughing with Aiden at lunch.

-Cracking up at Nate's terrible math jokes.

-Dozing off in the middle of studying.

Tyler

Mom and I settled into the rhythm of talking often. Not always long or happy, just always there. She told me about regulars at the bakery who argued about which concha is best. I told her about algebra and that Coach said my first step looked mean this month, which was a compliment. Some nights we were both too tired to talk. We would made make the call short and say goodbye.

It's soup season, that's what mom called it. She said she missed the food, just not the bitter cold. Grams and Gramps bundled up and made it to even more school things than before. I worried about that now—them on the icy roads and sidewalks.

Emilia

We were at an away game; the gym smelled like orange soda and school cleaner. Fourth quarter of a tied game, Aiden shot a three-pointer. My dad shouted, "Nothing but net!" Tyler sank two free throws, then stole the ball twice. Nasty and sneaky but clean. We won by five. I acted like Tyler and stole candid shot after candid shot. Too many to send—*all* good.

> **Me:** Game's over; Coach keeps talking on & on...

Picture Attached: Tyler, hair damp, eyes soft, listening to Coach dissect the game.

Me: He's okay. He really is. Even when he's not. You know?

Luz: Sí, Mija. That is exactly him.

Tyler

We finished basketball season with a winning record, not a flashy one. Felt like building up to more, instead of losing less than half. Coach clapped me on the shoulder after the last horn.

"Proud of you," he said. "You got stronger without upping the flash." I realized my joking side has made people think there's no serious.

Emilia

The farm thawed, froze, thawed, froze. Miggy and Sofía demanded pictures of them be sent to Tía Luz. She replied to those with strings of heart emojis. I remembered how Miguel cried when we came back without her. He had nightmares about someone taking our mom and dad. We didn't tell Tyler or Luz—neither one needed more.

It got better. Tía Luz was their pen pal and wrote to them with stories that had Miggy rolling around laughing. Fía joined in because Miggy's big laugh is impossible to ignore.

I remembered Tía Luz's green thumb and sent her pictures of spring farm beginnings.

Me: Babies!

> Picture Attached: Seedlings in neat rows

Tyler groaned and said, "Don't give her ideas" and I blushed bright red.

More pictures sent.

> Tyler's hand holding paint card samples, colors for La Bestiecita—faded blue, hopeful gray, stubborn silver.

Tyler

The Beast was a gazillion small fixes away from running—and so close at the same time.

"Hoy aprendí a trenzar el pan," she said on a call—today I learned to braid the bread.

"I painted sample colors on La Bestiecita," I replied. She laughed.

"Mira nomás." We are artists.

I agreed—not fancy, but good at beautiful from the regular and the hard.

Emilia

We made it through holidays, games won and lost, tests and studying. And many regular Tuesdays and Thursdays. Tyler showed me a text from his mom. Beautiful but painful.

> **Luz:** Mijo, every night I go out when the stars are brand new, then I blow you a kiss and send it north on the wind.

He needed me to hug him to hold his pieces together. The first time in a long-time cracks showed. He read the text again and didn't speak for a long time.

"What do I say back?"

I looked up and saw new stars, then reached out and opened my hand. I imagined her love streaming here to find Tyler. I swear I captured something feathery and warm.

"Tell her you caught it."

Then I put it in his palm and folded his fingers over it. "And when you're too sad or too worn to reach out, I'll be there to help you catch."

Tyler: I caught it Mamá. And I'll keep catching.

And he kept catching her love night after night.

69

Then Chuck Norris Drew a Chicken

Tyler

Miggy shoved a piece of paper at my stomach like it was a legal document he'd brought to court. And even though I'm usually the court jester, this time I had to do something serious.

"Tyler, write down my chicken," he said. "For the granted stuff. Meela and Papi need it."

"Your... chicken," I said, glancing at the drawing. It had a jet pack and a serious face. "So, official chicken notes. Where are we working, boss-man?"

He dragged me to the kitchen table and cleared a space with a one arm sweep I thought only happened in movies. Crayons and pencils rolled onto the floor.

"I'll pick those up later. After the chicken work. Now write the speck-vacations. You know—special vacations for my chicken to do farm security."

I figured Miggy meant specifications. Growing up on a farm, he'd heard it once or twice. I didn't correct him. Speck-vacations? Way better.

Miggy climbed onto the chair next to mine and scooted so close his knee kept bumping my leg. He smack-smoothed the paper flat with both hands, leaving a smudge of fingerprints. Just made it more Miggy.

"Okay," I said, flipping open a clean notebook. "What's this chicken dude all about?"

"He's a Jet Pack Security Chicken," he said without blinking. I wrote it. He watched my pencil move like it was a magic trick.

"Spelled security right?" he asked.

"Absolutely," I said. I hoped.

"Now do the parts," he said, tapping the drawing. "Start with the fire."

I wrote "1) Fire." Then waited.

"It goes whoooosh," he said, very seriously. "That's how he goes fast. Not flappy. Flappy is silly."

"Not flappy," I said, writing it down. "Whoosh is faster."

"Write 'super-fast.' Faster than cars. But not inside the house."

I wrote that, too. Miggy nodded, relieved.

"Safety first," he added, and pointed to a tiny circle on the chicken's head. "Helmet. Write helmet. And seat belt. Chickens need click."

"Helmet and seat belt," I said, adding little boxes. "Click."

He leaned in, finger traveling to two rectangles strapped to the jet pack. "These are corn tanks. He eats corn but it's not sharing corn. It's secret corn for the tank."

"Fuel: secret corn," I said. "Not snack corn."

"Right," he said. "Don't eat it."

I drew a tiny skull next to "snack corn." He grinned.

"What's his job?" I asked.

"All the jobs," he said. Then he sorted them, because four-year-olds like lists even when they pretend they don't. "Garden first. He guards the lettuce. Bunnies don't get it because he is watching with his eyes." He squinted at me to demonstrate. "Write 'watching with eyes.'"

"Watching with eyes," I wrote, because that was important.

"And shoes," he said.

"Shoes?" I asked.

"For bad guys," he said. "He pecks shoelaces. Then they trip and go home and say, 'No more farm, too many chickens.' Write that part."

I wrote: "Pecks shoelaces → bad guys go home."

"And he guards the fridge," Miggy added. "No snack bandits."

"Fridge guard. No snack bandits." I underlined it twice. "Any rescue missions?"

"Yes," he said immediately. "If Papi's hat flies away, he gets it. If Meela's going to get yelled at because she forgot a school book he blasts and brings the book. And if Sofía drops Wobby, he gets Wobby fast, no dirt."

"That's a lot of good work," I said, writing as fast as he talked. "Hat retrieval. Forgotten book delivery. Bunny save."

Miggy's feet swung under the chair, heels thumping the rung. He studied the drawing again, fingertips gentle on the jet pack flames.

He nodded, satisfied, and went back to business. "Do rules now."

"Rules," I repeated, ready.

He held up four fingers. "One: Helmet. Two: Outside whoosh only. Three: No blasting cows or chickens or people. Four: Ask Meela first. Always ask."

I wrote the rules down, numbered, neat. "What about landing?"

Miggy brightened. "He does a superhero pose. Like this." He slid off his chair, bent one knee, put his fist on the tile, and made a small explosion noise with his mouth. Then he popped back up and climbed into the chair like a squirrel.

"Landing: superhero pose," I wrote, and drew a little starburst.

"Also night eyes," he added, pointing at the chicken's pupils. "Green. Like glow sticks. That's so he can see if the raccoon is doing sneaky stuff."

"Night vision eyes. Raccoon surveillance," I said. "Excellent."

Miggy leaned his whole weight into my shoulder, watching my pencil. "You're good at writing, Tyler."

"Thanks," I said, and meant it more than he knew.

He drummed his fingers on the table. "Put my name at the top so the grant knows it's a real plan."

I looked at him. "Your name as author?"

"As boss," he said. "You're the writing guy. I'm the boss guy."

I wrote: "Project Lead: Miguel Preston (Boss). Scribe: Tyler Alred (Writing Guy)."

"And the granted people gotta know his name so they can talk to him."

Miggy tapped the drawing like it was a birth certificate.

"I got two—wait, no, three names. Cause I'm Miguel Ángel Preston, so he needs that too."

I raised an eyebrow. "His name is Miguel Ángel Preston?"

"No, Tyler. He needs chicken names. Not my people names." And then he did a four-year-old version of Emilia's eye roll. Scarily good.

"So write down Jetty Whoosh-Boom Chicken." He said whoosh-boom together, so I guessed it counted as one name. Miggy counted silently on his fingers and I saw him mouthing the names.

"Okay, yep that's three." He tapped the paper again. "Is his name down there? Cause that makes it not not-legal and he can do chicken work anywhere."

If only writing down all three names helped to make all the other stuff not not-legal.

He beamed. " Now write the ending."

"The ending?"

"Put 'This chicken helps our farm be safe and good and happy. Please do the granted for Meela and Papi.'"

"Then when we get the granted I'm gonna get a bigger jet pack for him. That takes him all the way to Mexico. Then he'll let Tía Luz pull a feather. And the feather will make the softest, goodest dreams for her to have that night. And Jetty will sit and keep her warm while she sleeps too. He'll make sure to turn off his whoosh so she's safe."

Emilia stepped into the doorway and leaned her shoulder against the frame, watching us. "What are you two up to?" she asked, voice soft like she didn't want to scare the moment.

"Granted," Miggy said without looking up. "I'm helping."

"He's the boss," I told her.

Emilia's eyes flicked to the page and got shiny in that way she pretended was just the kitchen light. "Looks perfect, jefe," she said.

Then Miggy slipped from his chair and ran out of the kitchen yelling, "CHUCK NORRIS TELLS THE..." He didn't look back because he was already sure his chicken could hold up the whole world. And I was sure too.

Maybe the jet pack burned secret corn fuel, but Jetty Whoosh-Boom really ran on Miggy's love. If Mom and I had to face the worst, the love here was more than enough to give us both the softest, bestest dreams and keep us warm for ten years. Time wouldn't whiz by, but it could be hurried along by whatever crazy way Miggy dreamed up to show how big his heart was.

I looked at Emmy and my eyes were stinging because of the kitchen lights too. She smiled at me, then shook her head at the floor.

"Let's see if Chuck Norris can tell the crayons and pencils to get back on the table and put themselves away. Otherwise, Miggy's gonna have to pick up the slack."

Miggy's Jet Pack Security Chicken

Jet Pack–Fueled by secret corn, not snack corn

Green glowing glow stick eyes to guard the fridge!

Uses his beak to peck at bad guys shoelaces to make them trip.

How it starts

The chicken pulls it with his beak because he doesn't have arms and farm guy said sometimes bite-ceps don't work right anyway

The chicken doesn't need to use his wings. At all. Have you seen a chicken flap its wings —It's all flappy and the flappy looks silly.

Jetty Whoosh-boom Chicken

MAY

70

Will the Beast Roar?

Tyler

"Today's the day," I told The Beast, giving the hood a gentle pat as I stepped into the outbuilding. "No pressure, but we're going to see if you remember how to start."

Weeks of work had led here—new battery, rebuilt starter, fresh plugs, flushed fuel. I'd double-checked every connection, wiped the dash, even polished the cracked vinyl. I wanted it right when Robbie walked in. Footsteps. Not Robbie's steady stride—Miggy's chaotic patter, plus Sofia's uneven toddle.

"FARM GUY! IS TODAY THE DAY?!" Miggy burst through the door. Sofía wobbled after him, bunny clutched to her chest.

"Day!" she echoed.

"Hey, guys." I couldn't not smile. "Yeah, today's the day. Where's your dad?"

"Coming," Miggy said, already scrambling onto the workbench. "He's bringing Meela too. And Mamá. EVERYONE is coming to see The Beast WAKE UP!"

My stomach flipped. An audience. An Emilia audience.

Sofía held out her bunny. "Wobby help."

I took it solemnly. "Thank you. Wobby is officially our good-luck charm."

"Wobby lucky," she confirmed.

I set the bunny on the dash, facing the wheel—co-pilot secured. Miggy dug in his pocket and produced a cloth bundle: two quarters, a button, a blue feather, a smooth gray stone.

"My payment. For my ride."

"I'll keep it safe," I said, tucking it into the glove box.

The door opened again. Robbie. Mariella. And Emilia.

"So, it's the big day," Emilia said, smiling in a way that made my heartbeat do jitterbug dance, "Miggy hasn't talked about anything else."

"No pressure," I laughed.

"None at all," Robbie said, clapping my shoulder. "Even if it doesn't start, we're closer than yesterday."

Mariella settled on a stool with Sofia.

"Process?"

"Fluids, then make sure there's no hydro-lock," I said, falling into explanation.

"Water in the cylinders that can't compress," Emilia finished. At my look, she shrugged. "I listen when you talk."

Warmth bloomed in my chest.

"Then we prime the carb, turn the key, and hope."

"It will work," Miggy declared. "The Beast wants to run again."

"From your lips to God's ears, Miggy-man," Robbie said.

Fifteen minutes of last checks blurred by—Robbie steady at my shoulder, Miggy absorbing everything, Mariella keeping Sofía busy, Emilia watching with that quiet attention that made me both nervous and better.

"Okay," I breathed, sliding into the seat. Leather creaked. For a second I pictured my dad's hands on this same wheel.

"Don't flood it," Robbie said. "Three pumps. Turn and hold no more than five seconds."

Miggy chanted, "GO BEAST GO!" while Emilia anchored him with one hand.

Three pumps. Turn. The starter ground; the engine turned over twice and died.

"Again," Robbie said. "One more pump."

This time: stronger whirr, a cough, a sputter—then a rough idle that smoothed into a steady rumble. Alive.

"YOU DID IT!" Miggy screamed, sprinting circles. "IT'S ALIIIIIVE!"

Sofía clapped. "Beast go vroom!"

Robbie grinned wide. "Well done, Tyler." I couldn't speak. The vibration traveled up through the bench seat and into my bones, like a circuit finally closed. Emilia's smile hit her eyes. She gave me a small thumbs-up, and something in me unraveled in the best way.

Robbie leaned in, voice low. "He'd be proud. Really proud."
I nodded, swallowing hard. After a few minutes I shut the engine
off. The silence was heavy in a good way—the after a hard job
done.

"When do I get my ride?" Miggy demanded at my elbow.

"Soon," I said, laughing. "We still have to test everything."

"But I will be first," he insisted.

"You will," I said solemnly. "Promise."

As everyone drifted out, Emilia lingered. She traced the fender
with her fingertips. "It's really something. Watching you bring it
back."

"It's not done yet." My voice came out rough. "Lot of work
left."

"That's not what I meant." She met my eyes. "You look...
connected. I like it."

"Couldn't have done it without your dad," I said.

"He says you think problems through like your dad did," she
said. "He means it as the highest compliment."

The words landed deep. "Yeah?"

"Yeah." She turned to go, then paused. "Oh—and I call second
ride. After Miggy."

I grinned. I grabbed her hand and pulled her into my arms.
"Miggy, gave me a rock, a quarter, and a feather."

Her cheeks pinked. "I'm fresh out of feathers."

I leaned in, "Having you sitting next me is enough. I could
always use good luck to get this thing to start though." We both

moved in and no matter what Miggy thought there was nothing gross about it. I heard a noise outside and pulled back. I looked at her pinked cheeks and watched her eyes flutter open my favorite part of the *after-kiss.* Evidence this beautiful, brilliant girl got fuzzy when I kissed her.

"You get the first second ride then, deal?"

"Deal Farm Guy."

— A week later —

"Is it ready YET?" Miggy bounced beside The Beast.

"Almost," I said, tightening the last bolt on the passenger seat belt. "Safety first."

He sighed like safety was a conspiracy by grownups to ruin all the fun of childhood. Robbie checked tire pressure.

"Patience is a virtue, Miggy-man."

"I gots virtues," Miggy declared. "Mamá says so. She says 'Bless You,' when I go 'aaachoooo!' So that's why I should get my ride now."

Robbie laughed "Yep, you've definitely got some virtues Miggy man. Safety means you get to keep having them."

Truth was, we could've done this two days ago. I'd kept adding checks because driving it on the road made my stomach twist—excitement braided with fear.

Robbie dusted off his hands. "Ready for the maiden voyage?"

I took a breath. "Yeah. Ready."

"FINALLY!" Miggy whooped. "I'll get my helmet, in case we blast off!"

Miggy returned in a bright red bike helmet.

"Safety and style," I said, fighting a smile. With Robbie spotting, I backed The Beast into the sunlight. Patchwork—faded blue, gray primer, bare metal, spots of rust—but somehow dignified.

"It's beautiful," Miggy breathed.

"Your chariot awaits," I said, opening the passenger door.

He scrambled up, helmet tilting over his eyes. "I can see EVERYTHING!"

I buckled him in, slid behind the wheel, and turned the key. The engine caught on the first try. Gauges looked good. I eased us down the gravel at a crawl.

"I'm the first passenger! I'm making history!"

"That you are," I said. "The first official ride in The Beast 2.0."

"We should go to town! Or the mountains! Or SPACE!"

"Let's start with the end of the driveway."

Even at ten miles per hour, every squeak and rumble felt like a line back to my dad.

"Look! It's Meela!" Miggy pointed down the lane. Emilia stood by the mailbox, surprise shifting into a smile as we rolled up. I tapped the horn. It bleated, tired but proud.

"Fancy meeting you here," I said, unable to wipe the grin off my face.

"If it isn't North Riverbend's newest chauffeur service," she said, peering in.

"MEELA! I'M THE FIRST RIDE!" Miggy announced. "I PAID WITH MY LUCKY ROCK!"

"Excellent investment Miggy."

"Did I pay enough to share the ride back with Meela?" Miggy asked.

"More than enough, should we invite her into the chariot?"

"MEELA, get in the beastie chariot with us!"

She glanced toward the house, then shrugged. "Sure! It's so sweet of you to share your ride back with me."

She leaned over like she'd give him a peck on the cheek.

"AAUGH, no kisses, just says thanks Meela!."

I laughed quietly when her eyes slid to mine over Miggy's head. *More for me* I mouthed to her and her cheeks did the pinking up thing again.

"Onward, Farm Guy," Miggy commanded. "To the barn and BEYOND!"

"Your wish," I said, putting us in gear, "is my command."

We rolled back even slower—precious cargo, and I wanted to make this moment last. Robbie and Mariella waited by the outbuilding; Sofia, sleep-flushed, perked at the sight.

"Beeeeast!" she squealed, grabby hands toward the truck.

"Next time," Mariella promised. "When you're bigger."

I shut the engine off. Silence roared again.

"Well?" Robbie asked.

"Like a dream," I said, not bothering to hide the pride.

Miggy tumbled out. "WE ALMOST WENT TO SPACE!"

"Sounds about right," Mariella said, smiling at Robbie.

Emilia met my eyes. "Congratulations. It's... pretty amazing."

"Thanks." The words caught. "All of it means a lot."

She seemed to hear everything I didn't say—about my dad, about their family, about bringing something back.

"So," she said lightly, "when is the official first second ride scheduled?"

My heart did that flip again. "Whenever you want."

"Tomorrow? After supper?"

"Deal," I said. As the Prestons headed in, Miggy narrating his heroics, I slid The Beast back into the outbuilding, climbed down, and leaned back against the warm door.

-The Next Evening-

Emilia

The dinner dishes were barely stacked when The Beast rumbled into our driveway like an impatient animal. I was absolutely not watching from the kitchen window.

"Right on time," I said on the porch, aiming for casual.

Tyler leaned against the fender, hands in his pockets, looking both nervous and pleased with himself. "Your carriage," he said with a ridiculous little bow.

"Meela! Is that Farm Guy?" Miggy thundered toward the door. Sofía tottered after him. Tyler's eyes widened.

"Quick, before he demands another ride."

"Too late."

Dad appeared behind them. "Not tonight, Miggy-man. This one's just for Meela."

"But I'm the official Beast co-pilot!"

"You'll always be official co-pilot," Tyler said. "That's in the history books. Tonight I need to test windows, if they're clear enough to see the view outside."

Miggy weighed the science, then nodded. "Fine. But I get to inspect it when you get back."

"Deal," Tyler said.

He beat me to the passenger door and opened it with a flourish.

"Such a gentleman." I said.

"I'm occasionally civilized."

Inside, the cab looked different—dash wiped, cracked vinyl polished to a dull shine. A tiny bundle of wildflowers was tucked into an ancient air vent.

"You polished up in here," I said as he slid in.

"Maybe." He flushed. "The flowers were Mom's idea."

"They're perfect."

The engine coughed once, then settled into a steady rumble that climbed through the floorboards into the seat. Instead of turning toward the road, he eased the truck across the yard, past the machine shed and the round bales stacked like giant coins.

"Where to?" I asked.

"The ridge," he said. "One of the reasons you should open up a spa out here, it's the best sunset in town. Also a good trip for evaluating the suspension," he added. "Bumpy field road."

The Beast lumbered up the rutted path that wound along the edge of the cornfield. Dust rose in lazy swirls behind us, grasshoppers springing out of the way as we bounced through the tracks. Each bump jolted us a little closer together until the ridge opened wide, prairie rolling out in every direction and the sky already stained with streaks of orange.

"How does it feel?" I asked. "Driving your dad's truck."

He was quiet. "Like I'm learning a piece of him. Turning the key, shifting—thinking how he did these same things."

"Sharing something," I said. "Even though he's gone."

"Exactly."

We switch backed up toward the ridge. The shocks were not impressed; I braced a hand against the dash.

"Sorry," he said after a pothole. "Shocks are on the list."

"It adds character to the ride."

He pulled into the gravel lookout and killed the engine. Quiet fell as orange and pink light flooded the cab.

"Wow," I said. "It's been awhile since I've been out here. I almost forgot the view."

"Gramps and I have stopped here. He told me the land belonged to family friends when I asked if it was alright."

The connections we had before we barely knew each other twined gently around us. The new ties we'd been creating pulled us towards each other on the bench seat. I snuggled into him with sigh. We sat with connections, old and new, in our minds.

Then his voice went softer. "I wish my mom could see The Beast running. She'd be so happy."

"Did you tell her yesterday?" He nodded. "She almost cried. But... it's not the same." A pause. "...ten years. She said it's a blink. But that's not how it feels."

I hated the wall of years sitting between them.

"Let's take some pictures of the sunset and the Beast. We can be all artsy with the light."

His face brightened. "That's a great idea."

We slid out. I posed him beside the truck, angled for the light. He started stiff but loosened up.

"Perfect," I said, scrolling. "These are good."

He stepped close to look. Warmth radiated off him; the space between us shrank.

"You made The Beast look almost cool," he said.

"It is cool," I said. "Vintage, seen-some-things cool."

"Let's get a couple together, my mom loves you more than me now, so I'd better make sure I pull you into some pictures."

"You're ridiculous."

"Good thing you're getting fonder and fonder of ridiculous then," he said.

He lifted my phone, arm out, pulling me in at his side. The Beast and the sky framed us.

"Ready?" he asked.

After scrolling through and seeing some good shots, he tucked his camera away. Leaning back on the Beast he pulled me into his arms face to face. The disappearing sunset lit up his edges like a purple and pink sun corona

"Em…," he cleared his throat. "I…" He took a deep breath in.

Feelings that I'd examined, made peace with, and welcomed flowed through me. "I'm not just fond of your ridiculousness. I love you Tyler," I rushed out.

"Oh, thank God! Em, I'm so crazy in love with you, if you didn't feel the same… I don't know what…"

"I thought I might spontaneously combust if I waited any longer to say that."

'You need to let off some steam." He smirked, then his lips touched mine. The setting sun lit the back of my eyelids with bright purple. The setting sun colors and the feel of Tyler combined felt almost surreal as we kissed leaning against the Beast.

Back in the cab, he studied the photos again. "I'll send these to her tonight. She'll love them."

The Beast moved through the not-quite-night and Tyler flicked the headlights on. I wondered if his dad had driven around the farm with his headlights carving a path through the dark. Wondered if the Beast's rumble was louder or softer.

The noise and vibration combined into a low rumbling purr as Tyler drove. Like a mythical creature in a fairytale awoken after a long-enchanted sleep, pleased that it was a prince of the royal line that had brought it to wakefulness.

71

Grant Awarded

Emilia

The auditorium hummed with anticipation as the benefit concert reached its intermission. I stood at the back, watching as people mingled in the aisles, their voices creating a warm buzz beneath the soft orchestral music playing through the speakers.

We'd hear about the grant decision tonight. We were bodily present because we'd made it the final round of decision making. Not everyone here would be selected though. I fought off resentment that our grant application was wrapped up in this show. I'd prefer we were just notified yes or no through a boring old email.

"It's all part of the spectacle Meela-Mi," Dad said. "A three-ring circus to gather an audience to raise more money to give more grants." Except I hated being part of a circus and had run out patience an hour ago. Lila Sandstrom, a rising folk-country singer from this part of the state was working with the Western Plains Recovery Fund. The decisions would be announced after the second half of the concert.

Lila had recruited area high school musicians to be part of the concert. There had been choral pieces, strings, guitar, and a small orchestra. Ivy's cello teacher knew Lila so Ivy had recruited to work her butt off as Artistic Director-in-raining. It was good she and Aiden had started using their "big kids words" consistently. The rest of the school year had been busy with sport, music, and regular studying.

Tyler appeared at my side, two paper cups of punch in his hands. "One extremely fancy fruit punch for the most anxious farm girl in North Dakota," he said, offering me a cup.

"I'm not anxious," I protested accepting a cup. "Just.."

Tyler gave me a knowing look and pulled me into a one armed hug. "Your knees have been bouncing or your toes have been tapping since this started. You're either nervous or you have been dying to get down to a string ensemble."

I sighed. He wasn't wrong. "We worked so hard on that grant proposal. If we don't get it..."

"You will," Tyler said with such certainty that I almost believed him. "You and your dad know your stuff and you made that proposal so tight it didn't even need Miggy's tractor claws. Though I assume that's something we're not telling him."

"No, it's definitely not," I relaxed against him.

"When are they announcing the recipients?" Tyler asked.

"After the second set," I replied, scanning the crowd. "Right before the finale."

The lights dimmed and brightened again, signaling the end of intermission. People began moving back to their seats.

"That's our cue," Tyler said. "I'm going keep Aiden company, do you mind?"

I shook my head. "Of course not, I'll sit with my mom again."

Tyler hesitated, then surprised me by dropping a kiss on my forehead. "Good luck. Not that you need it."

"I think that boy likes you Emilia," my dad came up behind me putting his hands on my shoulders.

"Dad... hush," I could feel my face heating. I heard my dad chuckle. They didn't tease me about Tyler very often, maybe because Sofía was convinced that Fahm Die still belonged to her.

"Any word, or hints?"

"Nope, no one's letting anything slip," Dad move to put an arm around my shoulder.

"Ugh, this is torture."

"That's suspense. Makes for a better show."

"Our livelihood isn't supposed to be entertainment," I muttered.

"It's not our whole livelihood, Meela-Mi," he reminded me gently. "It's one project. An important one, but still."

I knew he was right, but it felt bigger than that. The regenerative agriculture grant wasn't just about money—it was about validation. About proving that our approach to farming mattered. That my ideas mattered.

"You should get back to your seat," Dad said. "I'm staying backstage since they asked me to come up if we're among the recipients."

"If?" I raised an eyebrow. "Don't you mean 'when'?"

I made my way back to my seat just as the lights dimmed. Mom gave me a questioning look as I slid in beside her, Miggy on her other side with Sofía half-asleep in her lap.

"Nothing yet," I whispered.

Lila Sandstrom's voice filled the auditorium, her songs weaving stories of prairie resilience and renewal. The crowd was entranced, and despite my nerves, I found myself caught up in the music. When the final notes of "Prairie Light" faded, Lila stepped forward to address the audience.

"Thank you all for being here tonight," she said, her voice warm and clear. "This concert is about more than music. It's about community. It's about resilience. And it's about finding beauty and strength in unexpected places—like the humble dandelion."

A soft murmur rippled through the audience.

"Many of us grew up thinking of dandelions as weeds—something to be pulled up and discarded," Lila continued. "But these resilient plants have deep roots that hold soil together. They provided early food for pollinators. They can even help heal damaged ecosystems."

On the large screen behind her, images appeared—close-ups of dandelions, bees collecting pollen, and side-by-side photos showing flood-damaged land versus restored prairie.

"Tonight, we're not just celebrating music. We're celebrating a new way of seeing. A new way of working with the land instead of against it." She gestured to the wing of the stage. "I'd like to invite Maura Thompson from the Western Plains Recovery Fund to share some exciting news about how your support tonight will directly help our community rebuild after last year's flooding."

Maura walked onstage, thanking Lila before stepping to the microphone.

"Good evening, everyone. When the Little Missouri flooded last year, many of us wondered how long it would take to recover. But what I've witnessed in this community is not just recovery—it's renewal."

She gestured to the screen behind her, where a slide appeared titled "Fields of Dandelions the Western Plains Recovery Fund."

"The Western Plains Recovery Fund established three grant initiatives to support sustainable recovery: Dandelion Defense for riparian buffer restoration, Rooting Resilience for soil health improvement, and Dandelion Meadows for pollinator habitat creation."

I leaned forward in my seat, heart pounding. Mom reached over and took my hand.

"We received over thirty applications from local farmers and ranchers, all with innovative approaches to rebuilding our landscape," Maura continued. "After careful consideration, I'm pleased to announce our grant recipients."

The room went completely silent as Maura began reading names for the first initiative. With each name, the person would stand briefly, acknowledging the applause. I didn't recognize all of them, but there were familiar faces—Mr. Wilson from the farm equipment store, the Johansens who ran the orchard on the county line.

My pulse pounded in my ears as she moved to the second initiative—Rooting Resilience. This was the one we'd applied for, focusing on implementing cover cropping systems and strategic integration of deep-rooted plants to heal our flood-damaged northern pasture.

"For Rooting Resilience, we're pleased to award grants to the following farms," Maura announced.

"Jensen Family Farm. Riverdale Ranch. Blue Creek Homestead." Mom's grip on my hand tightened. "Preston Family Farm."

I gasped. Mom squeezed my hand so hard it hurt, but I barely noticed. Miggy, who'd been half-asleep, perked up.

"That's us! That's us!" he whisper-shouted, loud enough that several people turned to look. I swiveled in my seat, searching for Tyler. He was already looking at me, grinning broadly and giving me a thumbs-up.

Dad walked onto the stage with the other recipients, looking surprisingly comfortable in the spotlight. When the applause died down, Maura continued with the third initiative. The remainder of the ceremony passed in a blur. I was barely aware of the final performance, too caught up in the swirl of emotions—pride, relief, excitement. We'd done it. Our approach had been recognized. Validated.

As people began filing out after the finale, I pushed against the tide to make my way backstage. I found Dad surrounded by well-wishers, including several farmers who had initially been skeptical of our regenerative methods.

"There she is," Dad said, spotting me. "My sustainability expert." I rolled my eyes at the title but couldn't suppress my smile as I joined him.

"Congratulations, Emilia," said Mr. Henrikson, an older farmer who had once dismissed cover cropping as "fancy nonsense."

"Your father tells me you were the brains behind the soil aeration system."

"It was a team effort," I said, glancing gratefully at Dad.

"Well, I'll be watching your results closely," Mr. Henrikson said. "If it works as well as your proposal suggests, you might have a convert."

As the crowd around us thinned, Dad pulled me into a quick hug. "You did good, Meela-Mi," he said softly. "Really good."

"Thanks, Dad," I replied, my throat tight with emotion. "You too."

"Your mom's taking the little ones home," he said after glancing at his phone. "She said to tell you she's incredibly proud and that we'll celebrate properly tomorrow."

I nodded, glancing around the now-emptying backstage area. "I should find Ivy, congratulate her on the concert."

"And I should go thank Maura properly," Dad agreed. "Meet you by the truck in fifteen minutes?"

I found Ivy in the green room, directing the cleanup with the same efficiency she'd brought to the entire production.

"Congratulations, cuz!" she exclaimed, breaking away to give me a hug. "I was so excited when they called your name!"

"Thanks," I said. "And congratulations yourself. The concert was amazing. Every single performance."

Ivy beamed. "It came together even better than I hoped. And the fundraising total already exceeded their goal, which means they'll be able to fund even more projects next year."

As we chatted, I spotted Tyler through the doorway, talking with Drew near the exit. He must have noticed me too, because he excused himself and headed our way.

"There's the grant winner," he said, joining us. "Told you that you'd get it."

"You did," I admitted. "Though that doesn't mean I believed you."

Ivy glanced between us, a small smile playing at her lips. "I should go check on the orchestra breakdown," she said, not particularly convincingly. "See you guys later."

"You should believe me," he said, his expression. "I wouldn't say it if I didn't believe it. So, Farm Executive, what's next for the Preston Family Farm now that you've got the big grant?"

"First, implementation planning," I said. "Then ground prep. Then planting the cover crop mixture. Then—"

"Whoa, I was asking conversationally, not for the full agricultural breakdown," Tyler laughed. "Though I'm not surprised you have it all mapped out already."

I shrugged, suddenly self-conscious.

"Hey," he said softly. "I do want to want to know the details. Just not at the end of a long day and when your dad asked me to bring you to his truck."

His put his arm around my shoulder and began to steer me towards an exit. "Ah, perfect." Looking up I saw a darkened empty stairwell. "I also wanted enough time for this." He pulled me up a couple steps, he stayed on step lower. He tugged me to the edge of the step and leaned in.

"Congratulations. I never doubted it." He pulled back and cupped my face in his hands, "You're so brilliant it makes me dizzy sometimes. Come on your dad's waiting."

72

A Bonfire View of the Future

Emilia

The bonfire crackled in the center of our back field, sparks rising like fireflies against the darkening sky. Spring evenings in North Riverbend still carried a chill, but gathered around the flames, our circle felt perfectly warm.

I glanced around: Ivy and Aiden huddled together, his arm slung over her shoulder; Jenna animatedly telling a story to Aria and Nate; Tyler patiently toasting a marshmallow to golden perfection. The usual suspects—plus a few unexpected additions.

"Harper, don't eat that," Drew called, swooping down before his youngest sister could pop a pebble into her mouth. He'd arrived with four sisters, looking overwhelmed. I told him of course they could stay.

An hour later, they'd blended in. Mia, twelve, was peppering my dad with farm questions. Zoe, eight, critiqued everyone's marshmallow skills while hoarding charred "fire rocks." Lucy, six, crouched with her sketchbook, capturing the flames. And

Harper, four, might be Miggy's soul mate as she listened raptly to Miggy's ridiculous chicken jokes.

"Not my egg, that's my breakfast!" Miggy shouted. Harper squealed, clutching her rabbit. Sofía joined in, stamping her little foot. "Bad carrot!" she announced, pleased with herself.

Tyler slid onto the log beside me, offering a marshmallow toasted to perfection. "Trade you for that hockey puck you're torching."

I groaned at my flaming mess. "Something's wrong here."

"It's like a Freaky Friday mini-me—Bonfire Marshmallow Toasting Edition," he said. "Wait. Emilia Preston, did you get distracted?"

I smacked his chest. "I can't believe you insinuated my brain isn't functioning perfectly."

He grinned and handed me his marshmallow anyway. "Seriously. Yours is a biohazard."

I surrendered mine. "Fine. Sustainability and all that."

"Reduce, reuse, recycle," he agreed, tossing it into the fire.

Across the flames, Mia called, "So... are Ivy and Aiden together-together?"

Aiden choked on his s'more. Ivy patted his back, laughing. "Yes."

Sofía had been wandering around looking at the group in wonder. "Lotsa big kids!" she'd shouted earlier. Then, grabbing Nate's pant leg, she declared, "Dis my Nate!"

The group cracked up. Nate looked startled. "Uh, hi?"

Tyler pressed a hand to his chest in mock betrayal.

"Dis my Nate!" she repeated proudly, patting his knee before scampering back to Miggy.

Tyler leaned close. "This is nice."

"The chaos?"

"The everything," he said simply.

Drew seemed to feel it too, finally relaxing as his sisters disappeared into the circle's rhythm.

Sofía toddled over to Nate again. She grabbed Nate's arm and tugged insistently. "Up, Nate!" She stretched up making grabby hands. Nate blinked, then stood up and gamely hoisted her onto his shoulders. Sofía squealed in delight, clapping her hands. "I so high! Higher dan Farm Guy!"

"Not gonna lie, I'm both relieved and little bit hurt," Tyler told me. "But the world feels in balance now. Nate needs a Sofía goblin in his life. It's easier to people with littles."

By the time Drew rounded up his sisters, Harper was drooping in his arms, mumbling about dizzy chickens. Zoe scooped up her rocks, Lucy hugged her sketchbook, and Mia waved her notebook of farm facts at my dad. Sofía stayed perched on Nate's shoulders until Dad went to peel her off. From Dad's arms her tiny hand still pointed at him she yelled happily, "Dat my Nate!"

Dad walked to the house with Sofí, who must have remembered her first love before she yelled, "Night, night Farm Guy! Lub you! Mwah."

"Night Sofí, I caught it, thanks!" He pretended to catch the kiss she threw and plant in on his cheek. "Okay, that eases the sting."

Everyone drifted off—until only my family and Tyler remained. My mom shepherded Miggy inside to join Sofía and Dad.

"Did you see the picture Lucy drew of us?" He asked. "She told me we were telling secrets."

I couldn't help smiling. "Lucy has an active imagination."

"True," he agreed. "For the life of me, I can't think of what the secrets might have been."

"Oh? Well maybe you didn't know this... I think I've loved you a little bit more every year since third grade."

"Third grade?" Tyler looked genuinely shocked. "When you called me Prince Butthead?"

"Especially then," I admitted. "You were so nice to Ivy when those other boys were teasing her. Even after I yelled at you, thinking you were part of it."

"I remember that" he said, smiling now. "You marched right up to me, hands on your hips, and told me to leave your cousin alone."

"And instead of getting mad, you just asked if she was okay." I shook my head, feeling my cheeks warm. "Nobody else would have done that."

Tyler took another step forward, close enough now that I could feel the warmth radiating from him. "So you're saying I had a chance this whole time?"

"I wouldn't go that far," I teased,

He laughed, the sound warm and real in the quiet night. Then his expression softened again, his hand reaching up to brush a strand of hair from my face. The gesture was familiar now, but it still sent a flutter through my chest.

"Come here," he murmured. "The whole world probably already knows this, but..."

"Knows what?" I asked, barely breathing.

He looked at me for a long moment, then something shifted in his expression. A decision made.

"What I want for my future." he said, voice quiet but steady. "About how all of this—your family, this place, you—it feels right. It feels like forever. And if there were other forevers to choose from, I'd pick this one. Over and over again."

The honesty in his voice caught me off guard. No jokes. No deflection. Just Tyler saying what he meant.

"You already know I love you, Emilia. I love that in a world where I didn't think I'd have much of a future to choose, I get to tell you you're my future."

The words hung in the air between us, simple and enormous. For a moment, I couldn't speak. Every clever remark, every teasing joke I might normally have made vanished. There was just Tyler, looking at me with those honest eyes, waiting.

"Tyler," I finally managed, my voice barely above a whisper. "I want that too. I'm so glad you love it here and... I've been so worried you might not want to put down roots here. Because this is where I'm rooted, but I see the future when I look at you."

His eyes softened, a smile spreading slowly across his face. He cupped my face in his hands and leaned in. "There is absolutely nothing better than looking my future in the eyes."

Epilogue

Sometime Close to the End of the School Year

I'd felt off all day, smiles forced. Even smiles aimed at Emilia took effort. I'm sure she noticed, I saw her forehead furrow when she looked at me. She didn't push and probably wouldn't. Usually there was no need, she read me well and I didn't mind telling her stuff. Today, though I wasn't sure what was up, what I was feeling, why I was feeling it.

The *offness* lasted all day and accompanied me home. Gramps and Grams were out with friends. I kicked off my shoes and shuffled into my bedroom. I looked at myself in the dresser mirror and sighed, then fell back onto my bed. My cell rang and I dug it out of my back pocket. Pretty certain it was a miniature pro baseball player calling.

"Hello?"

"Hola, Farm Guy."

I sighed and rubbed my face, "Hola, Miguel Cabrera."

"Are you sad?"

I blinked and sat up, "Uh... what?"

He sounded insistent now, "You sound sad. Don't be sad. But if you gotta be sad that's okay too. Feelings are okay, you just can't be mean because of them."

I laughed at myself getting emotional advice from a four year philosopher.

"Meela says when I'm sad, I should talk to someone. So you should talk to Meela."

I let out a breath, "You give good advice Miggy."

"I know, Mamá says, I'm 'Un viejo en cuerpo de niño.' * So I gotta let the old man say smart stuff to get him out of my body."

I smiled a little, "I think most of the smart stuff comes from you Miggy, but thanks for the Old Man advice."

"Okay, bye Farm Guy."

I stared at my phone for a moment, then hit Emilia's number. I was a little frightened by how smart Miggy was, we needed to keep him using his powers for good.

"Hi Tyler," Emilia answered.

Smart kid. I felt better hearing her voice and I knew she'd help me figure myself out.

"Hey Emmy-kins."

"Gag!"

"Emmy-bear?"

"Yuck!"

"Emmy-poo?"

"Tyler," she warned, not really mad.

"Hi Em, Girlfriend, Love, Brilliant One, Goddess of Regenerative Agriculture, Apple Empress…"

"I love you too, Tyler," she interrupted.

Yeah, Miggy was right.

*Literally "an old man in a child's body.

Sometime Close to the End of Summer Before Tenth Grade

Emilia

Tyler's phone buzzed, again. He glanced at me with a wary look on his face. Then he answered.

I was close enough to hear, "Farm Guy, put me on speaker phone."

Oh, Miggy, no….

Tyler sighed and looked at me. I grimaced and shook my head. He shrugged helplessly.

"It's important, Farm Guy."

"Oh-kay, you're on speaker now, Miggy."

"Is Meela there?"

"Yep, I'm here, Miggy." I braced myself for a disaster to follow his words. Tyler and I exchanged looks.

"Meela, I think you should marry a basketball player."

Silence.

Tyler ran a hand over his face. "Wow. Just wow."

I stifled a laugh at the same time I gave thanks it was just the two of us at the moment.

"Miggy...why?"

Miggy sighed, overwhelmed by the work of having an older sister. The *duh* had been implied in his sigh. "Because they're the best."

Click.

Tyler stared at me. "I'm really not sure what I'm supposed to do with that."

I smiled at him. "Well, he's not wrong."

"Yeah, but I think he expects it to happen this weekend. I love you, but I'm so concerned for my future."

I finally broke down into laughter. "Lucky for you he's not the ultimate authority in my family. If you're really going to pop the question you've got to talk to my mom and dad first."

Tyler shook his head. He looked a little green. "Um, you're not expecting that anytime soon...are...you?"

I leaned closer, pressing my shoulder against his. "Relax, Farm Guy. I'm sixteen. I think we've got a little time."

He let out a breath like he'd just been released from a death sentence, and I couldn't help but laugh again.

"But," he said, eyes brightening "if I did have to plan something—purely hypothetical—I might get Miggy involved, maybe a choreographed chicken dance?"

"Or Jet Pack Chicken 2.0?" I asked.

"Oooh, I like that, maybe in the form of a floating Chicken blimp trailing a banner," Tyler said.

We both grinned. Then he squeezed my hand, the kind of small, steady pressure that mattered more than any speech.

"Okay," he said, quieter. "I won't let Miggy's expectations pressure me into acting yet. And I'll talk to your folks first. Or I'll at least write a very respectful letter and shove it under their door."

"Just take my dad for a drive in the Beast and go down memory lane. Then slip it in."

"That's a plan, I'll remember that."

He looked at me. "I still see the future in you though Em."

"Me too, Tyler," I replied quietly. "Me too."

We start there on the ridge watching the sunset from the Beast's bench seat. The future had never felt scary to me, but now next to Tyler it also felt more sure than it ever had. Not something to be worried about or rushed into. Not a cliff to fall over, but a field we'd walk together, one step at a time.

Afterword

Were you frustrated by Emilia's classroom experiences? Should I have addressed the results of the Preston's actions more in-depth? Should Robbie and Mariella's actions have resulted in a more significant change? Yes? Yes!

Is that realistic and representative of how changes take place within our educational system? No. Emilia was experiencing the effects of an educator's implicit bias. Implicit bias is the ingrained tendency to devalue the work of black and brown students. In Emilia's case the teacher unconsciously labeled her voice and opinions as less trustworthy and authoritative.

Is Mr. Klein just a really, really bad guy and a terrible teacher? No to the first and probably not to the second. Here's the thing- we all tend to negatively judge others. We all have implicit bias regarding groups of people different from us. Children as young as four can focus on the race of other children as the origin of "bad." The children who look different are more likely to be identified as causes of trouble and as aggressors.

Why? You've heard the saying *Do as I Say, Not as I Do?* Unfortunately, for adults young children will learn from and repeat both. Our unspoken but real bias impacts our actions and our words.

Why do well-meaning adults carry bias and act upon it? Do teachers walk into school thinking, "Today's the day I'll respond more positively to the efforts of white students? Consider their academic responses as more valid?" Of course not.

The vast majority of teachers want only the best for their students. Implicit bias is complicated. Dealing with our implicit bias takes hard work and courage. Teaching is challenging. It's even likely teachers, such as Mr. Klein, have participated in professional development training about bias.

It's not sitting through a training session that brings changes. A 2020 study assessed what impact implicit bias had on teacher evaluation of student writing. Student writing graded or scored using vague rubrics consistently scored white students as having higher competence. When teachers adhered to clearer evaluation criteria there was no demonstration of racial bias. The application of a clear writing rubric seemed to have mitigated the effect of implicit bias (Quinn, 2020).

Real life is complicated and there is no rubric that we can simply put on like a pair of glasses to correct our vision. It is here that we must make a concerted effort to understand that bias is institutionalized. We must clearly look at our systems. Like Friday Night Lights – *Clear Eyes, Full Hearts, Can't Lose.* We look at our systems not to protect them or ourselves but to see with clarity. We fill our hearts with the desire for all to flourish. This will be hard work. This will require teamwork. This will hold all of us to a higher standard. In the end we will all be better.

It is the generations to come that I am depending on to look at the world with clear vision and full hearts. Hold yourselves not to an image or a worn catchphrase. Hold yourselves to high standards of how you see others and the world. Hold yourselves to the high standard of everyone flourishing. My generation has been complacent. My generation has used addressing the issue of bias to gain or keep power.

Your generation can change, learn, grow, refuse to be comfortable with the way it is.

And now, undocumented immigrants –

I almost wrapped that storyline up in pretty wrapping paper and tied it up with a pretty bow. A marriage license surfaces! Luz and Adam were married before he was deployed and subsequently killed in action. I wanted this so deeply – to not deal with the pain my characters would experience.

I couldn't. I had to stay true to myself and show the messy complication of "dizzy chickens" that is our immigration system. Should immigrants enter the country legally? Yes, of course. Do we currently have a clear, efficient way this happens? Nope. If you want to doubt my words, that's okay. Who do you believe? And where do they get their information? What do they use the "facts about immigration" to accomplish?

Is it possible that immigration has become an issue that is bandied about to gain political power? You'll have to answer that question for yourself. We're at a time when the chasm between major political parties is wide and deep. There appears to be no way to bridge the divide. We don't trust those others over there, we don't accept their facts. The only opinions we trust are those of people like us.

Do you know the story of the emperor's new clothes? He listened to the voices that told him what he wanted to hear. He chose to live in an echo chamber in which all that echoed was praise for the new garments he wore. Invisible garments that could be seen only by those with exactly the same opinions. But when the emperor went to parade in his new clothes? Different voices pointed out an uncomfortable truth.

Below are some links to information about immigration. All the organizations are nonpartisan. Saying something loudly in the name of political power doesn't make it true or untrue. Just loud. The voices may not say the exact same thing you're used to hearing. Or they might. You'll need to discern what it is you're hearing. It's easier in the short-term to leave issues like immigration unexamined. The generations to come can deal. That's what's been happening before you. I hope this generation and the next and the next will be better.

The Pew Research Center Pew Research Center - https://www.pewresearch.org/about/

The Migration Policy Institute – https://www.migrationpolicy.org/about/aboutmigration-policy -institute

The Immigration Research Initiative -
https://immresearch.org/

The American Immigration Council –
https://www.americanimmigrationcouncil.org

The Migration Policy Institute
https://www.migrationpolicy.org/about/aboutmigration-policy
-institute

Breese, A.C., Nickerson, A.B, Lemke, M., Mohr,
R., & Heidelburg, K. (2023) Examining Implicit
biases of pre-service educators within a professional
development context. *Contemporary School Psychology.*
https://doi.org/10.1007/s40688-023-00456-6

Hu, X., & Hancock, A. M. (2024). State of the science:
Implicit bias in education 2018-2020. The Kirwan Institute for
the Study of Race and Ethnicity.
https://kirwaninstitute.osu.edu/research/state-science-implicit-
bias-education-2018-2020

Quinn, D. M. (2020). Experimental evidence on teachers'
racial bias in student evaluation: The Role of grading scales.
Educational Evaluation and Policy Analysis, 42(3), 375-392.
https://doi.org/10.3102/0162373720932188

Staats, C. (2015). *Understanding Implicit Bias What
Educators Should Know.* American Educator, Winter 2015-16.

Acknowldgements

Family, of course you're first. I wouldn't be doing any of this without you. Your love, support, and care are blessings covering me daily. To all the indie authors – thanks for sharing what you know. To the reviewers, bloggers, Tik-Tokkers, Instagrammers, and FaceBookers wanting to support authors, thank you. To creatives trying to make the world a better place, don't stop. Dallas Willard, philosopher of faith and science – already undertaking the most real part of his adventure, thanks for leaving so much behind for those of us still stumbling along.

Wish Creative Writing Guidance

Mr. Henderson's In-depth Instructions

As you prepare to write, consider the following:

Who is wishing and why? This will help you build your character and their motivations.

What is the wish about? This is the heart of your story. Make it clear and compelling.

What are the consequences or outcomes of this wish?

This is where your creativity really comes into play.

Think about cause and effect and how it drives your narrative. You'll have three weeks to complete this project.

Next week, we'll spend some time brainstorming and outlining in class, and you'll have the opportunity to share your ideas and get feedback. This is your chance to be as imaginative as you want, so let your minds roam free. I'm looking forward to seeing what you come up with!"

Recipes

SPECIAL K BARS (AKA SCOTCHEROOS, ND POTLUCK ROYALTY) – Made with breakfast foods* so they could be a meal

Ingredients

1 cup light corn syrup

1 cup granulated sugar

1 cup creamy peanut butter

6 cups Special K cereal (or any crisp rice/corn flake blend)

1 cup semi-sweet chocolate chips

1 cup butterscotch chips

Instructions

Prepare the pan: Lightly butter or spray a 9×13-inch baking dish.

Make the base: In a large saucepan over medium heat, combine corn syrup and sugar. Stir until the sugar dissolves and the mixture just starts to bubble.

Add peanut butter: Remove from heat and stir in peanut butter until smooth.

Add cereal: Pour in the Special K cereal and stir until evenly coated.

Press into pan: Transfer mixture into the prepared baking dish. Use a buttered spatula or wax paper to press it evenly into the pan.

Melt topping: In a small saucepan or microwave-safe bowl, melt the chocolate and butterscotch chips together, stirring until smooth.

Top and cool: Spread the melted mixture evenly over the cereal base. Let cool at room temperature until firm (or chill briefly to speed things up).

Cut and serve: Slice into bars.

*My Grandma called cereal breakfast foods. That's a tiny memory that resurfaced recently. I'm glad to have it so I wanted to put it in writing.

I was looking at recipes that would likely be something Mariella Preston would make. I found the website Dora's Table. Everything looks so good. I haven't tired any of the recipes – I have a ridiculous collection of food allergies, so I'd have to do a lot of substitutions. Sometimes it's just not worth trying. I'd love to hear if you find a great recipe.

https://dorastable.com/

Also By

Almost Missed Our Shot
Riverbend High Happy Endings Book 1

I Always Saw You
Riverbend High Happy Endings Book 3
Releasing Fall 2025

Riverbend High Happy Ending Book 4
Releasing Early 2026
Riverbend High Happy Ending Book 5
Releasing Early Spring 2026

About the Author

M.C. Danielsen writes heartfelt YA rom-coms with equal parts humor, emotional depth, and small-town charm. A lifelong North Dakotan at heart, she pays close attention to the smaller places that often get overlooked. Her current series delivers authentic rural vibes, slow-burn romance, and fiercely loyal friendships.

Her stories follow girls finding their voice, boys growing into heart, and the emotional chaos that comes with figuring out who you are—especially when feelings, playlists, and group chats get in the way.

When she's not writing, you can find M.C. playing merge-three games, rabidly cheering for the Minnesota Twins, the Minnesota Vikings, and the Buffalo Bills by marriage (she admits they're worth following).

By training, she's an expert in child development, trauma, and resilience. She believes every teen deserves a safe place to land and to have people who light up when they walk into the room. She's certain that today's young people are capable of more than any generation before them.

Find Me

Explore my website:

https://mcdanielsenyaauthor.com/

https://www.facebook.com/author.mcdanielsen#

https://www.instagram.com/mcdanielsenyaauthor/

https://www.tiktok.com/@mcdanielsenya_author

Join the crew and signup for my newsletter through my website.